D1707473

Lullaby

Lullaby

Sherry Scarpaci

FIVE STAR

An imprint of Thomson Gale, a part of The Thomson Corporation

Detroit • New York • San Francisco • New Haven, Conn. • Waterville, Maine • London

This novel is a work of fiction. Names, characters, places and incidents are either the product of the author's imagination, or, if real, used fictitiously.

Set in 11 pt. Plantin.

LIBRARY OF CONGRESS CATALOGING-IN-PUBLICATION DATA

Scarpaci, Sherry.
Lullaby / Sherry Scarpaci. — 1st ed.
p. cm.
ISBN-13: 978-1-59414-583-4 (alk. paper)
ISBN-10: 1-59414-583-0 (alk. paper)
I. Title.
PS3619.C27L85 2007
813′.6—dc22 2007012340

First Edition. First Printing: September 2007.

Published in 2007 in conjunction with Tekno Books and Ed Gorman.

Printed in the United States of America on permanent paper
10 9 8 7 6 5 4 3 2 1

This book is dedicated to:
Patricia McKeague, the teacher who started me down this road.

My parents, Mike and Mary Scarpaci, for instilling in me a love of books.

And my children, Jennifer and J. T. Selvage, you are my greatest joy and blessing.

ACKNOWLEDGMENTS

"I think you can write."

Those simple words spoken to me by college professor Patricia McKeague gave me a star to reach for and changed my life. Seeing *Lullaby* in print is the fulfillment of the dream that started with those words.

Many years have passed since I first started writing *Lullaby.* There were unforeseen detours and speed bumps that may have stopped me if not for the unfailing encouragement, support and help from the wonderful people I am blessed to have in my life.

My deepest gratitude to Patricia McKeague for starting it all.

To my children, Jennifer and J. T. Selvage, thank you for believing in me and making me laugh and smile even in the roughest of times. You inspire and make me proud every day.

Endless thanks to my parents, Mike and Mary Scarpaci, brothers and sisters-in-law Mike and Diane Scarpaci, Jim and Lori Scarpaci, and their broods, for being there for every hill and valley in my life.

Dear friends and personal cheerleaders, Kathy Bennett, Betty Siadak, Lynn Saso, Kathe McElherne, Saundra Slusher and Marilyn Smitas, thanks for the laughs and the shoulders. You have saved me thousands on therapy.

To my Linear Electric friends and cohorts, Tony Fimbianti, Dorothy Fimbianti, Bob Fimbianti, Mike Woolf, Bill Doerr, Rick Contreras, Tony Hundseder, Jerry Magdziarz, Laura Gora, Cathy Del Nagro, Al Henninger, Joe Witry, Dave Naylor, Stan

Moskal, and Bob Burnett, thanks for always being there.

A thousand thanks to the talented Southland Scribes, Helen Osterman, Nancy Conley, Linda Cochran, Sandi Tatara, George Kulles, Ryan O'Reilly, Joan Marie Poninski, Lydia Ponczak, Michael A. Black, Ralph Horner and Jane Andringa. Your suggestions, opinions and help made *Lullaby* better than I could have made it on my own. You are all golden. I am so glad I joined the group.

Merci, gracias and dankeschon to fellow Southland Scribe, talented writer and editor extraordinaire Julie Hyzy, for believing *Lullaby* "had legs." Without you, this day might never have happened.

My profound thanks to John Helfers, the people at Tekno Books and Five Star Publishing, for seeing the value in my work and giving *Lullaby* a chance.

Thanks to my cousin and fellow writer retired Chicago police officer, Harvey Keefner for his information on police procedure. Any mistakes are mine.

My deepest thanks to the Writers' Fellowship, Jan Haberichter, Ben Greenberg and Nancy Grasso. Over our many years together, we have become more than writing peers and friends, you are my family, too. And of course, endless thanks to our fearless leader Mary K. Fliris. Dear friend, you are my rock and trusted first reader. You nudged, pushed and gave me the occasional kick in the pants that kept me going. Without you, I would have probably given up long ago. I am so grateful to have you all in my life and to be a part of such a talented group of people.

And to J.K., you make my heart sing and my spirits soar. The angels truly smiled on me the day you asked me to walk. Thank you a thousand times over for coming into my life at just the right time.

I am truly blessed and I love you all.

Prologue

The first ring of the phone jolted Vicky wide awake. She sat up in bed, heart thudding. Each ring was like nails raking a blackboard, but she didn't reach for the phone. Maybe he'd give up if she just let it ring. She let out a sharp laugh at the thought.

Fat chance of that. Just pick it up and get it over with.

Her heart went into overdrive as she lifted the receiver.

"I'm coming for you, Vicky," the man whispered. "Do you hear me, bitch? I am Death, and I'm coming for you." His voice sounded like the rustle of dry leaves and sent a shiver down Vicky's spine. She bit back the scathing words on the end of her tongue, resisted the urge to slam down the receiver, and instead, left it off the hook. He wouldn't bother her any more that night. But what about tomorrow night and the night after that? How long before he made good on his threats? Hugging her knees to her chest, Vicky chewed her lower lip. In the beginning she tried convincing herself it was just some sicko who didn't have anything else to do at one in the morning. In her heart, she'd known better. This guy was serious trouble, and it was time to get the police involved. Of course Vicky knew Frank Paxton, the chief of police, would give her twenty kinds of hell when she confessed what she'd been up to. She'd heard it all before.

"Are you out of your goddamn mind, Victoria Langford?" he'd say. "Keep your nose out of things that can get you hurt."

But she couldn't do that this time—not when she was so close to finding the truth. She'd give it another day or two—see what else she could dig up before talking to the chief. Slipping back under the covers, she lay staring at the ceiling.

I am Death, and I'm coming for you.

She sat up again and snapped on the bedside lamp. Snowball, her white Persian cat, lifted his head and blinked lazily at Vicky from the foot of the bed. He stretched, then curled back into a ball and closed his eyes.

"Wish I could go back to sleep that easily," Vicky said.

She told herself she and her little boy, Josh, were safe, but she couldn't shake the sick, fluttery feeling in the pit of her stomach. She reached under the bed for the nightstick she kept there, and then went through the house checking doors and windows for the third time that night. Vicky checked the alarm, too, though she had set it before turning in. As she headed back to her room, she heard her son whimpering.

Eighteen-month-old Josh was sitting up in his crib rubbing his eyes. He raised his arms and cried, "Mama."

"What's the matter, sweetie?" Vicky murmured. "Bad dreams?"

Scooping him up, she settled in the rocker beside his crib. Josh quieted instantly and snuggled against her. Vicky leaned her cheek against his downy head. She was starting to relax when she heard a soft tapping at the window. Her head snapped back up and her breath caught in her throat.

It's only a branch from the old box elder, Vicky reminded herself, but her heart still hammered. Sensing his mother's fear, Josh began crying again.

Vicky kissed him and whispered, "It's all right, punkin. You go back to sleep now."

She sure as hell wasn't. Her gaze darted to the window once

more. Uneasiness nibbled at the back of her mind. It was going to be another long night.

Outside, a man peeked through the window of Josh's room. This was his nightly ritual. He couldn't stop himself from coming here any more than he could make himself stop breathing. His dark eyes bored into Vicky as she rocked her son.

Poor mommy. Another sleepless night? He pulled his cell phone from his pocket and punched in her number again. The sound of the busy signal vibrated in his ear. He shook with rage. Stupid bitch. Did she really think she could avoid him by leaving the phone off the hook? He should go in there right now and snap her neck like a dry twig.

"I am Death, Vicky, and I'm coming for you."

But not tonight—it wasn't time. The fun was just beginning and he would savor every moment of it. He deserved that. He stood at the window until Vicky tucked a sleeping Josh back in his crib.

Such a loving mother.

In that instant an idea took root in his mind and he smiled. This was going to be even better than he had imagined.

Chapter 1

"Darkness and death are all around you."

The woman who said it didn't look like a fortune-teller. Vicky had expected her to come to the table sporting a thick Slovak accent, flowing robes, and maybe a wart on her chin. Still, Madam Zoya was anything but ordinary looking. Hair that was more salt than pepper framed a chiseled face with wide-set hazel eyes and a hawkish nose. She had a linebacker's shoulders, and even with her black flats she was well over six feet. Vicky guessed she weighed a good 240.

The Southern drawl, smooth as a bottle of Kentucky bourbon, seemed out of place with her large frame. If Vicky had heard that voice over the phone she would have pictured a blond bombshell, not the Amazon sitting across from her.

Madam Zoya frowned as she peered intently into Vicky's teacup. "The wolves are waiting."

The hair rose on the back of Vicky's neck. Suddenly, the red brick walls and flickering candlelight in the Tanglewood Inn didn't seem as warm and inviting as when she and her best friend, Mary Renfield, first arrived. Vicky had hesitated when the hostess had stopped at their table to ask if they wanted their fortunes told. It was Mary who talked her into it.

"You've never had it done before," she'd said. "It'll be fun."

Fun wasn't exactly the word that crept into Vicky's mind now. Eerie was more like it. She had never put much stock in fortune-telling, but Madam Zoya was making a believer out of her as she targeted events in Vicky's past with the accuracy of a sharpshooter.

"Wolves?" Mary twirled the straw in her glass and chuckled nervously. "Are we talking the four-legged or the two-legged variety?"

The fortune-teller shot her a hard look, and Mary's smile quickly faded. Madam Zoya picked up the gold-rimmed cup and studied the tea leaves again. Her eyes widened slightly, and her face drained of color. Vicky saw her large hands tremble as she put down the cup. "What is it?" Vicky asked, her gaze darting from the teacup to Madam Zoya's troubled face. "What did you see?"

"I'm sorry." Madam Zoya pushed abruptly away from the table. "There are other people waiting. I've already taken too much time."

She started to walk away, then suddenly turned back and looked at Vicky with frightened eyes. Clamping a shaking hand on Vicky's arm she whispered, "You must be careful. You're surrounded by death."

Vicky's heart skipped a beat, but before she could respond, Madam Zoya hurried from the table. Blowing out a breath, Vicky raised her eyebrows and glanced at Mary.

"What a terrible thing to tell you." Mary shivered and rubbed her arms.

"I thought you said this would be fun."

"It usually is. Most of them tell you good things or general stuff that could be true for anybody."

"Well, she certainly didn't do that with me." Vicky chewed her lower lip and glanced around the room. Madam Zoya was seated at a table with an elderly couple. She watched as a smile spread across the old woman's face. "Looks like they're getting better news than I did. I want my twenty bucks back."

"What she said about you being surrounded by death and

darkness made me think of those creepy phone calls you've been getting. You *did* talk to Frank Paxton about them, didn't you?" Mary skewered Vicky with her gaze. Seconds went by as she drummed her fingertips on the table, waiting for an answer. "It's a simple yes or no question."

"I haven't had a chance."

"That's bullshit, and you know it." Mary balled her white napkin and tossed it on the table. "Dammit, Vicky, you promised."

"I'll do it tomorrow."

"That's what you told me two days ago. What the hell are you waiting for? What if this nut decides to skip the phone call and make a personal appearance?"

"Look, Mary, I'm onto something really big. I just need another day or two and it could bust wide open."

"I knew it. They aren't just crank calls. It's got to do with something you're working on." Mary leaned back in her chair and plowed her fingers through her coppery hair. "God, I thought I could stop worrying about you when you left the police force."

"Let's just drop this for now, okay?"

"Drop it? After everything Madam Zoya just said?"

"Oh, come on," Vicky chided, with more bravado than she felt. "You're too levelheaded to take this kind of stuff seriously."

Mary's green eyes widened. "So are you, but I wish you could have seen the look on your face when she told you why you left the police department."

"I'll admit that took me by surprise, but let's keep this in perspective." Vicky was quiet a moment, casting around for a reasonable explanation, but there wasn't one and they both knew it. Still, she gave it her best shot. "My picture was in the paper and on the news for weeks after what happened. She must have recognized me."

"That was seven years ago, Vicky. How could she possibly recognize you?" Mary frowned harder. "This is more than a little creepy. A total stranger just gave you the condensed version of your life, for Christ's sake."

"Coincidence."

"Neither of us believes in coincidence."

"No. And we don't believe in this stuff, either, remember?" Vicky signaled for their waitress. "Let's get out of here."

"Dessert ladies?" the waitress asked, flashing them a toothy smile. "We have killer turtle cheesecake tonight."

"That's just what I need," Mary said, slapping an ample thigh. "I'll pass. Vicky?"

"Just the check, please."

As the waitress tallied their bill she said, "I noticed Madam Zoya with you. She's fantastic isn't she?"

"She's done readings for you?" Mary asked.

"Several, and she's always dead-on."

"Dead-on?" Mary repeated, giving Vicky an I-told-you-so look.

The waitress nodded and arched her brows. "Sometimes it's positively spooky."

"Jeez," Vicky said as the waitress left their table. "That's just what I wanted to hear."

Tugging on their coats, Vicky and Mary shot anxious glances at Madam Zoya again. She was still locked in conversation with the elderly couple.

Vicky grabbed Mary's arm. "Come on. Let's forget about Madam Zelda."

"Zoya," Mary corrected, following her friend through the maze of tables toward the exit.

The next day started out with a bang—literally—for John Wexler. The snitch had gotten whacked early that morning in his bed in the Lexington Hotel. It wasn't the news that shocked Vicky so much—the Wexlers of the world didn't have a long life expectancy. It was the timing that blew her mind.

Madam Zoya's words nagged at her. *You're surrounded by death.*

This morning Vicky felt as if it was her shadow.

She'd known Wexler since her rookie days on the Westport Police Department and kept in touch with him after she changed careers. His services came in handy for her new job as an investigative reporter. While Vicky never made the mistake of counting the wiry, bug-eyed snitch among her friends, Wexler had always come through for her when she needed him.

Rain came down in a solid sheet, obscuring her vision, making the roads slick. Vicky eased up on the gas pedal and kicked the wipers up a notch. She stopped for the light on Avery Street and glanced at Gaffney's Coffee Shop on the corner. She had been on her way to Gaffney's to meet Wexler when she'd gotten a page from her editor, Tom McDonald.

"Meet Dalila Sinclair at the Lexington and cover a breaking story," he'd said, when Vicky called him. "Some hooker and a guy by the name of John Wexler were killed there this morning."

Vicky felt as if she'd gotten smacked in the chest with a two-by-four. That Wexler should be whacked now was no coincidence. He had the information she needed to finally nail Richard Blackwell. She had Wexler's money in her purse. Two thousand dollars in crisp new bills. She would have paid ten times that amount.

Blackwell probably thought he was going to get away with murder again, Vicky thought bitterly, but he was wrong.

"I'm going to get you this time, you murdering bastard," she whispered. "I swear you'll pay for everything you've done."

The street in front of the Lexington was jammed with police

cars and news vans by the time Vicky arrived. With no place left to park, she drove around the corner, swearing under her breath. This was one of the most crime-ridden areas in Westport. Not a neighborhood to be walking around in, but she didn't have a choice.

She finally found an empty spot one block down in front of a dilapidated liquor store that had a metal accordion grate across the front. She'd have a short trek back to the Lexington, but at least the rain had stopped. That was the good news. The bad news was she'd probably get mugged on her way there.

Switching off the engine, she quickly scanned the street. A mangy, old mutt trotted down the sidewalk, paused long enough to raise his leg on a rusted Buick at the curb, and then moved on. Fido was the only sign of life at the moment. All the other neighborhood residents were probably still in bed or in front of the Lexington.

She set the alarm and climbed out of the Blazer, hoping it would still be there and in one piece when she returned. The wind bit her face and she shivered. It was only October, but already the specter of winter hung in the air. Pulling her coat collar tighter, she hitched her purse up on her shoulder and hurried up the cracked and buckled sidewalk.

A few minutes later, she was searching the sea of faces in front of the Lexington for *Herald* photographer Dalila Sinclair. She wasn't usually difficult to find. At fifty-five, she had hair that was still naturally black. Cropped short, it curled around her face, accentuating sculpted cheekbones and emerald green eyes. She was the kind of woman who stood out in a crowd, if not because of her drop-dead features, then certainly for her taste in fashion.

Vicky rolled her eyes when she finally spotted Dalila leaning against the building. Today's ensemble included a neon-green floral skirt that grazed the tops of Dalila's black combat boots.

Her hands were shoved into the pockets of the prized raccoon coat she'd picked up at a rummage sale over the summer. A tattered mink hat—complete with black beady eyes and bared teeth—was perched at a jaunty angle on her head. Dalila broke into a relieved smile when she saw Vicky pushing her way through the crowd. "I couldn't wait for you to get here," she announced, shivering. "This weather is positively brutal."

"It is a little brisk," Vicky said. "Anything happening yet?"

"Just a lot of people coming and going."

"I guess we'd better get up there if were going to scoop the *Banner.*"

Dalila gave a wry laugh. "Speak of the devil, look who just showed up."

Vicky looked over her shoulder and groaned. "You know what's going to happen now, don't you?"

"I don't care. I actually get a little satisfaction out of seeing you get under Warren's pasty skin."

Mumbling apologies, they elbowed their way through the mass of bodies, heading toward the yellow police tape that cordoned off the six-story building. Vicky cast a glance at Warren Mott, her former co-worker, as she made her way past him. His bulldog face was pinched with cold. The wind lifted wisps of a bad comb-over he'd secured beneath a pair of brown earmuffs. His eyes narrowed behind his black-rimmed glasses when he spotted Vicky.

She pulled out her press pass, caught the attention of an older cop behind the police tape, and held it up for him to see. "Can we go up, Sulley?"

Sulley waved it away. "Go on. You know you don't have to show me that thing."

Vicky and Dalila ducked under the tape and were almost to the door when a familiar voice shouted, "Hey! I thought you said no one was allowed in the building!"

The two women stopped and turned around. Warren pushed his way through the crowd.

"She's got special clearance from Chief Paxton himself," Sulley snapped. "Not that I have to explain anything to you."

"If she can get in, so can I!" Warren shot back, his jowls quivering with anger.

Sulley drew his nightstick and slapped it against his gloved palm. Warren screwed his mouth into a defiant knot and started to duck under the tape.

"You've been warned," Sulley said. "And I don't repeat myself."

Warren paused, his gaze darting from Vicky to the nightstick.

"Don't be stupid," Sulley said. "No story is worth taking a crack from one of these."

Scowling at Vicky, Warren let the tape drop back in place and said, "It must be nice to be the goddaughter of the police chief, but not all of us have that advantage."

Vicky strode back to him, her face tight with anger. "That's not why I get to visit crime scenes, Warren, and you know it."

"If I were you I'd want to *forget* that I was ever one of Westport's finest and I sure as hell wouldn't take advantage of it, especially since you have innocent blood on your hands."

Vicky's pulse quickened and she took a step closer to Warren. "What's that supposed to mean?"

A sly smile curled his rubbery lips. "Surely you haven't forgotten poor Connie Springer. Can it really be seven years since that nasty little accident?"

"You son of a bitch," Vicky said, grabbing Warren by the lapels of his coat.

"Take your hands off me, Langford, or I'll have you thrown in jail." Warren's dark eyes blinked rapidly behind his glasses. "That's where you belong anyway, after what you did."

"Let him go," Dalila said, prying Vicky's hands away. "He's

not worth it."

Warren straightened his coat and grunted. "You cost me my job at the *Herald,* but you'll get yours, Langford. You're going to be sorry you ever crossed my path."

"Get a life, Warren," Dalila said, with a short laugh. She took Vicky's arm and steered her toward the building.

Vicky trembled with anger as she pulled open the door to the Lexington. "I don't know why I let him get to me like that."

"The little weasel just knows which buttons to push, and unfortunately you let him push yours big-time."

"It's hard not to when it comes to Connie Springer," Vicky replied quietly.

They crossed the threadbare cabbage rose carpeting to the front desk. The man behind it eyed the two women and gave them a toothless grin. His face was covered with a beard almost as heavy as the stench of alcohol and body odor that clung to him. Wearing a holey stained T-shirt, he leaned his flabby arms on the counter and asked, "What can I do for you, ladies?"

"What floor are the victims on?" Vicky asked.

"Fourth. You two cops or something?"

"Or something," Vicky answered, heading for the elevator. She jabbed at the CALL button, waited and pushed it again.

"Out of order." The clerk smiled. "Say, you want to ask me any questions? We could have a drink together. I have a bottle in the back room."

Scowling at him, Vicky turned to Dalila. "I hope you're up to a climb."

The dimly lit stairwell reeked so strongly of urine and booze it made their eyes water. They ran up the creaking steps, coat collars pulled over their mouths and noses. By the time they burst through the door on the fourth floor, Dalila was puffing like a steam engine. Peeling off her raccoon coat she leaned against a cracked pea-green wall and wheezed, "That's it. I've had my last Twinkie. I remember when I could run up twice that many stairs and not even break a sweat."

Vicky gave Dalila a minute to catch her breath. "You know I won't be able to get you in the room, but you can get a few pictures of the guys working—maybe get one when they take the bodies out."

"That's fine by me," Dalila replied, holding up her hands. "I wasn't keen on the idea of seeing dead bodies up close and personal this morning anyway. Lead on."

Vicky knew most of the cops she passed in the hall. They smiled and nodded in greeting, but she barely noticed. Her mind was focused on what she would see in Wexler's room.

As she moved toward the yellow police tape at the end of the hall, she let the veil of indifference she had perfected so well on the police department drop into place. It was the only way to do the job. She had to think of the bodies in there as just empty vessels—nothing more—not as people with hopes and dreams and family and friends who loved them. And even lowlifes like John Wexler and his hooker had someone somewhere who cared about them.

She turned to Dalila. "This is where we part ways."

"I'll be waiting right here," Dalila replied, removing the lens cap from her camera. Vicky ducked under the tape and stepped inside. The room was small, dingy and smelled of death. John Wexler's nude body lay spread-eagled on the double bed that took up most of the room. A pillow, apparently placed over his head to muffle the gunshots, still covered his face. It hid the gruesome sight, but the sheets and blankets beneath him were soaked with blood.

An officer was busily snapping pictures of Wexler's body from every possible angle while evidence technicians dusted for fingerprints.

One of the techs looked up at Vicky and grinned. "I was

wondering when you were going to get here. You usually beat us to these things."

"Find anything, Myers?"

"We're going to have a field day trying to identify all these prints. Some of them have probably been here for years. And forget hair samples," Myers said, rubbing his balding pate. "I've got enough to make a toupee for myself."

Vicky crossed the room and poked her head in the tiny bathroom. An officer kneeled over a nude woman lying on the white-tiled floor. Her hands and feet were bound with silver duct tape. Another piece covered her mouth. A clear plastic bag was wrapped tightly around her head.

The officer gave Vicky a weary smile. "Hey, what's shaking, Langford?"

"You ID her yet, Barley?" Vicky glanced away from the woman's wide-staring eyes, not allowing herself to think about what her last terrifying moments must have been like.

"We found her purse in the closet. Name's Livvie Summerfield." Barley drew himself upright and stepped back into the other room. He shook his head as he looked at Wexler. "Whoever did this was sure a sadistic son of a bitch. There are tiny cuts and what look like cigarette burns all over both of them. Neither Summerfield or Wexler were angels, but they sure as hell didn't deserve this."

"Who found them?" Vicky tried to keep her eyes on Barley's face, but they were drawn like a magnet to Wexler's body on the bed.

"A cleaning woman by the name of Gert Brinkman. She saw a man leave the room, assumed it was empty and used her key to get in. This is what she found."

"Any chance I can talk to her?"

Barley shrugged. "Fine by me, but you'll have to check it out with McCann. He's questioning her right now."

Vicky was about to ask who McCann was when the medical examiner arrived. Oliver Grant had been the ME for Westport for as long as Vicky could remember and well before that. His face was a spider web of wrinkles. White windblown hair clung stubbornly to his egg-shaped head. A man of few words, he nodded a greeting to them.

He tugged a pair of latex gloves onto his bony hands and let out a deep sigh. "Let's see what we have here."

Everything stopped as Grant shuffled toward the bed and took the pillow away. Not even Wexler's own mother would have known him. There was nothing left where his face had once been. One of the cops immediately lost his breakfast. Vicky felt her own throat close and her stomach churn. She clamped her teeth together so tightly they ached.

"What the hell are you doing in here?"

Vicky whirled around and looked up into the darkest blue eyes she had ever seen, but they looked hard as chips of granite and they were glaring right at her.

Chapter 2

Reporters. Detective Jim McCann felt the jackhammer in his head pound harder. As far as he was concerned, members of the press were one step above pond scum. He'd left strict orders that none be admitted into the Lexington. Somehow this one and the character in the hall had conned their way in.

He shot Dalila a look that made hardened criminals run for cover, and she immediately shrank from the doorway. Satisfied she'd be no trouble, he turned his attention to Vicky. Tall and slender, she had an almost fragile air about her, but there was a defiant lift to her chin and a determination in her dark eyes Jim knew in his gut spelled trouble.

"Out," he said, jerking his thumb in the direction of the door. "This area is restricted."

Vicky stepped back and sized up her opponent. In a split second she took in the broad shoulders, the dark hair that curled at the base of his neck, and his midnight-blue eyes. A head taller than her own five-feet-eight-inches, he wore a gray sweater and faded jeans that hugged lean thighs. He gripped a black leather jacket in one hand; the other was clenched in a tight fist at his side.

"You're obviously new." Vicky kept her voice even as she extended her hand. "My name is Vicky Langford. I'm a reporter with the *Herald.*"

"I don't care if you're the friggin' Queen of England. You're contaminating my crime scene. I don't know how you got past security, but you're out of here," the detective said, clamping a hand on her arm.

Vicky jerked it free, matched his glare with one of her own, and crossed her arms. Her confrontation with Warren Mott had worn her patience down to the bone. As far as she was concerned, this guy had just rung the bell for the first round and she was ready to jump in the ring with both feet. "Listen, pal."

"No, you listen. You've got to the count of three to turn around and walk out of here under your own steam."

Vicky started past him. "Where's Gil Fletcher? He can clear this up."

"Fletcher didn't catch this case, I did. And your time just ran out."

Dalila was already heading down the hall when the detective grabbed Vicky's arm again and steered her toward the door. The evidence techs stopped what they were doing and watched, their mouths agape. Heads turned as he pulled Vicky through the hall and down the stairs.

"You can wait outside with the rest of the vultures," he snapped.

When they reached the lobby Vicky tried to jerk her arm free again, but the detective's grip was like a vise. A moment later, she was sucking in frosty air as she stumbled unceremoniously onto the sidewalk outside of the Lexington. She caught a glimpse of Warren Mott who watched with a satisfied smirk on his face. She felt her own face flush with heat. The surly detective didn't know it, but he had just made Warren's day.

The detective stopped one of the uniformed cops holding back the growing crowd and jabbed his forefinger into his chest. "Don't let anyone in here, you got that?"

Turning on his heel, he stalked back into the Lexington. Vicky stared after him, her eyes blazing.

Sulley arched his brows and patted her shoulder. "Sorry, kid."

"It's not your fault, Sulley," Vicky replied. She turned to Dalila. "Do you believe that guy? He wouldn't give me a chance to explain anything."

Dalila pulled a pair of yellow-and-purple-striped gloves from her pocket and tugged them on. "If I were you, I'd get on his good side."

"He doesn't look like he has a good side. And as far as I'm concerned, the less I have to deal with him the better."

Jim clenched his fists as he let the door swing shut behind him. "Damn reporters," he muttered.

He knew all too well how far they were willing to go to get a story. What had this one done to get past security? Slip a few dollars in someone's hand or make promises for later that she might or might not keep?

An image of Mimi shot through his mind. More than a year had passed, but Jim still felt that same gut-wrenching pain now that he had the night he'd discovered what she had done.

"I don't know why you're making such a big deal out of it, Jim." Mimi had said it so casually. That had hurt just as much as the fact she had used him and betrayed his trust just to get a story. It turned out to be the story that made her career, even if it destroyed their marriage in the process.

In those first days after he'd left, Jim told himself that a month from then, a year from then, things would be better. That it wouldn't hurt so goddamn much.

He'd been wrong.

He was halfway across the lobby when Sulley's voice stopped him. The old cop marched over to him, his grizzled face indignant. "Do you know who you just threw out of here?"

"I don't give a damn who she is. She doesn't belong in here, and when I find out who let her and that other one in, I'll have his head on a platter."

"Well, you've found him."

Jim glowered at Sulley. "You deliberately disobeyed my orders."

"For your information, Detective, she has special clearance to visit crime scenes. She's Chief Paxton's goddaughter."

Jim kept his face a mask of indifference, but he groaned inwardly. On the Westport PD less than a week and he would probably be on the unemployment line by the end of the day, thanks to a reporter who happened to be in Paxton's hip pocket.

"I thought that would get your attention," Sulley went on. "Her old man and Chief Paxton go way back. He'd walk through fire for that girl."

The jackhammer in Jim's head beat against his brain with every word Sulley said. He dug in the pocket of his jacket for the bottle of aspirin, shook two out and swallowed them dry. "I get the picture. Next time I see Brenda Starr, I'll roll out the red carpet for her."

At three that afternoon, Vicky pushed through the revolving doors of the *Herald,* her mood as dark as the autumn sky.

"You look like you ate glass and nails for lunch," said Roxanne, the receptionist. She handed Vicky a stack of pink message slips.

"That would have been more pleasant than what I've just been through," Vicky said. She shuffled through the messages as she stepped into the elevator.

When she exited on the sixth floor, she headed straight for the break room. Pushing through the swinging door, she nearly collided with Dalila who was struggling to open a bag of Doritos.

"What took you so long to get back?" Dalila asked. "Did you

go back into the Lexington and have a chat with your new best friend?"

"I'd rather have lunch with Warren Mott than talk to that jackass again." Vicky dug in her purse for change and dropped it into a vending machine.

"I don't know. I thought he was pretty good-looking, myself."

"So was Ted Bundy."

Dalila chuckled. "Okay, so why are you so late?"

"After you left I stood in the cold and wind for two hours waiting for that Neanderthal to make his statement only to find out my tape recorder is broken. Then when I got back to my Blazer, all of the tires were slashed," Vicky replied, the anger still evident in her voice. She warily eyed the limp-looking ham sandwich she pulled from the vending machine. "I had to wait forever for a tow to the service station."

Dalila bit her lower lip, her face pulling into a frown. "I wish I'd have known you were in trouble. I would've waited around."

"Thanks, but don't worry about it. I walked back to the Lexington and got one of the uniforms to make a report."

"Vandals," Dalila said shaking her head. "I'll never understand why people destroy property for absolutely no reason, but I guess you're lucky the Blazer was there at all."

"Yeah, I guess." The cop who took the report had said the same thing, but Vicky didn't feel lucky. Too much was happening too fast. The phone calls, the sense she was being followed, Wexler's murder and now this. More of Richard Blackwell's handiwork?

Dalila started out the door, then stopped. "By the way, I meant to ask if you were still getting those horrible phone calls."

"Every night, like clockwork." Vicky dropped coins into the soda machine. She pushed a button and a cold can of Coke clattered down. "I haven't had a whole night's sleep in two weeks."

"Your caller ID doesn't show anything?"

"It comes up private caller with no number. He must be blocking it by pushing star-sixty-seven."

"Don't you think it's time to go to the police?"

"I'm going to stop by the station tonight and talk to Frank Paxton." Vicky reached into the bag Dalila offered and popped a chip in her mouth.

"Do you think they'll be able to trace the calls?"

Vicky shook her head. "I'd have to keep him on the line and that'll never happen. His calls are short and sweet—a little heavy breathing, then his usual, 'I am Death, Vicky, and I'm coming for you.' "

"Doesn't that scare you? It sure gives me a major case of the creeps."

"He's irritating the living hell out of me more than anything," Vicky replied flatly, not wanting to admit how unsettling she really found the calls.

She followed Dalila back to the newsroom where a stack of mail and a package waited on her desk. Wrapped in plain brown paper, the package had no return address or postmark. That meant someone had dropped it off at the *Herald.* Tearing it open, she found a black shoebox secured with tape.

Vicky raked a hand through her dark hair and swore under her breath. She'd been the unlucky recipient of packages like this twice before. The first had contained a cow's tongue and a note warning her that she'd have her tongue cut out if she didn't drop her investigation of a triple homicide. The other had contained a pile of dog feces and the message, "you're in deep." Vicky wondered what prize was in this box of Cracker Jack.

The stench of decaying flesh hit her as she removed the lid. Holding her breath, she pulled out the crumpled newspaper that was stuffed inside. Hands trembling, Vicky lifted a bloodstained note that lay beside a decapitated pigeon. She read the note over and over, until the words blurred and ran together.

Back off or you'll wind up like your pal, Wexler.

Fat rain drops peppered Vicky's windshield as she pulled into the parking lot of the Westport Police Department. Shuddering, she gingerly picked up the brown paper bag beside her and climbed out of the Blazer. As if on cue Mother Nature let loose again. By the time Vicky reached the steps of the station house she and the bag were soaked through. A perfect end to a perfect day. It just didn't get any better than this.

She waved to the desk sergeant who gave her a broad grin as she headed down the hall to the elevator. New faces passed her, making Vicky think of one new face she'd rather not see again. She scowled as she thought of the surly detective at the Lexington.

"Hey, Langford, you have some bad fish for lunch or something? You look like you've got a nasty case of indigestion."

"Just something that left a sour taste in my mouth," Vicky said to the officer who suddenly blocked her path.

Over six feet tall and built like a pro wrestler, Officer Nick Rizzo crossed his arms and flashed her an understanding smile. "Let it go, Langford. It's not worth getting your drawers in a bunch."

Vicky groaned, feeling heat creep up her face. "It's gotten around already?"

"We're taking bets on whether or not the chief is gonna call McCann on the carpet for it."

"He won't, unless I say something to him."

"Which you won't." Rizzo gave her an appraising look and added, "You're all right, Langford."

As he headed down the hall he called out, "You know something else? You're a good-looking woman, but you really gotta change your perfume."

Vicky looked down at the bag, sniffed and wrinkled her nose. The odor was getting worse and now the corner of the shoebox was poking through the bottom of the bag. She hoped it would hold until she got to the chief's office. Best not to wait for the rickety elevator. Vicky headed for the stairs, wishing all the while she had the new detective's head in the shoebox under her arm instead of a dead pigeon.

The aroma of coffee teased her as she slipped through the door of the reception area to the chief's office. She would kill for a cup right now—even the muddy concoction Frank Paxton prided himself on. An older woman with half-moon glasses perched on her nose looked up from her computer and smiled. "Vicky. What a pleasant surprise." She took the glasses off and let them hang from a silver chain around her neck. "How's the baby?"

"Fine, Laverne. Growing like a weed and getting into everything."

"You know Frank dotes on him the way he does his own grandchildren."

"I know, and he spoils him the same way, too," Vicky laughed. She pulled off her gloves and coat and laid them to dry on the hissing radiator by the window. Her clothes felt damp and uncomfortable, and she couldn't stop shivering.

"You look like you could use this," Laverne said, handing Vicky a steaming cup of coffee. "And don't worry. I made this pot, so it's safe for human consumption."

"You're an angel. Thanks."

"You just missed Frank, but he should be back in a few minutes." Laverne nodded in the direction of his office. "Why don't you go in and make yourself comfortable."

Frank Paxton's office smelled of tobacco, leather, and Old Spice cologne. Just like always, Vicky thought, closing the door behind her. Darkness crept across the room as the last of the late-afternoon sun faded. She turned on the lamp on the credenza and laid the bag down, glad to finally be rid of it.

Settling in one of the chairs in front of the chief's massive mahogany desk, she leaned back and sipped her coffee. What she wouldn't give for a hot shower and a warm bed right now. She couldn't wait to pick Josh up from Mary's and get home. Vicky decided to wait fifteen minutes. If Frank wasn't back by then, she'd leave the bag and a note with Laverne.

When the door opened a few minutes later, she turned in the chair and smiled, expecting to see the chief. Her smile faded instantly. Her eyes narrowed as they swept over the man standing in the doorway. She hadn't expected to see him again this soon. His eyes locked with hers and she saw a flicker of challenge in those blue depths that sent adrenaline coursing through her body.

The look on her face mirrored his own as Jim McCann stepped inside and quietly closed the door. He almost hadn't recognized her. Her dark hair was soaked and tangled. Mascara had smudged under her huge brown eyes. She looked tired, but from the defiant glint in her eyes, obviously not too tired to run to the chief and tell him what happened at the Lexington that morning.

Jim's jaw went rigid and his throat tightened. Dammit, he had come to Westport to do a job and that was exactly what he had done today. He hadn't been wrong to toss her out of the Lexington regardless of who she was, and he'd tell that to Frank Paxton.

"I just wanted to give Frank this report," Jim said gruffly. He laid a manila folder on the chief's desk, then headed for the door.

"Wait." Vicky rose from the chair and pointed to the bag on

the credenza. "I've got to get going and I was wondering if you could give that to Frank. You might want to take a look at it, too, since you're working the Wexler case."

Jim shot her a look that clearly said he didn't like where this was going already. He pulled the box from the bag. The sickeningly sweet scent of rotting flesh was unmistakable, and it was making the turkey sandwich he'd just wolfed down rumble dangerously in his stomach. Lifting the lid, Jim grimaced at the sight of the mutilated bird. He quickly read the note, then put it back in the box and replaced the lid. "What in the world do you have to do with Wexler?"

"I'm doing some digging on the Grayson Center fire and Wexler is—was—helping me."

"Whoa, back up," Jim said, holding up his hands. "You're going to have to start from square one. I don't have a clue what you're talking about. I'm new around here, remember?"

"Grayson Center was a forty-story office building still under construction. Someone toasted it two months ago. Eight people were killed, including a man named Peter Murphy who was accused of starting the fire. I think he was framed."

"Is it still under investigation?"

Vicky shook her head. "It seemed pretty open and shut. Murphy was a foreman on the construction crew working at the center. He was fired for drinking on the job, which he vehemently denied. A couple of his co-workers told police Murphy said he was going to find a way to get back at his boss. A few days later, Grayson Center burned and Murphy's prints were on the gasoline cans found at the scene."

"What's all this got to do with you?"

"I'm an investigative reporter," Vicky said evenly. "Murphy's wife, Lisa, came to see me a couple of weeks ago and asked if I'd help clear her husband's name."

"What makes you think he's innocent?"

"Lisa said he'd been upset for weeks because inferior materials were being used, and the company was hiring a lot of unskilled laborers. Nothing was up to code, but the building was passing inspection. That meant someone's pockets were getting lined big-time. When Murphy complained to his boss, he was canned. The night of the fire, he told Lisa he was going to get the proof he needed to go to the authorities. That was the last time Lisa Murphy saw her husband alive."

"Why not tell this to the police?"

"She did, but all of the evidence pointed to Peter. She needs proof of his innocence in order to reopen the case and clear him. I intended to get that proof and that's where Wexler came in. He had his ear to the ground for me. I was supposed to meet with him this morning. Obviously, he came up with something; otherwise he wouldn't be lying on a slab in the morgue right now."

Jim had been on edge ever since his confrontation with Vicky that morning. The more he listened to her, the angrier he got. He closed the distance between them in two strides.

"Why didn't you tell me all this, this morning?"

"You didn't give me a chance to say anything."

"If you would have come to me in the first place, instead of tromping in like you owned the place, I would have listened to you."

Vicky balled her fists at her hips. "No you wouldn't. You would still have tossed me out because you obviously don't like reporters. You have a chip on your shoulder the size of Rhode Island, Detective. I don't know why, and frankly I don't care. I just don't want you interfering with my job."

"Interfering with your job? You're the one interfering with a police investigation . . ."

"What the hell is going on here?" Frank Paxton's massive frame filled the doorway. He was a bear of a man with a thatch of snow-white hair and a face that was a road map of wrinkles. "I didn't think I needed a whistle and striped shirt in my own office. Why don't you two go to separate corners and cool down?" Striding into the room, he dumped an armload of files on his desk then wrapped a burly arm around Vicky. "How's my favorite goddaughter?" He pulled a crumpled pack of Camels from his gray suit coat, shook one out and lit up.

"Damp, tired, and ornery," Vicky replied. She took the cigarette from his fingers and stubbed it out in the ashtray on his desk. Frank scowled and Vicky gave him an exaggerated one right back. "Hey, Mister, this is a nonsmoking facility, and besides, you know you're not supposed to have those."

"And you know you're the only person who could do that and get away with it," he chuckled, shoving the pack of cigarettes back in his pocket. "How's Josh doing? You know it's been close to two weeks since Phyllis and I have seen him."

"I'll call Phyllis tonight about getting together."

"See that you do," Frank said with mock sternness. "If you wait much longer, Josh might not remember us."

Vicky rolled her eyes and shook her head. As if that could ever happen. Frank and Phyllis Paxton were Josh's surrogate "Papa and Gumma," as he called them.

"I'll be sure to show him your pictures to jog his memory," Vicky teased.

Frank turned to Jim. "I know you two have already met, but humor me. I'm from the old school and I believe in proper introductions. Vicky, this is Jim McCann. He just came here from the Seattle, Washington PD. Jim, this is my goddaughter, Vicky Langford. She's an investigative reporter with the *Herald.* You'll be seeing her around here from time to time."

"Detective McCann, it's a pleasure to meet you." As Vicky extended her right hand to shake Jim's, she snagged a lock of wet hair behind her ear with her left. Jim noticed she was wearing a wedding band. Pity the poor guy who tied the knot with this one, he thought. She was a regular Miss Congeniality. He hesitated a moment then took her hand in his. Her skin was soft and he could smell the warm, spicy scent of her perfume. An unexpected warmth spread through his body, and Jim felt the wall of hostility he'd built around himself slip just a fraction. It was a feeling he allowed to last only a second. Not only was she a reporter, she was married, too. He quickly dropped her hand, took a step back, and crossed his arms.

"I had a feeling you two would hit it off," Frank remarked. "Well, there's no better way to smooth the waters than to break bread together. I'm pulling a long shift tonight and I was just going to order something from Max's Deli. How about joining me?"

Vicky shook her head. "No thanks, Frank. I have to pick up Josh from Mary's and get home."

Frank put his arm around Vicky again and drew her close. "Do you remember the first time we all went to Max's?"

The tension in the room quickly faded as Vicky laughed. "How could I forget? You, Danny, and Gil took me there to celebrate my first collar."

"You looked like a drowned rat." Frank's leathery face broke into a grin. "Sort of like you look now."

"I'd just chased a perp on foot for three blocks in the pouring rain."

"You're the one who leaped out of the squad car to chase him!" Frank chuckled. "You nearly gave Gil a heart attack."

Jim's brows shot up as his gaze darted from Frank to Vicky. "Wait a minute. You were a cop?"

"Followed in her old man's footsteps," Frank said. "She was one of the best. She always had too much of the daredevil in her, though."

"I had to prove I was up to the job," Vicky countered. "No

one wanted to get stuck with a female rookie. I heard the fellas drew straws for me and Gil lost."

"You showed everybody, honey," Frank said softly. Then turning to Jim, he added, "Never should have lost her, but she's still helped us crack more than one case since she left the department."

"How did you go from being a cop to a reporter?" Jim asked.

He said the word *reporter* almost as if it were an insult. Vicky felt her temper rise, but she wouldn't get into another verbal wrestling match in front of Frank. She wasn't up to a round of twenty questions either. Let McCann get his answers through the department grapevine.

Ignoring the question, she turned her back to him and handed the shoebox to Frank. Vicky quickly repeated everything she'd told Jim about her investigation into the Grayson Center fire. The vein on Frank's neck started to throb—a sure sign his blood pressure was skyrocketing.

"Is there anything else I should know about?" Frank asked, the vein in his neck throbbing faster.

"My tires were slashed while I was at the Lexington today. It could have just been kids, but I don't think so. I'm pretty sure I'm being followed, too, and of course there are the phone calls."

"What kind of calls?" Jim asked.

"They're always in the middle of the night and he always says the same thing, 'I am Death, and I'm coming for you.' "

"Is there anything familiar about the voice?"

Vicky shook her head. "I only know that it's a man."

"And this all started when?" Frank asked, pulling out the pack of Camels again. Vicky frowned at him, but he lit up anyway.

"Just a few days after I started digging into the Grayson Center fire."

Frank puffed furiously on his cigarette as he paced the length of the room. "I want you to drop this investigation right now."

"I can't do that. I promised Lisa Murphy I would help her clear her husband's name."

"I don't give a rat's ass if you promised the Pope. I'm not asking you, Victoria, I'm telling you to drop this—now."

"Frank, listen to me. This could be our one shot at getting Richard Blackwell. If everything that's been happening to me is connected to this story, then I must be getting close to something and he must be running scared."

"Who's Richard Blackwell?" Jim asked.

"Westport's answer to an organized crime boss. He's got his fingers in every dirty deal in this town," Frank explained. "We know he's guilty of everything from extortion to murder, but we just can't pin anything on him."

"He's smart and very good at covering his tracks," Vicky added. "We've come close to nailing him a thousand times, but either our witnesses disappear or he skates on some technicality."

"How does he figure in with this fire you're talking about?"

"He owns the construction company that was working on Grayson Center," Vicky said. "Peter Murphy tried to go up against him and now he's dead."

"This guy sounds like he's bad news." Jim glanced at her wedding band. "It's none of my business, but what does your husband say about you chasing after a story that could get you killed?"

Vicky's spine stiffened and her shoulders went rigid. "You're absolutely right. It isn't any of your business, but just for the record, I'm a widow."

Jim rocked back on his heels and blew out a breath. "Look, I'm really sorry. I didn't realize . . ."

"Forget it. We were discussing Richard Blackwell, not my

marital status." She turned back to Frank. "I know I'm on to something with the Grayson Center fire. We can get Blackwell this time."

Frank slammed his fist on his desk and Vicky jumped. "You know what, Victoria? You're like a dog with an old shoe."

"Frank," she began, but his glare silenced her.

"The bottom line is this isn't about proving Peter Murphy's innocence, it's about proving Blackwell's guilt." Frank took a deep breath and rested his large hands on Vicky's shoulders. His tone softened as he said, "Listen, honey, I want Blackwell just as badly as you do and so does Gil Fletcher, but I don't want to arrive at a crime scene someday and find out you're the victim. If you're right and all the crap that's been happening is coming from Blackwell, then you're treading on dangerous ground. You of all people know Blackwell is no one to fool around with. Give up the investigation before it's too late, please."

"I can't do that and you know it."

"Let the past rest once and for all, honey. Revenge doesn't bring back the dead."

"It's not revenge I'm looking for, Frank," Vicky replied. "It's justice."

Chapter 3

"You're surrounded by death."

Madam Zoya's words continued to nag Vicky as she stared through the rain-spattered windshield at her rambling old farmhouse. With its wraparound porch and gingerbread trim it was usually a welcome sight at the end of the day. Not tonight. It seemed too isolated and lonely; the woods that surrounded it, too dark and forbidding.

Dammit! Why had she let Mary talk her into having her fortune told? It wasn't as if she didn't already have enough going on to give her a permanent case of goose bumps. Now she had Madam Zoya's predictions to contend with as well.

She fought the urge to drive back to the safety of Mary's house. You're being ridiculous, Vicky chided herself, but she sat there, peering into the darkness that swallowed up her yard, listening to the rain drum on the roof. Her pulse pounded in her ears and she swallowed hard.

"Oh, for God's sake, you can't stay out here all night," she muttered. Taking Josh out of his car-seat, Vicky ran for the porch. She tried to shield him from the downpour, but he howled in protest and squeezed his eyes shut as the cold rain stung his face.

"It's okay, sweetheart, you'll be nice and warm in a minute," she said, but she fumbled with the house keys and dropped them.

She couldn't shake the feeling someone was in the woods,

watching and waiting. It seemed like an eternity before she finally turned the key in the lock. Hugging Josh to her, Vicky cast a furtive glance over her shoulder and slammed the door shut. She quickly locked it and reset the alarm. Maybe it was time to get that dog she'd been thinking about. A big one that would attack on command, she mused. As she pulled off Josh's red corduroy coat and hat, Snowball stalked up to them. Tail held high, he wound himself around Vicky's legs.

Scooping Snowball up, she nuzzled his ears. He purred and buried his head against her.

"Who needs an attack dog when we've got you, huh, baby?" Vicky put the cat back down and he bounded toward the kitchen.

Josh immediately toddled after him, shouting, "Kitty! Kitty!"

Snowball was sitting on the counter staring outside when Vicky entered the room. She pulled back the lacy curtain from the window. The rain beat against the glass and, though Vicky tried, she couldn't see what held the cat's attention. She told herself it was probably just a raccoon, but the hair on the back of her neck prickled. She pulled the curtains closed and went through the house checking doors and windows.

"Get a grip," she said to herself, but as she warmed Josh's dinner, she found herself tensing over every little sound. When she heard a crash in the family room she nearly jumped out of her skin. Pulse racing, she ran to the doorway in time to see Snowball dart across the floor.

"Dammit, Snowball, you scared me to death!" Vicky sagged against the doorjamb and let out a long breath.

The cat had knocked two pictures from the mantel. Broken glass lay scattered on the champagne-colored carpet. Snowball peeked at Vicky from around the corner of her desk. Tail twitching, he bolted from the room. Snowball didn't come out of hiding until Vicky was tucking Josh in for the night. The cat skulked into the room meowing loudly and leaped on top of the dresser. Vicky scratched behind his ears then wound the teddy bear music box beside him. Snowball cocked his head, mesmerized by the three spinning bears, then swiped at it with his paw.

"Snowball, no!" Vicky caught it just before it slid off the edge of the dresser.

The music box had been the one and only thing her husband, Danny, had been able to give Josh, and Vicky cherished it. She smiled sadly, remembering how he had come home with it the day after she'd told him she was pregnant.

"I couldn't resist it," he'd said with a grin as he patted her stomach.

One month later, Vicky buried her husband.

Sighing heavily, she shooed Snowball from the dresser and flicked on the nightlight. She smiled at Josh who had one arm wrapped around his tattered blue bunny. He smiled back as she leaned over the crib and kissed him.

"Night, sweetie. Mommy loves you."

Snowball meowed and followed Vicky from the room. As she closed the door, he raced down the hall and around the corner. Vicky wondered what damage he would do next.

"If I was smart I'd put you in the basement," she said. Padding into her bedroom, she stripped off her things. The wind howled in the trees, reminding her of something else Madam Zoya said. *The wolves are waiting.* Were they the same wolves that killed John Wexler?

The fortune-teller's words kept nibbling at the back of her mind. If Madam Zoya had been right about Vicky's past, how accurate were her predictions about the danger in her future? Vicky thought they might be pretty damned accurate if you took John Wexler's death into consideration. If Danny were here he would hold her close and tell her everything Madam Zoya said was just coincidence. But how could the fortune-teller have known how Danny died or any of the other things about Vicky's past?

"It's not just coincidence, Danny," Vicky whispered to the silent house. "I wish to God it was."

A few minutes later, she was standing under a hot shower. She closed her eyes and willed herself to relax as the water pummeled her back and neck, but an image of John Wexler flashed through her mind and her eyes snapped back open.

"What did you find out, Wexler?" She couldn't suppress a shudder remembering the small, dingy room at the Lexington. The blood-soaked bed, the smell of death. She thought of the woman who died with Wexler that morning. Livvie Summerfield had simply been in the wrong place at the wrong time and paid the ultimate price.

The water was starting to run cold when Vicky finally turned it off. She toweled off, and then reached for the old red football jersey she slept in. As she slipped it over her head she heard the faint sound of breaking glass again.

Vicky rolled her eyes. "Dammit, Snowball, so help me when I get my hands on you . . ." The rest of the words died on her lips as the security alarm went off.

Vicky's stomach twisted into a knot and her mouth went dry.

Intruder!

The word slammed against her brain as she ran down the hall toward Josh's room. He was standing in his crib, his eyes wide and frightened, his little hands gripping the rail.

"Mama," he cried, but Vicky could barely hear him over the shriek of the alarm. Josh stretched out his arms to her. Heart pounding, she scooped him up and ran to her own room.

She tried to put Josh down long enough to get the nightstick from under the bed, but he wrapped his arms around her neck and wouldn't let go.

"Josh, honey, please," Vicky said, trying to pull him away.

When she finally succeeded, she dropped to the floor and groped under the bed for the nightstick. She found an old pair of shoes and a stuffed animal instead. Josh flung himself at her again, screaming in her ear. "I know, honey, I know," Vicky said, though she knew Josh probably couldn't hear her. She swore under her breath. Stretching further, she kept one eye on the doorway, expecting to see someone coming down the hall.

I am Death, and I'm coming for you.

How long before she came face to face with him? Her fingers closed around the nightstick and she was back on her feet. It was then she realized that the security company hadn't called to see if it was a false alarm. With Josh clinging to her legs, Vicky reached for the phone already knowing it was dead. She let the receiver clatter to the floor. If the security company couldn't reach her they would send the police, but how long would it take help to arrive way out there? Ten minutes? Twelve? Would she and Josh still be alive?

She picked him up again and held him tight. Screaming and sobbing, Josh clung to her. Vicky felt his heart beating hard and fast against hers. She kissed the top of his head. "It's okay, sweetheart. Mama's here."

For a brief moment Vicky weighed the idea of locking both Josh and herself in the bedroom, but she knew they wouldn't be safe. One kick would send the door flying open and she would never be able to fight off an attacker while holding Josh.

If there was going to be a confrontation, Vicky wanted it to be as far from her son as possible. She would put Josh back in his crib and go to the end of the hall and wait for the crazy son of a bitch to come to her. Whatever was going to happen would happen there, but Vicky would not let that bastard near her son. She started for the door.

The lights went out. It was as if someone put a blindfold over her eyes. Disoriented, she careened into the dresser, hitting her knee. Vicky cried out as white-hot pain shot up her leg. She ignored the throbbing and kept moving. She had to get to Josh's room before the intruder found them.

The nightstick felt heavy in her hand as she made her way down the hall. By the time she reached Josh's room, her eyes were finally adjusting to the darkness. Prying his arms from her neck, she kissed him and put him back in the crib.

"Mommy will be back," she said. "I promise."

She prayed she was making the right choice as she closed the door. Pressing herself against the wall, she wiped her sweaty palms on her jersey and began inching her way down the hall.

Back off or you'll wind up like your pal, Wexler.

Her legs turned to jelly as an image of the dead pigeon flashed through her mind, faded and was replaced with one of John Wexler. She forced herself to take slow, deep breaths and concentrate. She strained to hear a footstep, a creak of the floor, but she couldn't hear anything over the damned alarm.

She reached the end of the hall. Every nerve in her body was raw as she waited for someone to jump out at her. Keep the perp busy until backup arrives. That's what Vicky had been taught her first day at the academy.

"I'll keep you busy," she whispered through gritted teeth.

Vicky had faced armed perps alone during her six years as a cop. She had handled those confrontations then. It was fear for Josh that was making her half crazy. Beads of sweat rolled down her chest between her breasts. Her body was rigid, her knuckles white as she gripped the nightstick. Her gaze darted around, looking for some sign of movement.

Suddenly, a pair of high beams shined through the front hall sidelights. Vicky's shoulders sagged in relief. She made her way to the front door, fumbled with the buttons on the alarm and managed to shut it off on the second try. Peeking through the window, she saw a dark, low-slung sports car in the driveway.

Its engine was still running and the driver's side door hung open.

She didn't recognize the car, didn't really care who it belonged to. Help was finally there, but where was the driver? Moments later a dark figure ran up the steps and pounded on the door. Vicky started to unlock it then suddenly stopped. What if it was the intruder and not the driver of the car? The pounding became more urgent. A man was calling her name, but Vicky couldn't identify the voice. Leaving the security chain on, she held the nightstick ready and cracked the door.

Jim McCann stood on the front porch, silhouetted in the glow of the car's headlights. Vicky couldn't imagine what had brought him to her house and didn't really care. She was never so glad to see anyone in her life. Her hands shook as she slid the chain back and threw open the door.

Jim stepped through the threshold and grabbed Vicky by her shoulders.

"Are you all right?" he asked.

"I'm fine, but someone broke in."

"He's gone. I saw him take off toward the woods. Are you sure you're okay?"

"I'm fine, really."

Jim stepped back outside as a squad pulled up. Vicky saw him talking to two cops and gesturing toward the woods.

"He knocked the power out," she said, when Jim came back inside.

"I'll check the circuit breakers for you."

"The breaker box is in the basement. I'll get you a flashlight, but I have to get Josh first."

Vicky returned a moment later hugging Josh to her, trying to soothe him, but he was shaking and crying uncontrollably.

"Poor little guy is scared to death," Jim said. He ruffled Josh's hair. "It's okay, partner. You're safe now."

The gentleness in Jim's voice surprised Vicky. It seemed out of place with the gruff persona she had seen earlier that day. Maybe there was a good side to McCann after all.

She maneuvered her way through the dark kitchen and felt around in a drawer for the flashlight. The beam was weak when she tested it, but it would do. She shined the dim light on Jim and gasped. "What happened to you?"

Jim's face and clothes were streaked with mud and his jeans were torn at the knee.

"I had a little run-in with your visitor. No big deal," he replied tersely.

He took the flashlight from her. A wave of cold, damp air hit him as he opened the basement door and stepped onto the landing. "The breaker box is on the south wall," Vicky said. "Be careful."

Jim pulled the Glock from his shoulder holster. The wooden stairs creaked as he slowly descended them. He paused on the bottom step and played the flashlight beam around.

The basement was large, but appeared neat and organized, not the usual catchall most people used them for. No nooks or crannies for anyone to hide in that Jim could see. At first glance everything looked normal, then he spotted the broken window over the washing machine on the back wall. Frigid air gusted through the shattered glass, making the basement feel like a meat locker.

The door to the breaker box hung open, all of the switches in the off position. Jim used his pen to flip them back to avoid smudging any fingerprints, though he doubted there would be any. Immediately, a freezer in the corner began humming and the furnace kicked on.

"Vicky! Flip the light switch!"

Squinting against the sudden brightness, he kneeled on the

floor to examine the trail of muddy footprints that led from the broken window. Whoever came in here had gone straight for the breaker box, knocked the power out and left, but why? Had he seen Jim's lights, gotten spooked and run? It was a possibility, but there was another one, and Jim didn't like it. He headed for the stairs wondering what Vicky's reaction would be when he told her his thoughts.

"Whoever it was came in through the . . ." Jim stopped short as he entered the kitchen. Vicky was standing in the middle of the room, a much quieter Josh perched on one hip.

The red football jersey she wore clung to breasts that were firm and round. Barely skimming her knees, it revealed long, shapely legs. Desire stirred inside of Jim as he remembered how soft her skin had been when he touched her hand—how sweet her perfume had smelled. His breath caught in his throat when he tried to speak, making his words sound harsh. "Maybe you'd like to put something else on before the cavalry comes inside."

For the first time since Jim arrived, Vicky became aware of how she was dressed. She darted a glance at him, and the look in those midnight-blue eyes made her shiver.

"I'll be right back," she said.

She had a million butterflies in her stomach as she brushed past him. Vicky could feel his eyes on her as she headed down the hall. She grabbed the stuffed bunny from Josh's crib and gave it to him, then went into her room and closed the door. Josh clutched his toy as Vicky sat him on the floor beside her. Hands shaking, she pulled on jeans and a sweater, then brushed her hair into a loose ponytail. She tried to ignore the feelings that welled inside of her, but the look in Jim's eyes stoked embers of desire in Vicky that she thought died long ago.

"I must be out of my mind," she said to Josh. "I don't even like him." Josh flashed her a smile, showing off his two bottom teeth. Vicky picked him up and kissed his cheek. "You, on the other hand, I love very much."

Vicky had been able to quiet Josh down quickly, but his lashes were still wet with tears and he was making tiny hiccupping sounds. Every time she thought of what could have happened to him she felt sick inside. He's safe, she assured herself for the umpteenth time.

But things could have turned out differently.

Damn Richard Blackwell! She hugged Josh so tightly he began squirming.

"Sorry, punkin. Mommy didn't mean to squeeze you that hard. You ready to go back out there?" She took one last look in the mirror and said, "I wish I was."

Jim was looking out of the kitchen window when Vicky returned. She handed him the towel she grabbed from the linen closet and he grunted a thanks. He dried his face and ran the towel over his hair. When he pulled it away, Vicky saw blood on it.

"You've been hurt." Frowning, she gestured toward a chair. "Let me have a look."

"It's nothing. I'm fine."

Vicky's eyes narrowed. "Sit."

Jim scowled, but plopped down in the chair. Vicky strapped Josh in his high chair, handed him a cookie from the Big Bird jar on the counter, then turned her attention back to Jim. She gingerly parted his thick black hair and winced at the gash in the back of his head.

"It looks as if you could use a couple of stitches."

"I figured as much," he grumbled. Jim started to rise from the chair, but Vicky clamped her hands on his shoulders and pushed him back down.

"Stay."

"Sit. Stay. Did you run the department's K-9 Unit?"

She tossed him a look over her shoulder as she headed for the bathroom. She returned with cotton balls, antiseptic and a box of butterfly bandages.

Jim flinched as Vicky pressed the antiseptic-soaked cotton to his wound. "Damn, that hurts. Are you almost done?"

"Oh, quit being such a baby."

Jim twisted around in the chair and scowled. "Why do I get the feeling you're thoroughly enjoying this?"

"Because I am. Now sit still."

She carefully pulled the skin together, applied two butterfly bandages and examined her handiwork.

"I'm no Florence Nightingale, but I think that will do until you see a doctor."

Jim pushed back in the chair and stood. "Thanks for patching me up."

"Thanks for scaring off my intruder."

"I really can't take credit for that." Jim leaned against the counter, the towel slung around his neck. "He was already running from the house when I pulled up. I caught him in my headlights and jumped out of the car to chase him, but it was pitch-black out there. He was hiding behind the bushes by the garage and bushwhacked me."

"Thank goodness I've got an alarm system." She looked up at him, her face suddenly curious. "What are you doing here, anyway?"

Before Jim could answer there was a quick rap at the back door. Vicky opened it, expecting the two cops. Instead, Detective Gil Fletcher stepped into the kitchen. His sandy hair was plastered against his head from the rain and his camel-colored coat was soaked.

"Gil, what in the world are you doing here?" Vicky asked.

He held Vicky at arm's length, a worried look on his face. "The dispatcher paged me after the security company called.

Are you all right?"

She gave him a wry smile. "I'm no worse for the wear, I guess."

Gil nodded a greeting at Jim and extended his hand.

"The boys outside said the evidence team should be here any time," Gil said. "They also told me you responded to the call first, McCann. Thanks for taking care of Vicky."

"I think she was probably doing a pretty good job of taking care of things before I got here."

There was another knock. The two cops tromped in and stood by the door. Their badges said, "Van Dyke" and "Warchol." Vicky didn't know either of them, but thought they looked about twelve. Water dripped from their hats and jackets, forming a puddle around them on the almond-tiled floor.

"Man, it's colder than a mother tonight," Van Dyke said, cupping his hands and blowing into them. He gratefully accepted the coffee Vicky handed him and took a sip. "We took a look around, but it's too dark to see anything and this rain will probably wash away any footprints."

"Whoever it was, is long gone by now anyway. You can bet on that," Warchol added. He pulled a notepad and pen from his pocket. "You want to tell us what happened?"

Vicky went over every detail from the time she walked in the front door.

"But you never actually got a look at this guy?" Warchol asked.

"For all I know he could be five feet tall and weigh three hundred pounds," Vicky replied.

"More like six-feet and two hundred pounds from what I glimpsed," Jim interjected.

Warchol turned to him. "How did you wind up answering the call, Detective?"

"I was actually here to return a pair of gloves Mrs. Langford left in Chief Paxton's office. I heard the alarm and saw the perp run from the house as I pulled up. I chased him, but it was so damn dark I couldn't see. He clobbered me from behind and took off."

"Can you give us a description?"

"I only saw him for a split second when I caught him in my headlights. He was dressed in black and it looked like he was probably wearing a ski mask. Other than that, I can't tell you anything except he has a mean swing." Jim gingerly touched the back of his head.

"Do you need medical attention, Detective? We could run you over to Westport General," Van Dyke offered.

"I'm fine. Mrs. Langford was nice enough to take care of me."

"There's nothing else for us to do here then." Warchol stuffed the notepad back in his pocket. Resting his hand on the doorknob, he turned to Vicky. "We'll keep an eye on things for the next few nights and, in the meantime, if you hear so much as a squeak, Mrs. Langford, give a call."

The evidence team arrived not long after that and spent an hour in the basement. When they were done, Gil and Jim scoured the house and garage in vain for something to board up the broken window.

"Were you able to get ahold of anybody to come out to fix it?" Gil asked Vicky as he and Jim came back into the house.

"I'm batting a thousand. I got answering machines at all four places I tried," Vicky said, still holding her cell phone. She closed the thick yellow pages on the counter. "And I can't get anyone out here to repair the phone line until tomorrow."

"At least you have your cell phone, but we can't buy a piece of plywood to board up the window," Jim said, glancing at the clock on the stove. "Everything is closed by now."

"Why don't I just leave the front door open for him tonight?"

"Gil and I don't like it anymore than you do, but it can't be helped."

"I'm sorry," she said. "I didn't mean to snap at you."

"You're entitled to be edgy, considering everything that's happened." Jim held her eyes with his gaze and gave her arm a gentle squeeze.

The butterflies in Vicky's stomach returned in force. For an instant, she caught herself wondering what it would feel like to have Jim's strong arms wrapped around her.

Don't even go there. You don't need or want anything from this man.

Looking away, she took half a step back. Josh began squirming in his high chair and rubbing his eyes. Vicky was glad for the distraction.

"You're exhausted aren't you, punkin?" Vicky picked him up and Josh curled against her shoulder. "I'm going to put him back to bed."

"No, don't." Gil laid a hand on her arm. "I want you to pack up your stuff and stay at my place."

His pager went off just as Vicky was about to protest. Gil held up a hand as he looked at the pager, then reached for his own cell phone and punched in the number of the station house. "I've got to go," he said when he was done with his call. He took a spare key and laid it on the counter. "I'll expect to see you at my place later. McCann, will you make sure she gets there safely?"

"No problem."

Vicky shook her head firmly. "This guy is not going to run me out of my home, Gil."

"Dammit, Vicky. Why do you have to be so stubborn?"

"I've got the best security system money can buy, remember? You picked it out. And I'm getting drive-bys."

"And what good is that security system if that guy decides to come back and show you the business end of a gun? By the time help arrives you could be dead."

"I'm staying put. End of discussion."

Gil's jaw worked and he put his hands on his hips. "Why? Just because you say so? You were lucky tonight. They could have wheeled both you and Josh out of here in goddamn body bags."

Vicky flinched at his words. Hot tears pricked her eyes, but she blinked them away. "Don't you think I know that? But what good will running do?"

"Frank told me all about everything that's been going on. What the hell are you doing poking around Blackwell again anyway?"

"I'm trying to help Lisa Murphy clear her husband's name."

"You're trying to nail Blackwell!" he shouted. Josh screwed up his face and began crying. Gil reached out and stroked his cheek. "Sorry, big guy, Uncle Gil didn't mean to scare you."

Vicky held Josh closer, gently swaying back and forth to quiet him as she glared at Gil. "Yes, I'm trying to nail Blackwell, and by God this time I'm going to do it. That rotten bastard is going to pay for everything he's done."

"And if you're lucky you may even live to see it. Look, if you won't stay with me, then at least take this." He pulled a small revolver from his ankle holster.

Vicky shook her head and backed away from him. "I can't, Gil. Please, put it away."

"You used to be able to shoot the wings off a gnat, for Christ's sake."

"That was a long time ago. I thought you of all people would understand that." Tears welled in Vicky's eyes and she wiped them with the back of her hand. She was furious with Gil for bringing up what he knew was a taboo subject and even more furious with herself for showing how vulnerable she really felt.

She darted a glance at Jim. From the way his brows were pulled together, he was clearly puzzled over her reaction to the gun. And why wouldn't he be? Cops weren't afraid of guns. But she wasn't a cop anymore. A million questions must be running through his mind, Vicky thought. Questions that she didn't want to answer, especially tonight.

"Put it away, Gil, please," Vicky said again.

"Then I'm coming back after I'm through with this call."

"Don't worry about it, Fletcher," Jim interjected. "I'll stay."

"I don't need a baby-sitter," Vicky said. "I'll be fine."

"You've got two choices," Jim said. "Either I stay, or I get on the phone with Frank Paxton and he'll have a whole detail camped in your yard."

Vicky glowered at the two detectives, turned on her heel and stalked out of the room.

"She's scared to death you know," Gil said, his voice low.

"She'd never admit it, though, would she?"

"Not Vicky," Gil said with a wry laugh. "Never show fear and never ask for help. That's the motto she lives by."

"What's the deal with the gun?"

Gil pursed his lips. Finally he said, "I think it would be better if Vicky told you about that herself."

Chapter 4

Jim prowled the house, checking doors and peering through windows. Satisfied everything was secure, he went into the family room to wait for Vicky. It was a comfortable room with exposed ceiling beams and a natural stone fireplace that took up most of one wall. This would be a cozy room on a cold winter night with a fire crackling on the hearth, Jim thought. The kind of place that would be good to come home to at the end of the day. He settled on the sofa, but stood again a moment later. He was too restless to sit.

Pacing the room, he eyed the pictures on the oak mantel and end tables, catching glimpses of Vicky's life. Vicky holding a newborn Josh. Another of her and Frank Paxton standing on a dock with another man. Vicky's father? Jim wondered. A wedding picture, Vicky looking like an angel in white, smiling up at her husband.

After Vicky left the chief's office today, Frank Paxton had told him Danny Langford had been killed on the job. Before he could go into any details, though, the chief was called into a meeting. Jim had left Frank's office and gone straight to what the Westport PD called Officer's Row—a hallway on the first floor where photos of fallen officers were hung. On display with all the rest was a picture of Danny Langford. Now Jim's gaze settled on an identical photo of Vicky's late husband.

He found himself wondering what kind of life Danny and Vicky had had and how Vicky had managed to pull herself together after losing him. Obviously, she was one helluva strong woman. Once again he felt that grudging respect for her.

He was still looking at the pictures when Vicky came into the room carrying two steaming mugs. She set them on the coffee table and walked over to him.

"You really don't have to stay," she said quietly. "He won't be back tonight."

"Maybe not, but what about tomorrow night or the night after that?"

She folded her arms across her chest. "It's not like you can stay with me forever."

There was still a slight tremor in her voice when she spoke, and it tore at Jim's heart. If he left, she'd probably sit in a chair the rest of the night with that damned nightstick in her lap. She'd listen to every creak and groan in the house and who could blame her? Hell, he was spooked himself.

"I don't believe for a minute that you want to be alone tonight."

Vicky wouldn't look into his eyes. Jim wondered if she did, would he see how angry, vulnerable and terrified she truly felt in spite of the tough-as-nails façade she presented? A million thoughts must be running through her mind right now, Jim thought. He knew what was going through his. What if she had been ambushed as she got out of the car tonight? What if Josh had been hurt? The truth was she probably didn't want Jim to leave, but she couldn't bring herself to say the words. Confessing her fear, and to a stranger no less, would have made her feel even more vulnerable.

She turned away from him and settled in a chair. Taking a sip of coffee, Vicky tried to change the subject. "So you braved this storm and came all the way out here just to return my gloves?"

Jim smiled sheepishly. "I have to confess I did have an ulterior motive. I wanted to thank you for not telling Frank about what happened this morning. When I saw you in his office, I thought . . ."

Vicky shook her head as Jim's words trailed off. "I see. You thought I was going to make trouble for you."

"Well, it wouldn't be the first time a reporter gave me grief," Jim said bitterly.

"Listen, McCann, if I wanted to make trouble for you I could, but I don't work that way. And just for the record, Frank knows all about what happened this morning, but he didn't hear it from me. Gossip travels through that department faster than it does at a church social."

"Then why hasn't he said anything to me?"

"He won't step in unless I ask him to and I won't, unless you try to keep me from doing my job."

"What about my job?" Jim arched his brows and put his hands on his hips. "You could have contaminated a crime scene this morning. I'm not going to compromise a case just so you can get a story."

Vicky rose from the chair and took a step toward him. "I know better than to compromise the integrity of a crime scene, McCann. I was a cop—remember?"

"*Was* is the operative word here. You traded your badge for a pen—remember?"

The ringing of her cell phone was like a bell signaling the end of a boxing round. Vicky's spine stiffened as her gaze darted to the cell phone lying on her desk.

"It's probably Gil," Jim said. "Right before he left he said he'd call."

"It's not Gil," Vicky said, dread crawling across her skin like ants.

When she first answered there was nothing, then came the raspy voice that always raised the hairs on the back of her neck.

"I am Death and I'm coming for you, bitch."

She hit the end button to disconnect the call then slammed the phone closed. "Bastard. He's probably gloating over what he did tonight."

"You think it's the same guy who broke in here?"

"Who else could it be?"

She was shaking like someone with the DTs, but it was from anger now, not fear.

Jim's mouth pressed into a grim line. "There's something you should know about what happened. I'm not so sure he was scared off by the alarm or by me."

"What do you mean?"

"Think about it. The alarm would have gone off the moment he broke the window, but he didn't run. He came inside anyway, and from his footprints it's obvious he knew exactly where to go to shut off the power. He didn't make a move to come up the stairs, either. His footprints led right back to the window."

Vicky's voice was barely a whisper when she spoke. "He's been here before, scoped out the house."

"Unless it's a coincidence that he knew where to go once he was in here. Personally, I don't believe in coincidence. This guy has done his homework, and I think he's telling you he can get to you any time he wants."

"He'll be back then, won't he?"

"I know he will. If you're right about all of this being connected to the Grayson Center fire, then you'd better back off."

"Or I'll wind up like my pal, Wexler?" Vicky said, repeating the cryptic message in the shoebox.

She turned away from Jim and walked to the French doors. Thunder shook the house and rain pummeled the windows. Pulling aside a filmy curtain, she stared out into the darkness. A flash of lightning split the sky.

"As nasty as it is tonight, he's still out there watching me."

Vicky shivered and hugged herself. "I know it sounds crazy, but I can feel it."

Jim came up behind her and rested his hands on her shoulders. "Look, I know you don't want to give up on this, but there has to come a point when you ask yourself if getting a story is worth the price you might pay."

"You don't get it, do you?" Vicky wheeled around to face him. "I don't care about getting the story. I want to get Richard Blackwell."

"It sounds as if you'd like to personally wield the sword of justice."

Vicky's eyes narrowed as she walked over to the fireplace. She gazed at the photographs lined up on the mantel and reached for the one of Danny in his uniform. "If I held the sword of justice, McCann, I would gladly use it to cut out Richard Blackwell's heart."

"Just what did this guy do to you?"

Vicky hugged the picture of Danny to her breast. When she looked up at Jim, her eyes glittered with tears. "He killed my husband."

Minutes went by. Vicky could feel Jim watching her, waiting for her to explain. She didn't trust herself to speak or look him in the eye. She could barely swallow over the huge lump in her throat, but Vicky wasn't going to let herself go to pieces in front of him.

She gazed at the picture cradled in her arms. Danny had deserved to live a long and happy life—to watch his son grow up, but Richard Blackwell had taken all of that away from him and from Vicky. And she'd vowed to make Blackwell pay.

She took a deep breath and wiped the tears from her cheeks. Squaring her shoulders, she looked up at Jim and immediately wished she hadn't. The doubt was nothing more than a flicker crossing his face, but it was there just the same.

"You don't believe me."

Jim held up his hands. "It's not that. I just can't help wondering why Blackwell isn't sitting in a cell if what you're saying is true."

"I don't mean he actually pulled the trigger," Vicky said, placing Danny's picture back on the mantel. "Blackwell doesn't do his own dirty work."

"I see. There isn't any proof."

Vicky heard a note of challenge in his voice and it sparked her temper. She gritted her teeth. "Come on, McCann, you know as well as I do that guilty people get off all the time because of lack of evidence."

"Is that what happened?"

Vicky stuffed her hands into the pockets of her jeans and paced the room. "He was never even brought in for questioning."

"If the police don't think Blackwell's guilty, then what makes you think otherwise?"

"Some things you just know in your gut."

"You have to have more than that to convict someone, Vicky. It takes cold, hard facts."

Vicky quickly closed the distance between them. "You want cold, hard facts? Try this. The night Danny died, he and Gil were meeting a drug dealer who was going to help them sew up an airtight case linking Blackwell to the drug trade in Westport. It wasn't the dealer who was waiting for them in that alley, though. A man opened fire on them as soon as they got there. What does that sound like to you?"

"You think Blackwell ordered the hit."

"It makes sense to me. The next morning the dealer was found dead of an overdose. After that the investigation fell apart. Danny was dead and Gil was on leave for almost two months recovering from his wounds. Do I think Blackwell ordered the hit? I don't think—I know. And so does every cop in Westport."

Jim rubbed the line of his jaw with his thumb. "Okay, I'll admit Blackwell is the most obvious suspect, but something doesn't make sense. I would think Frank Paxton and Gil Fletcher would be out to nail Blackwell to a cross if they thought he was behind the hit."

"Like you just said, Jim, it takes cold, hard facts to get a conviction, and we didn't have any. What we did have was a triggerman with a grudge against my husband. Danny helped send Mark Leone to prison, and he spent four years telling everyone he was going to 'get' Danny as soon as he got out. Gil said Leone even shouted Danny's name as he opened fire. So as it stands right now, Danny was killed by an ex-con who got his revenge."

"Why is that so hard for you to believe?"

"It's too damn simple," Vicky said. "How did Leone know that Gil and Danny were going to be in that alley that night?"

"Did anyone ever ask him?"

"Dead men don't talk much. He and Gil exchanged gunfire and Leone was killed."

"Vicky, this could all be a horrible . . ."

Vicky glared at Jim, cutting off his words. "Don't you dare say coincidence. You just told me a few minutes ago that you don't believe in them."

"You're right," Jim said, holding up his hands. "I don't, but what if Leone acted alone? Maybe he'd been tailing Danny and somehow found out about this meeting he and Gil were going to have. Or what if someone other than Blackwell ordered the hit?"

"You're stretching."

"Am I, or is it that you don't want to admit I could be right?"

"Let me put it to you this way," Vicky drawled. "If I believed in Santa and the tooth fairy, maybe I could buy this idea of yours."

"Why can't you consider any ideas other than your own?"

"I could if they made any sense."

"I'll tell you what makes sense and what makes good police work—looking at all the angles. Since you were a cop I'd expect you to know that," Jim said, stabbing his forefinger in the air at Vicky. "From what you're telling me, Blackwell might be guilty of a lot of things, but he might not be guilty in this particular case."

"Why are you defending him?"

"I'm not. I don't even know who he is, but you're focusing all of your attention on him and you just admitted you don't have any evidence against him—just your gut feeling. In my opinion, you're just spinning your wheels."

"I don't recall asking for your opinion."

"You are one of the most stubborn and argumentative people I've ever met in my life." Jim waved a hand at her. "I don't know why I'm wasting my time trying to get anything through that thick skull of yours."

"Haven't you ever had gut feelings?"

He stared at her a moment then let out a long, slow breath and nodded. "Of course I've acted on instinct before. I don't know a cop who hasn't. But you're putting everything on the line, and there's no guarantee that you'll be more successful with this case you're trying to build against Blackwell than the ones in the past."

"I know I'll probably never get the evidence I need against Blackwell to convict him of Danny's murder," Vicky said. "I accepted that a long time ago, but he has to pay for the things he's done. The bottom line is I don't care why he does time, I just want him behind bars. The fire at Grayson Center could do it."

"I understand what you're saying," Jim said quietly. "But your little boy has already lost his father. Do you want him to lose his mother, too? Do you want him to just have photographs and other people's memories of you, like he does of Danny? Is that what your husband would have wanted?"

"I can't sit back and keep letting Blackwell get away with murder."

"Trust me, Vicky, guys like this slip up sooner or later," Jim went on. "They think they're untouchable, and that's usually their downfall. Blackwell will make a mistake, and when he does, I promise we'll get him."

Vicky looked Jim in the eye. "Why, when you don't even believe he's guilty?"

"Like I said, I believe in gut feelings."

Vicky sank down on the sofa and rested her elbows on her knees. Why did every encounter with this man have to turn into a skirmish of some kind?

"You're going to drop the investigation then?" Jim asked.

"I guess I don't have much of a choice. I'm certainly not going to endanger my son." She heard Jim sigh, and darted a glance at him. Was that relief she saw in his eyes? Why should he care one way or the other what happened to her? He didn't like her any more than she liked him, and it was no secret that he didn't respect what she did for a living. Don't worry about it, Vicky told herself. You have more important things to do than play armchair psychologist to Jim McCann.

He plopped wearily into the chair opposite her, and Vicky heard his stomach rumble. She arched a brow at him. "Sounds like you're starving."

Jim gave her a half smile and said, "I didn't have a chance to eat dinner and it's finally catching up with me. How about if I spring for a pizza?"

"It takes too long to deliver out here."

Snowball stalked into the room and perched on Vicky's desk, his tail swinging back and forth like the pendulum of a clock.

Jim nodded in the cat's direction. "How fond are you of her?"

"It's him," Vicky replied, looking at Jim in mock horror. "And we don't have to resort to that. I'll throw an omelet together."

"Works for me. You need a hand?"

Vicky declined his offer of help. She doubted they could even prepare a simple meal without the kitchen turning into a war zone. She did have the feeling, though, that they had called an unspoken truce. How long it would last, of course, was anyone's guess.

Turning on the TV, she tossed him the remote. "Surf for a while."

She busied herself peeling potatoes and cracking eggs, relieved to be away from Jim's brooding eyes. Something about him left Vicky feeling off balance, unsettled. She prided herself on always being in control, but ever since she first locked horns with the surly detective her emotions had been all over the charts.

She remembered the way he looked at her tonight when she was wearing that old jersey and the unexpected warmth flooded her body all over again. Stop it! Vicky chided herself. She slid the potatoes into a frying pan and turned up the flame.

Okay, so he was good-looking in a rugged sort of way, and he filled out his Levis really well. He was also rude and had the disposition of a grizzly. And for all she knew, he could be married. What was wrong with her anyway?

"You're thirty-four not fifteen," she muttered.

Wasn't she the one telling Mary just last week that she had no time in her life for a relationship—that she was happy with things the way they were? That wasn't altogether true, though. Vicky kept herself busy so she wouldn't have time for another relationship. She had dated a few times over the last year, but never anything serious. In fact, if she sensed anyone getting a little too close, Vicky pulled away. She wouldn't risk her heart again. It hurt too damn much to lose someone you loved. Whatever it was she was feeling for Jim would pass. She would make sure of it.

The aroma of potatoes, onions, and peppers frying drew Jim into the kitchen. Leaning against the counter, he watched Vicky expertly flip an omelet in the pan. He found himself slowly dragging his gaze from her head to her feet. Faded jeans hugged legs that were long and hips that were slender. Her breasts formed perfect peaks beneath the soft fabric of her sweater. She looked good. Too good.

"That smells great," he remarked, trying to keep his mind on food.

"I don't know how good it'll be, but it's hot and it'll stick to your ribs." Vicky nodded toward one of the upper cabinets. "Why don't you grab some plates? Silverware is in that drawer."

Her face was flushed from cooking over the hot stove. Wisps of dark hair had escaped from her ponytail. And at that moment, Jim thought she was the prettiest woman he had ever seen in his life.

"Earth to Jim," Vicky said, waving her spatula at him. "The dishes."

"Sorry. I was daydreaming."

He pulled two stoneware plates from the cabinet and handed them to her. They settled at the table, and Jim dove into his food, eating with gusto.

"This is great," he said, forking up a mound of potatoes.

"Not exactly gourmet fare, but it'll do in a pinch."

"I'm not much for fancy food anyway," Jim confessed. "Give me meat and potatoes any time."

Vicky laughed. "That's what my father always says every time my mother gets into a mood to experiment with her cooking. She'll knock herself out making some fancy French dish only to have him grumble about it and smother it in ketchup to cover up the taste."

Jim grinned as he slathered butter on a slice of toast. "So your old man was a cop?"

"For thirty years. Then a bum heart forced him into retirement. It was hard for him at first, but I think he's finally starting to enjoy himself."

"He and Frank Paxton have known each other a long time?"

"Since they were kids. Unfortunately, they only get to see each other a couple of times a year. My parents moved to Arizona because the winters here were just too hard on my dad's heart. Of course, they wanted to pack up and come back here after Danny died, but Frank convinced them that he and Gil would keep an eye on me."

"It seems like they really look out for you," Jim said.

Vicky rolled her eyes and shook her head with a laugh. "I don't know who is worse, Gil or Frank. I know they mean well, but sometimes they drive me a little crazy."

"They obviously care a lot about you."

"And the feeling is mutual, but they both have a tendency to be mother hens. Gil watches me like a hawk, especially where Richard Blackwell is concerned."

"Tell me about Fletcher. I hear we might get partnered up."

"You can count yourself lucky if that happens," Vicky said. "Gil works hard and he's a good cop. He's even-tempered, easy to be around and more important, he'll go to the wall with you if he thinks you're right."

"How long have you known him?"

Vicky shrugged as she speared a chunk of onion with her fork. "I guess it's around thirteen years."

"You were partners with him when you first started on the force?"

"Just for a few weeks. I kind of got shuffled around, but I learned a lot from him in that short time."

"How long were he and your husband partners?"

"Ten years total. Eight years on patrol, two in the detective's unit. They went through the academy together, too, so they really had a bond. He was best man at our wedding and he's Josh's godfather."

"They were more like brothers than friends, weren't they?"

Vicky nodded with a half smile. "Gil always said Danny was the brother he never had. I know he blamed himself for what happened. I think he still does. To tell you the truth, I think that's the biggest reason he watches out for me the way he does. He couldn't save Danny, so he's determined to keep me in a protective bubble."

"Guilt is a heavy burden to carry around with you."

"Yes, it is," Vicky murmured.

An image of Connie Springer flashed through her mind. Lord knew Vicky was no stranger to guilt. For the last seven years it had been swimming beneath the surface of her own consciousness like a hungry shark waiting to rip a chunk from her heart. It always struck when she least expected it. Those moments that meant so much, like watching Josh take his first steps, always brought a sharp reminder of the woman who would never know the joy of watching her own son grow into a man.

"It hasn't been easy for Gil," Vicky replied, guilt pressing down on her.

"And what about you?" Jim asked. "I'm sure it hasn't been easy trying to raise a child on your own, work, and keep up with things around here."

"I manage," she said, pushing her food around on her plate,

her appetite suddenly gone.

Jim cast a glance around the large, cheery kitchen. "This is a great old house. How long have you been here?"

"Almost a year."

"What made you decide to move?"

Vicky laid down her fork. How could she explain how lonely the house in Westport had been with Danny gone? That she had kept waiting to hear his key in the lock. That when she woke up every morning she still expected to find him lying beside her. How could Jim understand something like that?

"The city is so dangerous," she said finally. "I wanted Josh to grow up in a place where he would be safe. I guess that one has come back to haunt me after tonight."

"It must get pretty lonely at times."

"Not at all. It was the quiet and solitude that drew me out here."

"I know what you mean. I had a weekend place in the woods when I lived in Seattle. It wasn't much, just a one-room cabin on a small lake, but I loved it. I went there every chance I got." He pushed back from the table, grabbed the coffeepot from the counter and topped off their mugs. "Most women would be afraid to be out here all by themselves, though."

"I've never had a reason to be afraid until tonight. This was the first time I realized just how isolated this house is."

"Do you think you'll move now?"

"Of course not. I love this place. I've got the alarm system and the security lights. And I'd like to think this whole thing will come to a quick end once I get the word out that I'm dropping the investigation."

"Do you really think it'll be that simple?"

"Why wouldn't it be?" Vicky's mouth tightened in irritation. She'd already gone over all of this in her own mind, wondering if Blackwell would truly stop his campaign of terror, or if this time she had pushed him too far. The last thing she wanted to hear right now were her own secret fears spoken out loud. Vicky's voice was clipped when she spoke. "Blackwell wants me to stop nosing around. That's what I'm doing. Once he knows that, things will quiet down."

"I hope you're right."

"You don't think so?"

"Frankly, no, I don't," Jim said. "Especially after what happened here tonight. And if you honestly believe it, then it's time to pull that pretty head of yours out of the sand. You've got too much at stake here to go underestimating this guy."

Vicky bristled. "I'm not underestimating Richard Blackwell," she said. "I know exactly what I'm dealing with. If he wanted me dead I'd be dead, trust me."

"I'd still keep my guard up if I were you."

"My guard is always up, McCann," she replied, giving him a steely look.

They ate in silence, the tension hanging between them until Vicky finally asked, "So how long have you been in Westport?"

"Two weeks."

She eyed Jim quizzically over the rim of her mug. "What made you leave Seattle?"

Jim continued to eat without looking up at her. "It was just time to make a move."

"Pretty big move. You pulled up stakes and traveled across the country. What made you pick Westport?"

"It seemed like as good a place as any."

"What about your family and friends. Don't you miss them?"

Jim wiped his mouth with his napkin and laid it on the table. "That's what the telephone is for."

"How does your wife like Westport?" Vicky told herself she was asking the question out of casual curiosity, but she felt her pulse quicken as she waited for his answer.

"I'm divorced." The reply was abrupt, cold. Vicky felt as if Jim had just slammed a door in her face.

"I'm sorry," she said quietly.

"Don't be. I'm not." He leaned back in his chair. "What about you? How did you go from being a cop to being a reporter?"

Vicky felt her hackles rise again. Every time Jim mentioned the word *reporter,* he made it sound as if it was a step above the scum he dealt with on the streets.

"Just what is it you have against reporters, McCann?"

Jim spread his hands. "I don't have anything against them."

"That's a crock and you know it. Did one do a hatchet job on you?"

Jim scowled. "Let's just say I don't like the methods they use to get information. I've arrested people who had more scruples than the reporters I've met."

"I'll admit there are reporters out there who can be insensitive and unethical, but most are hardworking people who just want to do a good job."

"That's your opinion and you're entitled to it, but I'm also entitled to mine." He took a sip of his coffee adding, "And you didn't answer my question. You obviously loved police work, and from everything I've heard about you, you were a helluva cop. What made you quit?"

Now it was Vicky's turn to close the door in Jim's face. Start asking questions and this is what you get, she thought. The last thing she needed tonight was to talk about the past.

"I guess it was pretty much the same reason you had for coming here. It was just time for a change."

"Pretty big change."

"No bigger than the one you made," Vicky countered evenly.

Jim sensed he was treading on thin ice now. He could hear it cracking all around him and knew he would plunge headfirst into icy waters if he pushed her any further, but he just couldn't stop himself. He asked the question that had been gnawing at him since earlier that evening.

"I was kind of surprised to see your reaction to Gil Fletcher when he offered you his gun. Why wouldn't you take it?"

Vicky rose from the table without a word and scraped the remains of her dinner into the trash. She ran water in the sink and began cleaning the kitchen.

"There are still more potatoes in the pan if you want them," she said crisply.

End of discussion, Jim thought. She was telling him to go to hell just as clearly as if she had spoken the words. If Jim was a betting man he would have put money on her reaction being exactly what it was. He cleared the table and wiped the counters, silence hanging heavily between them. The tide sure could turn quickly with this woman. He cast a glance at her. Obviously, her career as a cop was a taboo subject, but wasn't he just as guarded talking about his reasons for leaving Seattle?

I guess we both have skeletons we want to keep in the closet.

He remembered an old saying his father used all the time. Let sleeping dogs lie. Well, Jim wasn't going to nudge this old hound anymore. Vicky Langford had enough people watching out for her. She didn't need one more, and he certainly didn't need the headache.

Jim sipped his coffee and stared out into the darkness through the French doors in the family room. Vicky had gone to bed thirty minutes earlier, leaving a pillow and blanket on the sofa for him. It had been a long night, but he felt restless and uneasy. He told himself it was just concern that that lunatic would pay another visit. It was more than that, though, whether he wanted to admit it or not. It was Vicky.

He'd never met anyone like her. The woman had brains and from the way Frank Paxton talked, balls the size of a bull's. She certainly wasn't hard to look at, either. *Attraction.* The word skipped through his mind and Jim frowned. He'd allowed himself to be blinded by it once and it had cost him his self-respect and very nearly his job. Mimi had taught him some tough lessons, and they were ones he was determined not to forget. Never trust, never let yourself get close to anyone again. For the last year Jim had forced himself to be numb inside—until today.

It was just the luck of the draw he caught the call at the Lexington. He had expected it to be routine and it was, until he'd met Vicky Langford. After that he'd spent the rest of the morning telling himself the less he saw of her, the better off he'd be. Jim had nearly convinced himself of that, too, but then he ran into Vicky again in Frank Paxton's office.

Now Jim couldn't get her out of his head. Every time he looked into those huge, dark eyes of hers he felt like he'd been hit by a Mack truck. A wave of anger washed over him as he thought of what might have happened to her tonight. The sudden rush of emotion shocked him. What the hell was wrong with him?

He had come to Westport to get away from the pain and memories of one relationship. He wasn't about to run headlong into the arms of another. Especially when those arms belonged to someone with an acid tongue and fiery temper. And Jim certainly didn't need the headaches that Vicky's connections to Frank Paxton could make for him.

Yet here he was. He didn't have to stay the night. Frank Paxton would have assigned a patrol car to sit in Vicky's driveway, or Gil Fletcher would have come back in spite of her protests. Instead, Jim had jumped right in with both feet, all the while telling himself this was just another case and Vicky was just another victim. But that was a lie and he knew it.

This woman with the huge doe eyes and defiant chin had touched a chord in him for reasons he couldn't explain. He only knew that she was one of the most courageous people he had ever met, and she was reawakening feelings and a hunger in him that he had told himself he never wanted to feel again.

Jim pulled a red plastic truck from Josh's toy box, sat on the sofa and spun the wheels. Josh sure was a cute kid. Good-natured, too, with an infectious grin. Jim had always thought he'd have a brood of kids just like the family he'd grown up in. Instead, here he was thirty-eight, divorced, no family, no nothing. He felt a sudden pang, wondering what his own child would have been like if he and Mimi had had a family. He laughed and laid the truck next to him.

Mimi having a baby. Now that would take a real stretch of imagination, though Jim didn't think so when he first brought up the idea. Mimi hadn't skipped a beat. She'd thrown her arms around his neck and told him nothing would make her happier than to have his baby. That turned out to be just another lie in a very long list, but he hadn't known it at the time.

For months Jim waited for Mimi to tell him she was pregnant, but nothing happened. He couldn't understand why until the day he found her birth control pills. It was only then his wife confessed that she didn't want children.

"I've got a career to think of, Jim," she'd shouted, when he confronted her with the pill pack. "I can't go out to cover stories when I'm as big as a house!"

Jim still didn't realize just how important Mimi's career was to her or how far she was willing to go to further it. That bomb had hit later, and when it did, it had cost them their marriage. Love sure can make people blind and stupid, Jim thought.

Danny Langford had been a very lucky man. Obviously, Vicky had loved him fiercely, and she loved her little boy the same way. Reporter or not, she was as different from Mimi as fire was from ice. And that, more than anything, scared the hell out of him.

Vicky bolted upright, awakened by her own strangled cry. Chest heaving, heart racing, she struggled to brush the cobwebs of sleep away. Fragments of her nightmare flitted in and out of her memory as if playing hide and seek. She closed her eyes trying to recall it, but all she could remember was that her baby was in danger.

Dread coiled itself around her, squeezing like a snake, leaving her breathless. She flung aside the comforter and ran down the hall. Blessed relief washed over her when she opened the door to Josh's room. He lay curled on his side, his arm wrapped around his teddy bear. What had she expected to find?

Again the nightmare tugged at her memory. She took a blanket from the linen closet and settled in the rocker beside Josh's crib. Vicky knew she was being ridiculous. Josh was perfectly safe. Her heart was still racing, though, and she could taste the fear the nightmare had left behind. So Vicky stayed in Josh's room, keeping watch over her son until the first rays of light filtered through the blinds.

Chapter 5

At one o'clock sharp the next afternoon, Vicky left the *Herald* and headed for Texas Joe's Grill. The sky was pewter-colored and the wind bitter, but she decided to walk the six blocks. She needed time to think of how to break her news to Lisa Murphy.

Pulling up her coat collar, she fell into step with the steady stream of people. Guilt nibbled at her conscience as she hurried along. Vicky had promised to clear Peter Murphy's name. Now she had to break that promise, even though that also meant letting Richard Blackwell off the hook again. Dammit, she had been so close this time! Vicky could feel it in her gut.

Let it go, Vicky. Nothing is more important than Josh.

And that was the bottom line. No matter how badly she wanted to put Blackwell behind bars, she'd never risk Josh's life to do it.

The scent of grilling steaks and burgers greeted Vicky as she entered the restaurant. Pictures of Billy the Kid, Wyatt Earp and Doc Holliday hung from antique frames just inside the door where patrons sat on rough-hewn benches waiting for tables. Garth Brooks blared from the jukebox. The blender behind the bar whined as it cranked out batches of strawberry margaritas. The hostess, wearing a blue calico dress and black leather boots, asked Vicky if she wanted smoking or nonsmoking.

"I'm meeting someone," Vicky said, searching for Lisa. She spotted her in a back booth.

Making her way across the oak-planked floor, she slid into the leather seat across from Lisa and frowned. There were dark circles under Lisa's green eyes and lines on her face that Vicky hadn't noticed before. Her sweater and jeans were wrinkled and she'd barely taken the time to pull a brush through her blonde hair. An empty beer mug sat on the table in front of her. Another near-empty one was beside it.

"Been here long?" Vicky asked.

"Since around eleven."

"You should have called me. I could have come by the house rather than have you waiting here all that time."

Lisa shrugged and lit a cigarette. "It doesn't matter. Like I told you when you called this morning, I was going to be downtown anyway."

"How are you?" Vicky asked, though she already knew.

Lisa swallowed the rest of her beer and signaled for their waiter. "Okay, I guess."

The waiter clopped over to their table wearing scuffed leather boots and a Stetson. He placed two menus on the table and rattled off the daily specials.

"I'm not eating," Lisa said, her voice slurred. "But you can bring me another beer. Vicky?"

"Diet Coke is fine for me, thanks." Vicky handed the waiter her menu. "Why don't you bring us a couple of burgers."

"I'm not hungry," Lisa insisted.

Vicky told the waiter to bring the food anyway, hoping she'd be able to coax Lisa into eating.

When the waiter left, Lisa took a long pull from her cigarette and propped her elbows on the table. "I went to see Ray Abrons this morning."

"That's the city electrical inspector Peter thought was taking bribes from Blackwell."

Lisa nodded. "He threw me out."

"Oh God, what did you say to him?"

"That I had proof inferior materials were used on the job and that he'd taken bribes from Richard Blackwell so that Grayson Center would pass inspection. I told him I was going to the police."

"Jesus, Lisa, why did you do that? Do you have any idea what kind of danger you just put yourself in? He probably got on the phone with Blackwell as soon as you left."

"I had to do something." Lisa looked out of the window, her brow furrowed. Her voice trembled as she spoke. "I don't sleep. My mind never stops. I keep thinking about what that night must have been like for Peter."

"Look, I understand what you're going through . . ."

"No, you don't. You don't know what it's like to have people whisper behind your back when you're in line at the grocery store, or for your boss to tell you that clients are dropping you. You don't know what it's like to have friends suddenly stop calling. You lost your husband, Vicky, but he didn't die accused of murdering seven other people. There's a big difference."

"You're right. I'm sorry." Vicky reached across the table and laid a hand on Lisa's arm. "I know you want to find the truth, but threatening Abrons wasn't a good idea."

"Peter said Abrons was the weak link in Blackwell's chain of command and I think he was right. Abrons wouldn't look me in the eye and he kept fidgeting with things on his desk the whole time I was there. I shook him up, Vicky, and I'll bet if you went to see him today and applied a little pressure, he'd crack."

"I can't do that, Lisa," Vicky said evenly.

"Why not? The timing would be perfect."

"I'm dropping the investigation."

"What?" Lisa's voice grew louder and more shrill with every word. "You promised you'd get that bastard Blackwell and clear Peter's name. Isn't that what you said?"

Vicky darted a glance around the crowded restaurant. The other customers were glancing curiously in their direction. The hostess walked past, her eyes narrowed in disapproval.

"Keep your voice down, please," Vicky said. "I know what I said. I'm sorry, but I don't have a choice."

"Of course you have a choice. People always have choices."

"Not this time."

Lisa squeezed her eyes shut. Tears seeped through her lashes and rolled down her pale cheeks. She dropped her head in her hands. "Christ, what am I going to do? My kids can't even go to school. The other kids say such horrible things to them! Megan cries constantly and Pete is sick all the time. I can't let them suffer like this. Just coping with the loss of their father has been hard enough, but to have him blamed for murder, too . . . I have to clear Peter's name for them, Vicky. I don't have anyone else to turn to. Please, you've got to help me."

A lump the size of a grapefruit rose in Vicky's throat. Hot tears blurred her eyes. She could have handled Lisa's anger, but this was cutting her to ribbons.

Taking a deep breath, Vicky leaned forward and folded her arms on the table. "Lisa, I'm sorry. I don't want to give up, but did you read the paper this morning? Did you see the story about John Wexler?"

"The guy who was killed in that hotel on the west side?" Lisa reached for the paper napkin beside her on the table and wiped her eyes.

"I was supposed to meet him yesterday morning because he had information for me on the Grayson Center fire. He was working for me, and now he's dead. I've been getting threatening phone calls, and yesterday afternoon I got a threatening note, too. That's scary enough, but then there was an attempted break-in at my house last night. Josh could have been hurt. I can't risk his life no matter how much I want to help you."

Lisa's eyes widened. "I'm sorry, Vicky, I had no idea. I wouldn't want you to put yourself or your little boy in danger."

"I know that." Vicky sank back in the booth. "Look, if you go to Frank Paxton, I know he'll do everything he can to help you."

"How can he help, Vicky? The cop that handled the case, what's his name, Fletcher, said the evidence was conclusive. As far as the police are concerned, Peter was the one who set that fire."

"Talk to Frank anyway, please. Who knows, maybe between the two of us we can convince him to reopen the investigation."

"Do you really think so?"

"Anything is possible, but I want you to promise me that you'll stop nosing around. Richard Blackwell is a coldhearted bastard who won't hesitate to kill to protect himself. I'm certain he's behind everything that's been going on with me. If he's willing to threaten me, knowing my connections, just think what he would do to you."

Vicky stopped by the station house that night on her way home. As she cruised the lot for a parking space, she found herself looking for Jim's black Mazda. When she didn't see it, an odd mixture of relief and disappointment washed over her. She pulled into a spot and switched off the ignition. It was just as well he wasn't there. She was better off not seeing him anyway.

Jim had been back to his old cranky self that morning. Eye contact was avoided, and when Vicky handed him a mug of coffee, he gave a grunt, which she guessed was supposed to pass for a thanks. Vicky guessed the tension was a carryover from the way their conversation had ended the night before. And she'd thought they'd called a truce. Hah. She couldn't blame everything on Jim, though. They'd both gotten their noses out of joint, and maybe it was better that way. Vicky had found herself enjoying their simple meal a little too much. It would have been easy to relax, open up, start forming a bond. Thank God their conversation ended when and how it did. Bonding wasn't a good thing when it was with someone you knew you were better off not being involved with on any level.

Too much had happened in the last twenty-four hours. Vicky needed to take a deep breath and regroup. She had vacation time coming. Now would be a perfect time to take Josh and get the hell out of Dodge for a while. When she reached the chief's office, Vicky could hear him bellowing through the closed door. She exchanged a look with Laverne who shrugged and went on with her typing. A moment later a young rookie slunk out of Frank's office, his gaze cast down at the floor. Vicky felt a stab of pity for him.

"Go on in if you dare," Laverne said. "But I'm warning you, Frank was called in here at five this morning and it's been downhill ever since."

Vicky knocked on the door, then slowly opened it and poked her head in. Frank was standing at the window, staring at the snarl of early evening traffic on Winthrop Avenue. Vicky frowned when she spotted the ashtray on his desk overflowing with half-smoked cigarettes. Smoke curled from the one that dangled from his lips. His white hair was ruffled, his tie askew. He was scowling when he spun around. "What is it now?" he snapped. His eyes softened and his scowl faded when he saw his god-daughter.

"Got a minute?" Vicky asked.

"I've always got a minute for you." He held her at arm's length, a worried look on his face. "Are you sure you're all right?"

"Like I told you when you called this morning, no worse for the wear."

Frank wagged his finger in her face, his white brows knitted together. "You see, Victoria, this is exactly the kind of thing I was talking about yesterday. What if Jim McCann hadn't shown up when he did?"

Vicky laid her purse on the desk and pulled off her coat. "I had the situation under control, Frank, and the police arrived just minutes after Jim."

"That's not the point," Frank thundered.

Vicky held up her hands, her eyes pleading. "Okay, last night could have turned out differently than it did, but you don't have to worry. I'm letting the whole Grayson Center thing drop."

"Jim told me this morning," Frank said, blowing out a long breath.

"Last night was a real eye-opener." Vicky dropped wearily into a chair. "I've been so busy trying to get a hook into Blackwell I never stopped to consider all the risks involved. I'm done now, though."

"Thank God for small favors." Frank pulled off his tie and tossed it in the bottom drawer of his desk. "You know you've put more white hairs on this old head than my own daughters."

"I know, and I'm sorry." Vicky gave him a half smile. "But I put the word out on the street this morning, so I'm sure Blackwell has heard the news by now."

"Let's hope he decides to let things drop as quickly and quietly as you have."

There was a knock at the door and Gil Fletcher stuck his head in. The chief motioned him to step inside.

The detective planted a kiss on Vicky's forehead. "You look like road kill, kid."

Vicky made a face. "Thanks a lot."

"Ah, it's nothing that a good night's sleep won't fix." He sat in the chair beside hers. "I hear you're dropping your investigation."

"I broke it to Lisa Murphy this afternoon."

"How did she take it?" Frank asked.

"Pretty much the way you'd expect. I'm worried about her. She went to see Ray Abrons today."

"The city electrical inspector?" Gil asked. "Why?"

"Peter told her he's mixed up with Blackwell so she tried putting the screws to Abrons hoping he'd give him up. I'm afraid if Blackwell gets wind of that, Lisa will be his next target."

"Did you explain that to her?" Frank asked tersely.

"Of course, but I don't think it sank in. She wants answers, Frank, and she's determined to find them."

"She sounds like you."

"It's horrible having so many questions, knowing there's more to what happened than what seems to be. I tried to convince her to talk to you." Vicky paused and took a deep breath. "I also told her there was a possibility you would reopen the investigation."

"Why did you do that?" Gil demanded angrily. "We don't have any reason to reopen the case."

Vicky started to appeal to Frank, but he stopped her before she could get a word out. "He's right."

"Come on, do you two honestly believe Peter Murphy was responsible for that fire? The man never got so much as a parking ticket for God's sake."

"So he snapped," Gil replied flatly. "It happens."

"Bullshit."

"Vicky, he threatened two of his co-workers. His prints were the only ones found on the gas cans. I went over all of this," Gil pointed out. "If the state's attorney was satisfied, why can't you be?"

"Blackwell set Murphy up and killed him along with those other men. Please, just look at the case again."

Gil gave her a disgusted look, pushed out of his chair and went to the window. "I told you she wasn't going to give up on this thing, Frank."

"I'm not doing anything but asking you to take a second look at the case," Vicky shot back.

"All right, you two, pipe down!" Frank rubbed his face and heaved a sigh. "I'll take another look at the evidence for you, Vicky, but I'm not going to make any promises."

"Dammit, Frank . . ." Gil began.

The chief cut him off with a look that brooked no argument. "I don't want to hear another word out of either one of you."

"Thank you," Vicky said.

"Don't thank me. I haven't done anything yet, but you can do a favor for me."

"Anything."

"Give Jim McCann your full cooperation. I've assigned him to your case, so it's to your benefit to get along with him."

"Frank! Of all the people. Why not Gil or Fred Danby?"

"They have huge caseloads already. Besides, I really think Jim's the best man for this job. And as long as I'm making your day, you might as well know that I've assigned a man to stay at your house for the time being."

"You don't have the manpower to spare for something like that, and I don't need a baby-sitter!"

"It's a done deal, Vicky," Frank said. "Officer Bettis is on his way there now. When we know you're safe, I'll pull him off. Not a minute before."

Officer Clark Bettis jumped out of his cruiser as soon as Vicky pulled up in front of the garage. She climbed out of the Blazer as the lanky officer walked toward her. Vicky had seen Bettis around the station house, but didn't know him. He had joined the force after she left.

"Evening, Mrs. Langford," Bettis said, taking off his cap to introduce himself. He took the diaper bag and groceries from the backseat. "I've checked the house and grounds and everything seems to be in order."

Raw wind slapped their faces and gravel crunched under their feet as they hurried toward the house. Vicky was halfway up the stairs when she suddenly stopped.

"What is it?" Bettis asked.

Vicky's gaze was riveted to the white plastic bag looped around the handle of the storm door. "That bag. I have no idea what that is."

"It's just your newspaper, ma'am. It was here when I arrived. Nothing to be worried about."

"I don't have a paper delivered, I get them from work."

"I'll take another look." Bettis put down the bags, his boyish face serious. He removed the newspaper from the white plastic bag as Vicky hugged Josh protectively to her. "It's a copy of the *Banner.*"

Bettis handed her a note that was attached to it. Vicky instantly recognized the angular writing scrawled across the yellow Post-it. It read:

> Vicky,
> just a little something to whet your appetite for next week's installment in my series.
>
> Happy reading, Warren.

"What the hell is this all about?" Vicky muttered.

"Is it from the guy who's been stalking you?" Bettis asked. He studied her, his brown eyes filled with concern.

Vicky shook her head. What the hell was Warren Mott up to now? Officer Bettis followed her inside and put the bags on the floor in the front hall.

"Is everything okay?" he asked.

"As fine as it's going to be for now," Vicky said, tugging off Josh's coat.

"I don't blame you for being edgy, but you don't have a thing to worry about. That guy isn't gonna come around while I'm here."

"I'm sure you're right."

Snowball stalked down the hall, eyeing Officer Bettis curiously. The young cop reached out and scratched behind Snowball's ears. "Beautiful cat. I've got two dogs myself. I'm surprised you don't have one, living out here all by yourself."

"Actually, it's something I'm starting to consider."

"It wouldn't be a bad idea." Officer Bettis dropped down on one knee and tickled Josh under his chin. The toddler smiled shyly, hugging his mother's legs. "How old is this little guy?"

"He just turned eighteen months."

"I've got one just a little older than this at home. A girl, Brittany." He pulled a dog-eared snapshot from his wallet and showed it to Vicky.

"She's a beautiful little girl and you're obviously a very proud dad," she said.

"I'll tell you, Mrs. Langford, I can't wait to get home at night just to see her."

"I know exactly what you mean. And I'm sure you'd rather be home with her right now than sitting in that cold squad car."

Bettis shrugged. "It's all part of the job. No problem."

"Can I make you a sandwich and coffee?"

"My wife packed me enough stuff to feed the third battalion, but thanks for the offer." He turned toward the door. "I better get back to my post. If you feel at all uneasy about anything, give a holler."

Vicky locked the door and reset the alarm behind him. The house was silent, except for the ticking of the grandfather clock in the living room. Suddenly, the house seemed lonely, and Vicky wondered what Jim was doing. It had felt good to cook for someone again, like she'd done last night. And she liked having someone to talk to over dinner.

Until last night she hadn't realized how much she missed those little things. Vicky frowned. She had Jim McCann to thank for reminding her.

"We're going to have a nice, quiet night all by ourselves. I promise," Vicky said, snuggling Josh.

She fed him supper, then gave Josh his bath. She let him play in the tub a little longer than usual, enjoying the time with her son. By the time he was done, Vicky was as wet as he was, but it was the first time she'd laughed in days and it felt good.

After reading Josh a bedtime story and tucking him in, Vicky took a quick shower and pulled on a heavy robe and slippers. It started raining again as she settled at the kitchen table. She picked at a roast beef sandwich, her eyes darting to the newspaper on the counter. Finally, she pushed her plate aside and reached for the copy of the *Banner.* She thumbed through it, looking for Warren's byline. Vicky didn't have to look long—it was highlighted in bright orange.

"How considerate of you, Warren," she said.

It was the seventh installment of an eight-week-long series entitled, "Crimes of the Westport Police Department." This week's story was about an elderly woman who was struck and killed by a Westport cruiser during a police chase. Warren wrote, "Why should the police department be held blameless when they behave recklessly? Was Emily Waters's life worth the seventy-five dollars the perpetrator stole from Lambert's Dry Cleaners?"

"That's right, Warren. Only give partial details. You failed to mention that the bastard shot the store owner and left him for dead."

Shaking her head in disgust, she continued reading. The last paragraph seemed to jump off the page, knocking the wind out of her as she read what next week's installment was about.

"You rotten son of a bitch," Vicky hissed between her teeth. "Why don't you rub a little more salt in the wound, Warren?"

She looked at the calendar by the phone. Next week marked the seventh anniversary of that horrible night. Hadn't Warren reminded her of that just yesterday? Why the hell was he dredging this up? It was as if he was deliberately trying to torment her.

Memories she always tried to hold at bay tumbled through her mind. In truth, they were never far from her thoughts. They hovered in the shadows of her mind, like vultures waiting to swoop down on her when she least expected it. Wind rattled the windows and rain pounded the roof. This was so much like that night seven years ago. It had been colder, though. The rain had started to freeze, making the pavement slick.

The image of a young boy, his face dazed and confused in the harsh glow of a streetlight flashed through her mind. Vicky closed her eyes and pressed her fingertips to them, trying to block it out. She pushed back in the chair so suddenly she had to grab it to keep it from falling over. She crumpled the paper up and angrily stuffed it in the trash can. Hugging herself, she paced the kitchen.

"I can't do this again tonight. I won't. I can go over it a hundred more times and it won't change anything."

You can't undo the past. Isn't that what Dr. Parker had told her during those counseling sessions the department sent her to? Vicky sighed heavily. "No, you can't undo the past, Doc, but it doesn't mean you don't wish you could."

She built a fire and poured herself a glass of white wine. Downing it, she poured another. Maybe Lisa Murphy had the right idea. Get hammered so you don't have to think, don't have to hurt. Vicky wondered how Lisa was doing. She had only picked at the burger Vicky had ordered, opting for three more beers instead. Vicky had taken her home in a cab. The driver was nice enough to help get her into the house where Lisa's sister, Michelle, took over.

Darting a glance at the clock on her desk, Vicky reached for the phone. It wasn't too late to call. Michelle picked up on the fourth ring, sounding exasperated. She told Vicky that Lisa was passed out cold. Poor Lisa. Vicky could only hope she'd let the police handle things from here on out. Grabbing the remote, Vicky channel surfed. She needed to lose herself in something. She shut the TV off fifteen minutes later. Everything was murder and mayhem, blood and gore, and God knew she had enough of that in her own life.

She ambled over to the bookcase and pulled down a romance novel, thought of Jim and immediately put it back. The last thing she needed right now was to read about bulging biceps and passionate kisses. Vicky eyed the two months' worth of magazines stacked in a basket in the corner and grabbed the top one. Snowball jumped in her lap as she settled back on the couch and propped her feet on the coffee table. The wine and sheer exhaustion kicked in, making her eyelids feel heavy as anvils. She'd barely made it through the first page when she dozed off.

Vicky's eyes snapped open the first time the phone rang. She looked around, blinking rapidly. Glancing at the clock, she was surprised to see it was after midnight. There were only glowing embers left on the hearth where just hours earlier a fire had roared. The phone rang again.

"Dammit," she muttered, pushing Snowball from her lap.

When she answered it a raspy voice said, "I am Death, Vicky, and I'm right outside your door."

Her mouth went dry and her body trembled. Vicky slammed the receiver down and backed away from the phone. "Rotten son of a bitch."

Running to the front hall, she peered through the sidelight. She could see Officer Bettis' silhouette in the glow of the porch light. She had to warn him in case that guy was nuts enough to come back tonight. Vicky grabbed her raincoat from the closet and the can of pepper spray she always carried, from her purse. She cautiously poked her head outside and scanned the yard. Holding the raincoat over head, she dashed through the rain to the squad car.

At first Vicky thought Officer Bettis was sleeping. Reality hit her like a freight train as she pulled the driver's side door open and the overhead light came on.

"Oh my God!" Vicky cried.

The young officer's throat was slit from ear to ear. His brown eyes were wide and staring. His jacket, pants, and the front seat were covered with blood. Fighting nausea, she reached in to feel for a pulse she already knew wasn't there. Tears scalded her cheeks as her fingers came away stained with Bettis' blood.

"You fucking bastard!" Vicky screamed as she dropped her raincoat and ran toward the house. She was at the bottom of the steps when she saw the killer's calling card. This time nausea won and she retched as she scrambled inside. Scrawled above her front door in dark red letters was a single word. *Death.*

The man paced the length of the room, adrenaline coursing through his body. He was too wired to sit after his visit to Vicky's. What a rush that had been! He looked down at his shaking hands. There was still blood on them—on his clothes, too. He wished it was Vicky's blood, but that would happen soon enough—to her and her kid.

Going to the kitchen, he rummaged for the bottle of Dewar's in the back of the cabinet over the stove. He opened it and chugged it straight from the bottle. It went down like liquid fire.

He had only intended to watch the house as he always did,

but once he got the idea, he just couldn't stop himself. Vicky thought she was safe with her armed guard. And Officer Friendly was being so diligent, going around at regular intervals, shining his flashlight into the bushes. Boy, had he been surprised when he got sliced and diced!

He'd come up behind the cop as he made his rounds. It was over in a heartbeat. The cop had dropped to his knees. Clutching his throat with one hand, he'd grappled for his gun with the other, but it was no use.

"I'll bet you're sorry you got that job, pal." The man chuckled and took another slug of Dewar's.

He rolled his shoulder and swung his arm around in a circle like a pitcher warming up for a big game. The cop was skinny but heavier than he looked. Lugging that dead weight all the way back to the squad car had been more difficult than the man anticipated.

He took another drink from the bottle and wiped his mouth with the back of his hand. Walking to the sliding glass doors he stepped out onto the deck that overlooked Pine Lake. The rain had just stopped and the moon was a sliver of white in a black sky. A few more hours and the sun would be up. Oh, how he wished he could be there when Vicky went outside in the morning.

He wanted to let her know in a big way there was nothing she could do, no place she could hide to get away from him.

"It's almost time for you to pay, bitch. Do you feel me getting closer, Vicky? I am Death, and I'm coming for you."

Chapter 6

"Vicky, what in the world are you doing here at this hour?" Mary's red hair was a tangle around her freckled face. Her green eyes were still half closed with sleep as she looked at Vicky, clearly puzzled.

It was four in the morning and pitch-black outside. Mary clutched her tatty pink robe around her as Vicky stepped inside and dropped Josh's diaper bag on the floor.

As Mary closed the door, her eyes snapped wide open. "My God, what is that police car doing in front of my house? What happened?"

"I'm sorry to do this to you, Mary," Vicky said, her voice cracking. Her eyes were red and swollen. She felt sick with grief every time she thought of Office Bettis.

Josh squirmed in Vicky's arms and began crying. She put him down and took off his hat and coat.

"Mom, what's going on?" Mary's fourteen-year-old twins, Melissa and Melanie came down the stairs, rubbing their eyes. They had the same coppery hair as their mother. The oversized T-shirts and baggy plaid flannel pants they wore swallowed their slender frames.

"I don't know," Mary said, locking the door. "Go back to bed."

Rattling off questions, they instead followed Vicky and Mary into the kitchen.

"Girls, give Vicky a chance to breathe," Mary said, exasperated. She reached for the coffeepot and filled it with water. "Why don't you take Josh upstairs and see if you can get him back to sleep so Vicky and I can talk. Then the two of you go to bed."

"Come on, Josh," Melanie said, taking him from Vicky. "I'll read you a story."

"I'll read him the story," Melissa insisted. "You don't put enough expression into it."

"Well excuse me, Meryl Streep. I didn't know I was auditioning for a role."

"Girls," Mary snapped. "You sound like two-year-olds. Just take Josh upstairs."

The aroma of coffee brewing filled the kitchen as Vicky dropped into a chair. "Please tell me I didn't wake up Bill, too."

"You could set a bomb off next to that man and he wouldn't move a muscle. I'm not worried about Bill, but I am worried about you. What the hell is going on?"

Vicky dropped her head to her hands. Her voice trembled when she spoke. "Remember how Madam Zoya said there was darkness and death all around me? She was right."

"You know you can't put any stock in what she said." Mary leaned over Vicky and put an arm around her shoulders.

"What I know is that people are dropping around me like flies."

"What are you talking about?" Mary asked, sitting in the chair beside Vicky's.

"Things have been happening that I haven't told you." Vicky explained everything then, starting with the Grayson Center fire and ending with the murder of Officer Bettis.

Mary's eyes grew wider with every detail. When Vicky was finally done, Mary shook her head, her mouth pressed into a thin line. "You think this is all connected to the calls you're getting and to Richard Blackwell."

"It makes sense."

"I'm your best friend and you never said a word about any of this. Why?"

"Because I didn't want you to worry."

"Lord knows you give me plenty to worry about, Vicky Langford."

Vicky didn't miss the tremor in her friend's voice or the flicker of fear in her eyes. She wanted to tell Mary everything was going to be just dandy, but the truth was Vicky couldn't be so sure about that. The murder of Officer Bettis drove home that fact.

Vicky couldn't get the vision of the young cop out of her head. He'd been so proud when he'd shown her the photo of his little girl. Now, like Josh, Clark Bettis' daughter would grow up without her father, too. The poor man had only tried to protect Vicky and he had paid with his life.

"What the hell are you doing getting yourself mixed up in something like this investigation of Blackwell?" Mary said angrily. "Are you trying to get yourself killed?"

"It's my job, Mary."

"It's your job to report the news. You act like you're still a cop." Mary blew out a breath. "Look, this isn't getting us anywhere. Instead of arguing about why this is happening, let's figure out what to do about it. For starters, I think you should stay here until the cops catch this guy."

"I can't do that. This bastard wants me, but anyone unlucky enough to be around me is in danger, too. Two people have already died because of me. I'm not adding my best friend and her family to that list." Vicky leaned forward, her elbows on the table. "I'm worried about Josh, though. Can he stay with you for a few days?"

"You don't even have to ask, but what about you? If you

won't stay here, what will you do, where will you go?"

"Home."

"Are you crazy?" Mary asked, her voice climbing. "Have you talked to Frank Paxton about this?"

"He came to the house tonight after I called the police. At first, he sounded like you, but he realized I'm right. I have to play this out to the end."

"You're both out of your minds." Tears ran down Mary's cheeks and she didn't bother to wipe them. "So what does this mean, that you'll sit around like shark bait waiting for this guy to make his move?"

"That's exactly what it means."

Dalila Sinclair pulled white cardboard containers from a brown bag and lined them up on the counter. It was Monday afternoon and she and Vicky were in the break room at the newspaper. Three days had passed since the death of Officer Bettis.

"God, Dalila, I feel as if I'm losing my mind," Vicky said. She got two diet Cokes from the vending machine and went to a table.

Dalila gave her a sympathetic smile as she spooned fried rice onto a paper plate and placed it in front of Vicky. "Eat. It'll make you feel better. You look like you're withering away to nothing."

"I feel like I could jump out of my skin." Vicky pushed rice and pork around on her plate then laid down her fork. "I'm constantly looking over my shoulder, wondering when he's going to make his next move."

"That's what he wants you to feel," Dalila said. "It's all part of the fun of this little cat-and-mouse game he's playing."

"I can't believe this is happening to me."

Dalila dabbed her lips with a paper napkin. "What are the police doing to catch this guy?"

"Everything they can, and believe me they're out for blood

now that one of their own has been killed, but there's nothing to go on."

"Have they figured out what happened the night that cop was murdered?"

Hot tears stung Vicky's eyes and she swallowed hard. "It looks like Officer Bettis was surprised from behind while he was making his rounds. He died within minutes and was dragged back to the squad car where I found him."

"What about evidence?" Dalila asked. "Didn't they find any at all?"

Vicky shrugged and pushed away her plate. Just the sight of food was making her stomach churn. "They collected a few fibers from the squad car and Officer Bettis' jacket, but any footprints were washed away by the rain."

"You still think Richard Blackwell is behind all of this?"

"More certain than ever," Vicky replied. Her face was tight with anger, her fists clenched. "God, I want to nail that bastard!"

Dalila reached over and squeezed Vicky's arm. "You're wound tight as a spring. You need to relax, girlfriend. Why don't we go out for a while tonight, get your mind off this crap."

"Gil called this morning and made me the same offer, but I'm afraid I'm turning you both down. I'm going to Mary's for dinner so I can spend time with Josh, then coming back here to finish up a story I'm working on."

"How about after that? You, Gil, and I could go for a drink. The last time the three of us went out we had a ball and you could do with some fun right about now."

"Not tonight, Dalila, really. I'm just not up to it."

Dalila shrugged and picked at her egg roll. "That's okay, we'll do it another time. How's Josh doing at Mary's?"

"Great. He loves the girls. He probably won't want to come home when this is over." Vicky smiled, but there was an ache in her heart. Even though she saw Josh every day, she still missed him terribly. The last three days had seemed more like three years. She wanted her little boy back home with her where he belonged. She wanted his hugs and sloppy goodnight kisses, but more than that, Vicky wanted her son to be safe. Having him stay at Mary's was the only way she felt she could accomplish that.

"Do you really think this guy is a threat to Josh?"

"I'm not taking any chances," Vicky said shaking her head. "There's a showdown coming, I can feel it, and I don't want Josh anywhere around when it happens."

"Why not take him and visit your parents in Arizona?"

"I already considered that, but they're vacationing in Europe right now. Even if they weren't, running won't solve anything. This guy would wait for me to come back, or worse, look for me, and I'm not drawing my parents into this, too. What if he showed up on their doorstep? I can't take that chance."

Dalila cast a worried look at her. "I wouldn't mind staying with you a few days. You've got to be a nervous wreck even if the police are there."

"I appreciate the offer, but to tell you the truth, after what happened to Office Bettis I'd probably be more nervous," Vicky confided, raking a hand through her hair. "I'd be scared to death you'd get hurt."

"Believe me, Vicky, if that guy came back while I was there, he'd be the one getting hurt, or worse."

Vicky's brows knitted together. "What are you talking about?"

"I carry a gun."

"I didn't know that," Vicky said, her eyes wide. "Do you really think you could use it, Dalila?"

"I wouldn't have it if I didn't think I could use it. Don't you think you could use a gun again if you had to defend yourself?"

It was a question that played over and over in Vicky's mind the rest of the afternoon. Could she pick up a gun again and actually pull the trigger if she had to? The truth was she didn't know, and Vicky hoped to God she didn't have to find out.

Vicky looked up from her computer monitor and was surprised to see it was nearly 11:00 P.M. She hadn't meant to work that late. Rubbing her eyes, she stifled a yawn. She'd been at it nonstop since returning from her visit with Josh three hours earlier. She could have taken the work home and probably should have, but she just couldn't face her empty house.

She stood and stretched, looking around. In spite of the hour, the phones were still ringing and people were busy pounding away at their keyboards. No matter what the time, or day of the week, the newsroom always bustled with activity.

"You pulling an all-nighter or what?" a gravelly voice asked from behind her. Her editor, Tom McDonald, stalked toward her, his hands on his hips, the sleeves of his wrinkled blue shirt rolled up to his elbows. His burgundy-colored tie had come off hours ago. McDonald's steel gray eyebrows were drawn together as he looked at her over the top of his gold-rimmed glasses. "Why don't you get the hell out of here and go home?"

"I will, right after I make a trip to the archives."

"It can wait," he snapped. "You look like you're dead on your feet. Get your stuff together and I'll take you downstairs."

"It'll only take me a half hour at the most, then I'll go home."

"Yeah, sure you will."

Vicky crossed her heart and held up her hand. "I give you my word."

"Come on. I'll go up there with you."

Vicky shook her head as she pulled her can of pepper spray from her purse. "There's no need. Al Delany and Roland Becker are already up there, so I'll have plenty of company."

When she stepped off the elevator on the eighth floor, Vicky was greeted by the sight of red toolboxes, paint-speckled scaffolding and pieces of drywall. The remodeling work had been going on for months as Stone Construction made their way floor-by-floor through the building. *Herald* employees had already been warned, the multimillion-dollar renovation could go on for well over a year, so get used to the inconvenience and the thin veil of plaster dust that hung in the air.

Vicky's footsteps echoed down the hallway as she passed locked and darkened offices. During regular business hours, this floor that housed the accounting and advertising departments as well as the archives, was like Wal-Mart on a Saturday afternoon. Vicky usually didn't mind coming up here after hours. The quiet was always a welcome respite from the noisy newsroom, but tonight she found the silence eerie and unsettling. She was glad she'd have company.

"Hello!" she called out as she entered the archives and looked around. Al and Roland were nowhere to be seen, though microfiche machines were on in two of the cubicles and they'd left their spiral notebooks behind. They probably went to grab a sandwich and will be back any minute, Vicky thought. For a fleeting moment she considered leaving, then changed her mind. Al and Roland were obviously coming back and besides, people were always coming and going from the archives. She was as safe here as she was anywhere.

Settling in a cubicle she went to work. A short while later, as she was changing rolls of film, she heard footsteps. Vicky pushed back in her chair, wincing as it scraped against the tiled floor. She went to the door and poked her head out. The corridor was empty.

"Hello? Al, Roland?"

There was no response. The silence raised a bumper crop of goose bumps on her arms. Her mouth went dry.

His words whispered in her mind. *I am Death, Vicky, and I'm coming for you.*

"Don't panic," she murmured. "It might not be him."

But Vicky knew it had to be. Anyone else would have answered. Trembling, she quietly closed the door and backed into the room. The other night Vicky had told Jim McCann she never let down her guard, yet that was exactly what she'd done tonight. Stupid, stupid, stupid. Never underestimate the enemy. She grabbed the can of pepper spray. It didn't seem like much, but a squirt of this and a kick to the groin could take the wind out of anyone's sails. Since it was all she had to work with at the moment, she'd have to run with it.

The footsteps were closer now, stopping outside. She moved to one side of the door. Her knuckles turned white as marble as she gripped the can of pepper spray.

Make the first strike. He won't be expecting that.

The doorknob turned.

As the door opened Vicky lunged, letting out a war cry and depressing the button on the can. Nothing but a hiss of air came from it, but still the man shrieked and stumbled back into the hall, dropping his mop and nearly tripping over his bucket of water.

The maintenance man's brown eyes were wide, his thick blonde hair spilled across his startled face. He pulled a set of headphones off, letting them hang around his neck. "What in the world are you doing, Mrs. Langford? You scared the life outta me!"

Sagging against the doorway, Vicky looked up at him. "You shaved a few years off of me, too, Ralph, so I guess we can call it even. I thought you were someone else. Sorry."

"I'm glad I'm not whoever you thought. What do you have there?"

Vicky frowned as she looked at the can in her hand. "Pepper spray, but there's something wrong with this can. Nothing came out when I pressed the button."

"Lucky for me, I guess." He bent down to retrieve his mop, giving her a quizzical look. "You okay? I didn't mean to scare you."

"It's just that I heard someone and when I called out, no one answered."

Ralph gave her a lopsided grin. "Can't hear anything with the headphones on. Listen, I'll finish up here later. I wouldn't want you to slip and fall on the wet floor."

"Thanks. I'm almost done." Vicky watched as he turned and lumbered down the hall. She shook her head and looked down at the can of spray. "Fat lot of good this'll do me."

She settled back in the cubicle once more, feeling relieved to have Ralph around. Twenty minutes later she shut off her machine, grabbed her papers and headed down the corridor, intending to let Ralph know he could finish mopping. Rounding the corner, Vicky caught a glimpse of him getting in the service elevator just before the doors slid closed.

"Oh well," she muttered. "I tried."

She went to the main bank of elevators and pressed the CALL button. Stifling a yawn, she leaned against the wall thinking of what she had left to do on her story. A sound snapped her back to attention.

Footsteps again. She spun around.

Nothing.

"Who's there?" Vicky called, starting back toward the archives. It was then she noticed the open toolbox on the floor. It hadn't been like that when she'd gotten off the elevator earlier. She was certain of that. The first prickling of alarm raced down her spine. "Al? Roland?"

The footsteps drew nearer. An odd, scraping sound echoed loudly in the empty corridor.

What the hell?

She stopped short as a man stepped around the corner.

Powerfully built, he was dressed in black from head to toe. He dragged the claw end of a red-handled hammer along the wall.

Vicky's breath left her in a *whoosh.* Dropping her papers, she turned and sprinted down the hall. She jabbed frantically at the CALL button for the elevator.

"Vicky," the eerie voice whispered.

There was nowhere to go, nowhere to hide, nothing to do but run. Vicky bolted for the door to the stairwell. She hit the steps running, screaming for help. Someone would hear her and summon the cop sitting in the car in front of the building, wouldn't they? She heard the door above her open and close. Her heart jackknifed at the sound of that damned claw hammer scraping along the wall and the man's slow and deliberate footsteps.

Vicky tugged at the door to the seventh floor, but it wouldn't open. She ran down to the sixth floor, but that door was locked, too. Screaming, she pounded on the door, but Vicky knew the chance of anyone hearing anything above the din in the newsroom was slim to none.

Blind fear propelled her as she ran, testing doors and finding them locked. Her chest burned and her legs felt weak, but she willed herself to keep moving.

"Vicky," the man whispered. "There's no where to run."

Oh, God. I'm trapped and he knows it. That's why he's not chasing me.

She reached the ground floor. If this door was locked, too, she'd have no choice but to face him and fight.

Please be unlocked, Vicky prayed, gripping the doorknob with both hands.

The door opened.

Relief washed over her as she stumbled into the lobby, screaming for help. Ralph was there, his back to her, swinging his mop in time to music only he could hear. Vicky lurched toward him and grabbed his arm.

Ralph jumped and spun around. He pulled his headphones off. "You must be trying to scare me to death today, Mrs. Langford."

"Ralph, someone chased me down the stairs," Vicky said breathlessly.

"What the hell," Ralph said, sticking his mop in the bucket. Hitching up his pants he headed for the stairs. "Stay right here. I'll take a look."

"No! There's a cop outside. Get him, please."

A moment later, Officer Grabski hurried into the building with Ralph on his heels.

"He's got a hammer and God only knows what else!" Vicky said, as Grabski drew his gun and disappeared through the heavy steel door to the stairs.

Ralph hurried to the reception desk to call for security. Within minutes the lobby was buzzing with activity. Vicky sank into one of the forest green chairs in the reception area.

"Jeez, Mrs. Langford," Ralph murmured, hanging his head. "I'd never have left you alone up there if I thought something like this was going to happen!"

"Don't apologize, Ralph. You had no way of knowing."

"I'm just glad you're okay. I don't know how all those fire doors got locked. They're not supposed to be."

"I'm sure my 'friend' had something to do with that," Vicky replied wryly.

"Well, well, well, Vicky Langford. What a surprise!"

Vicky turned in the chair to see Warren Mott sauntering toward her from the elevator. "Burning the midnight oil are we? You look a little harried."

"What the hell are you doing here, Mott?"

"I still have some friends here, believe it or not," Warren said, his voice tinged with sarcasm. "I was supposed to meet Brian Walker, but I was late and he was gone when I got here—not that it's any of your business. By the way, did you get the copy of the *Banner* I dropped off at your place?"

"I got it, and I'm only going to say this once, Mott. Stay the hell away from my house."

He gave her a thin smile. "Oh my, you're angry aren't you? And here I thought you'd be pleased with my work. After all, you were the inspiration for the series, Vicky."

"Too bad I can't inspire you to take a walk off the Westport Bridge."

Ignoring her remark, Warren went on, "My editor says this series is going to put me back on top. He thinks I may even get an award for my journalism. It's pretty compelling stuff, don't you think? And of course, I saved the best for last. That's why your story is the eighth and final installment."

Vicky narrowed her eyes and pushed out of the chair. "You have a brass set of balls to call yourself a journalist. You only give half the facts and the rest of the garbage you write borders on out-and-out lying. You'll be lucky if you and the *Banner* don't get sued."

Warren's pudgy face glowed with satisfaction as he took a step back. "Listen, I'd love to stay and chat, but I've got to run. I'll make sure you get a copy of next week's *Banner.*"

A string of expletives exploded in Vicky's mind. She bit her tongue to keep from saying them out loud. She was still standing there when Officer Grabski returned.

"Whoever it was is long gone, but I think you must have dropped these." He handed her the stack of papers she'd dropped and an envelope with her name scrawled across it.

Vicky sank back into the chair, staring at the envelope. Fear seeped into her bones like a winter chill. Her hands trembled as she tore the envelope open and read the note inside.

Remember John Wexler.

Chapter 7

Vicky poured herself a shot of apricot brandy, downed it, then splashed another generous drink into the glass. She sipped it as she went to her bedroom, relieved to finally be home. It was nearly one in the morning. She was exhausted physically and mentally, but at least she didn't have to worry anymore about Al Delany and Roland Becker. After her visit from Dark Man, as Vicky had come to think of her stalker, she'd feared that he had done something to her two co-workers. Instead, they'd run down to the Avalon for a sandwich, just as she had originally thought. When they finally walked into the lobby of the *Herald* Vicky had been so glad to see them she'd burst into tears.

Tossing her clothes in the hamper, she pulled her robe on and sank down on the bed. The fact Dark Man could have easily overtaken her on the stairs that night wasn't lost on Vicky. He could have made her head look like ground beef with that hammer, but he hadn't. Why? Tonight was the perfect opportunity for him to make his move. What in the hell was he waiting for? Why keep terrorizing her with this sick little game of cat-and-mouse?

Tears of anger and frustration blurred her vision. Dammit, she had felt so utterly defenseless tonight! It wasn't a feeling she wanted to experience again. Dalila's question to her at lunch echoed in Vicky's mind. Could she use a gun again if it meant defending herself? She wanted to believe that her instinct for self-preservation was stronger than fear, but she wasn't so sure.

Running a hand through her hair, she blew out a long breath and went to the closet. Pushing aside her clothes, Vicky dragged a large green metal chest into the room. She rummaged in a dresser drawer for the key, then sat on the floor and unlocked the chest.

Danny's old uniform lay inside, neatly pressed and folded. She pulled it out and ran her fingers over the dark blue fabric, then laid it aside. Memories of her husband's life were packed away in this chest—from his Boy Scout patches to his detective's badge. She paused to look at photos and skim old letters, anything to avoid what she had started to do. Finally, she gave herself a mental shake.

Quit stalling. You're not doing this so you can make a trip down memory lane.

She pulled Danny's ASP—a retractable police baton with a metal ball on the end—from the chest. She'd definitely keep this with her from now on.

Standing up, Vicky extended the weapon, listening to the whistle it made as she sliced the air with it. This baby was small enough to carry in her purse but could break bones when wielded. Too bad she hadn't had this with her tonight. Maybe this whole thing would have been over now. As she retracted the ASP, she made a mental note to get another can of pepper spray, too, but Vicky knew neither was a match for a gun. She quickly dug through the rest of Danny's things until her fingers touched cold metal. Nausea swept over her.

"You can do this. Just pretend Dark Man is here and it's either you or him." Swallowing hard, Vicky lifted the Sig Sauer out of the chest. It felt heavy and out of place in her trembling hand. Her mouth was dry and she licked her lips. Her heart beat like the wings of a trapped bird. She extended the gun with both hands and aimed at the lamp on the dresser. Shaking like a junkie in bad need of a fix, she struggled to keep the gun on her target.

"Shit, Langford, get with the program. You were one of the best shots in the department."

Suddenly, the gun slipped from her hands and clattered to the floor. Vicky sank down, put her back against the dresser and drew her knees to her chest. Could she use a gun to defend herself if she had to? Vicky glanced at the Sig lying next to her feet.

"I don't think so," she whispered, her eyes filling with tears. "Not in this lifetime."

Vicky's sleep that night was restless and full of nightmares of Dark Man. When she awoke with a start early the next morning, the bed sheets were tangled around her legs and one of her pillows was on the floor. Snowball, who always slept at the foot of the bed, had apparently gotten fed up with Vicky's thrashings. He was curled up, softly purring, in the chair in the corner of the room.

"Sorry I chased you away," Vicky murmured, scratching under his chin.

She was pulling on her robe when she heard a car drive up. She went to the front hall window and groaned at the sight of Jim McCann's black Mazda.

"God, don't I have enough problems to deal with without adding Mr. Sunshine to the list?" she muttered.

Early morning mist swirled around Jim's legs as he stalked toward the police cruiser parked in front of the house. He wore the trademark scowl Vicky was getting so used to seeing. Leaning into the squad, he spoke to Officers Foley and Lemont for a moment, then headed for the house. Vicky's heart thumped as she watched him walk up the steps. She opened the door before he got a chance to knock. A trail of cold air followed him as he stepped inside.

Jim's gaze swept over her and Vicky was suddenly aware of how she must look. Her dark hair was tousled and her robe hung open, barely concealing the red football jersey she wore. If Vicky lived to be one hundred she'd never forget the look on Jim's face the other night when he came up from the basement and saw her standing in the kitchen wearing nothing but the damn jersey. It was the same look he was giving her now.

Vicky felt her face warm under the intensity of his gaze. Turning away, she pulled her robe closed and tied it tightly. For an instant she wondered if Jim could hear her heart hammering, see it beating beneath the fabric of her robe.

She cleared her throat and folded her arms. "What are you doing here?"

The smoky gaze Jim had just worn suddenly disappeared. His jaw worked as he towered over her, his hands jammed at his hips. "What the hell is the matter with you? Don't you know better than to stay so late at the *Herald*?"

"I didn't think I had anything to worry about while I was there, and I had my can of pepper spray so I figured I could disable him long enough to get away even if he did show up. Unfortunately, I didn't expect the damn can to be faulty." She tilted her head and looked up at him. "How did you hear about what happened already?"

"I've been assigned to your case, remember? I went in to the station early this morning and the report was on my desk. Somebody is going to get reamed royally for not notifying me last night."

"If you've read the report then you already know what happened, so that brings me back to my original question. What are you doing here?"

"I want to hear every last detail from you, no matter how trivial."

"Then you're going to have to hear it while I have my coffee," Vicky groused, heading for the kitchen.

She self-consciously ran a hand through her hair, suddenly wishing she'd taken a minute to brush it before she answered the door. Her knees were trembling, her stomach fluttering, and Vicky hated herself for it. Of all the people in the world she could be attracted to, why did it have to be Jim McCann?

They had nothing in common whatsoever, unless you counted mutual desire—and there wasn't a doubt in Vicky's mind that Jim wanted her as much as she wanted him. It was written all over his face every time she saw him, regardless of how gruff and indifferent he tried to be. Was her desire for him as obvious? God, she hoped not!

Jim leaned against the counter, arms folded across his broad chest. Vicky felt his gaze on her as she scooped coffee into the basket of the coffeemaker. She began recounting events from the night before with clipped indifference. With each detail of her close call, Jim's face grew tighter with anger. When she was done she nodded at the piece of paper on the table. "That's a copy of the love note he left me, but since you've read the report you already know what it says."

Jim snatched it up and read it anyway.

"Did you hear from him last night?" he asked, tossing the paper back on the table.

"I decided not to give him the opportunity to gloat," Vicky said. She popped two English muffins in the toaster, then pulled mugs and plates from the cabinet. "I unplugged the phone."

"Good idea." Jim glanced over the counter into the family room then turned to Vicky, his head cocked. His tone softened when he spoke. "Your little guy still sleeping?"

"He'll be staying with my friend, Mary Renfield, for a while. After what happened to Officer Bettis, I thought it was best to get him out of the line of fire."

"You did the right thing, but it must be tough on you having him gone."

Jim's words instantly struck a nerve. Vicky caught her lower lip between her teeth as her eyes filled. Her voice quivering, she said, "It won't be much longer before he's back home where he belongs."

Vicky saw the look of pity in Jim's eyes as he started toward her. She immediately squared her shoulders and crossed her arms. She wanted her posture to say back off, I don't need you to comfort me, and it must have worked because Jim stopped. Thank God, Vicky thought. If he'd put his arms around her she'd have fallen apart on the spot, and she was absolutely determined not to do that in front of anyone.

As if trying to give her more space, Jim pulled out a chair from the table and sat down. "Listen, Vicky, this guy is becoming more daring, more willing to take risks. I think he's ready to make his final move."

"He's definitely becoming more aggressive, but I don't think he's done playing his little game yet. Last night proves that. He could have had me, McCann, but he didn't do a damn thing."

"But why didn't he?" Jim rubbed his hand across his jaw thoughtfully. "What's he waiting for?"

"Beats the hell out of me. I guess you'd have to ask Richard Blackwell that question. This guy is working on his time table, but trust me, when he comes after me again, I'll be ready for him."

"Like you were last night?" Jim's voice held a note of challenge.

"There won't be a repeat performance of last night," Vicky shot back. "Next time that bastard shows himself, you'd better believe I won't be running from him."

She leaned over Jim and put a jar of apple butter on the table, then turned away. In one swift movement he rose from the chair, grabbed Vicky by the arm, and spun her around to face him. His midnight-blue eyes pierced her straight through.

"You act as if you aren't afraid of anything and, dammit, you should be. Quit with the tough-as-nails routine already and let somebody help you."

Vicky's skin tingled beneath his touch and her pulse quickened. She told herself she didn't want or need anything from this man, but he was standing too close, making her feel things she didn't want to feel. Vicky trembled as Jim's gaze lingered on her mouth. He cupped her chin in his hand and brushed his thumb gently across her bottom lip.

A heartbeat of time passed. Vicky's breath caught in her throat. It would be so easy to lean into Jim, to lay her head on his chest and feel his arms around her, strong and reassuring, but she couldn't risk that small comfort. It would only take her down a road that would lead to heartache again. She wasn't about to go there.

Jim slowly lowered his face and Vicky realized he was going to kiss her. The thought excited and terrified her all at the same time. She suddenly jerked free and took a step back. "I can take care of myself, McCann."

"And you've done one helluva job so far, haven't you? At this rate you're going to get yourself killed. Why don't you just offer yourself up on a platter for him?"

Vicky gave him a withering glance. "That's exactly what I want to do."

"What the hell are you talking about?"

"I've thought about it, and I want him to come after me so we can bring an end to this."

"So what do you suggest? Staying late at the *Herald* so he can chase you down the stairs again?"

Vicky's nerves were frayed, her patience nonexistent. She fought to keep her temper in check when she spoke. "All I'm asking for is a little room so he can make his move—the one that will be for keeps. Pull some of this protection off of me and give the bastard that chance."

"Just what is it you're trying to prove?" Jim stared at her in disbelief. "Anyone else would be begging for police protection, but not you. You want to go it alone. Don't you get it? This guy will make his move whether or not you have police protection.

"He proved that last night and with the murder of Clark Bettis. You're on a collision course with a madman, Vicky. There's only going to be one of you left standing at the end and it's my job to make sure that one is you. So here's a news flash for you. Foley and Lemont will continue to stay here at night, and I'm personally escorting you wherever you go, starting now. I'll follow you to the *Herald* this morning and if you have to leave for any reason, you call me and I'll be waiting out front to follow you. Here's my cell number."

"You've got to be kidding," Vicky said, her mouth agape. "I've already got around-the-clock protection. What can you do that they can't?"

"Let's just say I'm taking your protection as a personal challenge. Frank Paxton told me to handle your case any way I see fit and this is it." Jim folded his arms and gave her a hard look that brooked no argument. "We're going to be seeing a lot of each other, so get used to it. I'll have to, and believe me it won't be any easier on me than it is on you."

Vicky worked the entire morning, not stopping for so much as a cup of coffee. The object was to lose herself in what she was doing. It had seemed like a good idea, but she couldn't focus, couldn't think about anything other than what was happening to her.

Pushing back from her desk, she sauntered into the hall and over to the set of windows that looked down at the *Herald*'s parking lot. She closed her eyes and Jim's face, rugged and handsome, leaped instantly into her mind. She shivered, remembering how it felt when he touched her. Jim would have kissed her this morning if she hadn't pulled away. Worse yet, she would have let him. She needed time away from him to sort out her feelings. She'd have to talk to Frank about putting someone else on her case.

As she started back to the office, Dalila came out of the ladies' room and fell into step with her. She looped her arm through Vicky's. "You look like hell, kiddo."

Vicky chuckled and shook her head. "So I've heard. Our esteemed editor said the same thing."

"You gonna take a lunch break soon?"

Vicky glanced at her watch. It was later than she realized, after eleven. "In about an hour."

"How about one of those greasy burgers down at the Avalon? I'll buy."

"Thanks, Dalila, but I'm going to Mary's to visit Josh. When this is all over, though, we'll go out and celebrate. My treat."

Her phone was ringing when she reached her desk. "Newsroom, Vicky Langford."

"How's Josh, Vicky?" the raspy voice on the phone whispered. "Have you checked on him lately?"

Vicky drew in a sharp, ragged breath. The line went dead before she could reply. Knuckles white, she clutched the receiver.

He's just trying to scare you. This is a call like all the others.

But in her heart, Vicky knew it wasn't. He had never mentioned Josh before. Hands trembling, she dialed Mary's number and counted the rings. Three, four, five. The answering machine picked up.

She called again, but got the machine once more. Mary never took Josh anywhere without telling her first, and she hadn't heard from Mary all morning. Vicky kept telling herself there were a million reasons her friend hadn't answered the phone. Maybe Mary was taking out a bag of trash, or she was too busy with Josh to answer the call.

Or maybe she can't because something has happened.

Grabbing her purse, she spun around and nearly collided with Dalila.

"Hey, where's the fire?" Dalila asked.

"I've got to go," Vicky said, panic gnawing at her. "Dark Man just called me again."

"Who?" Dalila said.

"Dark Man—my stalker. This time he asked about Josh. He's never done that before, Dalila. I know this is probably just my imagination working overtime, but I can't reach Mary and I'm afraid something's happened. I'm just going to take a run over there and make sure everything is okay."

"Let me take you," Dalila said. "You shouldn't be driving when you're upset like this."

"I'll be fine, really, but I've got to go."

Outside she sprinted toward the parking lot, oblivious to the stares of the people rushing by with their coat collars turned up. Vicky had left so fast she hadn't bothered to grab her jacket. Tires squealing against the blacktop, she sped out of the parking lot.

She kept telling herself she'd be back at her desk in less than an hour, feeling foolish for panicking like this. But she didn't feel foolish right now. She felt numb with terror. She caught every light, got behind every slow driver in Westport as she drove to Mary's. Vicky tried her number again and again, but kept getting the answering machine. Each unanswered call fanned her fear like a hot wind on a brush fire.

It seemed like an eternity before she finally swung her Blazer into her friend's driveway. Leaving the car door hanging open, Vicky ran up the front steps and pounded on the door. When

Mary didn't answer she twisted the knob, but the door was locked. Vicky's nerves felt tight as bowstrings as she ran for the back of the house. She heard the smoke alarm bleating before she reached the gate. Pushing through it, Vicky froze at the bottom of the steps. The back door was standing wide open, and she could see marks around the jamb that told her the lock had been jimmied.

Oh, God, please don't let this be happening.

She pulled the ASP from her purse and extended the weapon with a flick of her wrist. She took the steps two at a time and burst into the kitchen. Wisps of black smoke curled from the oven. A broken plate lay on the floor.

"Mary!" she called out. "Josh!"

Vicky held the ASP ready as she searched the first floor of the house. Chairs were overturned and drawers hung open, their contents spilling out. A lamp lay in the middle of the living room floor, the shade crushed, the porcelain base smashed.

She headed for the foyer and stopped dead. A reddish-brown stain trailed across the ivory carpet and up the stairs. Her chest tightened as she sucked in a breath. Reaching for the cordless phone on the foyer table, she dialed 911 as she ran up the steps. She was vaguely aware of giving the dispatcher her name as she followed the blood trail to the room at the end of the hall—Josh's room. Trembling, she pushed the door open. She screamed and the ASP clattered to the floor.

Mary lay beside the crib like a broken rag doll. The pale blue throw rug beneath her head was soaked with blood. Vicky lurched toward her. That was when she noticed Josh's white teddy bear hanging from the rail of the crib. Smeared with blood, the bear had a note pinned to its chest. Three words were scrawled across the paper.

Death is here.

Chapter 8

Vicky watched a paramedic work furiously to stop Mary's head from bleeding. Another paramedic hooked her to a monitor and ran an IV line. They were trying to stabilize her so she could be transported to the hospital, but weren't having much success.

Vicky had done what she could for Mary, checking her pulse and trying to stop the bleeding. She'd been terrified Mary would die before help arrived. Somehow she hung on—was still hanging on, in spite of her grievous wound and loss of blood. And she'd lost so much. The air was thick with its metallic scent. Vicky's clothes and hands were covered with it. How could a person lose that much blood and live?

Death and danger are all around you.

You were wrong, Madam Zoya. The danger was for everyone else, not me.

Now Mary was fighting for her life and Josh was gone. Dark Man had taken his game to a whole new level. Why didn't she see this coming? Sweet Jesus, where was her son?

Leaning against the doorjamb, Vicky squeezed her eyes shut. Hot tears leaked through her lashes and poured down her cheeks. Every horror story she'd ever heard about child abductions was tearing at the thin fabric of composure she was struggling to hang on to.

Vicky had numbly answered all of the questions the first two responding cops fired at her. When was the last time she'd spoken to Mary? What had Josh been wearing that morning?

What were the exact words the caller had said to Vicky? The two cops spoke gently to her, reassuring her they would find Josh, that more help was on the way. Vicky barely heard them over the terrified thoughts in her head.

She knew what carnage Dark Man was capable of. She was looking at it right now. If he could do this to Mary, what would he do to Josh? Vicky's legs turned to Jell-O and she felt as if she couldn't breathe. Precious minutes were slipping away. The trail was getting cold. Pressing her fist to her mouth, Vicky looked at Mary and stifled a sob. There was nothing more she could do for her friend, but she could damn well do something to find her son.

She burst through the front door and hit the steps running. The raw wind bit her face and through her green sweater, but Vicky kept going. Tearing past the cops swarming on the sidewalk, she headed to the house next to Mary's. She banged on the door, jabbed at the bell. No one home. Someone must have seen something. She tried the next house, and the next—ringing, banging, shouting—but no one answered. By the time Vicky reached the middle of the block she still hadn't found anyone home. No one to give a description of a strange car in the neighborhood. No one who could have seen Josh taken from the house. With no leads, how could she ever hope to find her little boy?

That thought brought a fresh wave of panic. It hit Vicky square in the chest and spread through her body. Hugging herself tightly she sucked in a breath of frosty air. Was Josh cold and frightened? Was he calling for her? Dropping to her knees, she buried her face in her hands.

"Oh, God, please," Vicky sobbed. "Someone tell me this is a mistake—a bad dream."

She wanted someone to put their arms around her and tell her that everything was going to be all right. She wanted someone to tell her that Josh was safe and sound. Suddenly, she was pulled to her feet and drawn into an embrace. Through a blur of tears she looked up at Jim.

"Jesus," he gasped, looking at her blood-covered clothes and hands. "I never should have left you alone. What the hell happened?"

"He's gone. Josh is gone," Vicky cried, clutching the front of his jacket. "That bastard beat the hell out of Mary and took my baby. She tried to protect Josh and now she might die. Why didn't Dark Man just come after me and be done with it? Why hurt so many other people? Now he has my baby! Oh God, what will he do to him?"

"Everything is going to be all right." The gentleness in Jim's voice belied the blinding rage he felt inside. Seeing Vicky's anguished face, knowing that Josh was with some nut job . . . God help the bastard that had done this if Jim got his hands on him.

Jim pulled his jacket off, slipped Vicky's arms into the sleeves and zipped it up. The black leather made her skin look even paler. The wind had torn her hair loose from its gold barrette. Her lips were tinged with blue. "Come here."

He pulled Vicky close and she buried her face against his shoulder. "There's no one around, Jim. No witnesses! How are we going to find Josh?"

"Someone must have seen something."

Vicky looked up at him with frightened eyes that were red and swollen from crying. "You know what kind of things happen to children who are abducted. Last year there was one little boy right here in Westport . . ."

Jim pressed his fingers gently to her lips. "Don't do this, Vicky."

"You've seen those things for yourself," she cried, her voice rising an octave. "How often are missing children recovered alive?"

"Stop it." He took her face in his hands. "Look at me. If you do an instant replay of every abuse or abduction case you ever worked on or heard about, you're going to make yourself crazy. You've got to get hold of yourself. Focus on getting Josh back. Do you hear me?"

"I thought I was keeping him safe by leaving him with Mary, but all I did was put her in danger, too." Vicky's shoulders heaved with fresh sobs. "I should have taken him and run, like Mary wanted me to."

"It's going to be all right, Vicky," Jim said. Resting his chin on the top of her head, he stroked her hair. "I promise you, we're going to bring Josh home."

The police converged on Maple Leaf Drive. Squad cars lined Mary's street. Radios crackled as cops canvassed the neighborhood. German shepherds from the K-9 Unit barked and strained at their leashes, eager to go to work.

Vicky watched from Frank Paxton's Cadillac as one of the handlers hurried from Mary's house carrying the sheet from Josh's crib. Kneeling, he let the dogs sniff the colorful fabric before they set off to join the search.

The air was thick with tension, anger and fear. Cops were supposed to remain emotionally detached from the cases they worked, but that was a tough order when it was a child abduction. This case would be especially difficult because it involved one of their own. And Vicky knew she was still one of their own whether she wore the uniform or not.

A knock on the driver's side window broke her thoughts. Gil Fletcher opened the door, leaned in and kissed Vicky's cheek. "Hey, kid, is there anything I can do for you?"

"You could spring me," Vicky said, gripping the steering

wheel with both hands. "It's killing me to sit here and do nothing. I should at least be helping with the canvass."

"I'm sure Frank will bring you up to speed just as soon as we have something."

"I don't want to just be informed, I want to be an active part of the investigation."

Gil took Vicky's hands in his. "Look, I know you're champing at the bit, but right now you just need to take it easy."

"That's all I've been doing for the last thirty minutes."

"Frank is worried about you, Vicky. You're still a target. What if you went out to help with the canvass and this nutbag grabbed you, too?"

"I feel so damn useless," Vicky said, blinking back tears.

"We're gonna get this guy," Gil said. His dark eyes smoldered with anger. "Everybody is volunteering to work double shifts, give up vacation time—anything to put more manpower on the street to bring in this son of a bitch. Everybody wants a piece of him."

"Nobody more than me," Vicky said, gritting her teeth.

"You know it's a good sign that the kidnapper took some of Josh's stuff."

Vicky blew out a breath and plowed her fingers through her hair. "I keep telling myself that."

"He wouldn't take things like clothes and toys and Josh's music box unless he intended to keep him alive."

"But for how long, Gil. How long?"

A squad car roared up the street, interrupting them. They watched as a cop jumped out clutching a black plastic bag. He ran toward Frank Paxton who was talking to Jim McCann and three uniformed cops in front of Mary's house. Frank threw down his cigarette, stubbed it out with the toe of his Rockports and opened the bag.

Vicky's heart rate kicked up a notch as she saw the pained

look on Frank's face. He turned and shouted for Rick Volpe, the head of the K-9 Unit, who immediately jogged over. Vicky scrambled out of the Cadillac.

"Vicky, hold up a minute!" Gil called. He reached for her arm, but she slipped from his grasp.

Her gaze locked on the black plastic bag, Vicky headed toward the group of men. Their conversation came to an abrupt halt when they saw her.

"You don't have to stop talking on my account," she said, looking pointedly at each one in turn. "I'd rather know what you know—good or bad, so just tell me, please, what's in that bag?"

Frank looked at her, his face ashen, his eyes sad. "Why do this to yourself, Vicky?"

"Frank, please."

He let out a long sigh and opened the bag. Vicky felt the world spin and her knees grow weak. She moaned softly, but didn't reach in to touch Josh's blood-spattered blanket.

"That's not Josh's blood," Vicky whispered, shaking her head. "It can't be."

"It's probably Mary's," Frank assured her. He stopped a technician who came out of the Renfield house and handed him the bag. In a low voice he said, "I want the report on this ASAP."

"Where was it found?" Vicky asked, her voice trembling.

"Draped over a trash can in the picnic area of Porter's Woods," Frank said.

"And I thought it was a good sign that he took Josh's things. He could just be using them to leave a trail . . ."

"Or to throw us off," Gil pointed out. "He could have planted this there knowing we'd have to search those woods now. That gives him time to put more distance between him and us."

"We're burning daylight here, people," Frank bellowed. "Volpe, you get dogs over to that forest preserve. I'm sending every available uniform over there to help."

Volpe nodded, gave Vicky's arm a squeeze and left.

"Have we been able to narrow down the time of Josh's disappearance?" Vicky asked.

"Based on the time of the delivery of the package we found on Mary's kitchen table, and the time the kidnapper called you, sometime between nine-thirty and eleven-fifteen," Jim said.

"Did you get to talk to the driver?" Vicky asked.

"Yeah. He said Mary seemed fine—not at all nervous. She was holding Josh when she answered the door."

"Did he notice anyone suspicious hanging around?"

"Nothing that caught his attention," Jim replied. "He was hurrying. He left his truck running, had Mary sign for the package and took off again."

"Dammit," Vicky said, biting her lower lip. "I was hoping . . ."

"We all were, honey," Frank said. "All right, let's see if we can get some volunteers to circulate copies of Josh's picture. I want to see that little boy's face everywhere. Gil, I want you to talk to Bill Renfield and get a detailed list of what was stolen from the house. Have it distributed to every pawn shop within a hundred-mile radius."

"That's the one thing I don't understand about this whole thing," Gil said. "Why did the perp take the time to ransack the place if his objective was to take Josh? It doesn't make sense."

"Who the hell knows," Frank spat. "But pray we get lucky and catch this bastard when he tries to unload some of that stuff."

The wind picked up and the temperature plummeted as the last of the late-afternoon sun faded. Streetlights winked on as Mary's neighbors returned home from work. Curious, some stood on their front porches, coats pulled tightly around them while others, unwilling to brave the cold, watched from their windows instead.

The police were still sifting through the fingerprints in Mary's house, trying to eliminate members of the household and people like Vicky who were regular visitors. If they came up with one print, even a partial one that didn't belong, they had a good chance of identifying the perp. Vicky knew that was too much to hope for. This guy was smart. He'd wear gloves to prevent leaving any prints behind.

What he couldn't help leaving behind, though, were the blood and tissue samples that had been collected from under Mary's fingernails. There'd been short, dark hairs and black fibers found clutched in her hands, too. She had obviously fought fiercely to protect Josh. Vicky hoped she would put up the same fight for her own life.

"The doctors have done everything possible. Now it's up to Mary and the Man upstairs," Bill Renfield said when he called Vicky on her cell phone from the hospital. Sobbing, he added, "I overheard one of them say it would take a miracle for her to pull through. I told him miracles happen."

A miracle was just what they needed right now. For Mary and for Josh. Every minute that slipped away lessened their chances of finding him. Her son had been missing six hours. It seemed like a lifetime.

She looked toward the end of the block where TV news vans were parked. Reporters pressed against the yellow police tape that was strung across the street to block it off. They shouted questions at the officers nearby and shoved microphones in the face of anyone who got close to them.

"Damn vultures, all of them," Jim said. "I wish Frank would tell them to get the hell away from here."

Vicky spun around. She hadn't even heard Jim come up behind her. He was wearing a dark blue Westport PD jacket and his trademark scowl.

"Those vultures, as you call them, can help me find my son."

Jim shook his head. "They aren't interested in helping us find Josh. This is a story to them—nothing more, and any one of them would run over their own mother to scoop it."

"You know, you make it sound like anyone who carries a press pass should be drawn and quartered, but how could I make a plea for Josh without them? How could we ask for the public's help?"

Jim cast a glance at the throng of reporters, then back at Vicky.

"I guess you're right. I'm sorry. We wouldn't get the tips we do if we didn't have the media to inform John Q." Jim reached for her hand. His voice was softer when he spoke. "Are you ready to make your statement?"

"More than ready." Vicky had gone over in her mind what she would say, and she had no doubt in her mind Dark Man would be listening.

The reporters strained at the police tape as Vicky, Frank and Jim walked toward them. Bright lights were turned on and cameras started to roll. Their questions came like a staccato burst of machine-gun fire. Frank asked for quiet, then held up a picture of Josh.

"This is Josh Langford. He's eighteen months old, approximately twenty-five pounds. He has blond hair and blue eyes. Josh was last seen wearing denim coveralls and a green-and-blue-striped shirt. He was abducted today between nine-thirty and eleven-fifteen A.M. from One-forty-seven Maple Leaf Drive.

"Mary Renfield, who was caring for Josh at the time, was viciously attacked. She's been airlifted to Manchester Hospital in Kensington where her condition is listed as grave. A reward of fifty thousand dollars is being offered for information regarding these crimes. We're asking the public to please step forward and help bring this little boy home. Josh's mother would like to make a statement now. Please hold any questions until she's through."

Bulbs flashed like giant fireflies as the attention shifted to Vicky. She swallowed hard, trying to keep her voice steady as she looked directly into a camera. "I'm asking for the person or persons responsible for my son's disappearance to please bring him back home. Your problem is with me, not him. I will do anything you ask. Meet you anywhere you want. Just bring my baby back safely."

The questions began as soon as she finished.

"There are rumors that someone has been stalking you, Mrs. Langford. If that's true, is it possible that same person is responsible for what happened here today? Chief Paxton, were there any witnesses? Was there a ransom note left? Are there any suspects? Is this connected to the murder of the police officer the other night?"

"I'm not at liberty to discuss any of the details of the case because it could jeopardize our investigation," Frank shot back. "But rest assured we'll find the person or persons responsible for these crimes."

As Frank spoke, Vicky scanned the crowd of reporters and stiffened. Warren Mott's gaze locked with hers and she saw a ghost of a smile tug at his lips. The sick bastard was enjoying this! That realization brought a frightening flood of thoughts to Vicky's mind.

Warren blamed her for his termination at the newspaper and had made veiled threats against her. He had been at the *Herald* last night when she was chased down the stairs. While Vicky was certain the short and pudgy Warren wasn't the man in the ski mask, he could have certainly hired someone to stalk her and abduct Josh.

Fury exploded inside of Vicky like a stick of dynamite as she watched Warren's smile turn into a full-fledged smirk. All eyes were on her as she slipped under the police tape and pushed her way to where Warren stood. He grinned at her. "Funny how fate works, isn't it, Langford? Seven years ago you took someone's mother away and now someone has taken your kid away. This definitely adds a nice little twist that I'll have to include in the last installment of my series."

Vicky lunged for Warren, grabbing him by the lapels of his brown tweed coat. His eyes were huge behind his thick glasses.

"You'd better watch what you're doing," he sputtered. "I've got witnesses here."

"I don't give a flying fuck who's here." Glowering at him, Vicky jerked Warren forward, knocking his glasses askew. He tried to pull free, but Vicky tightened her grip. She ground her teeth as she whispered in his ear, "So help me God, if you have anything to do with my son's disappearance, I'll kill you."

"Vicky, what in the world are you doing?" Jim shouldered his way through the crowd and pried her fingers from Warren's coat. The reporters pressed around them, hot on the scent of something new and unexpected.

"Mrs. Langford, do you think Warren Mott is responsible for your son's disappearance? Will he be questioned by the police? Do you think he's been stalking you?"

Warren shoved his glasses back on his nose and shouted, "I haven't done anything!"

"That'll be for us to decide," Jim said, giving Warren a look that made him take a step back. "I'll be in touch. And by the way, don't leave town."

Putting his arm around Vicky, Jim made his way back through the crowd. The reporters volleyed questions at them, but Jim and Vicky ignored them.

"This press conference is over," Frank Paxton bellowed. Pulling Jim aside, he whispered, "You heard Vicky's statement. She's offering herself up on a platter for this guy in exchange for Josh. Get her home, and don't let her out of your sight."

A bright yellow VW was parked in front of Vicky's house when she and Jim pulled up. Dalila scrambled out and slammed the car door shut. Her emerald green eyes were red-rimmed and swollen from crying.

"Tom McDonald made the announcement in the office right after you called him," she exclaimed, throwing her arms around Vicky. "I hope you don't mind that I'm here, but I was afraid you'd be alone. I know how stubborn you are. You'd never ask anyone to stay with you."

Vicky blinked back tears and returned the hug. "I'm glad you're here."

They climbed the stairs arm in arm, with Jim bringing up the rear. Vicky hesitated before unlocking the door. She had dreaded this moment all day. The idea of facing an empty house, of waiting and hoping for news of Josh was torturous.

Her throat thickened as she opened the door and saw one of Josh's jackets hanging on the coat tree in the front hall. She ran her fingers over the blue nylon fabric and thought of the heavier jacket the police had taken from Mary's house as evidence. Did Dark Man at least have a blanket to keep Josh warm? Had he bothered to feed him anything? Tears glided down her cheeks again. She didn't seem to have any control over them.

Vicky shrugged off Jim's leather jacket and hung it next to Josh's on the coat tree.

"Come on," Dalila said. "Let me fix you something to eat."

Vicky numbly followed her into the kitchen.

"So did anyone see who took Josh?" Dalila asked anxiously. "Do the police have a description of the man?"

"No," Vicky said, wiping her tears with the back of her hand.

"I'm sure someone must have seen something," Dalila said,

starting a pot of coffee. "They're just reluctant to get involved, but someone will step forward soon with information."

"I hope so."

"Tom said he's going to make sure Josh's picture is splashed across the front page of the morning paper and he had fliers printed up this afternoon." Dalila pulled a folded slip of paper from her purse and handed it to Vicky. "I brought one to show you. We rounded up volunteers to hang them up around town."

They had used the photo from Vicky's desk to make the flier. Her hands trembled as she looked at the grainy picture. She had seen children's pictures on milk cartons, watched talk shows where tearful parents recounted tales of their children's disappearance. Never in her life did Vicky think she would ever join those ranks. She let the paper flutter to the table.

Dalila exchanged a worried look with Jim as Vicky wandered aimlessly through the house. She touched Josh's toys, looked at his pictures. Each one made her heart ache a little more. She finally ended up in his room. Vicky reached for the blanket in his crib and held it against her face. The soft fabric smelled faintly of baby powder. Vicky dropped into the rocker and buried her face in the blanket, soaking it with tears.

"Oh, Josh, where are you?" she sobbed. "Why didn't Dark Man just come after me and leave you alone?"

But that was one question Vicky did have the answer to. Dark Man wanted to hurt her. What better way to do that than to take her child?

Mission accomplished, you sick bastard.

She felt eyes on her and looked up to see Jim standing in the doorway. He looked as helpless as she felt.

"Dalila fixed you something to eat," he said.

Vicky clutched the blanket to her chest and shook her head. "I'm not hungry."

"You should have something," Jim said, rubbing her shoulders. "You've got to keep your strength up if you're going to do Josh any good."

"I'd be a lot more help to my son if I was looking for him, instead of sitting in this house scarfing down sandwiches," Vicky snapped.

"I know you want to do something, but Frank thinks you're better off here right now. What if the kidnapper calls with a ransom demand?"

"This isn't about money," Vicky said, twisting around to look up at Jim. "This is personal. It's about revenge."

"That doesn't mean he won't ask for money. You have to be here to take that call if it comes."

Vicky stood up so quickly the rocker smacked the wall behind her. "And in the meantime, while I'm sitting around waiting, the trail is getting cold. I can be of more use out on the street right now."

Dalila poked her head around the door, her brows knitted together in a frown. "You two stop bickering and come and eat. Vicky, you look like you're about to collapse."

Vicky rubbed her forehead, blew out a long breath and glanced at Jim. "I'm sorry. I didn't mean to take anything out on you."

"No apology necessary." He took her hand. "Come on. Let's get some food in you."

Vicky reluctantly followed Jim and Dalila to the kitchen. Dalila had a plate of ham and cheese sandwiches in the middle of the table. A pan of tomato soup bubbled on the stove. Vicky sat at the table and put her head in her hands. Dalila ladled up the soup and placed a steaming bowl in front of her.

"You're going to eat that if I have to spoon-feed you," Dalila said. She filled bowls for Jim and herself and joined them at the table. "I can't believe the police don't have any leads. I'd think with all of the technology available today they would have found something."

"No one said we didn't have any leads," Jim observed irritably. "We collected a lot of evidence at the scene, and I know Frank put a rush on all of the testing. Now we just have to wait for the results."

"That's a nice way of saying the police don't have anything solid yet," Vicky said.

Leaning over, Jim pushed a stray lock of hair from her forehead and tenderly thumbed away a tear on her cheek. "We might get lucky with the blood and tissue, Vicky."

"Blood?" Dalila asked, pausing with her spoon halfway to her lips.

"Mary scratched the perp during the struggle," Vicky explained. "They were able to get blood and skin tissue samples from under her fingernails."

"So what will that tell you, exactly?"

"Hopefully, those samples will match one of our suspects," Jim explained.

"That sounds promising," Dalila said. "Are there a lot of suspects, Detective?"

"There's one I'm putting my money on," Vicky replied. "And for the life of me I can't understand why he's not in an interrogation room right this minute."

"You're talking about Richard Blackwell," Dalila said.

"It's not that simple." Jim put his sandwich down untouched. "We can't haul Blackwell in just because you think he's responsible. Frank, Gil and I discussed this. We have nothing to tie him to the case."

"Blackwell had Dark Man kidnap my son, just like he had him stalk me, and kill Officer Bettis."

"What good do you think it would do to talk to Blackwell?" Jim asked. "Do you think he's going to admit having Josh abducted?"

"Of course not, but if he thinks were turning up the heat on him, he'd make sure Josh was returned safely!" She abruptly pushed the bowl of soup away. "I'm sorry, Dalila. I can't eat."

Vicky rose from the table and began pacing the length of the kitchen. She stopped behind Jim's chair. "You could put a tail on Blackwell. I'll bet Frank would agree to that."

"Harassing Richard Blackwell is not the ticket to getting your son back. You're doing the same thing with this that you've done with the death of your husband—circle all your wagons around Blackwell. In the meantime, it's possible the real culprit is walking around scot-free."

Vicky crossed her arms and narrowed her eyes. "Do you mean to tell me you're not considering Blackwell a suspect in this? Even after everything we talked about the other night?"

"Dammit, I'm not saying that at all." He stood up and faced Vicky, his eyes dark with anger and frustration. "I'm sure we'll look at Blackwell, but there are other suspects we need to consider, like that guy you had the choke hold on earlier tonight. A few hours ago you thought he was responsible for Josh's disappearance. Now you're totally forgetting about him and focusing on Blackwell. I think if you want to get your son back, you'd better start looking at the whole picture—think of any possible suspects. Start thinking like a cop again—if you can remember how!"

Vicky's face blanched and her eyes filled with tears. Jim reached for her. "Jesus, Vicky, I'm sorry."

She took a step back and held up her hands to ward him off. "No, you're right. And if I was still on the force the first thing I'd do is make a list of all the possible suspects."

"Why don't we do that then?" Dalila suggested. Her green eyes darted back and forth between Vicky and Jim. "I'll get a paper and pencil."

She slid past Jim, went to Vicky's desk in the family room

and returned with a spiral notebook and pen.

"Okay, Vicky, think," Dalila said. "Who besides Blackwell could possibly have a motive?"

Vicky sat back down in her chair and shrugged helplessly. "Other than Warren Mott, I just don't know."

"I'm running a check on all the people you helped send to prison. We'll see who's been released recently," Jim said.

"That sounds like a good place to start," Dalila said. "How long will that take?"

"We should know something before too long." Jim took a slug of coffee and looked at Vicky. "What about your friend with the Coke-bottle glasses, what's his name, Mott? What's his gripe with you?"

"Warren Mott was fired from the *Herald* a couple of years ago. Tom McDonald moved me into Warren's position as lead investigative reporter, so he assumed it was my fault he was fired in the first place."

"Has he ever threatened you?"

"The old, 'you'll get what's coming to you,' kind of thing."

"Do you think he was the one who chased you down the stairs at the *Herald*?"

"No way," Vicky said with certainty. "Warren's shorter and fatter and besides, he didn't have so much as a bead of sweat on his pasty forehead when I saw him."

"That doesn't mean he isn't responsible," Dalila observed. "Maybe he hired someone to kidnap Josh."

"That same thought went through my mind when I saw that damn smirk on his face tonight." Vicky clenched her fists. "I wanted to punch him."

"Mott mentioned something that happened seven years ago," Jim said. "Is it possible that has anything to do with Josh's disappearance?"

Vicky twisted a crumpled piece of tissue in her hands. She

looked down at the table. "He's talking about the reason I left the department."

"Can you tell me about it?" Jim asked. He gently laid a hand on her arm.

Not a day had gone by in the last seven years that Vicky hadn't thought about what happened, but she never discussed it. It was too painful. Dalila, she knew, had heard the story through the grapevine at the newspaper. Now Vicky wished that Jim had already heard about it, too. At least she'd be spared the agony of talking about the night that took one life and changed so many others.

Vicky kept her gaze fixed on the table, not wanting to look at either Jim or Dalila. "It was a nasty night—frigid temperatures, freezing rain that covered the streets with a sheet of ice. My partner and I were chasing an armed perp who had just held up a convenience store. He cut down an alley, and I took off after him on foot, while my partner circled around with the squad car to head him off at the other end. The perp had already fired at us, so I had my gun drawn."

Vicky hesitated and sucked in a deep breath. Jim and Dalila remained silent, waiting. Reaching for a napkin from the holder on the table, Vicky wiped her eyes and blew her nose, then went on. "All of a sudden this woman and young boy came out of a yard and started across the alley. I shouted at them to get out of the way, but they just stood there. They were confused, I guess. Didn't know what to do. Then it was like the world turned upside down. I hit an icy patch and fell. My gun discharged and the woman was hit. Her name was Connie Springer. She died in her son's arms."

Vicky choked back a sob and her shoulders sagged. There, she had told Jim. Now what would he think of her? Silence hung in the room. He reached over and lifted Vicky's chin with his fingertips. She raised reluctant eyes to his and didn't see judgment there at all, only sympathy.

"It was a horrible accident," Jim said. "You didn't mean to hurt that woman."

"Do you think that made a difference to her family?" Vicky said quietly.

"Were you brought up on charges?"

"There was an investigation, of course, but the department ruled it an accidental shooting, and I was cleared."

"What's this got to do with Mott? Was he related to the woman?"

"It's my Achilles heel and Warren knows it. He reminds me of what happened at every opportunity. Next week is the anniversary, and Warren is doing a piece on it for a series he's working on."

"Okay. Warren Mott's name goes at the top of the list. Now what about this woman's family? Did they make any threats against you?"

Vicky vividly recalled the day of Connie's funeral. She had naively gone to pay her respects and offer an apology to the family. Connie's mother, Alice Graham, had dragged her grandson from his mother's casket over to Vicky and shouted, "Take a good look at this boy. Thanks to you he'll have to grow up without his mother, but we'll see the score settled. Some day you'll pay for what you've done." And deep inside, Vicky had known she would. What goes around comes around. Universal karma and all that crap. Was Josh's kidnapping payment for what happened back then?

"Connie's mother and son told me that someday I'd pay for what I'd done."

"What was the boy's name?" Dalila asked.

An image flashed in Vicky's mind of a young boy, his eyes wide with terror as he held his mother that cold night seven years ago. Those eyes had haunted Vicky every day of her life since then.

"His name was Bud," Vicky whispered. "He was barely fourteen years old."

Chapter 9

The evening dragged on. Every time Vicky looked at the clock, only five minutes had passed since the last time she looked. Frank Paxton sent a technician over to set up a recorder and tracer on the phone in case the kidnapper called. The phone rang constantly all night, but the calls were from friends and relatives offering help and prayers. Father Ryan from St. Michael's called to tell her he was going to hold a candlelight vigil for Josh the next evening.

"God willing he'll be home before then and we won't have to do it," the old priest had said. "In the meantime, you and Josh are in our prayers."

And we need all the prayers we can get, Father, Vicky thought.

Josh's disappearance made the ten o'clock news. Vicky, Jim, Dalila, and Sam Walsh, the tech, watched it on the small TV on the kitchen counter as they sat around the table. Vicky picked at a loose thread on the blue plaid tablecloth, feeling agitated and utterly helpless as she watched the broadcast.

"I wish there was something I could do," Dalila blurted when the news was over. She turned to Vicky, her green eyes glistening with tears. "I know what it's like to worry and wonder where your child is."

Vicky furrowed her brow. "I didn't know you had a child."

"It's not something I talk about very much." Dalila chewed her lower lip. "Even after all these years it's still so painful. I was barely sixteen at the time."

"It must have been hard for you to tell your parents," Vicky said.

"They were mortified—what would people say and all that."

"Same thing happened to my cousin, Maxine," Sam said, nodding in agreement. "Christ, I thought my aunt and uncle were gonna kill her."

"Did they let her keep the baby?" Dalila asked.

"She married the guy, kept the kid, and got divorced two years later. They were too young and didn't have any idea what they were getting themselves into. Her parents ended up raising the kid."

"That wasn't going to happen to my parents." Dalila laughed bitterly and played with her coffee cup. "That's why they made me give up my baby. It was a little girl. I named her Abby. She was adopted by friends of my mother's. They let me visit her at first, but then one day they just disappeared. They left a letter for my mother saying they didn't want Abby to know she was adopted."

"How horrible for you," Vicky said softly.

"I never stopped wondering about her or searching for her." Dalila dabbed her eyes and blew her nose with a paper napkin. "Every time I'd see a little girl on the street, I'd wonder if it was my Abby. I celebrated every birthday she had, bought her gifts for Christmas, wrote her letters. I saved everything for the day I would see her again. It took years, but I finally found her. It was the happiest day of my life."

"Where is she?" Jim asked.

"Gone." Tears slid down Dalila's heavily rouged cheeks and she hugged herself. "She died shortly after we were reunited."

"I'm so sorry." Vicky rose from the table and put her arms around Dalila.

"At least I was able to explain things to her and tell her I loved her. I know it's not the same as what you're going through right now," she said, looking up at Vicky. "I don't even know why I told you. I guess I just don't want you to give up hope. I never did and I finally found Abby, just like you're going to find Josh."

The phone rang, interrupting them. Vicky jumped for it and Sam started the recorder just as she lifted the receiver.

"Hey there, Girlie, you miss little Joshie?" asked a muffled voice.

Vicky felt the blood drain from her face. She swayed slightly and grabbed the counter for support. "Where's my son?"

"If you want to see him again, it's gonna cost you five hundred large."

"I'll do anything you ask, just don't hurt my baby."

"Shut up and listen. I'm only gonna say this once. You're gonna take the money to Crescent Park in Westport. There's a fountain in the middle of the park. Put the money behind the bench that's directly across from the fountain. You understand?"

Sam caught Vicky's eye and whispered, "Keep him talking. We've got people on the way."

"Yes, I understand," Vicky said to Sam and her caller. "But I need time to get that kind of money together."

"You got three days. Leave your house at exactly ten o'clock Friday night and deliver the dough to the park at eleven on the dot."

"I want proof my son is alive," Vicky said, clutching the phone. "Let me talk to Josh."

"Don't call the cops." The man went on as if he hadn't heard her. "Do as you're told, and Joshie comes home. Screw this up, Girlie, and pieces of your kid will turn up all over the city."

The line went dead and Vicky let out a cry. Her face was the color of bone, her lips, bloodless. Jim pulled the receiver from her hand and hung up.

"You'd better sit down. You look like you're going to pass

out." Jim turned to Sam. "Did we get him?"

The tech glanced at Vicky whose desperate eyes were riveted to him and shook his head. He laid his two-way radio on the table. "He called from a pay phone at Sixth and Clark, but he was gone when the cruisers got there."

"Christ," Jim said, pounding his fist on the counter. "Did you recognize his voice, Vicky?"

"Would you play the tape, Sam?" Vicky asked.

Sam hit REWIND, then PLAY and turned up the volume. The muffled voice echoed in the quiet room. "Hey there, Girlie, you miss little Joshie?"

"Oh, God," Vicky said, shuddering. "That's Arlo Pace. I'd stake my life on it. He's the only one who ever called me Girlie."

"Who is Arlo Pace?" Jim asked.

"Officially, he was Richard Blackwell's chauffeur."

"Unofficially?"

"He was one of Blackwell's enforcers." The color was slowly starting to seep back into Vicky's face. She forced herself to take a deep breath, stay in control.

"Is he the same guy who's been calling you?" Jim asked.

"I don't think so, but I can't be totally sure."

"I remember Pace," Sam said. "About six feet, built like a tank, liked to use knives?"

"That's him."

Sam's brows knitted together and he shook his head. "He was a killing machine, but the DA's office could never get a murder charge to stick."

"That's because the witnesses always disappeared," Vicky explained. "He finally got time for armed robbery. I helped send him away."

She rubbed her arms to ward off the sudden chill that swept over her body. The last time she'd seen Pace was at his sentencing ten years ago. As two guards led him away, he'd shouted,

"You haven't seen the last of me, Girlie. Not by a long shot."

"He's not due out for at least another year, though, and I'm supposed to be notified of his release."

"Josh's disappearance has been all over the news," Dalila pointed out. "Pace probably saw it on TV and decided to play a sick joke on you."

"I hope that's all it is." An edge of panic crept into Vicky's voice. "He's a violent and cruel man. If Pace is out on the street again and has Josh . . ."

Jim grabbed her by the shoulders. "We're not going to jump to conclusions."

"He's right," Sam said. "And even if Pace is out on the street again, it doesn't mean he has Josh. He could be playing a sick joke on you like Dalila said, or maybe he sees this as a chance to squeeze you for some cash. Don't go thinking the worst."

"I can't help but think the worst," Vicky cried.

"If this ransom demand is real, where in God's name are you going to get that kind of money?" Dalila asked.

Vicky plowed her fingers through her hair and shook her head. "I don't know. Danny's insurance money will cover most of it. The rest . . ."

"I'll bet the *Herald* will take care of part of it," Dalila said.

"Everybody on the department will chip in, too," Sam said, "And you know Frank will help you. Don't worry, kid, it'll be taken care of."

"I hope you're right." Vicky turned back to Jim. "Look, I know in my heart that Blackwell is involved in this. Bring him in for questioning!"

"I can't do that."

"Why not? You're going to question Connie Springer's family and Warren Mott."

"They've actually made threats against you. Has Blackwell?"

Vicky shook her head. "I've never even spoken to him."

"Then let's concentrate on the people who are the most likely suspects: Pace, if he's out of prison, Springer, Graham, and Mott. We'll look at Blackwell, but right now these other suspects look a hell of a lot more promising than he does."

"Don't you see? If Pace is out of prison, he's probably still working for Blackwell. Everything goes back to him and my investigation into the Grayson Center fire."

"Let's take this one step at a time, starting with a call to Frank. He'll be able to find out if Pace has been released, and if he has, we'll find him."

"It won't be that simple," Sam said. "He'll be so far underground we'll need a backhoe to dig him up."

"Someone will turn him in for the fifty-thousand-dollar reward Vicky's offering," Jim said. "You can bet on it."

"If I'm right and Pace is still working for Blackwell, you'll hit a dead end," Vicky said. "No one is going to go against him. They wouldn't live long enough to spend the reward."

"We'll find Pace one way or the other, and if he's working for Blackwell we'll find that out, too."

"I hope to God you're right, Jim," Vicky replied, her eyes glistening with tears. "Because my son's life depends on it."

Vicky stood at the French doors in the family room and watched the morning dawn, bleak and gray. Dalila had left hours earlier. Sam was leaning back in his chair at the kitchen table, head thrown back, snoring loudly. Jim had finally given in and lain down on the sofa in the family room. Vicky tried curling up in a chair a few times, but every time she closed her eyes she thought she heard Josh calling for her. She rubbed her forehead wearily. Exhaustion gnawed at her bones. She was moving on automatic pilot now, numb with worry, sick with fear. It hadn't taken long for Frank Paxton to call back last night. The news wasn't good. Pace had been out on the street since September. According to

Warden Howell at Romines Prison, Pace had been a model prisoner who earned an early release.

"Earned, my ass," Vicky muttered. More than likely it had been bought by Blackwell.

"Screw this up, Girlie, and the cops will be finding pieces of your kid all over this city."

Pace's threat ran through Vicky's mind for the umpteenth time. Dammit, why had she gotten involved in the Grayson Center fire? Why couldn't she just leave things alone? She'd been so hell-bent on getting Blackwell, on getting justice for Danny, that she'd put their son in danger. What kind of mother was she?

Vicky pressed her hand to her mouth to stifle a sob. She felt so damned empty inside. Her arms ached to hold her little boy.

Behind her, Jim stirred on the sofa. She turned and watched him. Even in sleep his brow was furrowed, his handsome face tight with frustration. She had been angry with him last night for refusing to question Richard Blackwell. Deep inside, though, Vicky knew Jim was right. The police couldn't haul Blackwell in without cause. And no matter how much she believed that he was responsible for Josh's disappearance, she couldn't afford to focus on him alone.

Josh's kidnapping coincided with the anniversary of Connie Springer's death. Bud Springer and Alice Graham had had seven long years to let their hatred toward Vicky fester. What if they had finally gone over the edge and were out for revenge now? And what about Warren Mott? It was obvious he had a cruel, dark side. Maybe this was Warren's twisted way of getting back at her for taking over his job at the *Herald.*

She cut a glance at the clock over her desk. It was almost six. It had been a long night and an even longer day stretched before her if she did what everyone wanted her to do, which was nothing. Well, Vicky had a news flash for them. She still had her contacts on the street and she still knew how to do the job.

"I want to be there when you question Connie Springer's family and Warren Mott," Vicky announced when Jim woke up. She plunked a fresh cup of coffee in front of him, stepped back and crossed her arms.

Sitting on the edge of the sofa, Jim cast a sleepy eye at her and rubbed his face. She had already showered and changed into a pair of jeans, white sweater and boots. Her hair was pulled back into a ponytail, her face pale and void of makeup.

Jim scowled. Vicky was ready to rock and roll and he felt like something that crawled out from under a rock. His mouth tasted like a sewer and sleeping on the sofa had left his back feeling as if he'd been kicked by a mule. He was barely awake, but Jim had to gear up for what he knew was going to be their next skirmish.

"Vicky, you know Frank wants you here."

"I know what he wants, but the bottom line is I can do more good being a part of this investigation than I can sticking around here wearing a hole in the carpet. You told me last night to start thinking like a cop. I want to do more than that. I want to act like one." Her gaze was unblinking, her tone rang with a certain finality. "I won't be cut out of this."

Jim took a sip of coffee then stood up slowly, working the kinks from his back and neck. He looked over the counter that separated the family room from the kitchen. Sam was leaning dangerously to one side of his chair, still snoring.

"You're too close to the situation," Jim said evenly. "You can't think or act objectively. You're better off here."

"Doing what?" Vicky let her hands slap against her thighs. "My son has disappeared, for Christ's sake."

"I understand how you must feel . . ."

Vicky cut him off with an angry glare. "No, you don't! It's

not your child who's missing."

Sam woke up abruptly, nearly falling off the chair. Vicky and Jim turned in his direction. Sam glanced around, startled, trying to orient himself. Then pushing away from the table, he gave them a nod and headed to the bathroom.

Jim turned back to Vicky. The helplessness in her eyes was like a knife in his heart. She was right. He didn't have a child. He didn't know how she felt. Who was he to tell her what she should or shouldn't do right now? She wanted to be in the loop, needed to participate in some way for her own sanity.

"Frank said the station is being bombarded with phone calls about Josh. How about if I take you to the station for a while to field some of them?"

"I'll do that after I go with you to question the suspects."

"Oh, yeah, I can just see you questioning Warren Mott," Jim snorted. "What would you do Vicky, choke a confession out of him?"

She frowned then said, "I guess I can see your point where Mott is concerned."

"And do you really think Connie Springer's family will be willing to talk to you?"

"I have to try," Vicky said, adding, "You might as well know if I don't go with you, I'll go on my own."

Jim didn't doubt that for a moment and it was the last thing he wanted. He told himself if Vicky was with him at least she wouldn't get hurt.

"All right, we go see Bud Springer and Alice Graham," Jim said. "But you have to promise you won't interfere."

Vicky checked the phone book for Bud Springer's address before they left the house. There was no listing for him, but Vicky found one for his grandmother, Alice Graham. She was still at the same address that she'd been at when Connie died.

Alice Graham lived in a neighborhood of modest, but well-kept older homes on the north side of Westport. Towering oaks and maples lined the quiet street. Many of the houses were sporting bundles of cornstalks and bales of hay in anticipation of Halloween. Vicky's heart pounded as Jim stopped in front of a small, white Cape Cod–style house with black shutters. The tiny front yard was covered in a thick blanket of orange and gold leaves. A rake and a box of black plastic lawn bags lay at the bottom step of the porch.

The last time Vicky had come here was about a month after Connie's funeral. It had been a short visit. Alice didn't say a word when she opened the door to find Vicky standing there. She didn't have to. Alice's icy glare cut her to ribbons right before she slammed the door in Vicky's face. And Vicky hadn't blamed her. Why had she gone there then? What could she have possibly said to the poor woman?

Her apologies wouldn't have made Connie Springer any less dead. Because of Vicky, Alice Graham had lost her only child and Bud had lost his mother. How old would he be now, twenty-one, twenty-two years old? Maybe he was married with a child of his own. Maybe he wasn't even living in Westport any longer.

And maybe he has your son.

That thought propelled Vicky out of the car and up the steps.

Jim pressed the bell.

"It doesn't look as if anyone is home," Vicky said, noting the tightly closed drapes.

"We'll give Alice a little more time," Jim had his hand poised to ring again when the inner door suddenly swung open. Alice Graham looked just as Vicky remembered. Short gray hair the texture of steel wool framed a face creased with deep lines. Her mouth was tight and unsmiling. She eyed them suspiciously.

Jim reached for his badge and held it up to the glass in the storm door. "Mrs. Graham, I'm Detective McCann. I'd like to talk to you and your grandson, please."

Alice Graham's sparse brows arched in surprise. "I don't know what in the world you'd want to talk to Bud or me about."

"We can do this down at the station if you'd prefer," Jim replied.

Alice scowled at them as she thrust the storm door open and stepped onto the porch. Clutching her black sweater around her thin body, she gave Vicky a withering look. "I didn't recognize you at first. Your hair is longer."

"Hello, Mrs. Graham." Vicky found it hard to meet the woman's bitter gaze. Even after all these years, the guilt she felt was overwhelming. Then she reminded herself there was a possibility this woman had helped to kidnap Josh, and it was easier to return the hard look.

"Does Bud still live here?" Jim asked, drawing the older woman's attention back to him.

"No. Why are you bothering me? What is it you want?" Her ice-blue eyes honed in on Vicky. Suddenly, her lips curled into a knowing smile. "Oh, wait a minute. I heard about your baby on the news last night. You think Bud and I had something to do with it."

"I just have a few questions for you and Bud, Mrs. Graham," Jim said. "I'd appreciate your cooperation."

"Of course, I'll give you my full cooperation," Alice replied, her voice dripping with sarcasm. "You want to know where Bud is? I'll be glad to give you his new address."

They followed her inside. The house felt hot as a sauna and the air was thick with the cloying odor of floral scented candles.

"Wait right here, I'll just be a minute," Alice said.

She started toward a hall off the tiny living room, her brown slippers slapping against her feet.

Vicky's gaze swept the room as Alice disappeared down the

hall. Every table and wall was covered with various-sized pictures of Connie Springer. Clusters of flickering votive candles were nestled among them on the tables giving the darkened room an eerie glow.

But it was the portrait hanging over the fireplace that took Vicky's breath away. It covered nearly the entire width of the mantel that was draped in white velvet. White candles flickered on either side washing Connie's image in soft light.

She could have been a model. Shoulder-length blond hair framed a heart-shaped face and high cheekbones. Her almond-shaped eyes were green and fringed with a sweep of thick black lashes. She had turned thirty-two the week before she died.

Vicky felt the first pricklings of nausea and quickly unzipped her jacket.

"You okay?" Jim asked. "You look a little pale."

Vicky nodded, hoping she wouldn't throw up all over Alice's red shag carpet.

"I take it that's Connie," Jim said nodding at the portrait. Then from the side of his mouth he added, "Must have gotten her looks and smile from her father."

Vicky ignored the sarcasm and whispered, "Have you ever seen anything like this? It's like a shrine."

"Personally, I think Alice has a screw loose. What person in their right mind does this? We'll definitely be digging deeper into Alice Graham and Bud Springer. Which reminds me. What about Connie's husband? Where does he fit in here?"

Vicky's eyes darted back to the portrait. "From what I heard, he took off when Bud was a baby and Connie never heard from him again. She moved in here and raised Bud with the help of her parents."

Their conversation came to an abrupt halt when they heard Alice coming down the hall. Stalking into the room, she went to Jim and thrust a paper in his hand. Her voice was brittle when she spoke. "This is Bud's new address."

Jim scanned the paper then handed it to Vicky. She read it and gasped.

"I had no idea, Mrs. Graham. I'm so sorry." She handed the bill from Mother of Angels Cemetery back to the older woman. "What happened?"

Alice's eyes were bright with unshed tears as she slipped the paper into the pocket of her sweater. "Buddy was killed in a car wreck six months ago while he was visiting a friend in Colorado. He was burned so badly I couldn't have an open casket for him."

"I'm sorry for your loss," Jim replied evenly, "however, I still have some questions for you."

"I suppose you're looking for an alibi," Alice snorted, folding her thin arms across her chest.

"I'd like to know what you were doing yesterday morning between nine-thirty and eleven-fifteen, yes."

"Sitting right there," Alice said, pointing a bony finger at a plastic-covered chair angled in front of the television. "Just like I do every day at that time, watching my programs."

"In other words, there's no one who can verify your whereabouts."

"I'm all alone here. My husband died last year."

"Mrs. Graham do you have any idea what might have happened to Josh Langford?"

"If the Lord has answered my prayers, the child is with Him!" Alice's bitter words pierced Vicky like a spear. "I've prayed every day that you would get back the pain you doled out a hundred times over. It looks like the good Lord finally heard me."

Alice went to the fireplace, lifted her arms and gazed at Connie's portrait. "I've waited so long for this moment, my precious baby. I just wish Bud and your father were here to rejoice with me! You can finally rest, Connie. We can both rest now."

Vicky took a step back, her chest heaving. If the woman had stuck a red-hot poker into her chest it would have hurt less. Never in her life had she seen such hatred. The air vibrated with it.

Jim took Vicky by the arm and jerked the door open. Alice followed them outside and stood on the porch.

"God is punishing you for what you did!" she shouted, clutching the silver crucifix hanging around her neck. "He's evening the score!"

"She's a lunatic. Ignore her," Jim growled as he bundled Vicky into the car. He slammed the door and turned back toward the house. Alice met his gaze, her chin lifted in defiance. He climbed in the car and angrily jammed the key in the ignition. As they pulled away, Vicky glanced through the passenger window. Alice Graham was still standing on the porch, her face rigid with hate.

Chapter 10

"Yes, ma'am, I've got it. Blue spaceship, three little men with big heads and suction cups on their fingers." Officer David Coombs looked at Vicky as he cradled the phone on his shoulder and twirled his finger by his head. "You say they made off with Josh Langford and your cat, too? Uh-huh, orange-and-white tabby, answers to the name of Mittens. Yes, ma'am, we'll be sure to look into it. Thank you for calling."

He hung up and shook his head. "There must be a strong wind shaking the squirrels out of the trees today. That's the third call I've gotten like that this morning. How about it, Maroney?"

Pat Maroney, a beefy man with a bad toupee and a sour disposition, grunted his agreement from the other end of the table and gave Vicky an uneasy look. He had openly objected when she'd shown up to help man the hotline phones with the other volunteers. He said he was afraid she was going to come apart at the seams, and he didn't want to be the one to deal with it. Maroney twisted his mouth up in distaste, grunted again and went back to perusing the lists of calls that had already come in.

Every detail of each one was written down and all would be carefully followed up. Vicky knew that in spite of the number of nutty calls they were getting, there were also some promising leads coming in. The phones had been ringing nonstop since she arrived.

Jim had wanted to take her home after their visit to Alice, but Vicky had insisted on coming to the station to help. Frank had turned the conference room into a makeshift command post for the investigation, and they needed all the help they could get covering the phones.

She'd been at it for four solid hours. Her neck was sore, her back stiff. Every bone in her body was screaming for rest, but there'd be time for that later. Right now she had work to do.

The field of suspects had narrowed slightly with the shocking news of Bud Springer's death. Alice Graham, however, had become a serious suspect. Jim had called her a lunatic and Vicky had to agree. Seeing those photos of Connie, hearing the way Alice talked to her dead daughter's portrait, sent a chill up Vicky's spine. Had the loss of her grandson finally pushed Alice over the edge of sanity, or had she taken that plunge seven years ago?

"God is punishing you for what you did! He's evening the score!"

"Is it God evening the score or is it you, Alice?" Vicky murmured.

She dug the heels of her hands into her eyes and looked up at the timeline of the crime that was tacked to the wall. Beside it hung a photo of Josh and pictures of the crime scene that Vicky could barely bring herself to look at. She forced herself to study them now, trying to see something that would reveal the identity of the person who had her son.

Up until this morning, she had been positive that Richard Blackwell was behind Josh's disappearance. Now, she wasn't so sure. She felt as if she was trudging through a maze.

Alice Graham certainly had a motive older than time itself—revenge. And even if Bud wasn't around to help her carry out the kidnapping, she could have hired someone to do it. Vicky had to admit it was hard to imagine Alice skulking around in the places she would need to go to find a goon like that, but stranger things had happened.

Warren Mott, however, could have done the same thing. He had access to the scum who would hire out for this kind of job. Warren had also recently collected big bucks on a lawsuit he'd filed years earlier. He was always bragging about the investments he made with his settlement, so he certainly had the financial resources to pay someone to kidnap Josh.

And, of course, there was Richard Blackwell. He could have hired Arlo Pace for the job. Then again, Pace could be working on his own.

Or he might not have Josh at all.

Vicky reminded herself the ex-con might just be looking for a way to pick up some cash, as Sam suggested.

"Hey," a voice said softly behind her. Vicky turned around to find Gil Fletcher standing there. He'd worked on Josh's kidnapping through the night, and it showed. His shirt and pants were rumpled, his brown eyes bloodshot. A shadow of stubble covered his chin.

He held a plastic-wrapped sandwich from the vending machine out to her. "It's your favorite. Mystery meat on whole wheat."

"Maybe later," she said, managing a weak smile. She looked at him with hopeful eyes. "I don't suppose it would do me any good to ask if we've caught a break yet."

Gil tossed the sandwich on the table and pulled up a chair for himself. He took both of Vicky's hands in his. "We got nowhere with Warren Mott, as you could probably guess, but Frank is putting a tail on him. We're checking his phone and bank records, too. The same goes for Alice Graham. We're also looking into the life insurance policy she had on Bud. It shouldn't be too hard to find out how much it was for and what she did with it. If Alice never banked the money, I'd say that's a pretty good indication she might have used it to pay someone to take Josh."

"And Arlo Pace?"

"The results on the blood and tissue samples collected from under Mary's fingernails came back this morning. They don't match Pace's blood type, but that doesn't mean he wasn't one of the people at Mary's yesterday."

"*One* of the people?" Vicky sat back, dumbstruck.

Gil nodded. "It looks like there were two, and they both tracked blood. From the size of the prints, we're guessing both are men, and one set matched those found in your basement."

"What now?"

"It turns out we've been looking for Pace, anyway. He's supposed to check in with his parole officer on a weekly basis and he hasn't shown up for over a month."

"Pretty dumb on his part," Vicky said. "He drew attention to himself even before he made the ransom demand."

"We've got an APB out on him and his picture will be in all the papers and on the news. Somebody's bound to spot him and call it in."

"It sounds like you've got all the bases covered except for one."

"Vicky, please don't go there. You're beating a dead horse. We can't tie Blackwell to anything. The man has never even spoken to you."

"Okay, never mind," Vicky snapped, holding up her hands. "Forget I said anything."

"Look, I want Josh back, too. I love that kid like he's my own, and God knows I feel guilty as it is for what's happened."

"You feel guilty?" Vicky asked, her eyes wide. "But why, Gil?"

"I promised Danny I would watch out for you, and look what's happened," he said, his voice hoarse with emotion. "I've failed you. First with Danny, and now with Josh."

"You haven't failed anyone." Vicky's eyes filled with tears. "You've been a good friend. I don't know what I would have done without you the last two years."

"Jesus, listen to me. You've got enough on your mind without me dumping my crap on you. I'm sorry." He checked his watch. "I'd better get back to work. I'll check on you later, sweetheart. You take care."

Pace, Graham, Mott. The names whispered through Vicky's mind after Gil left. She stood at the window, thinking all the ducks were lined up except for one. Richard Blackwell. But the man lived in a cocoon, protected by hard-core people like Arlo Pace. The only way to get to him was through one of them. That would be no small feat. Most would go to prison rather than give Blackwell up, but there was always that one chink in the armor. Vicky just had to find it.

Her gaze drifted across the street to City Hall. She felt a jolt of adrenaline as she realized she knew exactly who that person was. Ray Abrons. Before Peter Murphy died, he'd told his wife, Lisa, that the city electrical inspector was one of Blackwell's flunkies. A weak link, Peter had said. Maybe if she went to see Abrons . . .

Vicky left her purse and jacket behind, so if Jim or Gil looked for her they wouldn't suspect she'd left the building. She knew they would go ballistic if they knew what she was doing.

Dodging traffic, she ran across the street. Pushing through the revolving doors of City Hall, she got in line behind the rest of the people filing through the metal detectors. Vicky shifted impatiently from one foot to the other as the people ahead of her emptied their pockets of change and keys. When she finally made it through, she ran to the directory to look for Abrons' name. Ignoring agitated looks and disgusted grumblings, she squeezed into a crowded elevator just before the doors slid closed.

Ray Abrons shared a suite of offices on the tenth floor with the building and fire inspectors. Vicky hesitated at the door, going over what to say. If she wanted Blackwell, she had to put the fear of God into Abrons. A young woman with sleek blond hair looked up from her computer as Vicky entered the reception area. The nameplate on her desk said, "Ms. Tobins." She flashed Vicky a smile, exposing perfect white teeth. "Can I help you?" she asked, her voice sugary. She wore a tight pink sweater that showed off her cleavage.

Vicky marched up to her desk. "Is Mr. Abrons in?"

"Do you have an appointment?"

"This is a surprise visit," Vicky said, taking a step toward the door with Abrons' name on it.

The young woman jumped to her feet, tugging at the short, black spandex skirt that had hiked up around her thighs. She narrowed her blue eyes. Gone was the toothpaste-ad smile. "I'm sorry, but Mr. Abrons doesn't see anyone without an appointment."

"He'll see me."

Ms. Tobins bolted awkwardly for the door on her black spiked heels in a feeble attempt to block Vicky's way. She was too late. Vicky threw open the door to the walnut-paneled office. Abrons' head snapped up from the work he was doing, his eyes wide, his mouth agape.

"Hey, what are you doing? You can't go in there!" Ms. Tobins shouted.

"Abrons, I want to talk to you," Vicky said, stalking into the room.

"Who the hell are you?" Abrons pushed back in his black leather chair and stood up. "What do you think you're doing, barging in here like this?"

"I'm sorry, Mr. Abrons, she ran right past me." Ms. Tobins gave Vicky a wide berth. "Should I call security?"

"My name is Vicky Langford. I think you're going to want to hear what I have to say."

"Langford," Abrons said thoughtfully. "You're the woman whose little boy was abducted yesterday. I saw you on the news."

"Mr. Abrons, what do you want me to do?" his secretary asked again. Her eyes darted back and forth between Vicky and Abrons.

"Leave us, Jeannie," Abrons finally said, coming around the desk. He waited until she closed the door, then he motioned for Vicky to have a seat.

She crossed her arms and glared at him instead. Abrons shrugged his shoulders and straightened his maroon-colored tie. Perching on the edge of his desk, he folded his hands in his lap. "I'm sorry about your little boy," he said. "Things like this don't generally happen in Westport. Do the police have any leads?"

"None yet. That's where you come in."

He scratched his head and squinted at her as if he hadn't quite heard her right. "Mrs. Langford, what can I possibly know about your son? I've never even met you."

"Maybe you don't know me, but your friend Richard Blackwell does."

Abrons averted his gaze and picked at a hangnail on his right thumb. "He's not a friend, Mrs. Langford. I don't know him at all."

Liar! There was just a flicker of panic in those steel-gray eyes. Let's see if I can turn up the heat and make this a three-alarm fire, Vicky thought.

"Really? You've never met Richard Blackwell?"

Abrons continued to pick at the hangnail. He licked his lips. "There's a difference between meeting someone in business and knowing them. I've met Richard Blackwell. I don't think there's a city official in Westport who hasn't met him at one time or another. He's a very powerful businessman."

"And he owns creeps like you."

Abrons glared at Vicky as he jumped to his feet. "How dare you!"

"What's wrong, Abrons? Did I hit a nerve?"

"I don't like your insinuations, young lady. You'd better be careful what you say."

"Careful isn't a word in my vocabulary right now."

Vicky closed the distance between them in two quick strides and jabbed her finger in his chest. Her voice was deadly quiet when she spoke. "Jerks like you take your quiet little payoffs from him and then innocent people die. People like Peter Murphy and those seven other men at Grayson Center. How do you sleep at night? How do you look at yourself in the mirror?"

"You're out of your mind."

Vicky picked up one of the pictures from his desk and studied it a moment. "Nice family. Are they the reason you hooked up with Blackwell? Did you want extra cash to take them on nice vacations or maybe you needed a little help with college tuitions?"

"I'm not going to listen to any more of this," Abrons said, plucking the picture from her hands and returning it to his desk. "I only let you stay this long because I was trying to be sympathetic. I understand you're distraught over your son, but this is ridiculous. I'm calling security."

He reached for the phone. Vicky swept it from his desk and it landed on the floor with a thud.

"If you know what's good for you, you'll listen to every word I have to say. Richard Blackwell is a jack-of-all-trades in the crime industry. Did you know that? He's been accused of everything from murder to drug trafficking, and now I believe he's added kidnapping to his resume."

"Wait a minute. You think he kidnapped your little boy?" Abrons blinked at her in surprise. "But why?"

"Because I've been getting closer to bringing him down. What you need to ask yourself, Abrons, is do you want to be around when it happens?"

"I, I, I told you I don't know the man. Please, Mrs. Langford. I can't help you. I wish I could."

"How would you like it if one of your children vanished?" Vicky asked. "What would you do, how far would you go to get that child back?"

Vicky grabbed him by his starched white collar and pulled him close. Beads of perspiration dotted his forehead. The scent of fear clung to him like aftershave. Vicky gritted her teeth but kept her voice calm. "Help me and I'll help you when the police finally knock at your door, because trust me, Richard Blackwell won't back you up. He'll cut you loose so fast it'll make your head spin."

"Mrs. Langford, I can't help you. I don't have anything to do with Richard Blackwell."

"Keep protecting him, Abrons. That'll make you as guilty as he is."

"I'm not protecting anybody!"

"I swear to God, if anything happens to my baby, I'll take you down with him no matter what the cost because I won't have anything else to lose."

She let him go. Abrons staggered back and grabbed the edge of his desk. His face was ashen, his chest heaving. He looked like he'd aged ten years in the last five minutes.

"Give your friend a message for me. If it's me he wants, then he can have me, but my son has to be returned safely." Vicky went to the door, paused and turned back to face Abrons again.

"Call me when you're ready to talk. I'm easy to find."

As soon as Vicky left, Abrons dropped to his knees and scrambled for the phone. Punching in a number with shaking hands, he mumbled, "What the hell have I gotten myself into?"

"Richard Blackwell's office," a young female voice answered.

"This is Ray Abrons. Let me talk to him." Abrons loosened his tie and undid the top button on his shirt. "I don't care how busy he is. This is an emergency."

A moment later, Richard Blackwell's irritated voice came across the line. "What the hell are you doing, calling on this phone?"

"I'm sorry, Richard. I have to talk to you. We've got trouble."

"What kind of trouble?"

"The other day Lisa Murphy was here snooping around and today it's that Langford woman." Abrons blinked rapidly as sweat rolled into his eyes. "I don't like this."

"What do you mean, snooping around? Was Langford asking about the Grayson Center fire?"

"She mentioned the fire, but that's not why she was here. She thinks you have something to do with her son's disappearance. Is she right?" Abrons asked, an edge of panic in his voice. "Are you involved in that, too? Because if you are, I want out, Richard. I'm in way over my head here. You promised no one would get hurt and look at everything that's happened!"

"Ray, Ray, Ray." Blackwell suddenly sounded like he was Abrons' oldest friend in the world. "You worry way too much. It's not good for you. Relax. Everything will be fine."

"How can I relax? A cop is dead and now this little boy is missing. This Langford woman is desperate to find her son, and that makes her dangerous. She threatened me, for God's sake."

"Have a stiff drink, Ray, and get a grip. This woman has got you rattled and there's no reason. She has no proof of anything unless you give it to her, and you wouldn't do that, would you." It was a statement not a question, and it was said so quietly it made the hair on the back of Abrons' neck stand on end.

Blackwell didn't give Abrons a chance to say another word. He depressed the button on the phone to break the connection. His face was tight with anger as he went to his well-stocked liquor cabinet and poured a generous glass of bourbon. He took it to the window and looked out, thinking as he drank.

Abrons was nervous and that was never a good thing. He could blow things wide open if he decided to spill his guts. Blackwell wouldn't take that chance. He finished his bourbon neatly and reached for the other phone on his desk.

When his party answered, Blackwell said, "Ray Abrons is ready to snap. I want him and Lisa Murphy taken care of, and quit screwing around and take care of Vicky Langford once and for all. She's been a thorn in my side long enough."

Vicky's heart hammered as she jerked open the door to the station house. Mission accomplished. Abrons was definitely shaken. The way he was sweating, Vicky figured it wouldn't take long for him to crack. Hurrying up the stairs, she pulled open the door to the third floor and ran straight into Jim.

She gasped and pressed her hand to her heart. "You scared me."

"I've been looking all over for you," he said, reaching out to steady her.

"I went to the ladies' room, then down to the cafeteria for a soda. I can only drink that mud in the conference room for so long."

"That's funny," Jim said, cocking his head and eyeing her suspiciously. "You look like you've been outside."

"I stood outside of the back door to get some air." A pang of guilt kept her from meeting Jim's gaze. "Why were you looking for me?"

"I just got the report on the ex-cons we've been waiting for."

Jim put his hand on her back and steered her into the conference room. Maroney looked up and grimaced like he had a bad case of gas. He stubbed out his cigarette, mumbling to himself, and turned back to his paperwork.

Jim scowled at him as he handed Vicky the one-page report. "There have been two men, other than Pace, released in the last year. Pace is the most recent."

Vicky scanned the report. "And he was released from Romines just before the Grayson Center fire."

Jim nodded. "We're tracking down the other two now. As it turns out, we've been looking for Pace anyway, because he hasn't reported to his parole officer for weeks."

"I know. Gil told me. Has anybody seen him?"

"No, but we've got people keeping an eye on all of his old haunts. We'll get him. He can't hide for long."

"Can't he?" She pressed her lips into a thin line as she looked up at Jim. "We're all hoping that Pace is still in Westport, that someone will see him and turn him in for the reward, but he could be in another state by now. Hell, he could be in another country."

Jim's gaze swept over Vicky's face. Fatigue and frustration were leaving their mark. She was pale and faint shadows bloomed beneath her eyes. Josh had now been gone twenty-four hours. Every minute that ticked by lessened their chances of finding him, and Vicky knew that. Jim wanted to give her some small shred of hope, but he didn't want it to be false hope. He'd decided not to tell her about the tip they'd gotten a little while ago, just in case it didn't pan out.

"We're ready to roll, McCann," Gil said as he poked his head into the room. Smiling, he gave Vicky a thumbs-up. "I've got a good feeling about this, sweetheart. We'll see you in a little while."

Jim swore under his breath as Vicky's eyes widened.

"What's happening?" she asked. "Where are you two going?"

"You didn't tell her?" Gil stepped into the conference room and pulled on his coat.

"I thought it would be better to wait and see what came of it," Jim replied.

"Wait for what? You don't think she'd get wind of what's going down?"

"Will someone please tell me what's going on?" Vicky's gaze darted anxiously back and forth between Gil and Jim.

"We got a call from one of Mary's neighbors, an Inez Winfield," Gil explained.

"Did she see who took Josh?" Vicky's fingers curled around the sleeve of Gil's coat.

"No, but she noticed a strange car in the neighborhood over the last couple of weeks. She figured the guy was checking out houses to rob, so she took down the plate number with the intention of reporting it to the police. She just didn't get around to it until today."

"Dammit, why didn't she tell us this yesterday?" Vicky asked.

"She was away all day," Jim said. "She didn't even find out about Josh until today. As soon as she heard, she came to the station."

"How long will it take to ID the car?"

"We've got it," Gil said. "Does the name Corky Higgins ring a bell?"

Vicky frowned and shook her head. "I've never heard of him."

"That's the name the plates are registered to," Gil explained. "Higgins has a record a mile long, and he's served hard time in two different prisons. And get this, twelve years ago he was arrested for kidnapping."

Vicky pulled on her coat and headed for the door. "So where are we going?"

Jim grabbed her arm and spun her around. "*We're* not going anywhere. You're staying here manning the phones as agreed. Gil and I are taking some uniforms and paying Higgins a visit."

"You can't expect me to sit around waiting," Vicky said. She jerked from his grasp. "That man could have my son."

"We don't have time to argue."

"You're right, we don't," Gil said. "So we might as well let her come along. She'd get the address and show up there anyway. Better she's with us. At least we can keep an eye on her."

Chapter 11

Corky Higgins' dilapidated property butted up against an exclusive subdivision called Sandalwood Estates. Sean O'Connor and his assault team had been parked just inside the gated entrance of the development for an hour staking out Higgins' place. Those who weren't actively engaged in watching the suspect were pacing like nervous tigers, checking their watches, puffing on cigarettes.

"Let's get this show on the road," O'Connor said under his breath.

He chewed on the end of a Tiparillo as he strode back and forth in front of a white Georgian-style house. He had read the report on Corky Higgins. He was a badass who'd shot it out with the cops before. O'Connor didn't want it to come down to that if Josh Langford was in Higgins' house, but that would be up to Higgins.

O'Connor ground his fist in the palm of his hand. He could only imagine what Vicky must be going through. Last year some jag bag had tried to lure O'Connor's eight-year-old daughter into his car using a puppy as enticement. Thankfully, Colleen remembered everything she'd been taught about "stranger danger," and had run home and immediately told her mother. Even now, O'Connor trembled with rage when he thought of what might have happened to his little girl that day. He and his wife could be going through what Vicky was right now.

There but for the grace of God go I, he thought.

Hearing a car, O'Connor looked up to see a blue Ford Taurus stopping at the entrance. Gil Fletcher leaned out of the driver's side window, flashed his badge at the guard, then parked behind a police van. "It's about goddamn time," O'Connor muttered. He tossed the Tiparillo down on the asphalt and strode toward the Taurus.

Vicky immediately recognized the man with the orange-red hair coming toward them. With his freckled face and gaunt-looking frame, Sean O'Connor was often mistaken as being a wimp. Nothing could have been further from the truth. Beneath the Howdy Doody–face beat the heart of a lion. Don't give no shit, don't take no shit, was the motto he lived by. O'Connor had kids of his own. He knew what was at stake here.

"Hey, kiddo, how're you holding up?" O'Connor asked, giving Vicky a hug.

"Hanging in there, but I'm ready to get my son."

O'Connor nodded at Gil, introduced himself to Jim, then said irritably, "We've been waiting on you guys. What the hell took you so long?"

"Judge Warkowski didn't want to stick his neck out on this because Higgins doesn't have any outstanding warrants, and we don't have any physical evidence putting him at the crime scene," Gil explained. "Frank finally convinced him we had probable cause for a search because of Higgins' record for kidnapping and the fact his car was spotted in Mary Renfield's neighborhood several times over the last couple of weeks."

"If I know Frank, that's wasn't the only thing he said to convince Warkowski," O'Connor said.

Gil gave a half smile. "I don't think Frank said it in so many words, but he let Warkowski know that he'd let the press have him for lunch if Higgins did have Josh and Warkowski didn't move on this."

"Do we even know if Josh is in Higgins' house?" Vicky asked anxiously. She craned her neck in the direction of the ex-con's property, but her view was obscured by privacy fences and trees.

"We don't know shit right now," O'Connor said. "Higgins has been going back and forth between the house and garage since we got here, but he's got every shade drawn in the house so there's no way of knowing if there's anyone inside."

O'Connor's radio crackled, interrupting him. A voice said, "Heads up. I jumped the fence to get a closer look. Got right up to the window of the garage. Suspect has a Magnum on a workbench to the left of the overhead door."

O'Connor looked at Jim and Gil, his mouth set in a grim line. "Sounds like he's expecting company."

"Then we wouldn't want to disappoint him," Jim said.

There was a flurry of activity as Kevlar vests were slipped on and magazines were locked and loaded in assault rifles.

"In a way, Higgins is actually doing us a favor having the gun," Gil remarked. "If he doesn't have Josh, we'll at least have a parole violation to bring him in on, which will make Warkowski happy. I can't believe that prick was more worried that he would look bad if we came up empty than he was about getting Josh back."

"Let's just hope Higgins will be alive to bring in," Jim said under his breath.

"All right, Fletcher," O'Connor said. "Half of the team will go with me and take the house. The other half will go with you . . ."

"Vicky, what the hell do you think you're doing?" Jim said, as she pulled a Kevlar vest from the open trunk of a squad car.

"I know what this could turn into," she replied. "If you think I'm going to sit out here when my son could become a hostage, you're out of your mind. I'm going in with you."

Jim clenched his teeth. "We don't even know if Josh is in there."

"And we don't know he isn't."

"I'll send someone for you the minute we secure the scene, but you're not going in," Jim said. "You'll stay here like you're told or I'll lock you in the back of one of these squad cars. It's your choice."

Vicky looked at O'Connor and Gil, hoping they'd side with her, but the look on their faces said, "No way." Glaring at Jim, she turned on her heel and stalked back to Gil's Taurus.

"Trust me on this, McCann," Gil advised. "Vicky won't wait for you to send someone for her."

"Yeah, I know. I just hope she has the goddamn sense to wait until it's safe." He checked his Glock. "All right, let's do it."

Guns drawn, they crept to the edge of Higgins' gravel drive. The house Higgins called home leaned precariously to one side. The red-painted siding was peeling, the window frames rotting. Half the black shingles on the buckled roof slapped the tar paper underneath.

Country and Western music blared from the sagging white frame garage that stood twenty feet from the house. The overhead door was closed, but panels were missing and they could see Higgins with his back to them, puttering under the hood of an old Buick. They made their way quietly past the battered and rusted cars that dotted the weed-choked yard. As O'Connor split off in the direction of the house, Jim and Gil crept toward the side entrance of the garage, using the cars for cover.

Gil spoke into his radio, "Everyone in position?"

"That's a big ten-four," came O'Connor's reply.

Jim raised his foot and with one kick knocked the door off its hinges.

"Police!" Jim shouted as he, Gil, and four other officers

rushed inside the garage, weapons drawn.

Higgins snapped his head up so quickly he banged it on the underside of the Buick's hood. His gaze darted to the Magnum on the workbench, but he didn't make a move for it. Dropping the wrench he was holding, Higgins immediately laced his hands behind his head.

"You ain't got no right to come bustin' in here like this," he shouted. He glared at Jim with eyes the color of watered down coffee. "I ain't done nothin' wrong."

"Let us decide that, Higgins," Jim said. "You know the drill. Assume the position."

Jim holstered his Glock and quickly patted Higgins down. "He's clean."

"Can I let my hands down now?" Higgins demanded.

"Put them behind your back slowly."

"Behind my back?" Higgins' eyes grew wide as Jim reached for his handcuffs. "What the fuck! You're not arresting me!"

"Hands behind your back, Higgins. I won't tell you again."

"This is fuckin' unbelievable!" he shouted as Jim snapped the cuffs on him.

"Cornelius Higgins you're under arrest. You have the right to remain silent. Anything you say can and may be used against you in a court of law."

Higgins licked his cracked lips. "What the hell am I being charged with?"

Gil walked over to the workbench and picked up the Magnum. Holding it by the barrel, he said, "Parole violation."

"Fuck, I'm not stupid. You guys didn't come here because of a parole violation," Higgins spat. "You didn't even know I had that piece till you busted in here."

O'Connor stepped into the garage and Jim and Gil turned to him expectantly. O'Connor shook his head. "His place is empty."

"Well, of course it's empty," Higgins said. "What the hell did you expect to find?"

"We'll ask the questions, Higgins." Jim grabbed his arm and steered him toward the door.

"Aw, come on, man, don't do this."

As they stepped outside, Vicky came running up the gravel drive. Her eyes anxiously searched Jim's, hoping he'd tell her what she wanted so much to hear. The look on his face was all the answer she needed.

"Josh isn't here, is he?" she said, choking back tears.

Higgins flicked his eyes over the woman standing in front of him. "Who the hell is this? And who is Josh?"

"He's the eighteen-month-old baby you kidnapped from Mary Renfield's house yesterday morning," Gil replied, giving him a nudge.

Higgins planted his feet. "You mean that kid they've been talkin' about on the news? I don't know nothin' about that."

"Sure you don't," said Gil.

"Hey, man, you're not nailin' me for this," Higgins said, shaking his head. "I didn't kidnap no damn body."

"Tell it to your lawyer," Jim replied.

"This is a damn setup. I know how this shit works. The pressure is on and you ain't got no other suspects," Higgins snorted. "You're gonna plant evidence in my place to build your case and try to railroad me."

"If you're innocent, you've got nothing to worry about," Gil said.

"I *am* innocent," Higgins cried.

"And I suppose you didn't snatch that kid twelve years ago, either," Gil said. "Or shoot it out with the cops when you tried robbing that convenience store back in 'eighty-five. It was all a big misunderstanding, right?"

"I'm no fuckin' choir boy, but that arrest for kidnapping was bogus. My old lady was just trying to make trouble for me. I was a little behind on my support payments is all. One day I took my kid from the sitter's house for an ice cream and my ex called the cops and told them I kidnapped him. The charges were dropped. Check the records. You're not pinning this one on me."

"Yes, we are, dickhead," Jim snarled. He grabbed Higgins by the greasy collar of his coveralls and pulled him close. "We can put your car at the scene."

"Which car? Shit, man, look around," Higgins laughed. Half of his teeth were missing, the other half were blackened with decay. "I got all kinds of cars. I fix 'em up and sell 'em. What car are you talking about?"

"A 1987 Chevy Caprice, dark blue, with plates registered to you."

Higgins' shoulders sagged in relief. "Hell, I got rid of that thing weeks ago and I can prove it."

"I'll bet," Gil drawled.

"I've got a bill of sale," Higgins said anxiously. "I run a legitimate business. I don't want no trouble. I haven't had none since I got out of the joint, and I want to keep it that way."

"Please, Mr. Higgins," Vicky said. "It was my son that was kidnapped. Maybe you can help us find him."

"Yeah, Higgins, you could be the hero of the day and collect the fifty-thousand-dollar reward," Gil said, his voice dripping sarcasm. "And if you cooperate with us, the judge might go easier on you for the parole violation."

"There's a reward?" Higgins trained his rheumy eyes on Vicky.

"Yes, if the information leads to an arrest. If you're entitled to it, I'll make sure you get every dime," Vicky assured him.

"Let me go in the house and see what I can dig up."

The tiny house was dingy and smelled of sweat and stale beer. Faded gold curtains sagged at the grimy windows.

"Why the hell don't you let some light and air in this place?"

Gil asked, looking around with disgust.

"I'm entitled to my privacy like everybody else," Higgins said defensively as he headed for the kitchen. "I caught some kids from that fancy subdivision pokin' around, looking in my windows. So now I keep everything closed up."

Sidestepping a dip in the floor, he advised, "Watch it, that spot is a little spongy. I wouldn't want to get sued by the city 'cause one of you fell through my floor. And can you take these damn cuffs off me? It'll make it easier to look through my records."

"I'm warning you, Higgins," Jim said, removing the cuffs. "Don't get any ideas, or I'll put a hole in you big enough to put my fist through."

Higgins glowered at Jim, then pushed aside empty beer cans and fast-food wrappers to get to a black steel box at the back of the counter. He opened the box and thumbed through the papers inside. Finally, he pulled out a white slip of paper. He held it out to Jim, a smile of triumph on his grease-streaked face. "I told you I could prove I sold it. See, it's dated September twenty-seventh of this year."

"Lance Cahill," Jim said, reading the paper.

"It doesn't ring any bells," Vicky replied, shaking her head. "But then, it's probably not his real name anyway. Can you tell us anything about the man who bought the car, Mr. Higgins?"

"Shit, how do you expect me to remember somethin' like that? A lot of people come and go from here."

"Please try," Vicky said.

"Don't forget about that reward," Gil muttered. "Give it your best shot."

Higgins scratched his chin and squinted his eyes. "From what I can remember, he was kinda strange, real quiet. He looked over everything I had in the yard, and he didn't dicker at all when he decided he wanted the old Chevy. That's really the only reason I remember him. You know, it just struck me kind of odd. Most people figure they can get the price down."

"What did he look like, Higgins?" Jim asked.

"Young, probably early to mid-twenties and I think he was about your size," he said, nodding at Gil. "He had short hair that reminded me of a military cut. I don't remember what color his eyes was though, or nothin' like that."

"Come on!" Gil bellowed. "You've got to remember something else about this guy!"

"I didn't take a fuckin' Polaroid of him!" Higgins pushed his cap back on his head. Then furrowing his brow, he snapped his fingers. "There is something else. It was warm the day he was here so he wasn't wearing a jacket, just a T-shirt. He had this funny tattoo of a two-headed wolf on his right arm."

Vicky gasped and everyone in the room turned questioning eyes in her direction.

"What is it, sweetheart?" Gil asked.

"You won't believe me," Vicky murmured. She stuffed her hands in her jacket pockets and chewed her bottom lip. "Mary and I had dinner at the Tanglewood Inn a week ago. There's a woman there named Madam Zoya who goes from table to table reading tea leaves and palms—stuff like that. She said darkness and death were all around me and that the wolves were waiting. When Mr. Higgins said this guy had a wolf tattoo I thought maybe . . ."

"For Christ's sake, Vicky." Gil rolled his eyes. "You know those people are nothing but scam artists. I don't believe you let yourself get sucked into something like that!"

"I was skeptical at first, too, but Madam Zoya knew why I left the force and other things she couldn't possibly know."

"So you want her to tell your fortune again?" Gil asked irritably. "You think that's going to help us get Josh back?"

Vicky looked at him, her eyes pleading. "I know it sounds

crazy, but the police have used psychics to solve crimes before. Why can't we talk to her? If she knew all those other things about me, maybe she could help us find Josh!"

"There's only one thing that's going to help us find Josh, and that's good old-fashioned police work."

"I don't care how ridiculous you think it sounds. It certainly can't hurt to talk to Madam Zoya again."

"Yes, it can!" Gil thundered. "You'll follow up on everything she says, waste your time, get your hopes up, and probably put yourself in danger in the bargain."

"I'm willing to try anything—do anything to get my son back."

"Why the hell am I wasting my breath? You always do what you want anyway." Gil frowned as he pulled out his handcuffs and turned to Higgins. "Turn around, asshole."

"You're still takin' me in?" Higgins cried.

"You're still in violation of your parole," Gil said. He looked at Jim and added, "I'm taking our friend here down to the station. I'll have him look through some mug shots."

"You're gonna help me out with that parole violation, right?" Higgins asked. "After all, I am cooperating."

"Yeah, yeah, Higgins. Let's go." Without saying another word, Gil grabbed Higgins' arm and steered him toward the front door.

Vicky shook with anger as she watched them disappear outside. She wanted to throttle Gil. She knew what she was saying sounded nuts, but Gil was always so open-minded about everything. If Madam Zoya could offer a slim thread of hope, that was better than nothing at this point. Why did Gil want to take that away from her?

"Well," she said to Jim, her voice brittle. "Aren't you going to say anything?"

Jim shrugged. "Let's go see your fortune-teller."

Vicky glared at him, her hands balling into tight fists at her sides. "Don't patronize me, McCann. I saw the look on your face. You think I'm half a bubble off, stressed out, not thinking straight."

Jim brushed his fingers along her jaw line and pushed a stray lock of hair from her forehead. "You don't have to be angry with me. We're both on the same side, remember? I'll admit this isn't the same street I'd go down, but if this woman could impress you, then I think we should give her a chance. So, come on." Jim took her hand and twined his fingers with hers. "Let's go get our fortunes told."

The Tanglewood Inn was bustling with the early dinner crowd when they arrived. Vicky and Jim wended their way through the waiting patrons to the hostess station where two other couples stood in line. Busboys and waitresses carrying heavy trays laden with drinks and steaming platters hurried past on their way from the kitchen to the dining room. Though she hadn't eaten in nearly twenty four hours, the scent of garlic and grilling meat did nothing to stir Vicky's appetite.

As the other couples headed into the packed bar, the hostess flashed them a smile with ruby-colored lips. Over the din of conversation and the rattle of dishes she said, "It's going to be a long wait tonight, folks. Your name?"

"Were not here for dinner," Vicky said. "We were wondering if we could speak with Madam Zoya a moment."

"I believe she's with a customer right now."

"This is a police matter," Jim said, flashing his badge.

The hostess's eyes widened slightly. "Let me see if she's free."

She paused at the entrance to the dining area and glanced around. Vicky followed her movements as she headed for a booth at the far side of the room where Madam Zoya was seated with a young man and woman. The hostess bent close to Madam Zoya. The fortune-teller looked up, her brow creased with a puzzled frown. Saying something to the couple, she rose from the table and followed the hostess to the front of the restaurant.

Tonight her salt-and-pepper hair was swept back from her face. Large gold hoops dangled from her ears. She wore a long, orange-print dress that hid her sturdy legs but did nothing to disguise her broad shoulders.

She stopped short when she saw Vicky and smiled stiffly. "I understand you wanted to see me?"

"My name is Vicky Langford, and this is Detective Jim McCann."

Even with her black flats on, Madam Zoya still looked Jim in the eye as he extended his hand.

"What can I do for you?" the fortune-teller asked in her husky southern drawl.

"I was in here about a week ago," Vicky said. "Do you remember me by any chance?"

"You were with another woman and you sat at that corner table, right?" She nodded in the direction of where Vicky and Mary had sat that night.

"It's so noisy and crowded out here," Vicky said as a waitress bumped into her. "Is there some place we could talk?"

Madam Zoya's hazel eyes darted around the crowded waiting area. She glanced at her watch. "I really don't have time right now."

"Please, I promise it won't take long."

The fortune-teller led them down a narrow hall, to an office marked "Manager." Without knocking, she pushed the door open and flicked on the overhead light switch.

The room was small and windowless, the air heavy with cigarette smoke and the scent of aftershave. Dark paneling made the room seem even smaller. Madam Zoya crossed to the black metal desk and touched the curled edges of a spider plant fighting for space among the papers scattered there. She glanced pointedly at her watch again, and Vicky took her cue.

"You read my fortune when I was here. There was so much you knew about me. It was phenomenal. You said something about there being a lot of danger around me. Do you remember?"

"Yes, I do," Madam Zoya said. Her hands shook as she plucked a dead leaf from the plant and dropped it in the wastebasket beside the desk.

"My son was abducted yesterday. I'm sure you probably heard about it on the news."

"I was afraid it was your baby," Madam Zoya said sadly, shaking her head. She pressed her large hands to her chest. "I'm so sorry, honey. You must be worried sick."

Vicky's pulse began to pound. She remembered how Madam Zoya had refused to say what else she had seen in the bottom of the china teacup. Had she known Josh was going to be abducted and failed to warn Vicky?

"Did you know it was going to happen?" Vicky asked, trying to keep a reign on her temper. "Is that what frightened you that night?"

The fortune-teller's face drained of color. "No, of course not. I would have warned you about something like that!"

"What then?" Vicky closed the distance between them. "Tell me, please. My son's life is at stake. I'm desperate. I'll pay you anything you ask."

"It's not a question of money," Madam Zoya insisted, her breath quickening. Her eyes filled. She pulled a tissue from the box on the desk and dabbed them. "Please understand. I can't help you."

"I don't have anywhere else to turn." Choking back tears, Vicky reached for Madam Zoya's arm.

The fortune-teller shrank from her touch. She tried to take a step back, but was stopped by a file cabinet. Her eyes were as big as half-dollars, and she shook uncontrollably.

"Look, if you're worried you'll be putting yourself in danger by helping us, I can make sure you have protection," Jim assured her.

Madam Zoya turned her frightened gaze to him. "There's nothing you can do to protect me anymore than you can protect her or her son."

"What is it you're so afraid of?" Vicky asked.

"I have to get back to work now." Madam Zoya pushed past Vicky and Jim.

"Wait!" Vicky grabbed a business card from her purse, quickly jotted down her home address and phone number and handed the card to her. "I'll be home all night if you should change your mind."

Madam Zoya's large hands trembled as she took the card. Casting a last frightened glance at Vicky, she hurried from the office.

Chapter 12

Vicky pulled back the curtain at the living room window and peered outside, hoping to see headlights coming around the bend in the drive. Disappointment gnawed at her heart. Madam Zoya wasn't coming. Why did she keep thinking she would? The woman had looked at her like she had an infectious disease—what was it about Vicky that frightened Madam Zoya so much?

"I've built a fire," Jim said softly, coming up behind her. "Why don't you come and sit in the family room? Try to get some rest."

"In a little while."

Jim frowned, thinking he finally understood why Gil had been against the idea of Vicky consulting Madam Zoya. She had gotten her hopes up—just as Gil had said—only to have Madam Zoya tear them to pieces with her refusal to help. The woman was terrified of something and Jim had a feeling it wasn't anything in this world, but from the other one the fortune-teller dealt with. She wouldn't come within ten miles of Vicky now, even if she were wearing ropes of garlic and had the Pope himself in tow.

"Do you think looking out that window is going to make Madam Zoya magically appear?" he asked gruffly. "It's time to give up on her."

The grandfather clock struck eleven. Sounds drifted from the kitchen as Sam, the technician, made himself a snack. Snowball sauntered into the living room and rubbed against Vicky's leg, purring softly.

Vicky let the curtain fall back into place, bent over and scooped up the cat. "I keep hoping she'll change her mind. She could help us, Jim. I know she could. Maybe if we went back to the Tanglewood Inn . . ."

"Forget it, Vicky. I could hear her knees knocking for Christ's sake. She's not going to change her mind any time soon."

Taking her gently by the arm, he led Vicky to the kitchen. Sam was sitting at the table, his hands wrapped around a ham and Swiss on rye. He tore into the sandwich, consumed half of it with one bite and washed it down with a drink of Coke. Wiping his mouth with a paper napkin, he said, "It's a shame that Higgins guy couldn't identify anybody in the mug shots."

"Another dead end," Vicky murmured, her throat tightening. What if they kept hitting dead ends? What if there were no other leads? What if she never saw Josh again? Those thoughts brought a fresh wave of silent tears. Putting Snowball down, she reached for one of the napkins on the table and wiped her eyes.

"We still have the lead about the tattoo," Jim reminded her.

"Yeah, but Gil said the database of tattoos came up with nothing."

"He also said they've already gotten calls from the public on the hotline since the announcement was made on the six o'clock news and . . ."

A knock at the door cut Jim short. Vicky started out of her chair, her pulse pounding in anticipation. "It's Madam Zoya. She came after all!"

"She wouldn't come this late," Jim said. "It's probably just one of the patrolmen. I'll get it. You stay put."

Jim peered through the peephole, then twisting the locks, pulled open the door. Madam Zoya stood bathed in the soft glow of the porch light.

"Well, I'll be damned," Jim muttered.

"That makes two of us, Detective." She cast a glance over her shoulder at the squad car parked in front of the house. "They told me I could come on up."

Hesitating a moment, Madam Zoya gingerly stepped inside. She looked around as if expecting someone or something to jump out at her.

"I knew you'd come," Vicky exclaimed from the kitchen doorway.

"Then you knew something I didn't. Maybe you're the real psychic here." She cut a guilty look at the grandfather clock. Her tone softened just a bit. "I know it's late . . ."

"I don't care," Vicky said. "I'm grateful you came."

"I don't feel good about this at all, but I won't be able to live with myself if I don't at least try to help."

"Should I make tea so you can read my leaves again?"

"I don't need to read your tea leaves, honey," Madam Zoya said nervously. "I'd like to roam around the house and spend time in your son's room, if that's all right with you."

"Can I take your coat?" Jim asked.

"No, thank you." Madam Zoya clutched her coat around her as if it was a protective shield. "I won't be staying long."

The fortune-teller went from room to room, circling each one slowly. From time to time she'd stop, close her eyes and touch an object, then move on again. She finally went to Josh's room and closed the door.

Minutes passed. Vicky paced the family room. "Do you think she's getting anything?"

"You mean vibes? Images? Hard to say," Jim said. He sat on the sofa, elbows resting on his knees. "This is a long shot, Vicky, you know that. I don't want you to pin all your hopes on this woman."

Vicky narrowed her eyes. "Why did you bother to go with me tonight if you're so skeptical? Were you just humoring me?"

"Pull the claws back in," Jim said, holding up his hands. "I just think you need to keep this in perspective. Don't expect her to rattle off the address of where Josh is."

"I know, but I can't help feeling Madam Zoya is going to give us a clue that will help us find him."

Suddenly, an anguished cry tore through the house.

"What the . . . ?" Vicky headed for Josh's room, Jim and Sam on her heels. She ran smack into Madam Zoya in the hallway. The fortune-teller's face was milk-white.

"What is it?" Vicky asked, her stomach twisting into a knot. "Oh, God, please don't tell me he's . . ."

"No, no! I believe your little boy is alive and not far from here, but he's in terrible danger."

"Can you tell us where he's at?"

"I saw woods and water, but that's all," Madam Zoya said as she made a beeline for the door.

"Can't you tell us anything about who has him?"

"I've told you all I can. I'm sorry, I know you were hoping for more." Madam Zoya opened her purse and dug around. A cry of frustration escaped her lips. "Where did I put those damn keys?"

"Maybe if you took a little more time," Vicky said, taking a step toward her.

"I've done all I can." Madam Zoya shoved her hands in her pockets and relief washed over her face as she pulled out her ring of keys. Jerking open the door, she stepped outside.

"Why are you so afraid of me?" Vicky cried.

Madam Zoya whirled around to face her. "Don't you see? It's not *you* I'm afraid of! It's what's *around* you!"

"I don't understand."

"I don't expect you to, but I'm telling you I can feel something evil around you. I felt it the first night I saw you at the restaurant, and I can feel it now. It frightens me to death to even be here."

"But where is it coming from?"

"I don't know, but it's very strong and very dangerous. You must be careful about what you do and whom you trust. The wolves—I see them all around you!"

"Is there anything else?" Vicky asked. "I have to know!"

"Sometimes we're better off not knowing what the future holds for us, honey."

"Is it about my son?" Vicky asked. "Please, tell me what you saw tonight."

"The same thing as before," Madam Zoya whispered. "I saw you, Mrs. Langford. I saw you dead."

They watched from the doorway as Madam Zoya sped off, her station wagon spewing gravel. When her taillights disappeared, Vicky closed the door.

"Well, at least I know why she wanted to get away from me at the restaurant, and why she was so reluctant to come here. If a lightning bolt strikes me, she doesn't want to be around in case it ricochets."

"You can't put any stock in what she told you," Jim said. "She's just a superstitious . . ."

Vicky wheeled around and faced him. "You're wrong, Jim. I never believed in this kind of stuff, either, but that night at the Tanglewood Inn made a believer out of me—at least where Madam Zoya is concerned. She told me specific details about my life she couldn't possibly know. I don't understand why she couldn't tell us more tonight."

"Maybe that evil force was scrambling her signals," Jim said irritably. Shit, why didn't he listen to Gil Fletcher? "I told you not to count on her."

"She gave us a lead didn't she? She said Josh is close by and near woods and water."

Jim raised his brows and snorted. "You call that a lead? What are you going to do, check out every house that fits that description?"

"If I have to."

"Come on, Vicky. Where is that practical, levelheaded woman I keep hearing about?"

"She's away at the moment," Vicky said. "But she'll get back to you just as soon as she finds her son."

"You're really going to do this, aren't you?"

"Anything is better than just sitting here waiting for the phone to ring. At least I'll feel like I'm doing something to get my son back."

"Okay," Jim said, raising his hands, palms up in mock surrender. "If you want to pound on doors, then that's what we'll do."

"*We'll* do?" Vicky tilted her head back and looked up at Jim.

"That's right, *we'll*. I went along with you on the Madam Zoya thing, didn't I? Why stop there? We can't keep fighting each other. We have to be a team if were going to find Josh. So you tell me what you want to do, and we'll do it."

"Thank you." A tear glided down her cheek. She raised her gaze to meet his and saw the same desire in those smoky blue depths that she had seen the other night. Vicky felt a shiver of anticipation as he drew her close and lowered his face. He was going to kiss her and, God help her, she was going to let him. She wanted a moment—no matter how brief—to lose herself in, to get away from the hellish existence her life had become. It didn't matter that Sam was in the next room. Right now, she and Jim were the only two people in the world.

The phone rang, breaking the spell. Reality returned like a cold bucket of water thrown in her face. Vicky broke away and darted toward the kitchen. Sam gave her the go-ahead to pick up the phone as he turned on the recorder.

"Do you miss Josh?" a whispered voice asked. Then suddenly, Josh's cries came across the line.

Vicky's legs felt weak. She clutched the receiver tighter and choked back tears. "Josh, honey, mommy is here. I love you, sweetheart."

The crying faded and the whispered voice came back on. "He misses you, Vicky. He cries for you all the time."

"Give me back my son, you bastard!"

His voice was so quiet when he spoke, that Vicky had to strain to hear him. "I am Death, Vicky. And I'm coming for you."

"You're sure this is what you want to do?" Jim asked, casting a sidelong glance at Vicky. They were sitting in his Mazda in front of City Hall. The clock on the dash read 9:00 A.M.

"I don't know any other way."

Jim dropped a few coins into the parking meter and they went inside. Vicky hoped she didn't run into Ray Abrons. If she did and he confronted her, there would be a lot of explaining to do to Jim. That wasn't likely, though. There was no doubt in her mind she had scared Abrons shitless. If he happened to see her, he'd probably run in the other direction. But maybe he was tougher than she thought. As fearful as he appeared yesterday, he still hadn't rolled over on Blackwell. That wasn't a good sign.

The clerk for the county recorder's office stepped off the elevator with them on the second floor. Juggling her purse and a large cappuccino, she fumbled for her office keys.

"I'm running a little late this morning," she said, giving them an apologetic smile. "Traffic was backed up for a mile on the turnpike. Give me a minute to get settled and I'll be right with you."

Jim and Vicky leaned against the marble counter as she disappeared into a back room. She returned a moment later, tugging her plaid suit into place over her ample backside. Her nametag identified her as Evelyn Keys, County Recorder. Patting her mousy brown curls, she smiled at them.

"What can I do for you folks?"

"We'd like to have a look at the records for property owners at Lake Katherine, Big Bear Lake, and Pine Lake, please," Vicky said.

"Well, ma'am, I can let you see addresses and lot descriptions, that type of thing," Ms. Keys explained. "You might want to take pictures of homes that are comparable to yours, too. It can be a big help when you're trying to get your taxes lowered."

"This isn't about taxes," Vicky said. "Please, I need to see those records."

The corners of Ms. Keys' lips pulled down and she blew out an exasperated sigh. "I'm sorry, but the names of homeowners are confidential."

"My name is Vicky Langford. My little boy was kidnapped two days ago and there's a chance that he might be at one of those places."

"Oh my," the woman gasped. "I saw that on the news. How terrible."

"We just want to look at the records to see if a name rings a bell. It won't take long, I promise." Vicky touched the woman's arm. "Please, this is the only hope I have right now."

Ms. Keys furrowed her brow. Clasping her hands together, she said, her voice almost a wail, "It's not that I don't want to help, but I could lose my job."

"There's no one else here right now," Vicky said. "My little boy's life could depend on this."

"Well, all right." Ms. Keys unlatched the gate beside the counter to let them in. "The other girl won't be here for quite a while. Root canal, poor thing."

She led them to her desk and motioned for Vicky to have a seat. Glancing nervously at the door, Ms. Keys went to a cream-colored file cabinet and fished three disks from the top drawer.

Popping a disk in her computer, she handed the other two disks to Vicky. "This is everything you need, but hurry, please."

Vicky sat down and quickly began scrolling through the list. Jim leaned over her shoulder, reading the names flashing by on the screen. They went through the entire list for Lake Katherine, but not one name was familiar to Vicky.

She sat back in the chair and chewed her lower lip. "What if the person didn't use his real name when he purchased this property? I could look at a hundred lists and not recognize any of the names."

"You want to give up?"

"No way." She popped the disk in for Pine Lake and began scrolling down again. Halfway through she swore out loud.

"What have you got?" Jim asked, looking over her shoulder.

"Check this out." Vicky pointed to a name on the screen. "I've got the bastard now."

Pine Lake was a maze of winding gravel roads that led to houses deep in the woods. Jim and Vicky drove around for nearly thirty minutes before finding Warren Mott's address on a mailbox at the end of a driveway. They could barely glimpse the log house that was nestled in a cluster of pine trees about fifty yards from the road. Jim drove around the bend and killed the engine. Vicky had her hand on the door when he stopped her.

"We can't go charging in there like the seventh cavalry. I know you're anxious, but you have to remember procedure."

"The hell with procedure."

"If Mott is the kidnapper, we don't know how many people he might be working with. Arlo Pace could be involved in this somehow, and there has been at least one other person calling you. They could all be in that cabin right now. We don't want to put Josh in any more danger than he is already."

"What are you saying?"

"That we quietly check this out, and if need be, wait for backup."

Vicky narrowed her eyes and looked at Jim. He was asking—no expecting—her to think like a cop again, but she wasn't a cop right now. She was Josh's mother, and she was terrified.

"We have to do this right, Vicky, for Josh's sake," Jim said.

She shifted her gaze and stared through the windshield. Her emotions warred with common sense. "Okay. I promise I won't break down any doors."

"Remember that," Jim mumbled, checking his Glock. From the corner of his eye, he saw her pull the ASP from her purse and slip it into her deep coat pocket. "How long have you been carrying that?"

"Since the night my friend paid me a visit at the *Herald.*" She stowed her purse under the front seat. They climbed out of the Mazda and headed for the woods. "That bastard won't catch me unprepared again. The next time we hook up, he's in for a surprise."

Jim grabbed her arm and spun her around. "I'd like to think there won't be a next time. And there shouldn't be, as long as you don't go off on your own. I want you to promise me that."

"I won't promise anything," she replied flatly. Without saying another word, Vicky left Jim standing ankle deep in leaves as she plunged into the woods.

It was cold in the shelter of the trees, and the sun did little more than dapple the ground in places. The air was thick with the scent of moist earth, and crows called out from the trees. Branches slapped their faces and tore at their clothes and hair as they made their way through the heavy undergrowth. By the time they reached Warren's property, their faces were scratched and leaves were stuck in their hair.

Crouching at the edge of the woods, they looked for some

sign of movement in the house. "It doesn't look like anyone's here," Jim said. "Let's take a closer look."

They made a dash for the one-story structure, pressing themselves against the rough log wall. Vicky's heart was pounding so hard it felt as if it would jump out of her chest. Jim edged to a window, cupped his hands around his face and peeked in. "Looks like the place is empty."

"Jim," Vicky gasped, pointing over his shoulder. A playpen was folded up and leaning against the wall in the living room area. "That's enough for me!" She bolted for the door. Jim stopped her just as she raised her foot to kick it in.

He shot her a look of exasperation. "In the future, I'll remember how well you keep your promises."

Digging in the pocket of his jacket, he pulled out a small black billfold. Vicky watched anxiously as he removed two thin tools from it and picked the lock. A moment later the door swung open.

They brushed off their jackets and wiped their feet on the straw mat in front of the door, not out of courtesy to Warren, but to keep from dragging in anything with them that might alert him to the fact someone had been there. Jim pulled a red-gold leaf from Vicky's hair and ran his hands through his own. They gave each other a last quick glance, pulled on latex gloves, and stepped inside.

Vicky couldn't imagine Warren Mott living in this cozy cabin. It was too clean, too homey. Lace curtains hung at the windows, and brightly colored braided rugs lay on the polished wooden floor. No, this place wasn't Warren at all.

Jim crossed to the double balcony doors on the other side of the room and gave a low whistle. A huge deck overlooked the sparkling waters of the lake and Warren's boat launch. "Now we know what Mott's been doing with most of the settlement he got from that lawsuit. It must cost a small fortune to keep this place and his condo in Westport."

"Maybe not so much that there wasn't enough left over to pay someone to kidnap my son," Vicky said, sifting through a stack of bills and letters on an end table. Laying Warren's mail back down, she went into the kitchen. An open box of animal crackers sat on the butcher block counter, and she found two baby bottles filled with milk in the fridge.

"I'd like to think if he has Josh, he's feeding him better than this," she muttered angrily.

She followed Jim into the bedroom. He looked under the four-poster bed and pulled out a small mesh bag filled with toys. Shoving it back, he smoothed the ivory-colored coverlet and looked up at Vicky. She was standing at the antique dresser, holding a child's brush in her hands. She turned around and held it out to him.

"Look," she said, her voice choked with tears. Wisps of blonde hair clung to the bristles. She laid it back on the dresser and went into the living room. "Josh has been here, but where is he now?"

"We'll get that answer when we arrest Mott." Jim took one last look around to make sure everything was left as they found it. "Let's get the hell back to the car and call Frank."

They were on the porch when they heard a car coming down the driveway.

"Shit!" Jim said. Grabbing Vicky's arm, he pulled her around the side of the cabin. He held her close in case she got any ideas about putting another choke hold on Mott. "Pray he doesn't drive around here."

Gravel crunched and dust flew as a Ford Expedition screeched to a halt in front of the cabin. Climbing out of the vehicle, Warren slammed the door. His cell phone was pressed to his ear.

"So cut to the chase already," he snapped. "I don't have all day."

There was silence as he listened. "You're bringing him here tonight at eight o'clock? Yeah, yeah, that's fine." Warren kicked at the bottom porch step and grumbled, "I'm sorry I ever let you talk me into getting mixed up in this. I'll be glad when it's finally over. I can't stand that kid."

Vicky squirmed in Jim's arms. He held her tighter and whispered, "We'll have nothing but trouble if you go out there now. Don't lose your head."

"That bastard has Josh," she hissed.

"We have to do this the right way. Don't blow it."

Warren shoved his cell phone in his pocket and climbed the steps. The front door slammed shut. Jim peeked through the window and watched Warren cross the living room and go down the hall.

"Let's move," he said, grabbing Vicky's hand. They bolted toward the woods and didn't stop running until they were back at Jim's car.

Within hours, the woods surrounding Warren Mott's property were teeming with police. As time inched slowly toward eight o'clock, a fine mist started falling. The wind howled mournfully around them as Vicky and Jim crouched in the woods watching Warren's cabin. Frank Paxton was just a few feet away, search warrants tucked safely in the pocket of his down jacket.

The chief's face had turned fire engine red when he found out Jim and Vicky had illegally entered and searched the cabin. He had blustered about the ramifications if that information was leaked. He hadn't asked what led them to Warren's property in the first place. Vicky suspected he didn't want to know. As it stood now, the story released to the press after everything was over would simply be that an anonymous tip was phoned in about Warren Mott.

Vicky shifted slightly and wiggled her toes, trying to get the feeling back in them. She pulled her green knit cap down tighter over her ears and folded her arms across her chest in an effort to keep warm. "Isn't it time yet?" she asked.

Jim turned toward her. He could barely make out her image in the inky blackness. Reaching out, he took her hand. "It'll be over soon, Vicky."

"I'm almost afraid to let myself believe it," she said, shivering.

Jim poured coffee from a thermos and handed it to her. "We both heard Mott on the phone."

"What if he found out the police are staking out this place? What if he changed his plans?"

"There's no way he could know unless he's a mind reader. He's smart, though, I'll give him that. We've had a tail on him and haven't caught him doing a damn thing to raise suspicion. There's nothing in his phone records to implicate him, either."

Suddenly, Frank Paxton's radio crackled. He turned to them. "There's a car turning in as scheduled. Nice of them to be prompt."

Vicky's pulse raced as she heard tires crunching on the gravel road. Just a few more minutes and she would have Josh back. She watched as a battered Olds Cutlass rolled to a stop in front of the cabin. Vicky was barely able to restrain herself as a woman climbed from the Olds and pulled a toddler from the backseat.

"Hold steady," the chief ordered, speaking low into his radio. "Wait till Mott opens the door."

With a diaper bag slung over one shoulder and the child balanced on her hip, the woman knocked at the door. She shifted the child to her other hip as minutes dragged by. Banging impatiently at the door, she shouted, "Come on, Warren, it's cold out here!"

The door finally swung open, and Warren Mott appeared wearing a Notre Dame sweatshirt and faded jeans. His glasses were pushed on top of his head. "Christ, can't you wait a second?"

He offered no help as the woman started inside.

She had one foot over the threshold when Frank Paxton stood up and shouted, "Police! Freeze, Mott!"

Suddenly, the area was lit up like a night game at a baseball stadium. Warren shielded his eyes with his hand and blinked against the harsh lights.

"What the hell is going on?" he shouted, as the police converged on the house.

"Hands up, Mott!" Frank Paxton bellowed.

The woman's eyes widened in terror as a police officer slammed Warren against the side of the cabin. She shrank back as two other officers came at her, one reaching for the child, the other holding a pair of handcuffs. The woman clutched the child tighter and the toddler wailed.

"What are you doing?" she screamed as the officer pulled the child from her arms.

Vicky stumbled from the woods calling Josh's name, but even before she reached the crying child, she knew something was wrong.

"Oh, no," she cried. Disappointment twisted her heart as the child squirmed and turned, reaching for his mother. It had all been a mistake. Vicky didn't know who this little boy was, but she knew who he *wasn't.*

"Oh, this is a sweet one, Langford," Warren sneered, when he saw Vicky. His eyes bored into hers. "You actually thought I took your kid? This is my sister and her kid. I agreed to baby-sit for her while she works a night shift. Oh, yeah, this is real sweet. I'm gonna hang you out to dry!"

"There's nothing you could possibly do to me that would be

worse than what's already been done, Warren," Vicky said numbly. "So take your best shot. I don't care anymore."

She turned away from him and headed down the road. Fear was like a noose around her neck, getting tighter and tighter. Josh had been gone two days and they'd had no solid leads. What if they never found him? Tears blurred her vision. A cry escaped her lips, then another and another.

"Vicky, wait!"

She stopped short and spun around. Jim was standing in the middle of the road, his arms hanging helplessly at his sides. "I'm sorry."

He went to her and drew her into his arms. Vicky didn't pull away. She leaned into him, welcoming his strong, comforting arms around her.

"Where do we look now? We still don't have a clue where Josh is."

"We're not beaten yet. We've just narrowed our list of suspects again."

She buried her face against his shoulder and sobbed. When her tears were spent, she tilted her head back and looked up at him. "I want to talk to Madam Zoya again. I want to see if she's been able to come up with anything else."

Jim groaned. "You're just grasping at straws now."

"I know that, and I don't care," Vicky said. "Straws are all I have left."

As soon as they reached Vicky's house, she called the Tanglewood Inn. The disappointment was evident in her face when she hung up the phone.

"Madam Zoya couldn't tell you anything more, right?" Jim asked.

"She's gone. The manager said Madam Zoya called in this evening and told him she was leaving town and didn't know when she'd be back."

"She didn't say where she was going?"

Vicky shook her head.

"Why would she leave town out of the blue?"

"You saw her last night. She was terrified. She probably took off for some place safe."

"Maybe," Jim said. "Or maybe she's just a good actress and Madam Zoya is mixed up in this whole thing somehow."

"Hey," Sam called from the family room. "Come and look at this."

Frank Paxton was on the news giving a statement about the fiasco at Warren's cabin. The camera swung to Warren Mott, whose eyes were blazing with indignation. He held his nephew in one arm and his other was wrapped protectively around his sister who was still sobbing.

A reporter thrust her microphone in Warren's face. "Mr. Mott, are you going to take any action against the Westport Police Department or Vicky Langford for what happened here tonight?"

"I'll let my lawyer do my talking for me, but I will say this. Someone is going to answer for what we've been put through. The police can't be allowed to continue to harass innocent citizens in the name of the law."

"Mr. Mott," the reporter pressed. "Do you think what happened tonight is in retaliation for the series on the police department you're doing for the *Banner*?"

"Anything is possible, Fran," Warren responded, lifting his chin. "And speaking of my series, the last and most powerful installment will be in the paper this Sunday . . ."

Vicky reached for the remote and hit the POWER button. Warren's image faded as the screen went black. Vicky wished she could make the real Warren Mott disappear just as easily.

"You know Mott's going to try his best to make your life

miserable," Jim warned.

"He's the least of my problems right now," Vicky said flatly, stacking kindling in the fireplace.

She reached for the matches on the mantel as the phone rang. Wheeling around, she looked at Sam who hurried to the counter where the recorder was. He gave her the go-ahead and Vicky lifted the extension on her desk.

"I just watched the news," a muffled voice said. "You think you're smart, don't ya? I'm warning you, no stunts like that when you make the drop tomorrow night. If I smell a cop within ten miles of that park, I promise you, Girlie, the next time you see your kid, it'll be in the county morgue."

CHAPTER 13

Dalila swept into Vicky's house bright and early the next morning, a bag of fresh bagels in hand. She shrugged off her tattered mink and eyed Vicky with concern. "I know you probably haven't eaten a thing since Josh disappeared. I thought I could at least get one of these into you."

"Oh, Dalila, it's not that I don't appreciate it," Vicky said. "I'm just not hungry."

"Hey, I'll take one of those," Sam said as he and Jim came into the kitchen. "I'm starving."

Dalila stacked the bagels on a plate and put it in the middle of the table. "I saw what happened last night on the news. You must have been devastated when you realized that baby wasn't Josh."

"That's an understatement," Vicky murmured.

"You know Warren will probably slap a lawsuit on you."

Jim frowned and folded his arms. "I think Vicky has enough on her mind right now without adding something else, don't you?"

"Of course," Dalila said, her thin brows arching in surprise. "I didn't mean anything by what I said. What led you to Warren anyway?"

Dropping wearily into a chair, Vicky explained about Madam Zoya's visit and what she and Jim discovered during their trip to city hall. She omitted the part about illegally searching Warren's cabin. Not that she didn't trust Dalila, but the fewer people who knew about it the better.

"This fortune-teller couldn't tell you anything at all about the person who took Josh?" Dalila asked. She slathered cream cheese on a toasted onion bagel and took a generous bite.

"Nothing."

Dalila swallowed her food, dabbed crumbs from her mouth with a paper napkin and frowned. "I tried going to a psychic when I was looking for my Abby. They took my money and gave me a lot of false hopes just like that Madam Zoya person did to you. Don't see her again, Vicky. It only makes it worse."

"I couldn't even if I wanted to." Vicky gave a bitter laugh and pushed away from the table. "She's gone, headed for parts unknown."

"It's probably a blessing in disguise," Dalila said.

Going to the window, Vicky looked out at Josh's brightly colored jungle gym. She could almost see him out there, crawling through the tunnel, scrambling up the little slide. Her parents were supposed to visit next summer. Her father wanted to build Josh a playhouse. What was she going to tell them? They were still away on vacation in Europe and had no idea what was going on. Vicky wanted to keep it that way for the time being because of her father's heart condition. If Josh wasn't found soon, she'd have to tell them somehow.

"By the way," Dalila said, "have you heard any news about Mary?"

"No change. She's still in ICU." Vicky reached for the dishrag on the sink and started wiping the counters, the microwave, and the front of the fridge. Anything, just to have something to do besides look at the clock.

"Poor woman," Dalila remarked, brushing crumbs from her zebra-print blouse.

"She's going to pull through," Vicky said with a certainty she didn't really feel. Mary was still in a deep coma and her doctors were offering little hope.

Dalila turned to Jim. "I noticed the patrol car was gone from in front of the house."

"They're only coming at night because there's always someone here, whether it's Sam, his relief, or me." Jim's beeper went off. He looked at the number displayed and said, "It's Frank."

He reached for his cell phone to call the station. Vicky's gaze was trained on Jim's face, watching for a reaction to news, good or bad, but he remained impassive as he spoke.

"Where was he found?" he said, reaching for the pen and notepad lying on the counter.

"Oh, God," Vicky gasped. She pressed her hand to her chest, breathing hard.

Jim shook his head and mouthed, "Not Josh," then jotted down an address and hung up. Vicky leaned over the counter and covered her face with trembling hands. "You okay?" Jim asked.

She pulled herself upright and gripped the edge of the counter. "I thought . . ."

"I know, but this has nothing to do with Josh, I swear." Jim put his arm around her and pulled her close. "The city electrical inspector was found murdered in his home this morning."

"Ray Abrons?" Vicky looked up at Jim, her eyes wide. "What else did Frank say?"

Jim shrugged a shoulder. "Nothing much, except that it looks like a robbery. The cleaning lady found him in the den. I guess the house was pretty well trashed."

"What about the rest of his family?"

"Kids are away at college and his wife is out of town on business." Jim shot her a questioning look. "Did you know him?"

"I met him for the first time just the other day."

"So why all the interest?"

"Abrons wasn't killed in a robbery, Jim."

"What are you talking about?" he asked uneasily.

Vicky leveled her gaze at him. "Blackwell had him killed."

Sam furrowed his brow and licked cream cheese from his fingers while Dalila braced herself for Jim's reaction.

He slammed his fist on the table making the mugs bounce and coffee spill. "Dammit, Vicky, every crime in this city is not connected to Richard Blackwell!"

"Trust me, Jim, this one is. Blackwell was afraid Abrons was going to crack, so he eliminated him."

"What's going on?" Jim asked, putting his hands on his hips. "What do you mean Abrons was going to crack?"

"I went to see him."

Jim groaned and rubbed the back of his neck. Suddenly, his eyes snapped wide open as realization dawned. "That's where you disappeared to while you were at the station."

"No one else is working the Blackwell angle, so I am. Abrons is—was—one of Blackwell's patsies."

"And you know this because?"

"Lisa Murphy told me, and she got it from her husband before he was killed. I thought if I could get to Abrons, he'd roll over on Blackwell. Check Abrons' phone records, Jim. I'll bet there was a call from his office to Blackwell the day I saw him."

"Even if there was, what would it prove? Nothing. Look, Vicky, Frank has a tail on Blackwell and he's trying to get a court order from Judge Warkowski to have Blackwell's lines tapped. We're doing everything we can right now where he's concerned, so just stay out of it."

"That's not enough," Vicky insisted angrily.

"Right now our best bet is to find Arlo Pace and that's what I'm going to concentrate on doing. I have to meet Gil at Abrons' house now. We'll finish this discussion later." Jim grabbed his jacket and looked pointedly at Sam. "Don't let her out of your sight."

The door slammed behind him, echoing through the house. Vicky shot Sam a glare and he spread his hands defensively. "What did I do?"

"Guilt by association," Dalila explained.

Vicky stalked into the family room, pulled open the French doors and went out onto the deck. Dalila followed her, hunching her shoulders and folding her arms tightly against the cold wind.

"I'm going to search Blackwell's office," Vicky announced. "He's involved in this somehow. I just know it. Someone has to check him out, and if McCann won't do it, then I will."

Dalila shifted from one foot to the other, trying to stay warm. "Detective McCann said the police have Blackwell under surveillance."

"That's not enough."

"What do you think you're going to find?"

"Maybe nothing," Vicky admitted. "But I have to do it for my own peace of mind."

"Do you want me to go with you?" Dalila asked warily.

"No. I just want you to keep Sam busy long enough for me to sneak out of here."

"How are you going to get into Blackwell's office without being seen?"

"Don't worry," Vicky said. "I already have a plan."

"But you don't know what time Blackwell leaves, and you have to deliver the ransom tonight."

"That's not until later," Vicky replied. "I'll have plenty of time."

"I don't think this is a good idea, Vicky. Detective McCann doesn't want you to leave the house."

"Yeah, well, it's not his son who's missing. It's mine."

"Vicky, this is crazy. What if Blackwell finds you?"

"That's a chance I'm willing to take."

Later that afternoon, as Dalila plied Sam with a heaping plate of steak and eggs, Vicky made the necessary phone calls, then sneaked out of the house. Her first stop was Webster's, the store where Park Plaza purchased all of its uniforms. From there, she went to the mall where she bought a short blonde wig. Her next stop was a gas station where she used the restroom to change into her disguise. Vicky looked in the mirror and smiled. Her own parents could pass her on the street and not recognize her.

At five-thirty sharp, she pulled into the employee parking lot at Park Plaza. The door to the service entrance was wide open and a delivery truck was backed up to it. The driver came out of the building and started to close the door when Vicky called to him.

He gave her a commiserating smile as she jogged toward him. "I'm running late, too," he said, holding the door for her. "It's been that kind of day."

Vicky thanked him and hurried inside. She had no idea where she was going and hoped she didn't run into anybody. She didn't need people asking questions. Rounding the corner, she saw a door marked "Maintenance."

The odor of ammonia assaulted her as she stepped inside the room and looked around. Large bottles of various cleaners lined gray metal shelves. Brooms and mops were stuck in a wide-mouth barrel. Two carts with cleaning supplies were parked against the wall.

She took off her coat and stuffed it behind a stack of boxes in the corner. Then, grabbing one of the cleaning carts, Vicky headed out the door. She didn't know what, if anything, she was going to find in Richard Blackwell's office. She only knew she wouldn't rest until she searched it.

She found the service elevator with little trouble and took it to the twelfth floor. According to the receptionist she had spoken to earlier, Richard Blackwell's office suite occupied the entire north corner of the floor. Parking the cleaning cart against the wall, Vicky took a spray bottle and rag so she'd look legitimate in case she ran into someone. She prayed Blackwell was gone for the day. From the quiet and darkened offices she passed, it looked as though everyone else was.

A burst of laughter and voices—one of them all too familiar—stopped her before she reached the end of the corridor. *It can't be,* Vicky thought. Creeping forward, she peeked around the corner. Her heart skipped a beat and her mouth went dry.

Vicky sagged against the wall. There had to be a reasonable explanation for what she was seeing, but for the life of her, she couldn't think what it could possibly be. Jim McCann was supposedly from Seattle and had never heard of Richard Blackwell. So why was he standing in the hall with Blackwell acting as if they were long-lost friends? There was only one explanation for that. Jim had been lying all along. And why would he do that unless . . .

"Oh, God," Vicky breathed. Backing away, she turned and ran down the hall.

Downstairs, she grabbed her coat from the maintenance room and bolted out of the building. A wave of nausea hit her like a battering ram as she ran across the parking lot. *Damn him! Damn him! Damn him!* Vicky climbed in her Blazer and slumped against the seat.

Anger burned like hot coals in the pit of her stomach. She had trusted Jim, believed in him. Was she really that gullible? *We have to be a team, Vicky.* Isn't that what he'd told her? He'd drawn her in, made her believe he was trying to find Josh, and all the while he was helping Blackwell.

Vicky knew her evidence against Jim McCann was circumstantial at best, but there were too many coincidences to ignore. Jim blew into town almost three weeks ago, which happened to be the same time she started getting those damn phone calls. He had shown up on her doorstep the night her house was broken into. For all she knew, Jim could be the one stalking her. Just as likely was the possibility that he was working with Dark Man and had timed his arrival so he could come to her rescue and gain her trust. But then, what about the man with the wolf tattoo who'd bought the Chevy from Corky Higgins? How many people were involved in this? Vicky's mind tumbled with possibilities, but one thing was certain. If Jim accompanied her to the drop site tonight as planned, she wouldn't make it back home alive. She had to talk to Frank Paxton, and she had to do it before she made the trip to Crescent Park.

Vicky paced the kitchen, her back ramrod straight, her arms folded tightly across her chest. The half sandwich she'd eaten was sticking in her throat like a horse-sized pill that wouldn't go down. At least she'd gotten Frank to listen to her—which was no small feat. She'd barely gotten the words Park Plaza out of her mouth when his temper exploded. He blustered at her, and then turned on Dalila and Sam. Vicky had to force her vocal cords to a level she didn't know she possessed in order to get Frank's attention.

Her revelation had stopped his tirade as effectively as if he'd run headlong into a brick wall. At first Frank had risen to Jim's defense, just as Vicky knew he would, but in the end, he agreed they needed to take a closer look at his newest detective.

Now Jim leaned in the kitchen doorway, his face stony, the muscles in his jaw working furiously. Vicky suspected it was taking every ounce of self-control he could muster to keep his anger in check. Frank had pulled Jim aside as soon as he arrived. Vicky could only imagine Jim's fury when he discovered that he was no longer riding to Crescent Park—that Frank would be taking his place—and that Gil was now in charge of the investigation.

Jim and Vicky's eyes locked and she quickly averted her gaze, fearful she would blurt out what was running through her mind. She'd have her chance, but now wasn't the time. She turned her attention to Frank, who looked as tense and grim as she felt.

"I don't like this," Frank said sharply, dropping the last bundle of cash into the brown paper bag on the table. "This whole thing hasn't smelled right from the beginning. I think we should call this off."

"No!" Vicky cried. "If Pace does have Josh, I don't want to give him any excuse to hurt him."

"I'm afraid he's going to pull some kind of double cross. He has to know we'll be watching the park. How does he think he's going to get the money without getting caught?"

"Frank, nobody ever said Pace was the sharpest knife in the drawer," Gil reminded him. "He just might be dumb enough to think he can waltz in there and pick up the money."

"I don't care. There are too many risks." Frank shook a cigarette from the crumpled pack in his pocket, lit it and took a long pull. "I'm shutting this down."

"Don't do it, Frank," Jim interjected, pushing off the doorjamb and walking toward the chief. "We've got men stationed along the route to the park, inside of it and all around the perimeter. Vicky will be wearing a Kevlar vest. She'll have more protection than the president."

"I thought you didn't like this idea, either," Frank said.

"I don't, but what if this is our only chance to nail this bastard?"

Or nail me, Vicky thought.

"Frank, I agree the risk factor is over the top," Gil said, "but I think this should be Vicky's call. She's the one who has everything at stake and the one taking all the risks."

"I don't have to ask what she wants to do." Frank turned to Vicky and blew out a long breath. "You'd better get ready. It'll be time to leave soon."

Vicky walked out of the kitchen, sweeping past Jim without so much as a glance.

A scowl tugged at Jim's mouth as he watched her leave the room. Vicky had been avoiding him ever since he arrived, and if looks could kill, he would no doubt have a dagger in his heart right now. At first he thought her foul mood was just tension over tonight, and he couldn't have blamed her. Hell, they were all edgy. But then Frank had given Jim his little news flash, and now he had a whole different picture of what was really going on. Vicky Langford was pissed at him over their argument this morning, and she'd used her influence with Frank to have everything changed.

Oh sure, the chief had tried giving him some bullshit excuse about Vicky feeling more comfortable with him as her backup in the car. Jim could almost buy that, but why pull Jim off this case and put Gil in charge of it? There was only one explanation. Vicky had pulled strings as effortlessly as a master puppeteer and not only interfered with his job, but with his whole reason for coming to Westport in the first place. He had to find a way to fix this mess and finish what he came here to do.

Jim ground his teeth together and clenched his fists, his temper threatening to erupt. Jerking open the front door, he stepped onto the porch. The frigid air chilled him to the bone and snatched his breath away, but it did nothing to cool his anger. The idea that Vicky Langford could put his nuts in a vise any time she pleased infuriated him. Now wasn't the time or place to confront her, but Jim would be damned if he'd let it go.

"Sorry about the changes, McCann."

Jim was so deep in thought he didn't hear Gil Fletcher come outside. He shrugged, but couldn't keep the edge out of his voice. "Frank calls the shots and the rest of us are supposed to do as we're told, right?"

"I'd be pissed, too, but shit happens." Gil pulled a black knit cap over his sandy-colored hair and tugged on a pair of gloves. "It's nothing personal. Take me, for instance. I thought for sure Frank would have me ride with Vicky to Crescent Park, but then he decides he's the man for the job. Do I like it? No. But what am I gonna do?"

"Hey, it's no skin off my nose," Jim said, holding up his hands. "I don't have the time or patience to baby-sit her for the rest of this case."

Gil lifted a brow. "You sound just as disgusted with Vicky as you do with Frank. I thought you two were finally getting along a little better. Guess I was wrong."

That makes two of us, Jim thought bitterly. Dammit! He'd had his life tied up in a neat little package, then Vicky Langford came into the picture and turned everything upside down. He cared about her and he'd stupidly allowed himself to think she felt something for him as well. How could he have been so blind? I'm probably better off anyway, Jim told himself. Vicky was a huge distraction and distractions were something he didn't need or want in his life right now.

"Since you're in charge of the Abrons case now, I'll make sure you have all of the reports on your desk first thing in the morning," Gil said.

Glad for the change in topic, Jim sat on the porch rail and folded his arms. There'd been something gnawing at him ever since his conversation with Vicky that morning. The more he thought about what she'd said, the more he was beginning to think she could be right. Now was the perfect time to get

Fletcher's input. "Speaking of the Abrons case, I want to run something by you. Do you think it's possible it was a professional hit and not a robbery?"

"Hell, no." Gil's brown eyes were quizzical. "Where'd that idea come from?"

"Vicky thinks Richard Blackwell had him killed."

"Why would Blackwell want to whack Abrons?"

"Seems that Lisa Murphy has her convinced that the two are—were—connected. Vicky went to see Abrons, thinking if she could get him to roll over on Blackwell . . ."

"It could help her get Josh back since she thinks Blackwell is behind the kidnapping." Gil finished Jim's sentence and shook his head. "Don't get me wrong, McCann, Blackwell is as bad as they come—everybody knows that. But that doesn't mean he's behind every murder in Westport."

"Maybe not every murder, but more than likely he's behind John Wexler's killing."

"Wexler was also trying to dig up something on him. That's not a real healthy thing to do."

"So wouldn't Blackwell have Abrons hit if he felt threatened by him?"

"Probably, but we don't know for a fact they knew each other. Don't forget where Vicky is getting her information. Lisa Murphy is in denial over what happened at Grayson Center, and I guess I can't blame her."

"She could be telling the truth," Jim pointed out.

"I worked that case myself, McCann. Peter Murphy is the one who set that fire, not Richard Blackwell. And as far as Abrons goes, I doubt Blackwell even knows he existed. Abrons was killed during a home invasion, end of story. His house was the third to get hit in that part of town in the last month. Compare the reports on the other robberies with this one. The MO was the same. They used a glass cutter on the patio door and trashed the house before they walked away with anything that wasn't nailed down."

"No one was killed in the other two."

"Abrons just had the bad timing and bad luck to walk in while they were tossing the place."

"What if Vicky is right?"

"Come on, you were there. You know what it looked like."

Jim knew what it looked like, but as he'd knelt beside Abrons' body, Vicky's words kept buzzing inside his head. Abrons and Wexler had both talked to Vicky and now they were dead. Coincidence? Jim didn't think so. He was about to tell Fletcher that when the front door swung open.

Frank Paxton stepped outside; worry lines etched in his face. "It's time."

Chapter 14

Darkness and death are all around you.

Madam Zoya's words nibbled at Vicky as she followed Frank outside. She shivered in spite of the heavy Kevlar vest she wore under her jacket.

"You watch yourself out there," Gil said. Pulling Vicky close, he gave her a hug that could break bones.

She pressed a kiss to his cheek. "You don't have to worry about me. I've got nine lives."

Vicky started across the porch. As she went past Jim, he laid a hand on her arm. "Vicky, wait."

Without wanting to, she looked into his eyes. Where she'd seen anger and resentment just minutes earlier, she now saw hurt and worry. This man had consoled her and opened the door to feelings she'd kept locked away for so long. Her breath caught in her throat, and for a moment her heart threatened to betray her. She wanted to be wrong about him. She wanted to trust and believe in Jim. Then she remembered what she'd seen at Park Plaza that afternoon.

She looked pointedly at his hand that held on to the sleeve of her jacket, then back up at Jim. "I've got an appointment to keep."

"Vicky, I . . . Be careful."

"Frank's got my back. I'll be fine."

Without saying another word, she pulled from his grasp and got into her Blazer where Frank was already crouching in the backseat. As she drove away, Vicky looked in the rearview mirror. Jim was still standing on the porch, watching them. She quickly turned her attention to the road, willing herself not to look back again.

She couldn't afford to trust Jim McCann, much less have any feelings for him. Besides, it wasn't as if he truly felt anything for her, Vicky reminded herself. Whatever emotion he'd managed to plaster on his face just now was there as a ploy to make her trust him, nothing more.

As she turned from her driveway onto the highway, she hit the gas, spewing gravel and throwing Frank against the back door.

"Jesus, Vicky, take it easy."

"I'm sorry. Are you okay?" She gripped the steering wheel with both hands and edged the speedometer to seventy-five.

"Yes, goddammit," Frank shouted. "But slow down. We've allowed plenty of time."

"I'm just anxious to get there."

"If you put this thing in a ditch we won't make it at all."

Vicky eased up on the gas as her cell phone rang. She flicked a worried glance at Frank, who'd poked his head over the seat.

"I'd put money on that being Pace," Frank said.

Vicky answered on the second ring.

"You don't listen very well do you, Girlie? That park is crawling with cops, so there's a change in plans," a muffled voice said. "Go north on Route 9 instead of south. When you come to a fork in the road make a right and follow it all the way to a small clearing. Leave the money in the middle of the clearing, then take a hike. When I see all the cash is there, I'll call you back with instructions about where to pick up your kid. Be there in fifteen minutes. Do exactly as I say, or I swear little Joshie won't live to see his next birthday."

"I'll do anything you want," Vicky cried. "Just don't hurt Josh!"

The line went dead.

"You were right," Vicky said to Frank. "That was Pace and he's changing everything. He's making it impossible to have backup."

"We'll be okay, honey, I promise." Frank reached for his radio to call Gil Fletcher. Vicky could hear Gil swearing when Frank told him what Pace had pulled. "Gil is sending backup," Frank said when he broke the connection. "But slow down a little. Give them time to catch up with us."

"If I slow down, we won't get there in time. You know as well as I do that Pace will follow through on his threats to Josh without giving it a second thought."

"If he even has Josh."

"I don't want to put Pace to the test," she shot back.

"Then it looks like it's you and me."

When Vicky got to Route 9 there was still no sign of headlights behind her. "Where the hell is our backup?"

"They'll catch up, but just in case, you'd better take this." Frank pulled a gun from the pocket of his jacket and laid it on the seat beside her. "Gil told me to give this to you. I didn't want to do it if I didn't have to, but like it or not, you're probably going to need it if we run into Pace before our backup arrives."

Vicky licked her lips and glanced at the gun beside her. It might as well have been a rattlesnake, coiled and ready to strike. Tiny beads of sweat dotted her brow and her mouth went dry, but she didn't protest. *You'll use it if you have to.*

She repeated the words in her mind as she wrapped her hands tighter around the steering wheel. It felt as if the Blazer was standing still, but time was doing anything but that. She nudged the speedometer up again as she glanced at the clock on the dash.

Vicky drove down the black ribbon of highway for nearly eight more miles before finally coming to the fork in the road. She turned right, as Pace had instructed. Within minutes the paved highway turned into a single-lane dirt road. The Blazer bumped along as Vicky tried to steer around deep ruts. Frank let out a string of obscenities as his head smacked into the door handle. Suddenly, Vicky slammed on the brakes.

"What's going on?" Frank asked. He chanced a peek over the backseat.

"We've hit a dead end." Vicky stared at the huge orange-and-white barricade that blocked the road. "There was probably a barricade like this back at that fork in the road, too."

"Let's get the hell out of here. We're sitting ducks like this."

Suddenly, a man dressed in black and wearing a ski mask jumped out of the trees and yanked open Vicky's door. She cried out, her hands tearing at his, as he dragged her out of the Blazer by her ponytail.

Frank sprang from the backseat, Glock drawn, but the man wrapped a muscular arm around Vicky's neck and pulled her in front of him to use as a shield.

"Put it down or I'll blow her fuckin' brains out," he shouted.

Vicky gasped as the cold barrel of the gun was jammed against her temple.

"Just take it easy," Frank said. "Nobody has to get hurt."

"Then do as I say," the man shouted.

Vicky's eyes were frantic as they met Frank's. It made her skin crawl to be that close to Arlo Pace, and there was no doubt in her mind that's who held her in an iron grip.

"Put the gun down or I swear the bitch is history!" The man's arm tightened around Vicky's neck.

"All right." Frank laid the Glock on the ground then put his hands in the air. "You're the one in charge."

"Damn straight I'm in charge. Now kick it under the truck."

Frank did as he was told as the man growled into Vicky's ear, "Too bad little Joshie has to pay for Mommy's mistake."

"Please don't hurt my baby. I've got the money!"

"Where?"

"Where's my son?" Vicky shouted. She jammed her elbow into his stomach but his muscles were rock-hard. He didn't grunt in pain, didn't move an inch. Reaching behind her, she ripped off his ski mask and clawed his face. He cried out and loosened his grip just enough so that Vicky was able to turn her head and look at him. The stubble-covered face was leaner than she remembered, the dark hair shorter, but the eyes were still the same. Cold, evil. A shiver went down her spine. Arlo Pace was the original Grim Reaper. A harbinger of death. Blood seeped from the scratches on his cheek as he glared at her.

"I'm glad you took it off. I want you to look into my eyes when I put a fuckin' bullet in your head." His lips twisted into a maniacal grin. "I've waited a long time for this. It's payday, Girlie."

The wail of police sirens sounded in the distance.

"You bitch! I warned you!" Pace roared. He backed toward the woods still holding Vicky in front of him. Cocking the hammer, he said, "I'll give little Joshie a kiss for you right before I slit his throat!" Pace shoved Vicky away and pulled the trigger. She dove for the ground as the bullet whizzed past her shoulder.

"Are you hit?" Frank shouted, pulling his spare gun from his ankle holster.

"I'm fine, just get him!"

Vicky heard the rustle of bushes and snapping of branches as Frank disappeared into the woods. She was pulling herself to her feet when another shot rang out. Swearing, she dropped to the ground again. The shot hit a tree, splintering wood and sending bark flying in all directions. It was quickly followed by another that stung the ground beside her.

Willing herself to move, Vicky scuttled to the passenger side of the Blazer. She pulled open the door. The dome light shone down on the gun on the seat. She reached for it, intending to follow Frank, but suddenly her fingers felt thick and clumsy. Her arms and legs were heavy as lead pipes. Nausea sank its teeth into her as she stood up.

Just put one foot in front of the other and do it now, she commanded herself, but her feet remained firmly rooted to the ground.

Where was her training, her cop's instincts? Dammit, where were her guts? It was as if her body was fighting what her mind was telling her to do.

Four cruisers screeched to a halt behind her Blazer. Her backup poured out onto the road, guns drawn. Gil and Jim scrambled out of Gil's Taurus and ran toward her.

Gil grabbed her by the shoulders. "Are you okay?"

"I'm fine, just get Pace. He went in that direction," Vicky shouted, pointing the way. "Frank went in after him."

Vicky watched as they darted into the woods, then looked down at the gun in her hand.

"You blew it, Langford," she said out loud. Hugging herself, she sagged against the truck. Thanks to her, Pace would probably get away, taking with him what may be their last chance of finding Josh.

The grandfather clock struck six as dull-gray light streaked the morning sky. Vicky sat in the family room, staring at Josh's picture and feeling totally defeated. She'd been home for hours with nothing to do but wait and worry. The police had set up roadblocks and combed the woods looking for Arlo Pace. All they found were fresh tire tracks on an old service road that cut through the woods. The ex-con had vanished into thin air. Vicky knew it would take a miracle at this point to find him. *"I'll kiss Joshie for you right before I slit his throat."*

Pace's words were like a knife in her heart. Whatever happened to her son now rested squarely on Vicky's shoulders. If only she'd taken the gun and gone after Pace, he might be in custody right now. Instead she'd frozen, just as she'd always known she would if she had to use a gun again. It was that fear that had driven her from the department after Connie Springer was killed. After all, what good was a cop who couldn't use a gun? Her partner would never be able to depend on her, and now the most important person in her life hadn't been able to depend on her, either.

What kind of mother was she that she couldn't overcome her fear for her own child? One tragic moment in time had altered the course of her life and taken Connie Springer's. Seven years later, would it take Josh's as well?

No, dammit, she wouldn't let it! She'd screwed up royally last night, but Pace was out there somewhere and she was going to find him. Vicky tiptoed past Dalila who'd insisted on staying the night and was now dozing on the couch. She went into the kitchen where Sam was slumped in a chair at the table snoring, his head lolling to one side.

The poor guy had caught twenty kinds of hell from Frank for letting her sneak past him and go to Park Plaza. Vicky hated to tell Sam he was going to be knee deep in it again today, but she had places to go and people to see.

Vicky spent the day scouting every flophouse in Westport and came up with nothing. She'd checked all of Pace's old haunts as well, but again drew a blank. If people knew where the ex-con was, they weren't talking. Making matters worse was the fact that none of her snitches were answering her pages, either, and hadn't been since Josh's disappearance. Keeping an eye on the traffic ahead, she reached for her cell phone. She punched in Louie Patella's number again, adding the 911 she'd been using each time.

The phone rang back almost immediately, making Vicky jump.

"What the hell do you want, Langford?" Patella snapped when Vicky answered.

"Where have you been? I've been paging you for the last four days."

"I'm telling you straight up I don't want nothin' to do with you right now. I thought you'd get the hint when I didn't call you back the first hundred times you paged me."

"I need your help, Louie."

"Helping you ain't so healthy lately. Just ask John Wexler. I hear his mother had to have a closed casket for him."

Patella's words hit a nerve, and Vicky cringed remembering Wexler sprawled across his bed in the Lexington Hotel. She pushed the image away. There was nothing she could do for Wexler, but she could still save her son. This man could help her do it if she could only convince him.

"What makes you think Wexler was helping me?" Vicky asked.

"Shit gets around."

"My son is missing."

"I heard," Louie replied coldly. "Tough break."

"I think Arlo Pace has him."

"That psycho?" Patella whistled softly.

"Have you heard anything? Do you have any idea where Pace might be holed up?"

The silence on the other end of the phone seemed to last forever. Patella knew something, otherwise he would have just said no.

"I ain't heard nothin', 'cept your kid was gone," he finally replied.

"That's bullshit, and we both know it."

"Think what you want, Langford. I don't know nothin'."

"My son is just a baby. Where's your conscience?"

"Alive and well, thanks, unlike some people I know."

"Help me, Louie, please."

"Are you fuckin' nuts? You think I want a facelift like Wexler's?"

"I know I'm asking you to take a risk, but you're the only one who can help me now." The traffic light turned red and Vicky stopped her Blazer. She glanced at the street sign. "I'm at the corner of Fourth and Waverly. I can be at our usual spot in fifteen minutes, twenty tops."

"Sorry, Langford. I hope you find your kid, I really do, but you'll have to do it without me."

He hung up before Vicky could say anything else. She tossed the phone down on the seat and slammed her fist against the steering wheel. Tears rolled down her cheeks. Whom else could she ask for help? Where else could she look for Pace?

The car behind her honked and Vicky looked up. The light had turned green and the driver was gesturing angrily at her. Vicky waved an apology at him as her phone rang again. She snatched it up, hoping it was Louie and he'd changed his mind.

"Vicky, this is Lisa Murphy."

Vicky's brows shot up. She hadn't spoken to Lisa since the day they met at Texas Joe's for lunch.

"I have to talk to you about Josh," Lisa sobbed. "But I can't do it over the phone. Take down this address."

Vicky pulled over and threw the Blazer into park. Cradling the phone on her shoulder, she jotted down the address that Lisa gave her.

"What's going on?" Vicky asked, but there was no response. Lisa had already hung up.

★ ★ ★ ★ ★

Darkness was falling as Vicky turned onto Winslow Avenue. It was one of eight square blocks that had been condemned and slated for the wrecking ball in the spring. According to the sign posted at the corner, the site would soon be the new home of Bradford Square Mall. Right now it was just an abandoned neighborhood that was quiet as a ghost town and just as eerie. Vicky's senses had been on full alert since Lisa's call; now they went into overdrive. This was not the kind of place Lisa would go to voluntarily. The wind picked up. Unlocked doors banged back and forth. Debris skittered across the pavement. She strained to see addresses as she drove slowly past the dilapidated structures lining the street. Stopping at 486, she switched off the engine and peered through the passenger window. The three-story apartment building rose like a specter against the darkening sky. Reaching for her phone, Vicky dialed the station. Neither Frank Paxton nor Gil Fletcher were in.

"I'll try to reach the chief for you," the dispatcher said, "but is there anyone else who can help you in the meantime?"

Vicky identified herself and explained about Lisa's call. "I don't want to leave if there's a possibility she's really here."

"I'll send help. Just sit tight."

Checking her door locks, Vicky glanced around. The street was empty, but she felt eyes on her. She took the ASP and a new can of pepper spray from her purse and laid them in her lap. Drumming her fingers on the steering wheel, she checked her watch. Five minutes had gone by and there was no sign of the police.

Great response time.

Suddenly, screams came from number 486. Vicky swore under her breath and reached for the door handle, then hesitated. The screaming woman might not be Lisa Murphy, but someone trying to lure Vicky into the building.

"Stay away from me!" a woman shouted. "Someone help me!"

The woman's desperate cries tore at Vicky's heart. She knew she'd be walking into a trap if she went into the building, but what choice did she have? If it was Lisa in there, Vicky had to do something, backup or no backup.

Her hands shaking, she shoved the ASP into her pocket and grabbed the can of pepper spray. Cement crumbled beneath her feet as she raced up the front steps.

"Don't, please! Don't!" the woman sobbed.

One last horrible scream echoed in the night as Vicky's hand closed around the doorknob. Holding the can of pepper spray ready, she shouldered the door open. In the faint light that spilled in from the streetlight, she saw a set of sagging stairs.

She started toward them, the rotting floorboards creaking under her weight. Suddenly, the wind grabbed the door behind her and slammed it shut. She spun around. Her pulse roared in her ears.

Her gaze darted around the vestibule, trying to detect some movement. The shadows seemed to shift and change, and she blinked hard as she focused her eyes. Her palms were damp, her chest tight. She started toward the stairs, ducking to avoid the rafters that hung from the ceiling like lifeless arms. She heard a sound and stopped again. The hair prickled on the back of her neck. Someone was breathing, soft as a whisper. The front door seemed like a million miles away as she turned and bolted for it. She made it halfway there when a set of powerful hands grabbed her from behind.

Dropping the can of pepper spray, Vicky clawed wildly at the hands around her throat. They squeezed harder. Blind terror washed over her as she struggled to breathe. Panic gave way to resolve. A burst of adrenaline shot through her body. She brought the heel of her boot down hard on top of her attacker's foot. Twisting around, Vicky thrust her knee up, catching him square in the groin. He grunted in pain and let go of her. She pulled the ASP from her pocket, extended it with a flick of her wrist and swung. She heard a thud as it struck home. He cried out and fell to the floor swearing.

She stumbled away from him, gasping for air. Her legs felt like jelly and her chest burned. She scrambled for the door, frantically tugging at it, but it wouldn't budge. Vicky glanced over her shoulder. She could barely make him out as he got to his feet. Dressed in black from his ski mask to his shoes, he was like something from a nightmare.

Vicky darted for the stairs, but he was right behind her. She made it to the first landing when he grabbed her ankles and pulled. She went down and her head slammed against the edge of the step. Pain shot through her like a lightning bolt. She dropped the ASP, and it clattered down the stairs.

"Do you think you can get away from me, Girlie?" He reeled her toward him.

Vicky cried out as the rough wooden step scraped her cheek. She kicked, making contact with his head. Her boot found its mark again and he tumbled to the bottom of the stairs, landing in a heap.

"You're dead, bitch!"

Vicky grabbed the banister and struggled to her feet. She hugged the peeling wall as darkness, thick as quicksand, threatened to pull her under.

She made it to the top of the next flight of stairs and staggered down the hall into one of the empty apartments. He came charging behind her, sending Vicky sprawling across the dirty floor. A broken two-by-four lay just a few feet away. Vicky's arms ached as she strained to reach it. Her fingers closed around it just as he grabbed her. Rolling over, Vicky swung the board and was rewarded with a satisfying crack. Crying out, he stumbled back, holding his side.

Vicky staggered to her feet as he started toward her again. She blinked blood from her eyes, clutched the board tighter, and took a batter's stance. "Come on, Pace, you rotten son of a bitch!"

He was breathing hard and about to charge again when they both heard the sirens. Blue and red lights bounced off the walls, illuminating the room. He hesitated a moment, as if considering what to do. He stood with his fists clenched at his sides, his ragged breathing echoing through the room.

At first Vicky thought he was actually going to chance another attack, but instead he turned and ran out of the apartment. Vicky's shoulders sagged in relief, and she let the board clatter to the floor. Bruised and bloodied, she slowly made her way downstairs.

Vicky sat huddled in her Blazer with the heater blasting. Her head throbbed. Reaching in her purse, she pulled out a bottle of aspirin and swallowed three of them dry. She leaned back, closed her eyes and pressed a wad of tissue to her forehead. The bleeding had almost stopped, but she had a nasty bump and she'd probably be black and blue for a month. All things considered, she'd gotten off easy.

The police had scoured the building and the neighborhood to no avail. Pace was long gone, but he'd left behind a gruesome souvenir of his presence—the dead body of Lisa Murphy. Vicky identified her. Poor Lisa, Vicky thought, her throat tightening. All she had wanted to do was clear her husband's name. Instead, she wound up another casualty in the war against Richard Blackwell.

A car pulled up behind her truck and Vicky glanced in the rearview mirror, expecting to see Gil or Frank. She swore when she saw Jim McCann climb out of his Mazda and stalk toward her Blazer.

He jerked open the door and stood glaring at her. Vicky sat up, blinking against the brightness from the dome light. The sudden movement made her feel as if someone had just hit her in the head with an ax. Gritting her teeth against the pain, she glared right back at him. "What are you doing here?"

Jim's mouth was tight, his blue eyes dark with fury.

"It's my job to respond to calls," he said tersely. "Neither Frank nor Gil were around, so you're stuck with me for the time being."

"Gee, lucky me."

"Cut the sarcasm, dammit," Jim replied. His troubled gaze swept over her and he frowned. "Was it Pace who attacked you?"

"Yeah, wearing his best black outfit and ski mask again."

"What the hell are you doing here anyway?" Jim shouted. "What would make you come to a place like this?"

"Lisa Murphy called and asked me to meet her here because she had information about Josh."

Jim slammed his fist on the roof of the Blazer. "And you didn't smell a setup?"

"Of course I did. I called the police as soon as I got here, and I was waiting for them when I heard Lisa screaming."

"And, of course, you couldn't resist the urge to play Wonder Woman. Vicky the invincible," Jim said, throwing up his hands.

"Don't patronize me, Jim McCann."

She climbed out of the Blazer, but her head started to swim when she stood up. She sank back against the seat. "How could I stand around while she screamed for help? Maybe if I hadn't hesitated she'd still be alive."

Vicky watched as Lisa's body was loaded into the back of an ambulance. It pulled slowly away. No need for sirens or speeding through traffic. Lisa Murphy was beyond anyone's help now. Vicky turned her head away and blinked back tears.

"You couldn't have saved her. Deep inside you know that," Jim said, his voice softening. He reached for her hand, but Vicky shrank from his touch. "Look, I understand you've been through a lot, but don't take it out on me. I'm one of the good guys, remember?"

Vicky folded her arms and glowered at him. "Really?"

"How about cluing me in on what this sudden attitude change in you and Frank Paxton is all about? He yanks me from your case with no explanation, then keeps me running around like a chicken with my head cut off. You've been treating me like a leper, and goddammit, I think I deserve to know why."

Vicky lifted her chin and gave him an accusing look. "I went to Park Plaza yesterday with the intention of searching Richard Blackwell's office. You'll never guess who I saw when I got there."

"That's what this is all about? You saw me there with Richard Blackwell." Jim furrowed his brow. "So what? I went there to informally question him."

"It sure as hell didn't look like an interrogation," Vicky said. "It looked more like old home week."

"I can explain. I just can't do it now."

"Of course, you can't. Well, I'm not interested in your explanations. I just want you to tell me where my son is."

Jim stared at her in disbelief. "Do you honestly think I could kidnap your son? Do you think I'm that much of a monster?"

Vicky's response was an icy glare.

"Answer me, dammit! Do you really think I could march into Mary Renfield's house, beat her nearly to death and take Josh?"

"Here's what I think, McCann. You and Richard Blackwell are old pals and you've been lying about it, which would explain why you've been doing your best to throw me off the track."

"I haven't been lying to you, at least, not intentionally."

"That's backpedaling if I ever heard it."

"Look, there are things about me that you don't know," Jim said.

"That was pretty obvious to me when I saw you and Blackwell together."

"You are unreal." Jim narrowed his eyes and jammed his fists at his hips. "You'd rather think that I have something to do with Josh's kidnapping than believe there's a reasonable explanation for what you saw at Park Plaza. I think that hit you took to your head must have scrambled your brains."

"This conversation is over. I'm going home."

She reached for the handle of the door, but Jim stopped her from pulling it closed. "The only place you're going right now is the nearest hospital to get checked out. Why the hell wasn't an ambulance called for you anyway?"

"I didn't want one. I'm fine."

"Don't be ridiculous. You're going to the hospital."

"Then I'll drive myself."

"You're in no condition to drive." He reached past her and pulled the keys from the ignition. "I'll take you."

"I'm not going anywhere with you."

"Half of Westport's finest are going to see you leave with me," Jim said sarcastically. "I promise you'll make it there in one piece."

Chapter 15

Jim paced the length of Westport General's emergency room, his stomach knotted. Things were going from bad to worse with lightning speed between him and Vicky. He'd wanted to take her in his arms the moment he saw her tonight, tell her how relieved he was that she was all right, but the look on her face had stopped him. And here he'd thought she was angry with him over the Ray Abrons incident. Jim laughed and shook his head, earning curious glances from the other people in the crowded ER waiting room.

Ignoring them, he went to the vending machine, dropped change into the slot and pushed the button for black coffee. He couldn't get over the idea she actually thought he was involved in Josh's disappearance. That hurt more than he cared to admit. He thought they had gotten to know each other over the last few days, had gained trust in each other. What a jerk he'd been.

It was amazing how life could turn completely around in the blink of an eye. Twenty-four hours ago he was envisioning the possibility of life with Vicky after Josh was found safe and sound. Now it looked like there were better odds for snow in Jamaica than for the two of them hooking up. He never should have let his guard down. That little voice in his head had warned him he'd get hurt again, but did he listen? No.

"Detective McCann?" A pudgy, middle-aged doctor waddled into the waiting room and looked around at the weary and frustrated faces.

"I'm right here." Jim put the scalding coffee on the windowsill.

"I'm Dr. Ahearn." The doctor extended his hand. "You're here with Vicky Langford?"

"Yes, is she all right?" Jim asked, following the doctor down the hall.

"She took a pretty good blow to the head and the gash on her forehead required a few stitches, but I'd say she's in good shape, considering what she went through. I've advised Mrs. Langford to see her family doctor for a follow-up in a few days, but in the meantime, if she should experience any dizziness, nausea, blurred vision, that type of thing, bring her back in."

"Wait a minute." A worried frown creased Jim's brow. "Isn't she at least staying overnight?"

"That was my recommendation, but she's a very stubborn and determined young woman," Dr. Ahearn sighed. "When I left Mrs. Langford, she was getting up to change back into her clothes."

As if on cue, Vicky walked around the corner, a bandage over the gash in her forehead, her face pale. Looking wobbly as a new colt, she headed toward them. Dr. Ahearn signaled for an orderly and asked him to bring a wheelchair. Vicky frowned, but she eased herself into it with the doctor's help.

"By tomorrow morning you're going to feel like a freight train hit you," Dr. Ahearn said. He pulled a prescription pad from the pocket of his lab coat and began writing. "If aspirin doesn't help you manage the pain, this will. And remember, as hard as it might be, you need to get as much rest as possible."

"That'll be the day," Jim said under his breath.

"You'll just have to sign discharge papers and then you can go."

In spite of her protests that she could walk from the exit to the car, Jim brought it around and helped her in. As he reached for the gearshift, she laid her hand on his arm.

"You said you could prove you're telling the truth about Blackwell," she said quietly. "Do it."

"I thought I'd already been tried and convicted. What brought on this sudden change of heart?"

Vicky shrugged her shoulder and chewed a thumbnail. "I had a lot of time to think while I was waiting to see the doctor."

"So now, all of a sudden, I'm not the crazed maniac you thought I was?"

Vicky huffed an exasperated sigh. "Look, I'm just saying that I'd be interested in seeing your proof of innocence, okay? Unless you really don't have any."

"I've got proof, but you're not going to see it tonight. It's getting late, and I have strict orders to get you home so you can rest."

"What difference can a few minutes make? Besides, it's not like I'm going to go home and go to bed."

"Of course not," Jim said. "Why would you do something sensible like take care of yourself?"

"My body will get all the rest it needs. It's my mind that needs to be put to rest right now."

When they got to his condo, Jim didn't bother to ask if Vicky wanted help in, he just swept her up in his arms and carried her. She started to argue, but she was just too tired. She felt bruised from head to toe and every part of her body was screaming for a long soak in a hot tub.

When they reached his second-floor unit, he had to put her down long enough to unlock the door, but he kept one arm wrapped protectively around her. Vicky hated to admit it, but it felt good to have his arms around her. He pushed open the door to his condo and started to pick her back up again, but she held her hands up. "I think I can make it from here."

Jim shrugged as if he couldn't care less and let her go in first. She stood in the small foyer, her arms folded across her chest.

"You might as well make yourself at home. It's going to take me a while to find what I want to show you." He pulled off his jacket and tossed it over the back of a chair. Pointing in the direction of the kitchen he added, "By the way, if you feel the need for a weapon, you should be able find a skillet or a meat mallet in there that you can clobber me with. I'll be back."

Vicky narrowed her dark eyes at him as he turned and went down the hall. Minutes ticked by as she heard Jim rummaging around and swearing occasionally. Exhaustion weighed on her, heavy as a boulder. She looked at the overstuffed leather sofa in the living room. Part of her wanted to give in to the fatigue and curl up there and sleep, but she couldn't. There was too much to do. She went to the dining room, sat at the glass-topped table and buried her head in her hands. She couldn't help wondering if there was something she could have done to save Lisa Murphy's life.

Common sense told her no, that Pace had brought Lisa to the building on Winslow Avenue to kill her, just as he had intended to kill Vicky. But her heart said yes. If she would have gone in right away, Lisa might still be alive. Vicky had been too late to save her, just as she'd been too late to save Josh or help Mary. Tears seeped through her lashes. She brushed them away as she heard Jim coming back down the hall.

"Sorry it took so long. I haven't gotten around to unpacking everything yet. I had a ton of boxes in the spare bedroom to look through, but I found what I was looking for," Jim said, placing a framed eight-by-ten photo and copy of the *Herald* on the table. The front page carried the story of the tragic fire at Grayson Center.

"Turn to page three," Jim said. "The story is continued there."

"I wrote this story," Vicky said, pointing to her byline. She sat back and looked at him. "I know what's on page three. And you'll excuse me for saying this, but the first day I met you, you said you didn't know anything about the Grayson Center fire."

"I lied."

"That's supposed to make me feel better?"

Shaking his head, Jim blew out a breath and flipped to page three. Splashed across it were photos of the eight men who were killed in the fire. Jim jabbed his finger at one of the pictures. "That guy, Terry Simmons, was my brother-in-law."

Jim pulled the framed color photo toward Vicky. It was of a wedding party of twelve. The groom was the same man in the newspaper photo. Standing next to him was Jim McCann.

"He married my kid sister, Bridgette, five years ago. Terry was originally from here, so they moved back after the wedding. He went to work for Blackwell's construction company a year before the fire. Not long after that he started telling me about some of the things he suspected were going on."

"He sounds like Peter Murphy."

"Except Terry went a step further than Murphy. He talked to the feds. Seems they already had Blackwell under investigation. They were looking to get an agent on the inside. Terry offered to help, and they took him up on it. He was already working there, he had a pretty good idea of what was going on and access to places and information that someone new coming in wouldn't necessarily be able to get. Terry was working with the feds for a couple of months when Murphy started spouting off to people about what he thought was going on. Terry was afraid something was going to happen. He tried talking to Murphy, told him to keep his mouth shut. The feds didn't have enough at that point to make an arrest stick, and they knew that the situation was about to explode because of Murphy, so they pulled the plug on the whole thing and told Terry to give his notice to Blackwell. They told him too late. He did give his notice, but it was the same day as the fire."

"Why didn't you tell Frank? Why didn't you tell me?"

"How could I know who to trust? For all I know Frank could be on Blackwell's payroll."

Vicky shook her head and said angrily, "No way. Not Frank. He would never . . ."

"It's a possibility, Vicky. You'd better face that. A guy like Blackwell doesn't get away with the kind of crap he's been doing for as long as he's been doing it unless he has friends in the department."

"Just who are your suspects?"

"Sorry, but Frank's number one."

Vicky stood up and began pacing the room. "I'm telling you, it's not Frank."

"Take off the blinders. He's got the connections and the power to do whatever Blackwell needs him to do."

"Who else?"

"So far there are two other names that surfaced more than any others with cases that are connected to Blackwell. Your friend Sean O'Connor and a patrolman by the name of Nick Rizzo."

"I can't believe it's either of them."

"You asked. I'm telling," Jim said. "Now I'm asking that you keep this to yourself. Let me do what I need to do."

Vicky waved a hand in the air. "None of this explains why you seemed to be so chummy with Blackwell the day I saw you at his office."

"I met him at Terry's funeral," Jim said. "Bridgette told me Blackwell gave each of the families several thousand dollars to help out with expenses. I made it a point to sit with him at the funeral luncheon and tell him what a great guy he was and how lucky Bridgette and the other wives were that their husbands worked for such a generous, caring boss. We hit it off pretty good. I went to see him before I flew back to Seattle, too. Both times I tried to drop what I hoped were subtle hints that I might be interested in working for him. I was trying to lay some groundwork to get inside, because I already knew I was coming to Westport not just to give my sister a hand, but to bury that bastard, too."

"You came here to do the same thing that I've been trying to do for the last two years."

"Nail Blackwell. I need to do this for Terry, my sister, and their kids." Jim took her hand in his and searched her face with his gaze. "You do believe me, don't you?"

Vicky tilted her head back and looked up at him. She knew he was telling the truth. She could see it in his face, the way his eyes pleaded with her to believe him.

"Yes," she whispered.

"I want this to be over for you," he said, pulling her gently to her feet. "I want Josh home."

Vicky touched his cheek. The four days' growth on his face felt rough as sandpaper against her fingertips. His eyes were bloodshot and there were lines of fatigue in his face. He'd been trying so hard to find Josh. How could she have ever doubted him?

Vicky melted against Jim as his arms encircled her waist. He pulled her close and buried his face in her hair. She slipped her arms around his neck and clung to him. She could feel the warmth of his body, the beating of his heart. Its rhythm matched her own.

Jim gave her a whisper of a kiss that left her weak. Then his mouth grew more demanding. Vicky could feel his desire against her and her breath quickened as she returned the kiss hungrily. She pressed herself against him as he feathered kisses across her face, tasting her tears.

His lips brushed the bandage across her forehead and he

suddenly drew back. He looked down at the ugly purple bruises blooming around her neck, a grim reminder of what had happened earlier.

His voice was husky when he spoke. "I should get you home. You're exhausted and need to rest."

"Yes, rest," Vicky whispered. But even as she said it, she was twining her fingers in the dark curls at the base of his neck, pulling him closer. What she needed was to be held. What she needed was a reprieve, no matter how small, from the hellish nightmare of the last few days. What she needed was Jim.

Exhaustion faded as a flame of desire sparked and burned bright and hot inside of her. Jim kissed her again. Vicky slid her hands beneath his shirt and caressed the dark, silky hair that covered his chest. He swept her up in his arms, never taking his midnight-blue gaze from her face. He made it to the bedroom in a few quick strides and put her down next to the bed. She reached for the light to snap it off, but Jim stopped her.

"I want to see you." His very words, the need she saw in his eyes, sent desire coursing through Vicky's body. Their clothes came off in a flurry, dropping in a tangle at their feet.

"God, you're beautiful," he murmured. He gently ran his fingers down her arms, across the swell of her breasts to her flat belly. Vicky shivered with anticipation.

They fell onto the bed. His kisses seared her skin as he slowly moved from her lips, down her neck to her breasts. They tasted, teased and explored each other's body until each was dizzy with excitement, aching with the need for release. When they could hold back no longer, Jim thrust himself inside of her. Vicky arched into him and gasped as a shock of pleasure held her in its grasp. She began to move with him, faster and harder until they were both breathless. Sweet release came at the same time for each of them.

Jim gazed down at Vicky. She reached up and traced the line

of his nose, letting her fingers trail across his cheek. It felt so good to have someone's arms around her again. She'd missed it more than she had ever let herself admit, but she couldn't afford to get used to it. She didn't believe Jim wanted anything more from this and she told herself she didn't, either.

A feeling of sadness suddenly swept over her, washing away the warmth of their lovemaking. For a little while she had found an escape from the living hell her life had become. Reality was back now and she knew this had been a mistake.

"What is it?" Jim asked. He tried to pull her close, but Vicky twisted away from him. He cupped her chin in his hand and forced her to look at him. "Don't say you regret what just happened."

"Don't you?" she asked quietly.

"Why would I regret what we just shared?"

"Because it happened for the wrong reasons. Because neither of us wants anything more."

"What if I said I did?"

"What if I said I didn't?" she challenged.

"I'm falling in love with you."

Vicky looked at him, dumbstruck. For a moment she didn't say anything, then she shook her head and blurted, "It couldn't possibly work."

"Don't say that," he said softly, pressing a kiss to her temple. "I didn't plan on telling you now. I wanted to wait until Josh was back home, but I just had to say it."

"We have nothing in common. Our personalities are totally opposite, and you hate what I do for a living."

Jim propped himself up on one arm and slung his other one across her, trapping Vicky's body next to his. "I'll admit I'm not fond of your profession, but don't try to use that as a reason for why this wouldn't work. There's more to it than that, isn't there?"

He searched her face, but she stared at the ceiling and refused to meet his gaze.

"It's the job isn't it?" Jim said. "You think it carries too many risks."

"I don't think—I know. I've lived through the worst of what the job can bring, and I don't think I could stand to lose anyone else. If I ever do get involved again, I want it to be with someone who has a normal job with no risks."

"Every job carries an element of risk nowadays. We live in an era where disgruntled people gun down co-workers and kids shoot up their schools, so stop using that as an excuse, Vicky. The truth is, you're afraid of being hurt again. You put up walls and refuse to let anybody in. I know, because that's all I've done since my divorce."

"And now you've changed your mind."

"That's what I'm trying to tell you if you'd get it through that thick skull of yours. I want you more than I've ever wanted anyone else."

"Even if that's true, it doesn't change how you feel about my job. You don't respect what I do, and you can't be supportive of something you don't respect." Vicky looked at him curiously. "Why do you dislike reporters so much anyway?"

Jim lay back and folded his arms beneath his head. "I was married to one for five years. Her job was everything to her, and she was willing to sacrifice anything to get ahead, even our marriage. I came home early from work one day and found her in our bed with her editor. You know what she said? 'It's no big deal, Jim. It was just sex and it did more for my career than all the hard work I've put in for the last ten years.'

"After that I found out she'd been sleeping with him all through our marriage to get the plum assignments, not to mention sleeping with other people to get information, too. My whole marriage had been a lie, but I was just too damn blind and stupid to see it."

Vicky didn't know what she'd expected Jim to tell her, but it certainly wasn't this. Her heart ached for him. Betrayal was something she had never had to deal with. She and Danny had had their share of ups and downs during their marriage, but their commitment to each other and their relationship had always remained rock solid. She touched Jim's face with her fingertips. He turned toward her and she whispered, "I'm not like that."

"I know you're not, and that's why I'm asking you to give this a chance. I'm just as afraid of getting hurt again as you are, but I'm willing to take the risk." He gently stroked her cheek. "Life can be awfully lonely when you close your heart to people, Vicky."

He leaned forward and brushed his lips to hers. When Jim pulled her to him this time, Vicky didn't resist. Jim cradled her in his arms, softly stroking her silky skin.

Vicky moved closer, savoring the warmth and comfort of his nearness. The nightmare would continue until she held her little boy again, but at least she didn't feel quite so alone. Fatigue closed in around her and Vicky gave herself over to it. She drifted into a merciful sleep with Jim murmuring in her ear, "Don't worry, Vicky. Everything is going to be all right."

Two hours later they were awakened by the faint ringing of a phone. They bolted up, glancing at the clock on the nightstand. It was almost one in the morning.

"Is that yours or mine?" Jim asked, referring to their cell phones.

"Mine, I think." Her muscles screamed as she scrambled out of bed and ran to the living room. She swept up her purse from the floor and dug out her phone. With shaking hands, she pushed the SEND button.

"Arlo Pace just left a crack house on Eighth and Greenly," a muffled voice said.

Jim walked into the room tugging his jeans on and whispered, "Who is it?"

Vicky held up a hand and pressed the phone tighter against her ear. "I can barely hear you."

"Open your ears, goddammit. I don't have all day! Arlo Pace just left a crack house on Eighth and Greenly. He's driving a Pontiac Grand Prix, late model, dark blue, maybe black. I got his plate number."

"Are you sure it was Pace?" Vicky cradled the phone on her shoulder and pulled her notepad and pen from her purse.

"I ain't seen him since he's been out of the joint, and I didn't ask for no fuckin' ID," the caller said. "But I'm ninety percent sure it was him."

Vicky scrawled the plate number down and repeated it back to her caller. He hung up without confirming the number or saying good-bye.

Within minutes every patrol car on the street was hunting for the dark-colored Grand Prix. Of course, Frank Paxton wanted to know where Vicky had gotten the tip. She'd simply said it was anonymous, though, in fact, she did know who it was from. Louie Patella had come through for her after all, but he had risked life and limb to do it. She would never betray him, not even to someone she trusted as much as Frank.

It had been a helluva night for Officers Russ Selby and Manny Esposito. They weren't even halfway through their twelve-hour shift and they'd already had two domestics, one attempted suicide and a knifing at T.J.'s Pub over—of all things—a pinball game.

In between calls they'd kept their eyes peeled for the dark-colored Grand Prix. The call had gone out over the radio at one that morning. It was nearly 6:00 A.M. now, and there hadn't been a sign of it.

"I could go for a coffee and a couple of egg sandwiches," Selby said, stifling a yawn. "How about making a stop at the Burger Barn?"

Esposito grimaced. "That food tastes like shit."

"Yeah, but it's quick, and it'll help get us through the rest of our shift."

Esposito shrugged and headed in the general direction of the Burger Barn as they continued checking license plate numbers. He pulled into the Burger Barn's lot and headed for the drive-thru. They'd eat in the car with the engine running in case they got another call.

"I'll buy this time," Selby said, digging in his wallet.

Esposito wasn't paying attention; he was checking out the black Grand Prix parked on the other side of the lot. "Shit, I don't believe it."

"What?" Selby's head snapped up.

"We've got Pace." Esposito nodded in the direction of the car.

Selby reached for the radio to call for backup. "Do you think he has the Langford kid with him?"

"Christ, I hope not." Esposito made the sign of the cross. "Things could get ugly."

Arlo Pace was stuffing a hash brown patty in his mouth when he glanced in his rearview mirror and saw the cruiser coming toward him.

"Fuck," he spat, spraying the windshield with bits of potato and flecks of ketchup. He didn't think anyone would make him in this ride.

The cruiser stopped twenty feet behind the Grand Prix. Doors flew open as Selby and Esposito crouched behind them for cover. Esposito got on the loud speaker. "Step out of your vehicle with your hands in the air."

"Fuck you!" Arlo shouted. Tossing the food on the floor, he gunned the engine and shot across the lot to the exit. Another cruiser arrived, blocking his escape and Arlo slammed on the brakes. Cutting the wheels sharply to the right, he hit the gas and bumped across the concrete parking blocks that separated the Burger Barn's lot from the strip mall next door. He roared across the asphalt and out onto Davenport Avenue with the cops right behind him. He led them down alleys and up side streets as speedometers crept toward ninety.

Glancing in the rearview mirror, Arlo laughed. He was gaining distance and feeling like a regular Mario Andretti behind the wheel.

He headed for an industrial complex where he was certain he'd be able to lose his pursuers in the winding streets. He didn't count on the semi that was lumbering out as he was about to turn in. Still doing close to ninety, Arlo let out a scream and slammed on the brakes sending the car spinning like a top across the pavement. His world blurred as the car flew toward a steep embankment. He frantically gripped the wheel, his mouth hanging open in terror.

"Fuck me!" Arlo screamed as the Grand Prix crashed through the guardrail and hit the black water below.

CHAPTER 16

Thanks to Louie Patella, the net was tightening like a noose around Arlo Pace. Vicky found little comfort in that, though. If the ex-con was on drugs now, he'd be more dangerous and unpredictable than ever.

Keep busy, keep moving, don't look at the clock.

That was the only way Vicky would survive until she had word on Pace.

There was one positive thing that had happened that morning. Shortly after she returned home, Bill Renfield called to tell her that Mary was showing signs of coming out of the coma. The doctors were cautiously optimistic about her recovery. Vicky said a silent prayer of thanks as she picked up Snowball and cuddled him.

Sunlight slanted into the family room through the French doors. Another long day stretched ahead. How would she get through it? How much longer would she have to survive without her little boy?

She felt the familiar lump rise in her throat and the hot prick of tears sting her eyes. God, she had thought losing Danny was the worst thing that ever happened to her. She was wrong. This was worse. Her heart was being torn apart bit by agonizing bit. Vicky could feel herself getting sucked into that dull black void that had been her life in the days after her husband's death. It had been Josh that kept her sane.

Knowing she was carrying a tiny life inside of her had given her hope—something to look forward to. After suffering through three miscarriages, Josh had been her little miracle, the child Vicky feared she and Danny would never have. But even as she'd built a new life with her little boy, she was always waiting for the other shoe to drop. Now it had. Vicky pressed her hand to her mouth to stifle her sobs.

Get going, find something to do before you dissolve into a puddle, she commanded herself.

She absently thumbed through an unopened stack of mail on her desk, thinking there was probably twice as much jammed in the mailbox. When was the last time she'd checked it, two days ago, three? She couldn't remember. One day was fading into the next. She'd check it now. She wanted to get out anyway. Since Josh's disappearance, the house made her feel claustrophobic. She went into the kitchen, plopped down in a chair and pulled on her Nikes, which earned her a dubious glance from Sam's relief, Kyle Donner. A stout, unpleasant man with graying hair, Donner acted as if he carried the weight of the world on his rounded shoulders. He hated assignments like this and didn't do anything to hide it. When he wasn't pouting like a spoiled child, he was heaving great sighs and looking at his watch. Putting down the issue of *Time* he'd been perusing, Kyle exhaled one of his long-suffering sighs.

"Where do you think you're going?" he asked, his tone as sour as his face.

"Down to check the mail."

"Neither of us should leave in case a call comes in, and besides, you're not supposed to go out of the house alone. You'll just have to wait."

"Kyle, I'm just going to the end of the driveway, not Yucatan." She pulled her coat from the back of the chair.

"In case you've forgotten, that's at least a block away and can't be seen from here because of the trees." He folded his arms on the table and looked at her over the top of his bifocals. "Let's get one thing straight, Mrs. Langford. You're not going to pull any stunts with me. I'm not Sam Walsh."

"No, you sure aren't. And the last I heard I wasn't under house arrest, either." Vicky headed out the front door, letting it slam behind her.

She sucked in deep breaths of frosty air trying to tamp down her irritation. God, she was so tired of people telling her what to do, watching every move she made. She toed a large chunk of gravel, sending it flying into the trees, then stopped and listened.

Except for the sound of chirping birds, it was so quiet Vicky could hear the sound of her own breathing. This place was so beautiful and peaceful. It had been a safe haven for her and Josh.

Not anymore.

Shuddering, she glanced at the spot where Officer Bettis' squad car had been parked the night he was murdered. Vicky knew in that instant she couldn't live here anymore. When Josh was back home she would put the old place on the market.

But what if Josh doesn't come home?

The thought burst into her conscious like a gunshot—sudden, violent, jolting. She tried to push it away, then realized that on some level it had been in the back of her mind since the morning Josh disappeared. The thought alone crushed her heart.

Vicky started walking again, head down, breathing hard. She'd seen talk shows with parents whose children were missing. Some were gone for years, and their parents still didn't know where they were or what happened to them. She had listened and cried, her heart aching. How did anyone face one day after another, not knowing where their children were or what happened to them?

God, please don't let me become one of them.

Emptying the silver-colored mailbox, Vicky started back up the drive. She was fanning through the assortment of bills and advertisements when she heard a car coming. Gil's blue Taurus pulled up alongside her. Her heart started to gallop as the passenger window slid down. Would this be good news or bad?

Gil leaned across the black leather seat and gave her a thumbs-up. "We got Pace!"

"Thank God," Vicky said, exhaling in relief. She climbed in beside Gil. "When? And why didn't anyone call?"

"Early this morning, and I told them not to. I wanted to tell you the good news myself and see how you were doing."

"Has he said where Josh is?"

"He hasn't said jackshit," Gil snorted. He put the Taurus in gear. "His car went out of control during a chase, and he went into the retention pond over in that industrial complex off Keene Avenue. He was half out of it when they fished him out of the drink, but that son of a bitch still had the presence of mind to say he wasn't talking until he saw his lawyer. He's at Westport General now. Frank and Jim are waiting to question him."

"You know he killed Lisa Murphy last night."

"I heard." He pulled up in front of the house and turned off the car. Lifting her chin, Gil examined the eggplant-colored ring of bruises around her throat. "He could have killed you, too. You were lucky. That was a really stupid thing to do, Vicky, going there by yourself like you did."

"Please. I don't think I could take another lecture right now, not even from you."

"Okay, we'll put this conversation on the back burner for the time being, but you're not off the hook yet, sweetheart." He slid an arm around Vicky and kissed her cheek. "And don't look so down. We've got Pace now, haven't we? Once he starts talking, everything else will fall into place. We owe a lot to the person who called you. Without that tip, he'd still be out there. So, who was it anyway? The caller, I mean."

Vicky shrugged a shoulder and stared at the stack of mail in her hands. "Like I told Frank, he didn't identify himself and I didn't recognize the voice."

"Come on, Vicky. We both know it was one of your snitches. Which one was it?"

Guilt nibbled at Vicky for lying, but she had to protect Louie Patella at all costs. If word got out he was the one who fingered Pace, his life would be worth less than nothing.

"I don't know, and does it really matter anyway? The important thing is the information helped us catch Pace."

"I guess you're right," he replied and stifled a yawn. "Say, you got any coffee? I could sure use some."

"You look like you could use some rest even more," she admonished. She hooked her arm through his as they climbed the stairs. "You look like hell. When was the last time you got some sleep?"

"You're a fine one to be telling me to get some rest. What about you? Raccoons don't have circles under their eyes like you've got, and I've seen corpses that have more color."

"That's one of the things I love about you, Gil. You always know just the right thing to say to a girl."

"Seems like McCann must be the one saying all the right things. One minute he's off the case, the next he's back on. What's up with that?"

"I made a huge mistake, but I'll tell you all about it over that cup of coffee." Vicky cast her gaze down at the floor as she pulled off her coat. "I only hope I can make it up to Jim."

"I wouldn't worry about it too much." Gil wrapped his arms around her and gave her a squeeze. "I have a sneaking suspicion he'll forgive you."

★ ★ ★ ★ ★

Edmond Grafton elbowed his way through the throng of reporters camped outside of Westport General wishing he was on a golf course in Myrtle Beach instead. A rowboat in the middle of the Atlantic would do just as nicely for that matter—anywhere but here. He should have listened to his father and become a plumber like him, but no. Not Edmond. He didn't want to get his hands dirty, so he'd become a lawyer instead and had to deal with a different kind of dirt. The irony of it would have made him laugh if he wasn't so damn scared right now.

Edmond scowled at the reporters who pressed closer around him. Thrusting microphones in his face, they shot questions at him.

"Have you spoken to Arlo Pace? Is Josh Langford still alive? Is it true that Richard Blackwell hired Pace to kidnap the Langford baby?"

The last question stopped Edmond dead in his tracks. Arlo Pace might be the one under arrest, but thanks to Vicky Langford the finger of suspicion was now pointing in Richard Blackwell's direction. The bottom line was Edmond was here, less as Pace's attorney, than he was to do damage control for Blackwell. Running a well-manicured hand through his auburn hair, he faced the cameras trained on him.

"Mr. Blackwell is not involved in, nor does he have any knowledge of the crimes that Mr. Pace is suspected of," Edmond said in a voice smooth as glass. "He extends his sincere sympathy to the families of the victims. Now, if you'll excuse me."

His statement started a whole new line of questions which Edmond ignored. There would be time for a question and answer session later. Right now he had more pressing matters to attend to. As he rode the elevator to the third floor, Edmond thought about Vicky Langford. She'd created far too many problems for the Blackwell organization over the last few years. Edmond knew Blackwell wanted her out of the way a long time ago, but her ties to the police department had kept her from having some unfortunate accident.

Edmond had a sneaking suspicion her days were numbered now, though, in spite of those connections. That, however, was none of his business. He had to worry about his own backside. If he wasn't able to clear Blackwell of suspicion, Edmond would be the one whose days were numbered.

Blackwell had dumped this entire mess in his lap and told him to fix it. How the hell was he supposed to do that? A child had vanished, a cop had been murdered and a woman had been brutally assaulted. Another had been killed last night. On top of that, there were rumblings that there would be a deeper probe into the murder of Ray Abrons, too.

Edmond hadn't asked Blackwell if he was involved in Josh Langford's abduction. It didn't matter. Guilty or innocent, Edmond was paid to do one thing—keep his client out of jail. And he'd been successful at that for the ten years he'd worked for Blackwell. This time around, though, he had a feeling the shit was going to hit the fan. A lot of futures hung in the balance, and whatever happened depended on Arlo Pace.

He didn't think the ex-con would give up Blackwell, but then Arlo never had so much at stake before. If he was offered immunity in exchange for information and his eventual testimony against Blackwell, he might just go for it. And if Richard went down, so would everyone else in the organization. Including Edmond. That thought made the ham sandwich he'd wolfed down on the drive over rumble furiously in his stomach.

Arlo knows Blackwell would have him gutted like a fish before he could testify, Edmond thought as the elevator doors slid open. *There's no way he would chance it—would he?* Edmond flipped his wallet open to show his identification to the two cops stationed outside of Pace's room. He was shoving it back in the pocket of his black suit jacket when the door was suddenly flung open. Surprised, he took a step back as Frank Paxton and another man stormed out of the room.

"Well, it's nice of you to finally show up, Grafton," Frank snapped.

"I don't appreciate the sarcasm, Chief Paxton." Edmond's face colored slightly. "I got here as quickly as I could. I certainly can't help it if I got tied up in court."

"What? Blackwell didn't demand that you put everything on hold to come here and counsel Pace?"

"Mr. Blackwell doesn't have anything to do with this. He isn't the one who contacted me, and I'm not here to represent him."

"Better make room in your schedule," Jim interjected. "That's going to change."

Edmond gave him a narrow look. "And you are?"

"Detective Jim McCann," Jim replied, not bothering to offer his hand to Edmond. "I'm in charge of the case."

The name registered immediately. This was the cop who'd paid the visit to Blackwell. Edmond had been briefed on him. New to the Westport force and someone Blackwell thought might be an asset. Time would tell. They'd keep an eye on McCann. If he really was interested in becoming a part of the organization as Blackwell thought, it would be imperative that McCann keep up a believable front. From his attitude and the look on his face, Edmond thought he was doing a pretty good job. He'd give Blackwell a full report on how things went with McCann today.

"If you're insinuating you're going to arrest Mr. Blackwell in connection with this case, you'd better have rock-solid evidence, Detective. We've been down this road before and there's never enough to build a case. Just ask the Chief here." Edmond shot

Frank a look. "I'm sure he'll be glad to brief you on the past follies of the Westport Police Department."

"Maybe it'll be different this time," Jim replied, his voice low and dangerous.

"Try if you want, but Mr. Blackwell is guilty of no wrongdoing," Edmond stated with just a touch of indignation. He reached for the door. "If you pursue this, I promise you'll have the mother of all lawsuits on your hands."

"We might not have enough on Blackwell right now, but we've got enough evidence to bury Pace, and we'll do it if he doesn't cooperate." Frank looked at his watch. "You've got thirty minutes with your client, Grafton. After that we're coming in, and Pace better have some damn good answers for us, starting with the whereabouts of Josh Langford."

"Thirty minutes!" Edmond gawked. "That's not enough time for everything I need to discuss with my client."

"Tough shit, that's what you're getting," Frank said. "We've wasted enough valuable time waiting for you. I suggest you don't waste any more, Counselor. The clock is ticking."

Arlo was busy shoveling in pot roast and mashed potatoes, his eyes glued to the TV when Edmond walked into his room. He was a sorry-looking sight with his right arm in a cast, a purple jaw and eyes that looked like someone had drawn rings around them with a black marker. Wiping his mouth with the paper napkin that was tucked into the neck of his hospital gown he asked, "What, no flowers? No get-well card?"

"Shut up, Arlo. I'm not in the mood for any of your bullshit." Edmond slapped the briefcase down on the bed, reached for the remote and shut off the TV.

Arlo jammed a chunk of buttered roll into his mouth and said, "Hey, talk to that prick Paxton, will ya, and see if I can have this damn cuff off my good wrist, while I eat? I'm gettin' a backache hunchin' over this tray table."

"I don't give a damn if you starve while you're cuffed to that bed." Edmond narrowed his eyes and ground his teeth as he glared at Arlo. "Thanks to your colossal screw-ups we've got a mess on our hands, and there's no easy way out."

"Ah, it ain't so bad. They can't back up half the shit they're charging me with."

"Really?" Edmond lifted his brows as he popped open his briefcase. "Well, I've got news for you, Arlo. They do, and it's enough to make you a lifer this time."

"For what, makin' a few phone calls, carryin' a piece?"

"They weren't just phone calls dammit, they were ransom demands," Edmond shouted, then dropping his voice, added, "What the hell were you thinking? Mr. Blackwell didn't get you out of prison so you could kidnap Josh Langford."

"I didn't take that kid, so don't get your drawers in a bunch, Counselor," Arlo said, pointing his plastic fork at Edmond. "The cops are yankin' your chain. They got zip."

"Zip, huh? They found stolen goods from the Renfield house in your room at the Oak Ridge Arms. That puts you at the crime scene. That makes you the one who assaulted Mary Renfield and abducted Josh Langford. It's all right here." He tossed a copy of the police report at Arlo.

Arlo tossed it back at him with a glare. "I don't care what this fuckin' report says. I ought to know what I did or didn't do, goddammit!"

"You listen to me, you worthless idiot. Your neck is on the line because of this shit and that's just fine with me, but now Richard Blackwell's neck is on the line, too."

Every muscle in Arlo's body visibly tensed. "What are you talkin' about?"

"Thanks to Vicky Langford, the police think Mr. Blackwell hired you to abduct her son. They're watching him like a hawk."

Edmond pulled the orange-vinyl guest chair alongside the bed. "Have they talked to you about a deal?"

"Paxton mentioned some crap about the State's Attorney goin' easier on me if I'd be willing to testify against Mr. Blackwell, but I'd never rat him out," Arlo said anxiously. "He knows that, don't he?"

For the first time Edmond could recall, he saw a flicker of fear in Arlo's eyes. No worries here. Arlo's lips were zipped. There really was a God, and he had just smiled on Edmond.

He gave Arlo a reassuring pat on the arm. "Of course Mr. Blackwell knows that. You're one of his most trusted employees."

"Fuckin' A, man," Arlo said, relaxing a little. "I did everything I was told. I took care of that dickwad Peter Murphy, and everybody else I was supposed to. Blackwell wouldn't hold it against me 'cause I didn't get to clip the Langford bitch."

"I don't want to know anything about what you were supposed to do. What I do want to know is why you involved this other man. Where did you find him and have you told him anything that could hurt Mr. Blackwell?"

"What the fuck is all this other man stuff? Paxton and McCann have been bustin' my balls about that all goddamn day."

"The police know you've been working with someone. He was with you at the Renfield house when you abducted Josh Langford. They have his blood and tissue samples. Just give him up and tell the police where he and Josh Langford are. It's the only way to end this and the only way to put Mr. Blackwell in the clear."

"I ain't got no name to give you." Arlo speared two quivering red cubes of Jell-O and popped them in his mouth. "This is a solo act."

"Why are you protecting him? Do you want to take the blame for everything yourself? They'll lock you up and throw away the key."

"You ain't gonna let that happen."

"This has gone beyond anything I can do, Arlo. You kidnapped a child, you murdered a cop! Did you really think you could walk away from that?"

"I'm tellin' you I didn't do any of that shit."

"You're saying this other man is responsible?"

"Yeah, that's exactly what I'm sayin', and I ain't takin' the rap for none of it."

"Well, for the time being you're the one the police have got, so you'd better start talking." Edmond leaned toward Arlo. "A name. That's all it will take."

"But . . ."

"No more buts, dammit! If you don't give this guy up you're fucked six ways from Sunday. The cops have Mr. Blackwell under surveillance and his phones are tapped. He's not a happy man, and you know what happens to people who make Mr. Blackwell unhappy."

Arlo's face turned as white as the mashed potatoes on his plate.

"I don't care how you do it," Edmond went on, "but you've got to convince the cops that Richard Blackwell is not involved in this. The only way to do that is to give up this other man and tell them where Josh Langford is. Do we understand each other? This ends today, Arlo, otherwise jail will be the least of your problems."

"None of this is working the way it was supposed to," Arlo blurted miserably. He fell back against the pillows and stared at the ceiling. "All I wanted was a little extra cash. I didn't think Mr. Blackwell would mind if I squeezed the Langford bitch for a little before I whacked her. Where the hell did I go wrong?"

"In a few minutes those two cops are going to come back in here and they're going to expect answers," Edmond said. "Given your position, I'd suggest you give them your full cooperation."

Arlo continued staring at the ceiling. "Man, some choice I gotta make, huh? Get whacked or go to prison. If I tell the truth, you could cut a deal for me, and I wouldn't have to go away for that long, right?"

"I promise I'll do my best for you." Edmond leaned back in the chair, relaxing for the first time since he'd gotten the call about Arlo.

"I guess doing time is better than what I'll get if I fuck this up, huh?" Arlo snorted. "Okay, I'll tell the cops everything I know."

Frank Paxton leaned over the footboard of the hospital bed and glowered at Arlo Pace. Frank's face was red, and the vein in his neck was pulsing like a live wire. "I hope you've enjoyed the little bit of freedom you've had, you sorry son of a bitch, because you're going down."

"This is what I get for cooperating?" Arlo shouted, his blackened eyes darted from Frank Paxton to Edmond Grafton. "I thought we had a deal."

"There was a deal if you told the truth, dickhead," Jim interjected.

"It happened just like I said."

"So let me get this straight." Jim folded his arms and leaned against the windowsill. "You started following Vicky Langford a couple of weeks ago, and you just happened to notice someone else following her, too."

"Yeah, that's right."

"And, of course, you didn't recognize him."

"Nope," Arlo said, picking at his teeth with his thumbnail. "Anyway, the morning all this shit went down, I followed Langford as usual and right after I parked, this other car showed up and parked a couple of doors down from that Renfield chick's house. After Langford left, the other guy just sat there, so I decided to hang around."

"How long, Pace?" Jim asked.

"Three hours maybe."

"What was he doing all that time?"

"Spankin' the monkey," Arlo drawled. "How the hell should I know? I wasn't in the fuckin' car with him. He just sat there."

"And you hung around all that time. Since when did you become part of the neighborhood watch?" Frank asked. "Why didn't you follow Vicky like you'd been doing?"

Arlo shrugged. "I wanted to see what the fuck he was up to. I know this dude has been on Langford like flies on shit, then all of a sudden he's hanging around this house instead. I figured he was gonna rob it, and if I followed him when he left, I'd be able to, uh, you know, convince him to split with me."

"But he came out carrying Josh Langford instead of the silver," Frank said flatly. "So what did this guy look like?"

"I'd say he was in his twenties, maybe six feet or so with short, dark hair. He was driving a beat-up Chevy Caprice."

"Why didn't you follow him?" Jim asked.

"What the hell was I gonna do with a kid?"

"So you went into the Renfield house instead and robbed it."

Arlo held up his hands in supplication. "Hey, when opportunity knocks."

"And what was Mary Renfield doing while you helped yourself to her things?" Jim asked. The muscle in his jaw worked and his eyes grew dark with anger.

"Not a goddamn thing. Her head was mashed potatoes by that time, know what I mean?"

"You fucking worthless piece of crap." Jim's pulse roared in his ears as he pictured Pace kneeling beside Mary's still body, reaching for the gold chain around her neck. His anger picked up momentum as he stalked to Pace's bedside and glared at him, his chest heaving. "Now, let me tell you what really happened. Richard Blackwell wanted Vicky Langford out of the way, so he hired you and your partner to take care of the job, but then you two got this brainstorm to kidnap her son. That way you'd get ransom money from her, as well as whatever Blackwell was paying you to whack her. And what would Blackwell care as long as the job got done, right?"

"Blackwell ain't got nothin' to do with this," Arlo said. His gaze slid nervously to Edmond, then back to Jim. "I ain't even talked to him."

Jim went on, ignoring Arlo's protests. "You played your cat-and-mouse game with Vicky Langford for weeks and when the time was right, you went into Mary Renfield's house, beat her, ransacked her house and took Josh Langford."

"I swear to God I never laid a hand on that broad, and I didn't take that kid!"

"You made a ransom demand!" Frank said, slamming his fist on Pace's tray table.

"I figured it was worth a shot. That other guy did the work, but maybe I could pick up the payoff. I had nothin' to lose by makin' a phone call," Arlo reasoned. He gulped down a glass of water and wiped his mouth with the back of his hand. "From the sound of Langford's voice and the things she said, I knew the other guy hadn't contacted her, so I'm thinkin' I got it made. Get a cool half mil and I'm outta there."

"But the drop was botched and you never got your money," Frank said.

Arlo narrowed his eyes. "That fuckin' bitch screwed things up for me again."

"You wanted revenge on her. That's what this was all about, Pace," Frank said. "You blamed Vicky Langford because you went to prison and you were going to make her pay."

"Hell, yes, I wanted to make her pay! Do you know what it's like to be locked up like an animal? She stole ten years of my life. She owed me, and the way I saw it, half a mil could even the score."

"So this is all just a misunderstanding then, is that it?" Jim asked, his voice low, teeth clenched. "You didn't kidnap Josh Langford, you just made the ransom demand. You didn't try to murder Mary Renfield, you just robbed her. And, of course, you didn't kill Clark Bettis, either. The other guy did all of it, but you don't know who he is."

"Now you're finally startin' to get the picture."

"Where the hell is Josh Langford?" Frank bellowed, clenching his fists.

"You tell me," Arlo said. "You're the one with all the answers."

Edmond squeezed Arlo's shoulder. "Remember our conversation, Mr. Pace."

"Well, fuck," Arlo exclaimed, twisting from Edmond's grasp. "I'm telling the truth, but they don't want to believe a goddamn word I'm sayin'."

"You wouldn't know the truth if it jumped up and bit you in the ass," Frank said, waving his hand in the air.

Edmond Grafton cleared his throat. "All right, gentlemen, I think you've badgered my client enough. He's told you everything he knows."

"I'll say when we're through, Counselor," Frank snapped. "And we're far from it. You assured us your client would cooperate, and he hasn't given us one piece of information that will help us locate Josh Langford."

"I told you what happened that day, and I even described the dude for you. I can't help it if I didn't get right up in his face and take a fuckin' picture," Arlo protested.

"Your so-called description doesn't mean squat, Pace," Frank growled. "You probably heard it on the news. The bottom line is you're the one we have right now, and you're the one taking the fall for everything. As soon as the doc gives us the high sign, you're out of here and back in the can, you—"

A pager bleated, cutting off the rest of Frank's retort. Frank, Jim and Edmond all reached for theirs in unison.

"It's mine." Frank looked at the display window with a start then up at Jim. "We've got to go."

Without another word they headed for the door.

Arlo's mouth dropped and his eyes darted wildly to his lawyer. "Wait! I'm tellin' the truth. You gotta believe me."

Frank turned around and pointed a finger at Arlo. "You're done. I'm burying you, Pace."

Dark Man turned up the volume on the TV and leaned forward in his chair. A suspect had been arrested in the Josh Langford kidnapping case early that morning. Arlo Pace was in Westport General under police guard.

"Idiots!" He threw his head back and laughed. The noise startled Josh who had been dozing in the playpen. He sat up, rubbing his eyes and started to whimper like a kitten. Dark Man turned the volume higher to drown out his cries.

The cops think they're so smart. Just like Vicky Langford. Well, none of them are as smart as me, and they'll all know that when this is over.

Chapter 17

"Okay, baby, you're into me for six grand. Let's go another round."

Vicky heard the slap of the cards as Sam dealt another hand at the kitchen table. Thank God he was back. It was a small blessing, but she would take all she could get right now. She glanced at the clock on the nightstand and frowned. Pace had been in custody for hours. Why hadn't she heard anything yet?

A lifetime had passed since Josh's disappearance. Every minute that went by felt like a slow torturous death for her. Her mind was spinning with agonizing questions. Was Josh cold and hungry? Was he crying for her? Tears scalded her cheeks and she wiped them away. They had finally gotten the break they'd been waiting for. She had to stay focused on that—stay positive for Josh's sake.

She went into the bathroom and splashed cold water on her face. She was reaching for a towel when the doorbell rang. Face still dripping, Vicky raced down the hall and ran in to Sam who grabbed her by the arm.

"Let me check it out." He went to the living room window and nudged back the curtain. "It's a delivery service. You expecting anything?"

"No," Vicky replied.

Sam opened the door and examined the brown envelope the courier handed him. "It's from Warren Mott, so it's nothing good."

Vicky signed for it anyway and headed to the kitchen with the envelope. Inside was a copy of the *Banner* and a note that Vicky read aloud:

> I know I don't have to remind you that tonight marks the seventh anniversary of Connie Springer's death, but I will anyway. Here is a copy of my article hot off the press for this evening's edition.
>
> Happy anniversary, Warren.

"Slimy bastard," Sam spat. "I've scraped shit off my shoes better than him. What's this all about anyway?"

"He's been doing a series for the *Banner* on private citizens injured during police pursuits." Vicky tossed the paper and note on the table. "This is the last and 'the best installment in the series,' as he put it the other night. It's about Connie Springer."

"What a crock," Sam grumbled, checking the pot bubbling on the stove. "Hey, Dalila, the chili is hot. Why don't you clear the table and I'll dish some up for all of us."

Dalila scooped up poker chips and cards, put them back in a drawer, then sat at the table and opened the paper. Warren's article was a two-page spread complete with pictures of Connie Springer, her funeral, and a recent shot of Alice Graham putting flowers on her daughter's grave. He even managed to dig up a picture of Vicky taken just a few months before the shooting. There she was in her uniform shaking hands with the mayor as she received a commendation for pulling a man from a burning vehicle. The caption under it read, "Save a life, take a life; it's all in a day's work for the Westport PD."

Vicky swallowed hard over the lump in her throat. She wondered what horrid things lived inside of Warren Mott that would cause him to be so cruel. He did this series more as a way of taunting her than revealing any negligence or wrongdoing within the police department. The timing was just too perfect to be anything else.

"Connie Springer was a real looker," Sam said, glancing at her photo as he set the steaming bowls on the table.

"Yes, she was," Dalila agreed, looking at Connie's photo. "Such a tragedy to die so young."

Vicky stiffened. Sam shot Dalila a look. "Why don't you toss that crap where it belongs?"

"Of course," Dalila said, folding the paper and shoving it into the trash can. Her brow furrowed with concern as she looked at Vicky and gave her arm a squeeze. "I hope I didn't upset you. I didn't mean anything by what I said."

"I know, Dalila," Vicky replied, her voice cracking. "And you're right. It was a tragedy for everyone concerned."

"Warren certainly knows how to go right for the jugular, doesn't he?" Dalila shook her head, spooned up some chili and blew on it. "Why don't you eat before it gets cold?"

Vicky raised a full spoon but couldn't manage to get it past her lips. Her stomach knotted at the aroma of spices and tomatoes. She put the spoon back in her bowl.

Pushing away from the table, she went to the window and looked out. It was raining again, and the heavy black clouds that covered every square inch of sky didn't hold any promise of it stopping. Seven years ago on this day it had rained nonstop, too. A cold rain that started to freeze, coating everything in a thin layer of ice as temperatures plummeted.

Memories spun through her mind like a video on fast-forward. Her jumping out of the squad car to chase Ronnie Volkers who had just robbed a liquor store and shot the owner. Volkers stopping to take a shot before disappearing into an alley. The screech of tires as her partner floored the squad car to head Volkers off at the other end. Vicky pulling her gun, slipping and sliding, trying to run. Connie and Bud Springer stepping into the alley from a gangway. Vicky hitting an icy patch of cracked asphalt, everything seeming to be in slow motion as she fell. The crack of gun fire as her weapon discharged the fatal bullet. Connie Springer crumpling to the ground.

Vicky sucked in a ragged breath and wiped the tears that rolled down her cheeks. "Maybe Alice Graham is right," she said.

"What's that, kid?" Sam asked, looking at her.

"Maybe Josh's kidnapping is my punishment for what happened to Connie Springer."

"Come on, you're not being punished for anything," Sam said. He got up and awkwardly put an arm around her.

"Oh, but I am," Vicky insisted. "That's what revenge is all about, Sam. And make no mistake about it, the only reason Josh was taken was for revenge."

But whose, Vicky thought. Blackwell's, Mott's, Graham's? There could be a dozen people out there somewhere who want to get back at me for arrests I made, or stories I did.

Taking her by the arm, Sam guided her to a chair. "Come sit down and try to take it easy."

"Detective McCann is going to call any minute and tell us Josh is safe and sound," Dalila said, spooning up chili. "You have to believe that."

"It's taking too long," Vicky said. "If Pace said where he's got Josh, we would have heard by now."

"You mustn't give up hope," Dalila said. "There were so many times I felt like giving up when I was searching for my Abby, but just when I thought I'd never find her—bam—it happened. And that's the way it will happen for you with Josh. You're going to see him again soon, Vicky. I guarantee it."

Frowning, Vicky bit her bottom lip, trying to put a lid on the irritation she suddenly felt. She knew Dalila was trying to make her feel better, and God only knew what Vicky would have done without her these last few days, but Dalila's comparison of her experience to Vicky's struck a raw nerve. Dalila's ordeal had been heart-wrenching to be sure, but there was a world of difference between knowing your child was being loved and cared for versus having him in the hands of a maniac. Vicky was about to point that out when there was another knock at the door.

"I hope it's Detective McCann this time!" Dalila exclaimed.

"If it's not, I'm going down to that hospital myself," Vicky said, following Sam down the hall. Her shoulders sagged with relief when Sam opened the door and Jim was standing there. She went to him, her eyes searching his face. "Why didn't you call? I've been going out of my mind. What did Pace say?"

The look in his dark, tired eyes told her all she needed to know. Panic tightened icy fingers around her heart. Her legs turned to jelly and buckled beneath her. Jim caught her and helped her to a chair in the living room.

"Put your head between your knees," Dalila said, scurrying from the room. She returned a moment later with a damp washcloth that she placed on the back of Vicky's neck. Vicky gritted her teeth against the black dots that danced before her eyes and the sudden nausea that came all the way from her toes. This was all just part of the same bad dream. She should have known it would be this way.

"He totally denies having anything to do with the kidnapping, honey," Jim said, kneeling beside her.

"If he's so damned innocent, then why were Mary's necklace and wedding ring found in his room at the Oak Ridge? Frank called and told me that himself." Adrenaline and anger pushed Vicky unsteadily to her feet. "And why would Pace make a ransom demand if he didn't take Josh?"

"I know you've got a million questions, and I'll answer all of them on the way down to the station, if you think you're up to making the trip."

"Down to the station for what? What else happened, Jim?

What did Pace tell you?"

"This has nothing to do with Pace. Frank got a nine-one-one page while we were at the hospital. The principal of Kennedy High School, a Wes Heinrich, called the station this afternoon about a group of boys who went to Kennedy a few years back. They all had wolf tattoos like the one Corky Higgins described."

"The information on the tattoo was released days ago!" Sam interjected. "Why did he wait so long to call in?"

"He called before, but it takes time to sift through everything coming in. Thank God Heinrich had the sense to call again today when he didn't hear back from us."

"Do we know who these kids are?" Vicky asked anxiously.

"He all but handed them to us on a silver platter, and you're never going to guess who one of the kids was," Jim said, his eyes locking on Vicky. "Bud Springer."

"What?" she breathed.

"But I thought Vicky said Bud Springer was dead," Dalila said, blinking rapidly. "Why would that mean anything?"

"Maybe Springer planned this whole thing with his friends before he was killed and they followed through with it," Vicky said. "How long is it going to take to bring them in?"

"We're bringing one in to the station now and we've got uniforms out looking for the rest. Once they're all rounded up, we'll put them in a lineup and see if Higgins can identify one of them as the guy who bought that old Chevy from him."

Vicky went to the front hall and pulled on her jacket. She had her hand on the doorknob when Jim stopped her. Worry lines creased his face. "Are you sure you're up to this? I knew you'd want to be there for the interview. That's why I came by instead of calling, but you look like you're about to collapse."

"Just try and keep me away."

"Detective McCann is right," Dalila said. "You really don't look well at all. Why don't you wait here? He'll call you as soon as he has any news, and if you still want to go to the station, I'll take you there myself."

"Thanks, but I'd rather be there to hear what this kid has to say," Vicky said, opening the door. "You can come with us if you'd like."

"I really think you should stay here," Dalila said sharply.

"I'll call you as soon as I hear anything," Vicky replied.

Kenny Woods slouched in a metal chair in the interrogation room, jaw clenched, arms folded tightly across his narrow chest. Vicky studied the angry young man from behind the two-way mirror. His face was gaunt and framed by stringy brown hair that reached past his bony shoulders. Two silver rings adorned his right eyebrow. Another was hooked through his bottom lip. All in all, Woods was a far cry from the strapping guy with the crew cut Higgins described, but even if he wasn't the one who bought the old Chevy, that didn't let him off the hook for the kidnapping. Not by a long shot.

Barely past his twenty-first birthday, Woods had already had several brushes with the law. Frank had told her Woods was considered to be well on his way to serious trouble. Vicky perused the report on him. There had been time spent in the juvenile detention center, and his high school career was littered with everything from truancy problems to violence. He was a follower, the principal had told Frank Paxton, and he'd worshipped Bud Springer. Did Woods worship him enough to carry out Springer's wishes for revenge?

The door to the interrogation room opened and a detective stepped inside. He flashed Woods a warm smile and extended his hand. "Hey, Kenny, how're you doing? I'm Detective Fletcher."

Woods kept his arms firmly crossed. Perspiration soaked the

underarms of his tattered black T-shirt. Fletcher shrugged and asked if he could get anything for him, soda, coffee, a sandwich.

"I just wanna get the fuck outta here." Woods shifted uneasily in his chair. Shit, the cops were probably at the old warehouse on the edge of town right now going over it with a fine-tooth comb. He could kiss his ass good-bye, that was for sure. Why the hell did he let himself get mixed up in this shit, anyway?

"Cooperate and you could be out of here in less than an hour." Woods looked up as Fletcher sat across the table from him. "Where were you last Tuesday morning, Kenny?"

"What difference does it make?" Woods asked with a cockiness he didn't really feel.

The door opened again and another detective strode in, letting it bang shut behind him. With his bloodshot eyes and dark stubble covering his face, he looked like ten miles of rough road.

Fletcher introduced Detective Jim McCann to Kenny and said, "I was just asking Kenny where he was last Tuesday morning."

"So how about it?" Jim paced behind Woods, his hands at his hips. "Where the fuck were you?"

"At home, sick."

"Your boss down at Whittleton Shipping says you've been off a lot this week," Jim went on.

"I told you, I've been sick." Woods tossed a defiant scowl over his shoulder at Jim.

"You have someone to back up your story, I suppose."

"Sure, my old man was there, drunk as usual. He'll be glad to vouch for me."

"Look, Kenny," Gil said, leaning back in his chair. "There's no need to be so defensive. You're not in trouble. Just answer the questions."

Gil pulled out a pack of cigarettes, shook one out and held it out to Woods. Woods hesitated, looking at him suspiciously through his veil of stringy hair. He finally accepted the smoke and light Gil offered.

"We'd like to take a look at the tattoo on your bicep," Gil said.

"I don't have to let you look at shit. In fact, I don't even have to talk to you if I don't want to."

"Roll up your sleeve, Kenny," Jim said flatly.

"Fuck you. I'm outta here." Woods started to get out of the chair.

Jim shoved him back down and leaned over him. The scent of sweat and fear rolled off of Woods.

"We can make this as hard as you want, you worthless little prick," Jim said, grinding his teeth. "Now roll up your goddamn sleeve."

"You're a psycho, you know that?"

"You don't want to know how much of a psycho I really am."

"I'll have to take the shirt off," Kenny said. Standing, he tugged it over his head. Glaring at Jim, he thrust forward his bony arm. A two-headed wolf with bright red blood dripping from its fangs decorated his right bicep—exactly as Corky Higgins had described it. "Now are you satisfied?"

"Kenny, what kind of car do you have?" Gil asked.

"I don't. I can't afford to buy no car," Woods snorted. He pulled the shirt back on and plopped back down in the chair. "My old man drinks up most of my paycheck every week."

"You don't have an '87 Chevy Caprice?" Jim asked.

"Do you need a fucking hearing aide, or what? Didn't you hear what I just said?"

"Listen dickwad." Jim grabbed a fistful of Kenny's shirt and hauled him to his feet. "I'll mop this goddamn floor with your scrawny ass."

"Let me go!" Woods shouted. His eyes darted back and forth

between the two detectives. His mouth was dry, his pulse throbbing in his ears.

Gil jumped up from his chair. "Take it easy, McCann."

Jim scowled at Woods, then tossed him back down in the chair.

"Sorry, Kenny," Gil said. "It's just that this case has got everyone on edge."

"What case is that?"

"The big kidnapping we're working on. You must have heard about it."

"That baby that got snatched the other day?"

"That's right," Gil said. "His mother is Vicky Langford. Have you ever heard her name before?"

"I don't know." Woods played absently with the ashtray on the table.

"Sure, you've heard of her," Jim said, pacing again. "Your pal Bud Springer blamed Vicky Langford for his mother's death, didn't he?"

"What the fuck, man, wouldn't you?" Woods looked at Jim incredulously. "I mean she gunned Bud's ma down in cold blood."

"He ever talk about getting even with Vicky Langford?" Jim asked. He stopped pacing and leaned over Kenny's chair.

"I don't know. Kids say shit, you know."

"What kind of shit, Kenny?" Gil asked.

"Like he hated her guts, and he was gonna make her pay for what she did."

"Did Bud have a wolf tattoo like yours?"

"Yeah, a bunch of us got 'em back in high school."

"A bunch meaning you, Bud Springer, Cal Brookman, Tony North, and Gabe Wilkins?"

Woods nodded. "We all hung out."

Jim mentally flipped through the notes on Woods and the

other three boys. All were loners, kids who had been singled out their whole lives, picked on, until they fell in with Bud Springer. Bud had surrounded himself with misfits eager to belong and please.

"Bud didn't make fun of you like everybody else did," Jim said. "And once you started hanging around with him, nobody bothered you anymore. You looked up to him."

"Maybe a little." Woods took one last pull on his cigarette and stubbed it out. "We all did. He was a cool dude. I felt real bad when he went and got himself toasted like he did in that car crash."

"We hear he was the leader of this little gang of yours. What did you call yourselves, the Young Wolves?"

"It was just kid stuff."

"You call vandalizing teachers' cars and going after your classmates with baseball bats kid stuff?" Gil arched a brow as he leaned on the table and folded his arms.

"It ain't the way you're making it sound," Woods protested.

"Sure it is. Bud would get pissed off at somebody and send his four goons to take care of it. You'd do anything he asked, Kenny," Jim said. "You're a 'yes' man."

"I'm nobody's fucking 'yes' man," Woods sulked. "And I don't know where the fuck you're going with this or why you're asking all these questions about Bud. That was a long time ago, and he's dead. What does he have to do with anything anymore?"

"You guys still hung out together after high school," Gil said.

"We'd play pool, go to the drag races, shit like that."

"And maybe steal a few cars, strip 'em down and sell em for parts?" Jim asked.

Oh, fuck, here it comes, Woods thought. All this crap about the Langford broad was just to rattle him so he'd crumble when they got to the real meat of the matter.

"I, I don't know what you're talking about. We never did

nothing like that," Woods insisted. He sat up straighter in the chair, his gaze darting from Jim to Gil.

"We know all about the chop shop, but that's small potatoes," Jim said. "Yeah, you guys took a quantum leap right to the big leagues with this one."

Woods turned and looked up at Jim. His breathing came fast and hard. Licking his cracked lips, he swallowed. "What quantum leap?"

"To murder and kidnapping," Jim replied.

"What?" Woods' eyes grew round and his heart fluttered sickeningly in his chest. "You got the wrong guy. I didn't kidnap or murder no goddamn body."

"Bud Springer wanted to make Vicky Langford pay for what happened to his mother. You said that yourself," Jim said, matter-of-factly. "You two were working something out, but then Bud was killed. That didn't stop you from going ahead with your plans, though, did it? After all, it was for Bud, right?"

"You're fucking nuts, you know that?" Woods snapped.

"You went to Mary Renfield's house last Tuesday morning, attacked her, left her for dead and took Josh Langford." Jim banged on the table with his fist. "That's what Bud wanted you to do. That's what he planned before he died, didn't he?"

"No! It wasn't me!" Woods looked like a cornered animal. All attempts at bravado were gone as he crumbled right before their eyes, sobbing.

Jim placed his hands flat on the table and glared at him. "Then who was it?"

"I don't know."

"If you want to take the rap for this, that's just fine with me," Jim said. "Let's see, you're what, twenty-one, twenty-two? You may get out of the joint by the time you're fifty—if you live that long, and if you don't screw up."

Woods dropped his head in hands, his shoulders heaving with

sobs. After a few moments, he wiped his eyes and nose on his sleeve and ran his hands through his hair. "Can I have another cigarette?"

"Sure, Kenny, no problem," Gil said, handing him the pack.

He lit up and blew the smoke out through his nostrils. "I'm telling you straight up, I don't know anything about what happened. All I know is Bud hated the Langford bitch."

"Did he ever say anything specific about what he wanted to do to her?" Gil asked. Woods didn't answer. Gil leaned across the table and spoke to him like they were coconspirators. "Look, Kenny, you've got to understand something. Maybe you didn't take Josh Langford, but you could be an accessory if you have knowledge of the crime. That'll get you hard time and you don't want that. A kid like you wouldn't survive in the joint twenty-four hours."

"But I didn't do it." Woods' eyes filled up again and his nose started running.

"Help us and we can help you," Jim said.

Woods' gaze darted from Jim to Gil. Leaning forward, he propped his elbows on the table and rested his forehead in his hands. His whole body shook.

"Maybe one of the other guys did do it," Woods conceded after a moment. He sat back in his chair, drew in a deep breath and looked Gil in the eye. "I really don't know, and that's the truth."

"If we had to look at one of your friends for this, which one would it be?"

Kenny stubbed out his cigarette and reached for the pack again with trembling hands. He didn't answer.

"If you're worried about someone coming after you, Kenny, we'll give you protection. You've got my word," Gil assured him.

"You don't understand," Kenny said. "He's crazy. I mean really crazy."

"Tell us, Kenny, or you're an accessory," Jim reminded him. "And if you think this guy would do a number on you, wait until you get inside."

Kenny swore under his breath and looked up at the two detectives, his nose running, tears rolling down his cheeks. "Cal Brookman. He was obsessed with Bud when he was alive. They were built alike and sort of looked alike to begin with, but then Cal started dressing and acting the way Bud did, too. He even got the same haircut. Bud thought it was funny, but since he died, it's gotten worse. It's like Cal thinks he *is* Bud. To tell you the truth, it freaks me out."

"Brookman would be capable of committing these crimes?"

"Without a doubt, man."

"When was the last time you saw him?" Gil asked.

Woods wiped his nose with the sleeve of his T-shirt again. "I don't know. It's been a while—a couple of months maybe."

"He still lives at home with his parents?" Gil asked.

"Last I heard he was renting a house over on the east side."

"What does he look like?" Jim asked.

"I just told you. He looks like Bud. Here." Woods rummaged through his shabby wallet and pulled out a photo of five young men, arms slung over each other's shoulders. "That's Cal and Bud on the end."

"They could be brothers," Gil observed. "And he sure as hell looks like he could be the guy Corky Higgins described."

Kenny shoved his wallet back in his pocket. "I'll tell you who else you should look at, too."

"Who's that, Kenny?" Jim asked.

"Bud's grandmother. She's a crazy old bitch, and before he died, Bud told me they had a plan to get back at Vicky Langford."

Vicky paced Frank Paxton's office, too wired to sit. She wanted to scream and pound her fists against the wall. If she were still sane by the end of this day it would be nothing short of miraculous. Her nerves were in tatters, her patience worn down to the bone. Time was the enemy now, as much as Alice Graham and Cal Brookman.

Tears threatened again, and Vicky squeezed her eyes shut. Alice Graham's face with its cold, narrow eyes and tight mouth instantly loomed before her. Hatred had poisoned her soul and stolen every shred of joy from her life. That hatred had spread like a contagion to her grandson. It had festered in both of them until it drove them over the brink of reason. And what about Cal Brookman? He had to be as twisted as Alice and Bud to get involved in this. In his mind, was he now Bud Springer? Had Bud's revenge become his?

Vicky's cell phone rang. It was Dalila.

"Any news?" she asked.

Vicky gave Dalila the condensed version of what Kenny Woods had said.

"Gil and Jim are waiting to go to Alice Graham's, and Cal Brookman's, but Judge Warkowski is giving Frank a hard time about the warrants because of what happened with Warren Mott," Vicky explained. "Frank's been arguing with Warkowski for the last half hour. In the meantime, Alice and Cal probably have my son."

"Are you going with them when they finally get the warrants?"

"If I had my way about it I would, but Frank was adamant about me waiting until they know exactly where Josh is." Vicky choked back a sob. "God, every time I think about the possibility that Josh was at Alice Graham's while Jim and I were there the other day . . . I wonder did he hear my voice?"

"Don't torture yourself. He could be at Cal Brookman's, or they could be holding Josh someplace else altogether," Dalila pointed out. "Listen, it sounds like this could take a while, and I really don't think you should be alone. Why don't you wait it out at my place? I'll be glad to pick you up."

Vicky took only a moment to consider before accepting her offer. Dalila's house was closer to Alice Graham's than the station, so she'd be that much closer if Jim called from there.

Chapter 18

"Do you really think this Cal Brookman is in cahoots with Alice Graham?" Dalila asked. They were sitting at the dining-room table of Dalila's old Victorian house. Thunder rumbled, shaking the windows as she poured tea from a china pot.

"I don't know what to think anymore." Vicky wrapped her hands around the hot cup to warm them, but it did little to dispel the chill that had settled over her ever since she'd observed the interrogation of Kenny Woods.

"This Brookman guy sounds like he's deranged," Dalila said. "Do you suppose he really thinks he *is* Bud Springer?"

"It's possible, if everything Kenny Woods said is true." Vicky checked her watch and drummed her fingertips on the table. "I wish Jim would call. There should be teams on their way to Brookman's and Graham's by now. Jim called just before you picked me up to tell me Judge Warkowski was signing the warrants."

"I know waiting is hard, and I can see what a toll these last few hours have taken on you." Dalila bit her lower lip. "I'm so sorry I didn't go with you to the station. You shouldn't have been alone. It's just that I had some important personal things to take care of."

"You don't have to apologize. You've been a good friend. I don't know what I would have done without you through all of this."

"What are friends for?" She smiled and offered a plate of

butter cookies to Vicky. "Now drink your tea, it'll help you relax."

"Come on, dammit!" Jim pounded at the door of Alice Graham's white Cape. "Open up!"

Squad cars lined the curb. Patten Street was blocked off and everyone was in position. The wooden door shook as Jim banged on it again. The heavy red drapes at the living room window moved.

"Someone's home," Gil said.

Jim banged on the door once more, shouting, "Open up, or I'll break it down."

"Just a minute," came an indignant voice on the other side. The door opened a crack and Alice Graham peeked out at Gil and Jim. "What do you want? What's going on?"

"We're here to search your house, Mrs. Graham," Jim said, holding up his badge for her to see.

Flinging the door open, Alice Graham stepped outside. She pulled her gray wool cardigan tighter around her thin body. Her blue eyes were like blocks of ice. "Why are you doing this to me?"

"Lady, don't insult our intelligence," Jim said. Gun drawn, he stepped past her.

"What do you think you're doing?" Alice shouted. "You can't barge into my home! You don't have any right."

"Here's the warrant," Gil replied, holding up the papers. "And you can rest easy, Alice. I guarantee you're going to hear all about your rights in just a few minutes."

Turning to one of the patrolmen who followed him in, he added, "Baldwin, take her into the kitchen and keep an eye on her."

They searched the tiny house in a matter of minutes, but there was no sign of Josh. Jim and Gil met back in the candlelit living room looking defeated and frustrated.

"Jesus, this house is like a fucking shrine. Every room has pictures of Connie in it," Gil remarked. His gaze settled on the portrait over the mantel and he shook his head. "This broad is totally nuts."

"She's crazy all right," Jim agreed. "Like a fox."

Gil plowed his fingers through his hair. "Where do you suppose she's stashed Josh?"

"Unless there's a secret room somewhere, she doesn't have him here."

Jim went to the door and motioned for the evidence team to come in. Alice ranted from the kitchen as they began going through closets and drawers.

"I'll start going through the bedrooms with the techs if you want to talk to Smiley in there," Gil said, nodding toward the kitchen.

Officer Baldwin stepped aside to let Jim through, then stood just inside the doorway. Alice sat at the red Formica table, her face a mask of unconcealed rage. She waved her scrawny fist at Jim. "How dare you ransack my home. I didn't do anything to deserve this!"

"Where the hell is Josh Langford?"

"I don't know what you're talking about."

"You know, I've heard that a lot lately in connection with this case," Jim said. "Nobody knows a damn thing, but eventually everyone comes up with a little piece of the puzzle for us. Kenny Woods came up with one."

Alice canted her head. "That friend of Bud's?"

"He says you and Bud were planning on the old 'eye for an eye' with Vicky Langford."

"That skinny, little twerp is out of his mind. Where'd he get an idea like that?"

"He swears Bud told him." Jim leaned against the counter

and crossed his ankles. "Once Kenny started talking, we could hardly shut him up. He told us about Cal Brookman and how tight the two of you got after Bud's death."

"I never had anything to do with Cal. I didn't like any of that bunch my grandson hung around with." Alice's mouth twisted in distaste. "My Bud was a good boy, and they were a bad influence on him. They were always getting him into trouble."

"Sure they were, Alice."

"Hey, McCann, come here quick and check this out!" Gil shouted.

Jim found him in Bud's room. Gil thrust a photo at him as soon as he walked through the door. "I found this in the drawer of the nightstand. How the hell do you suppose Springer knew her?"

"What the . . . ?" Jim stared at the photo in disbelief. Then he compared it to the picture of Connie on the dresser and a cold chill settled deep in his bones. The women in both pictures had the same startling green eyes, the same heart-shaped face. The only thing different was the hair. Connie Springer's was blonde. The woman in the photograph with her arm around Bud Springer had hair that was raven black.

"This can't be," Jim gasped. "Oh, Christ, Vicky."

Heart galloping, he reached for his phone and punched in Vicky's cell phone number. Jim cursed himself for not noticing the resemblance before, but then he wasn't looking for it, either. What had he said the day they were here? Connie must have gotten her looks from her father. Wrong! She was the mirror image of her mother after all.

"I had a baby when I was sixteen," Dalila Sinclair had tearfully confided the night of Josh's abduction. "Her name was Abby, and my parents made me give her up for adoption."

"Come on, dammit, pick up," Jim growled. After six rings it went to voice mail. Dread washed over him. She would have answered her phone if she were able to. “Vicky’s with Dalila at her place.”

“So fill me in, McCann. How does she fit into this scenario?” Gil asked.

“I’ll explain everything, but we have to get units over there now.”

“I wish I knew what was going on.” The floor creaked as Vicky paced Dalila’s dining room. She checked her watch, then eyed her cell phone on the table. “I think I’ll try Jim.”

“Vicky, leave Detective McCann alone and let him do his job.” Dalila frowned and snatched the phone up as Vicky reached for it. “You have to be patient like I had to be.”

“What are you talking about?”

“When I was searching for Abby, of course,” Dalila exclaimed. Her mouth twisted into an angry red knot. “I told you that earlier at your house.”

“I’m sorry,” Vicky said sharply. The irritation she’d felt toward Dalila that afternoon returned, but Vicky reminded herself again of how helpful and supportive Dalila had been since Josh’s disappearance. Her tone softened. “I’m just worried.”

“Well, you don’t have to worry anymore. You and Josh will be together again. I guarantee it.”

“I hope to God you’re right.” Vicky looked at her watch again and held out her hand. “Give me my phone, please. I’m going to call Jim.”

Instead of handing over the phone, Dalila slipped it into the pocket of her purple tunic.

“What the hell are you doing?” Vicky looked at Dalila incredulously and started toward her. “Give me my phone.”

“You don’t need to talk to Detective McCann.” Dalila settled back against the Queen Ann chair, folded her arms and smiled at Vicky.

"Have you lost your mind?" Vicky asked, as puzzled as she was furious.

Chest heaving with anger, she shook her head and stalked to the kitchen to use that phone. She stopped short in the doorway. Her mouth went dry and her pulse roared in her ears. Sitting on Dalila's counter was the teddy bear music box that was taken from Mary's house the day Josh was kidnapped. There was only one way Dalila could have it, but that was impossible. What reason could she possibly have for doing such a horrible thing? Common sense warred with disbelief. Thunder cracked overhead and the cold wind moaned through the house as she slowly turned around. Nausea swept over her. Dalila was still seated at the table, but she had a gun trained at Vicky's head.

"Why, Dalila?" Vicky cried.

"You're being punished, just like you said this afternoon."

"For what? I'm your friend. What have I ever done to hurt you?"

Dalila's nostrils flared. Her jaw hardened. "You killed my daughter, and now I get to kill your son."

"What are you talking . . . oh my God." Vicky's breath left her in a whoosh. She reached with one hand for the buffet to steady herself as her other hand flew to her mouth. "Connie Springer?"

"Don't you dare call her that," Dalila shouted. Her hand tightened around the gun and her knuckles turned white. Her cheeks were flushed and her eyes shone like two bright green marbles. "Her name was Abby."

For a moment the room seemed to tilt, and Vicky felt as if she couldn't breathe. Her gaze darted toward the front hall and the staircase. Was Josh locked away in one of the upstairs rooms in this musty old house?

"Where's Josh?" Vicky started toward the front hall. "Josh!"

"Don't bother. He's not here."

Vicky leveled her gaze at Dalila and gritted her teeth. "Then where is he?"

"Safe and sound and waiting for his mama," Dalila replied in a sugar-sweet voice.

"So help me God if you hurt him . . ."

"Not to worry. We haven't touched a hair on his little blonde head," Dalila smiled. "We're saving that for later."

"Who's we? You and Cal Brookman?"

"Bingo!" Dalila exclaimed. "You see, Kenny Woods told the truth when he said Cal Brookman and Bud's grandmother were planning to take revenge on you. He just failed to tell you which grandmother."

"You'll never get away with this."

"Oh, honey, we already have." Dalila clucked her tongue and gave her a mock sympathetic look. "The wheels are in motion. There's no stopping us now."

"Take me to Josh."

"All in good time," Dalila said. "Cal's getting too anxious and hard to control. I'm afraid if I take you there too soon, he'll blow your brains out before I'm ready. I don't want that. I want to hear you beg for your son's life."

"What do you want from me?"

"What I want, you can't give me," Dalila said vehemently. "Unless, of course, you can raise the dead."

"I'm so sorry, Dalila."

"Sorry doesn't cut it. You didn't put a ding in my fender, or spill wine on my lace tablecloth. You killed my daughter."

Vicky's hands slapped against her thighs. "What happened to Con—Abby was a horrible accident. If I could go back and change what happened that night, I would."

"Alice and her husband took Abby all the way across the country to get away from me," Dalila said, her face crumbling. Tears ran down her heavily rouged cheeks. "All those years I spent searching and hoping, then I finally find her and she wouldn't even talk to me. Alice poisoned her mind against me. If I had had more time with her, I know I could have made her see how much I loved her, but a week later you took her away from me."

The words were like a spear that Dalila drove deeply into Vicky's heart. For the first time she looked into Dalila's eyes and saw the anguish of a mother's loss, but it was an anguish that had driven her over the brink of madness.

"Not a day has gone by that I haven't punished myself for what happened," Vicky said softly. Her legs felt wooden as she returned to the table and sat across from Dalila. "It doesn't change anything, and hurting Josh won't change anything, either."

"No, it won't." Dalila wiped her tears with the back of her hand. "So, I'll have to settle for the next best thing. I'm going to see the look on your face when you watch your child die."

"This is between the two of us, let Josh go, please."

"Not a chance. You know what's funny, though?" Dalila cocked her head to one side. "He wasn't even a part of this at first. Cal and I just planned to have some fun with you then blow your brains out, but a couple of weeks ago, on one of his nightly visits to your house, he came up with this wonderful idea about Josh, and I thought, how fitting. And I had the house to keep him at until we were ready."

"What house?" Vicky sat up straighter in her chair.

"A lovely A-frame on Pine Lake that I bought just for you." A sly smile tugged at Dalila's mouth. "You had half the police department camped out at Warren Mott's house, and all the time Josh was at my place directly across the lake. Cal and I got such a kick out of that."

Vicky dug her nails into the palms of her hands to keep from sighing in relief. At least she knew Josh was alive and where he was. Now all she had to do was get to him.

I'm coming, sweetheart. I promise mommy's coming.

"It was a pretty big risk buying a place so close to someone we both know," Vicky said, forcing herself to sound matter-of-fact. "What if Warren had spotted Josh?"

"I bought my place long before Warren bought his," Dalila said with a shrug. "And it really made no difference whether or not he knew about it as long as he didn't see Josh, and I can assure you he didn't. Cal is smart enough to keep the curtains drawn."

"How on earth did you convince him to get involved in something like this?"

"Piece of cake. Cal is unbalanced, to put it mildly." Dalila kept the gun pointed at Vicky as she sipped her tea. "He idolized Bud and wanted to please him, be like him, just as Kenny Woods said. Cal was devastated when Bud died, but he and I worked the Ouija board right at this table and with a little help from me, Bud told Cal that Bud's spirit was in him and that he had to carry out our plan."

"And Cal believed it."

"Completely."

Vicky clenched her teeth and covered her face with her hands. She thought of Mary who had been drawn into Dalila's plot for revenge simply because she knew Vicky. Then Officer Bettis' boyish face leapt into her mind. She looked at Dalila. "Cal murdered Office Bettis."

"He almost killed you that night. Cal said the urge was uncontrollable. He had to do something to satisfy it." Dalila shook her head and frowned. "Look at all of the innocent blood you have on your hands."

"Oh, God." Vicky's throat tightened and she felt the hot sting of tears again.

Dalila giggled as she eyed the teacup in front of Vicky. "I

wonder what Madam Zoya would say if she could read your tea leaves now. She was really very good—too good. I was so afraid she was going to ruin everything that I went looking for her right after she came to your house."

Vicky gasped, "Please tell me that you didn't hurt her, too."

"She'd already left town and I had no way to track her. Lucky for her."

"So many innocent people have been hurt already: Mary and her family, Officer Bettis and his. Don't add Josh to that list, please."

"Oh, cry me a river," Dalila said bitterly. "Do you really think I care about them? Did Alice and Ronald Graham feel bad for me when they took my baby and disappeared? Did my parents feel bad for me? No! I found out after you killed Abby that they knew all along where she was. They even had pictures of Bud that Alice sent them, but I made them pay for what they did."

"What are you talking about?" Vicky shifted uneasily in her chair.

"They were both killed in a horrible boating accident—with a little help from me."

Vicky sucked in a breath and suppressed a shudder. Dalila had killed her own parents with no more thought than she would a mosquito that landed on her arm.

Think what she'll do to Josh.

She fought hard against the nausea that crawled up her throat. She had to stay calm, had to stay focused. Josh's life depended on it.

"You certainly took your time for someone who was so hell-bent on revenge," Vicky said. "Why wait so long? What made seven the magic number?"

For the first time Dalila fell silent. Her gaze dropped to the table and her cheeks colored. She chewed her lower lip. "Things happened. I didn't have a choice."

"You had a breakdown, didn't you?" Vicky said quietly, though she suspected it was more than a breakdown. Dalila had probably been diagnosed as psychotic. "You were in a hospital."

Dalila's face turned stony. "Nearly six years, but it didn't stop me. As soon as I got out of the hospital I moved here, landed the job at the *Herald* so I could be close to you and put my plan into action."

"Did Bud welcome you with open arms?"

"Not quite," Dalila laughed bitterly. "Bud didn't want anything to do with me at first. He was all I had left, though, so I kept trying to see him until he finally broke down. I didn't want Alice to know I was living here, so we met secretly. The more time we spent together, the more he realized we both wanted the same thing, and that was to make you pay. We grew very close thanks to you. And then, of course, just when we started making our plans, he was killed."

Dalila glanced at her watch. "Time to go. We can finish our little talk in the car. Cal is waiting. I spoke to him just a little while ago and he said Josh has been crying for you."

Just then Vicky's phone rang.

Please let it be Jim, Vicky prayed. She held her breath and counted the rings. Four, five, six, then silence. He would know she was in trouble if she didn't answer. How long, though, before help arrived? She had to stall for time.

"Come on," Dalila said, getting up.

Vicky didn't move. Instead she leaned back in the chair. "Is Alice Graham involved in this? Did she help you?"

"Alice doesn't even know that I'm living in Westport," Dalila said. She motioned for Vicky to get up.

"What about Arlo Pace? How does he fit into this?"

"Whatever he was doing, he did on his own. In fact, once we realized he was after you, Cal started to panic. He was afraid Pace would get to you before we did, but Pace provided the ideal red herring. You were so focused on him and Blackwell, it made things easier for us. We planned the perfect crime. Who would ever suspect that I, your good friend from the *Herald*, had anything to do with it?"

"Perfect, until Kenny Woods pointed the finger at both you and Cal."

"Even if the police are smart enough to figure out it's me Kenny was talking about and not Alice, it doesn't matter. I'll still have my revenge and it really is sweet."

Trembling with rage, Vicky clenched her fists. She wanted to vault across the table and choke Dalila. How could she have been so unsuspecting, so naïve? She had invited this monster into her home. Dalila had even baby-sat for Josh a few times, and all the while she had been spinning this web of deceit to trap Vicky.

"Let's go, move it," Dalila said.

Vicky kneeled to tie her bootlace, trying to stall for time. She shifted her gaze to the heavy brass candleholders on the buffet. If she could divert Dalila's attention for just a second . . .

She glanced at the doorway behind Dalila and widened her eyes. Dalila craned her neck to see what Vicky was looking at. Vicky jumped up and grabbed the candleholder and flung it. Dalila spun around and fired just as the candleholder flew past her, narrowly missing her head. Vicky dropped to the floor as the mirror behind the buffet shattered, raining glass down on her.

"Killing you now isn't part of the plan, but I'm flexible so don't push me." Dalila pointed the gun at Vicky again. "I'm a pretty good shot and the next one will be right between those pretty brown eyes of yours if you try anything like that again. Now let's go."

Mind reeling, Vicky shook glass from her hair and carefully brushed it from her clothes. Dalila motioned with the gun for

Vicky to go in front of her.

When they reached the front hall Dalila said, “Put your hands against the wall and don’t move.”

Vicky did as she was told. Her purse was just inches from her feet. Glancing over her shoulder, Vicky watched Dalila slip on her coat. If only she could get to the ASP and pepper spray, but Vicky knew Dalila would drop her like a rock before she got the opportunity to use either. Maybe there would be a chance in the car.

“All right, you can put yours on now.” Dalila kept the gun on Vicky as she put on her jacket. She bent down to retrieve her purse and Dalila chuckled. “Bring it with you if you want, but your little arsenal of weapons is gone. I took the ASP and pepper spray and hid them earlier while you were in the bathroom.”

She tossed Vicky the keys to her VW. “You’re driving and I’m warning you, don’t try anything cute. If we don’t show up by midnight, Cal will assume something went wrong and he’ll kill Josh. I’d really hate for that to happen, because I want to see your tearful good-bye to your son.”

Dalila was right behind Vicky as she went down the steps and across the flagstone walk toward the driveway.

“Freeze! Drop the gun, lady!” Officers Nick Rizzo and Hank Baumann jumped out of the tall bushes beside the house, their guns pointed at Dalila.

She whirled around, her face contorted with rage.

“It’s over Dalila, just put the gun down,” Vicky said.

“It’s not over. Far from it! Today you’re going to find out what it feels like to lose a child and there’s nothing you can do to stop it.”

“Put it down, lady,” Rizzo ordered once more. “Don’t make things play out this way.”

“It doesn’t matter what happens here. In the end, things are going to ‘play out’ exactly as they should.” She smiled wistfully.

"I'm finally going to be with my daughter."

Vicky watched in horror as Dalila put the gun to her own head. "No, Dalila! Don't!"

There was a sharp crack of gunfire, then Dalila's legs crumpled beneath her. Vicky screamed and staggered back. Baumann rushed toward Dalila, kicked the gun away, then checked for a pulse.

"Ah, fuck," he sighed, shaking his head. "I'll call it in."

"You okay, Langford?" Rizzo asked, putting an arm around Vicky. "We thought the worst when we heard that shot. We were about to go in, but—"

"Rizzo, listen to me," Vicky said, grabbing the front of his jacket. "You've got to call Jim McCann and tell him what happened."

"McCann is the one who told us to check things out."

Vicky eyes were wide with fear, and her voice trembled. "Tell him Josh is at Pine Lake at an A-frame directly across from Warren Mott's place."

"Calm down, Langford. You'll get to tell him everything yourself. He'll be here any minute. You need to take it easy. You're white as a sheet and probably going into shock."

"You don't understand! There's no time. Cal Brookman will kill Josh at midnight unless someone is there to stop him!"

"What the hell are you doing, Langford?" Rizzo asked as Vicky twisted from his arms and made a beeline for Dalila's yellow Volkswagen.

She slammed the door shut and locked it before Rizzo could get to her. He barely had time to jump out of the way before Vicky gunned the engine and roared down the street.

Chief Calvin Leonard of the Garrett County Police settled his girth in his leather recliner and burped loudly. Damn burritos were going to talk to him all night long, he thought, making a face. Reaching for the remote, he flipped to the news. He was watching a live report from a house in Westport when the phone rang.

"Leonard here," he said, turning down the volume on the set.

It was one of his deputies, Fred Masters. "Chief, we just got a call from the Westport PD about a big kidnapping case they're working on."

"I've been following it. In fact, it's on the news right now." Leonard reached for his smoldering stogie in the overflowing ashtray and took a deep drag. "What's it got to do with us?"

"This Detective McCann who called thinks one of the suspects is holed up at a house on Pine Lake with the missing child," the deputy replied. "He wants us to check it out, see if the suspect is there. He gave me his cell phone number so we could report back to him. He's on his way out there now."

"That's a big case," Leonard said thoughtfully. And if this Detective McCann was right, it had landed right smack dab in Leonard's backyard. His florid jowls quivered with excitement.

"McCann says the suspect is armed and dangerous and, Chief, McCann was adamant that he doesn't want us to move on it, just assist the Westport PD in making the arrest. Riley and I are going to take a ride out there."

"No. You and Riley stay put. I'll do it myself, and I'll call in if I need you." Leonard pushed himself out of the recliner with a grunt. "Give me McCann's number and tell me where the hell I'm going."

It was nearly a quarter to twelve by the time Vicky found the entrance to Dalila's property. Leaning out of the window, she used the small flashlight on her ring of keys to check the name on the black mailbox. Sinclair and the address were plastered across the side in big gold stick-on letters. She parked at the side of the road and started to leave the keys in the ignition, then thought better of it. They could be used as a weapon, and right now they were all she had. She shrugged off her bulky coat so she could move more easily and started down the long drive that led to Dalila's house.

Low-hanging branches tugged at Vicky's hair as she stumbled along in the dark, hugging the side of the drive. Cold rain pelted her face and numbed her body. Her clothing clung to her like plastic wrap, but she was oblivious to it all. Her mind raced as she tried to formulate a plan. The road curved and as she came around the bend, she saw a police car parked in front of the A-frame. Its engine was running, and red-and-blue lights flashed against the trees. Help was there. With any luck, Brookman was already in handcuffs. Vicky was weak with relief, but the feeling was short-lived. As she neared the end of the drive, she saw a body sprawled in front of the squad car. The headlights shone on it like a macabre spotlight.

She darted a glance at the house, then crouching, ran to the downed officer. Nausea hit her as she looked at the gaping hole in his chest. His brown eyes were dull, his mouth slack. The gold name pin on his blood-spattered jacket said, "Chief Leonard."

Taking a deep breath, Vicky swallowed hard and pressed her shaking fingers to his carotid artery. Nothing. She glanced at the house. Brookman had probably sat at one of the windows and dropped this man like a duck in a shooting gallery. A chill ran down her spine. Was he watching right now, ready to do the same thing to her?

Vicky scuttled back to the squad car, using it for cover. She sat back against it, fists clenched, heart jackhammering. What now? For some reason Leonard didn't have his portable radio attached to his jacket, and she couldn't take a chance on opening the car door to use that radio. The dome light would come on and be a dead giveaway to Brookman that he had more company—if he didn't already know.

Dammit, where are Jim and Gil?

She should have waited for them. Vicky looked at the keys clutched in her hand. What the hell did she think she was going to do with these? She was such a fool to think she could do this alone.

If we're not there by midnight, Cal will assume something went wrong and kill Josh.

Dalila's threat gnawed at Vicky. It was almost midnight. If she waited any longer, it would be too late.

She swore under her breath. There was only one way for this to go down. She poked her head up and glanced at the house. Vicky didn't see Brookman at any of the windows. Keeping her gaze riveted to the house, she crawled to Leonard's body. Hands trembling, she grabbed the Sig Sauer that was still in his holster and hurried back to the squad car.

Vicky laid the gun down and sat back on her haunches. She looked at the gun lying on the ground beside her. Who was she kidding? Hand-to-hand combat was one thing. She could give Brookman a run for his money, but to use a gun again? No way. She'd probably end up shooting herself instead of him.

Vicky consoled herself with the thought that the dead officer had to have radioed his position before stopping here. If the dispatcher wasn't able to raise him, another cruiser would be sent out to check on him. How long before they came looking for him, though? How long before Jim and Gil arrived? Vicky checked her watch.

"Longer than I can afford to wait," she said aloud.

Dizziness washed over her and her chest tightened as she grabbed the Sig. Nausea threatened, but Vicky gritted her teeth against it. She couldn't afford for this to be an instant replay of the night of the ransom drop when she let Pace get away. Josh's life was stake. She took a deep, shuddering breath and grabbed the gun. Her hands shook as she checked to be sure there wasn't a round in the chamber, and then she stuck the gun in the back of her jeans.

This is it—my day of reckoning. God, please help me.

Crouching, she ran toward the house. Flattening herself against it, Vicky carefully peeked through a side window where the blinds were askew. The house was dark except for the light burning in the kitchen and one dim light in the living room, where Cal Brookman was loading a shot gun. He leaned it against the stone fireplace and placed the open box of ammo on the mantel. Suddenly he cocked his head, as if listening. Grabbing a revolver from the end table, he snapped off the light, went to the window and peered out between the blinds.

Vicky pulled back, and keeping herself pressed against the house, inched her way to the back door. She blinked rain from her eyes and pushed her soaked hair from her face. She hoped to God Josh was upstairs and out of the line of fire, because once she was in the house, it was going to turn into a war zone.

A flash of lightning illuminated the black sky, making it look like cracked glass. The kitchen light flickered. Vicky took a deep breath, pulled the gun from her jeans and raised her foot. The door burst open with one kick and she rushed into the kitchen.

"Freeze, Brookman!" Vicky stood in the doorway between the kitchen and the living room, legs spread, gun held at arm's length in front of her.

Brookman swung around and began firing as he dove for cover in front of the couch. Vicky pressed herself against the wall as bullets flew into the kitchen, splintering wood, shattering glass. As the volley of shots faded, she heard Josh's muffled sobs coming from upstairs. His cries tore at her heart, but at least he was alive.

"Mommy is here, baby," Vicky murmured.

The staircase leading to the second floor was on the other

side of the kitchen, but Vicky would have to cross the doorway between the two rooms to get to it. If she could do that, maybe she could barricade herself in a room with Josh until help came. It would be her only hope.

She made her move, firing as she vaulted across the doorway. Brookman sent a hail of bullets in her direction. Vicky shrieked as one ripped into her left shoulder. She dropped her gun and hit the floor on the other side of the doorway.

Pain seared her body as she reached for the dishtowel that hung over the edge of the counter. She pressed the towel to her bleeding shoulder while frantically looking for the Sig. It had spun under the table, but she would be in Brookman's line of vision if she went for it.

Her mouth was dry as cotton, her heart hammering, but she kept her voice strong and steady when she spoke. "Give it up, Brookman. Dalila is dead, and the police are on their way!"

"I promised Dalila and Bud that you would pay for what you did," he shouted. "I'm gonna see that you do."

His footsteps were heavy on the wooden floor as he walked slowly toward the kitchen.

Move, dammit! Don't sit here waiting for him to blow your brains out!

Head swimming, Vicky struggled to her feet. Dropping the dish towel, she pulled the keys from her pocket and positioned them so the sharp ends protruded between her fingers. Blood dripped steadily from her shoulder, and dizziness threatened to pull her under. She forced herself to concentrate.

When the toe of Brookman's black leather boot was through the doorway Vicky lunged at him, stabbing him in the face and neck with the keys. He cried out and stumbled back. Vicky aimed a kick at his groin, but it barely grazed his thigh as Brookman turned away. He drove his fist into her stomach and she fell to the floor, dropping the keys and gasping for breath. Grabbing Vicky by the hair, he yanked her back on her feet. She gritted her teeth and slammed the heel of her palm under his chin. He grunted in pain as his head snapped back. Vicky reached up and raked his bloody face with her nails.

"Bitch, you're gonna die," Brookman shouted, "but first you're gonna see your kid die!"

Adrenaline shot through her body. There was no fear, no pain, only the need to protect her son. She threw her full weight into Brookman. The momentum sent them crashing into the pine table and tumbling to the floor. Brookman pinned her down. Vicky squirmed and thrashed, trying to free herself. A flash of movement at the open door caught her eye. She hesitated for only a fraction of a second, but Brookman seemed to sense it. His grip tightened on the gun as he brought it around and fired.

Vicky screamed as someone fired back. Bullets flew into the kitchen, hitting cabinets, and stinging the oak floor. Suddenly, Brookman's body stiffened. Vicky smelled the metallic scent of blood. A dark red stain spread across the front of his white T-shirt. She watched as he sucked air and his eyes grew wide. He dropped his gun. Vicky screamed again as his body convulsed, then fell on top of her. Breathing hard, she struggled to free herself from the weight of his lifeless body. She looked up to see Gil Fletcher standing in the kitchen doorway.

"Thank God you're here," she cried. "It's over. It's finally over."

Spurred by Josh's frightened wails, she pulled herself to her feet. She swayed and clutched the table to steady herself, then staggered toward the stairs.

"Mommy is here," she called to Josh. "I'm coming, baby."

"Don't go up there, Vicky," Gil said quietly, tugging on a pair of black leather gloves. Vicky looked at him, dumbstruck as he holstered his own gun and picked up Brookman's. "We have some unfinished business."

"What the hell. What are you doing?" Confusion short-circuited her brain and the room spun. Lurching forward, Vicky reached for Gil, but he took a step back and leveled the gun at her.

"I was hoping dickwad would have taken care of you by the time I got here and save me the trouble, but no such luck." Gil's expression was flat, his eyes cold. The hand that held the gun didn't waver. Vicky met his gaze, searching for some sign of the man who had been her trusted friend for so many years. She felt as if she was looking into the eyes of a stranger. In that horrifying moment everything became crystal clear.

"I can't believe you would do this to me," Vicky said. "Why, Gil?"

"I don't have a choice thanks to that screw-up, Pace. Blackwell got him out of Romines to handle the problems at Grayson Center and he did just fine. He always did everything exactly the way Blackwell wanted, until it came to you. Pace fucked everything up royally, and now I have to clean up his mess."

As Gil spoke, Vicky's gaze slid to Chief Leonard's gun lying under the table. Her heart sank. There was no hope of reaching it before Gil dropped her. Then suddenly, she thought of Jim. Where was he? She glanced toward the kitchen door.

"If you're looking for McCann to come to the rescue, you can forget it." Gil jerked a thumb in the direction of the yard. "He's lying next to our brother in blue, out cold. I'll finish him off when I'm done with you."

The hell you will, you son of a bitch. I'm going to take you down first.

"Did you know that Dalila and Brookman took Josh?" Vicky asked.

"I thought Pace took him, like everybody else," Gil said. "I was supposed to take care of Pace and you both the other night at the drop if I got the chance, but that got screwed up when Frank insisted on going with you himself."

"How could you let yourself get involved with Blackwell?" Vicky said bitterly. "You took an oath, Gil! You're supposed to be one of the good guys!"

"I am one of the good guys," Gil said defensively. "I go out on the street every fucking day and put everything I have on the line."

"Except when it comes to Blackwell. Then you destroy evidence, frame innocent people like Peter Murphy—whatever it takes to get the job done."

"Blackwell makes it worth my while to do whatever I have to."

"That includes killing me?"

"Dammit, you put yourself in this position, not me! You have no idea how many times Blackwell wanted to have you whacked, but I saved your ass." Gil clenched his jaw. "Why couldn't you leave him alone? You're just like Danny."

"Danny?" Vicky gasped.

"He was such a goddamn do-gooder, too. I tried to bring him into Blackwell's organization with me—tried to show him the financial gains that were at his fingertips. He could have given you the world, but would he listen? No. Instead, Danny, the defender of justice, was ready to turn me in." Gil jabbed his chest with his thumb. "Me. His best friend and partner."

"You set Danny up," Vicky whispered. Bile rose in her throat as the horror of what Gil had done to her husband sank in. She thought about the last moments of Danny's life. Had they been like this? The feeling of disbelief, the mind-numbing fear? "He thought of you as his brother. He would have taken a bullet for you."

"And he did—in a manner of speaking."

Vicky shook with rage as memories flashed through her mind.

Gil sobbing at Danny's casket. Gil holding Josh as he was baptized.

Lying, murdering bastard.

Vicky clenched her teeth. "You're worse than Blackwell."

Gil moved closer to her, his back to the door. "Turn around."

"What's the matter?" Vicky lifted her chin defiantly. "Can't do it while I'm looking at you?"

Gil shrugged. "Have it your way. I was just trying to make it easier on you."

"You know me. I don't do anything easy." She staggered toward him, determined to fight, just as Jim crept unsteadily into the kitchen. His face was chalk white and blood trickled down the side of his face, but he grasped a nightstick with both hands.

Gil spun around just as Jim raised the nightstick. A shot rang out. Vicky screamed as Jim collapsed on the floor.

"You son of a bitch!" she shouted.

She threw herself at Gil, knocking him off balance, just as he fired again. The shot went wild, shattering a kitchen window. Vicky sank her teeth into his gloved hand. Gil yowled in pain and dropped the gun.

"Goddammit!" Balling his fist, he struck her in the side of the head. The blow sent her sprawling backwards across the floor.

"Leave her alone!" Jim shouted. He tried to get up, but his chest hurt like hell and felt as if it had a two-ton boulder sitting on it.

Gil sauntered over to him. Jim winced as Gil nudged his chest with the toe of his shoe. "When did you put on the vest?"

"Right before we left for Alice Graham's," Jim said, breathing heavily.

"Smart thinking."

Gil kicked him in the jaw. Bright lights exploded inside Jim's head as he fought to stay conscious. He saw Vicky dragging herself toward the gun on the floor and cast around for a way to keep Gil's attention on him. "How are you going to explain three dead bodies, Fletcher?"

Gil bent to retrieve Brookman's weapon. "Brookman shot you and Vicky, and I shot him—pretty simple since it's his gun that's going to kill you both. His prints will be the only ones on it."

"Frank will never buy it."

"Frank will buy anything I tell him. I'm his right-hand man, McCann. He'd never look at me for any of this."

Keep him talking, Jim, Vicky thought as she pulled herself another few agonizing inches across the floor. It felt as if she was being stabbed in the shoulder with a red-hot poker as she reached for the gun. Her fingertips brushed the barrel. Gritting her teeth against the pain, she stretched further and finally grabbed it.

Rolling over, she leveled the gun at Gil. "Drop it!"

Gil stopped short and whirled around. His sandy brows shot up when he saw the gun pointed at him.

"What do you think you're doing?" He chuckled, looking at her in disbelief. "You're gonna shoot me? Nice try, sweetheart, but look how you're shaking. You can hardly hold the damn thing. Give it to me."

Vicky blinked hard, trying to clear her blurred vision. She could barely hold her arms up. Her blood pooled on the wooden floor.

"Come on," Gil said. "We both know you can't do it. You were put to the test the night of the drop and you failed big-time—just like I knew you would. I know you better than you know yourself."

Still laughing, Gil raised his weapon and aimed at Vicky. Two explosions ripped through the room. Dropping to his knees, Gil looked at her in surprise just before he pitched forward and hit the floor.

"I guess you don't know me as well as you think," Vicky said.

Epilogue

"Is Vicky out of her mind?" Frank Paxton blustered when Jim opened Vicky's front door. Pulling off his coat, he stalked down the hall toward the family room. "What was she thinking, checking herself out of the hospital after just three days?"

"You know better than anyone, Frank," Jim said. "Common sense isn't necessarily a concept your goddaughter understands."

Vicky was propped on the couch, talking on the phone when they walked into the room. She gave Frank a crooked smile, held up her hand and mouthed, "I'll be off in a second."

Josh scrambled down from his place beside her and ran to Frank. He squealed in delight as Frank lifted him high in the air, turned him upside down, and put him back down. As soon as Josh's feet hit the floor, he made a beeline for his toy box and began rooting around.

When Vicky hung up, Frank gave her a kiss then stood back with his hands on his hips, scowling. Her eyes were sunken, and her face was mottled with dark purple bruises. A bandage was plastered across her forehead and her arm was in a sling. "You belong in the hospital, young lady."

"Tell her, Frank," Jim said, stacking kindling in the fireplace. "She looks like hell."

"Worse," Frank groused.

"I'll never get a swollen head hanging around the two of you," Vicky said.

"We're only looking out for you," Frank retorted. "Lord

knows you sure don't look out for yourself."

Josh toddled up to Vicky and held a Barney doll up for her to kiss. She brushed her lips first to the top of Josh's downy head, then the purple dinosaur's. "It's a known fact people don't rest in hospitals—all those nurses and doctors coming in at all hours, poking and prodding. I'll do much better here."

Frank grunted his disapproval and nodded at Josh who abandoned Barney and was now busy playing with some brightly colored blocks. "He doesn't seem any worse for the wear."

"The child psychologist thinks he may actually come through this unscathed." Vicky cast a worried glance at her son. "I hope she's right."

"That's more than I can say for you," Frank said, sitting in the chair beside Vicky. His tone softened as he put a beefy hand on her arm. "How are you feeling, honey?"

"I'm tough, I'll mend." She was quiet a moment, then she asked about Gil.

"He's improving. I spoke to him before I came here."

"Did he give up Blackwell?" Jim asked.

"He gave up the whole damn organization," Frank snorted.

"What was his price?" Jim sat beside Vicky on the sofa. He slipped an arm around her, careful not to touch her wounded shoulder.

"He'll serve time, but it will be a reduced sentence and in a white-collar crime facility, at that."

"A country club," Jim spat in disgust.

"According to the DA, it couldn't be helped. Everybody has a stake in this; the FBI, the DEA and the ATF. They want Blackwell and the rest of 'em, and Gil was the one man who could hand everyone over on a silver platter. He's smart, I'll give him that. He was setting up Sean O'Connor to take the fall for him. We're still looking at O'Connor, but I really think he's going to come up clean. Blackwell is going down big-time, though. Gil has got tapes and other forms of documentation that will make it impossible for him to weasel his way out of this."

"What else does Fletcher get?" Jim asked.

"A new face and identity before he starts serving his time. When he gets out, he'll have more plastic surgery, then go into the witness protection program."

"He should spend the rest of his life behind bars. Every time I think of what he did to Danny—what he would have done to me—I wish I would have killed him." She looked from Jim to Frank. "I know that makes me just as bad as Gil and Blackwell and all the rest of them, but I can't help it."

"It doesn't make you bad, honey," Jim said, gingerly planting a kiss on her forehead. "It makes you human."

"I trusted him," she said bitterly. Looking at a picture of her husband, she added, "And so did Danny."

"We all did," Frank replied gruffly, his bushy white brows furrowed. "I feel like a damn fool. I knew somebody in the department was dirty, but I never dreamed it was Gil."

"Don't feel too badly, Frank," Vicky replied. "I'm the one who cornered the market on foolish. I didn't have a clue about Gil or Dalila. I was blind to everything."

"There was no way you could have possibly known that Dalila was Connie Springer's mother," Jim pointed out.

"Maybe not, but what's my excuse for Gil?"

"He had everyone fooled, including me, but he'll pay for what he's done." He turned to Vicky and gently brushed his fingertips to her jaw. "They all will. You accomplished your goal and mine, by the way. You put all the bad guys away."

"Jim's right, honey," Frank said. "You finally have all your answers. You can put the past to rest once and for all and start looking at the future."

"Speaking of the future," Vicky said, brightening a little,

"That was Madam Zoya on the phone. She came back to Westport when she heard on the news that Josh had been found. She's going to come by tonight and read my tea leaves again."

"Ah, come on, Vicky," Jim groaned. "You're not going to start with that hocus-pocus stuff again."

"I know you're still not a believer, but Madam Zoya said the reason she left town in the first place was because she felt she was in danger herself."

"She was right about that," Frank said. "Gil told me this morning that he wanted her out of the way because he was afraid she was going to steer you toward him. He went to her house, but she'd already skipped town."

"Dalila was after her, too, so you see, this 'hocus-pocus stuff' as you call it, saved her life," Vicky observed. "And let me remind you, she did give us leads that helped us find Josh."

"Wait a minute," Jim protested, holding up his hands. "I never said I didn't believe. Who was the one who went with you to talk to Madam Zoya when we were searching for Josh?"

"Okay, so maybe you believe a little," Vicky conceded.

"Actually, I believe a lot." Jim reached across her for her cup on the end table and peered into it. "I never told you this before, but my grandmother was a tea-leaf reader from way back and she taught me how to do it. So you see, you don't need Madam Zoya to tell you about the future. You have me. I can tell you anything you want to know."

"That's coffee."

Jim shrugged. "Tea leaves, coffee grounds, what difference does it make? If it's in the bottom of a cup, I can read it."

Vicky rolled her eyes toward the ceiling and laughed.

"Hmm. I don't see any wolves, two-headed, or any other kind, so that's good news," he said, blowing out an exaggerated sigh of relief. "You have Josh back. Mary is expected to make a full recovery, and you put the bad guys away. All and all I'd say things are looking up for you, Langford."

"Absolutely," Frank said. He added cautiously, "And while we're on the subject of the future, I was wondering if you'd given any thought to what we talked about yesterday?"

"About me coming back to the department?"

"Like I said, honey, I know you would pass the detective's test with flying colors, and we have a position open now. I could sure use you."

"I've thought about it a little," Vicky said matter-of-factly, playing with the hem of her sweater. The truth was she'd thought about it a lot.

"If what you've been through these last few days and what you had to do to Gil doesn't prove you can still do the job, nothing ever will."

"I know, Frank, but that didn't have anything to do with the job," she admitted, casting a sidelong glance at Jim as she pulled Josh into her lap. "When people we love are in danger, we can do things we didn't realize we could."

"We'll talk more about it later. Right now you need your rest and I've got to get back to the station," he said, giving her and Josh both a kiss. He grabbed his coat, paused in the doorway and turned around. "You know, Vicky, you're a lucky woman. You've been given a second chance, and that doesn't happen very often. Don't let it pass you by."

Vicky curled her fingers around Jim's. "I know, Frank, and believe me, I don't intend to."

After Frank left, Jim reached for Vicky's coffee cup and looked into it again.

"What are you doing?" she laughed.

"I didn't get to finish telling you your future."

"So what do you see besides cold coffee?"

Jim put down the cup and turned to her. "A man who loves you and Josh very much and wants to be a part of your lives—if you'll let him."

A heartbeat of time passed. Vicky looked into Jim's eyes and saw her future there. She gently brushed her lips to his.

"You heard what I told Frank. I don't intend to let any second chances pass me by."

ABOUT THE AUTHOR

Sherry Scarpaci is the mother of two grown children whom she raised with much greater success than most of her houseplants. She collects husbands like some people might collect rare coins and old stamps. Currently between husbands, she hopes to gain custody of two of her four cats. *Lullaby* is her first mystery novel for Five Star. Sherry makes her home in the greater Chicagoland area where she is currently at work on her next novel. In addition to mystery writing, Sherry has written nonfiction articles for *Woman's World* magazine and the *Star* newspaper. Her favorite pastimes are eating Twizzlers, (Sherry thinks they should be their own food group), baking, reading, and thinking up new plots and innovative ways to kill people.